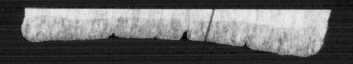

The Restless Dead

Also by Simon Beckett

Featuring David Hunter
The Chemistry of Death
Written in Bone
Whispers of the Dead
The Calling of the Grave
The Restless Dead

Other novels
Where There's Smoke
Stone Bruises

For more information on Simon Beckett and his books,
see his website at www.simonbeckett.com

The Restless Dead

SIMON BECKETT

BANTAM PRESS

LONDON · TORONTO · SYDNEY · AUCKLAND · JOHANNESBURG

TRANSWORLD PUBLISHERS
61–63 Uxbridge Road, London W5 5SA
www.penguin.co.uk

Transworld is part of the Penguin Random House group of companies
whose addresses can be found at global.penguinrandomhouse.com

Penguin
Random House
UK

First published in Great Britain in 2017 by Bantam Press
an imprint of Transworld Publishers

A CIP catalogue record for this book
is available from the British Library.

ISBNs 9780593063477 (hb)
9780593063484 (tpb)

Typeset in 11/14.5pt Sabon by Falcon Oast Graphic Art Ltd.
Printed and bound by Clays Ltd, Bungay, Suffolk.

Penguin Random House is committed to a sustainable
future for our business, our readers and our planet. This book
is made from Forest Stewardship Council® certified paper.

1 3 5 7 9 10 8 6 4 2

For Hilary

1

COMPOSED OF OVER sixty per cent water, a human body isn't naturally buoyant. It will float only for as long as there is air in its lungs, before gradually sinking to the bottom. If the water is very cold or deep, it will remain there, undergoing a slow, dark dissolution that can take years.

But if the water is warm enough for bacteria to feed and multiply, then it will continue to decompose. Gases will build up in the intestines, increasing the body's buoyancy until it floats again.

And the dead will literally rise.

Suspended face down, limbs trailing below, the body will drift on or just under the water's surface. Over time, in a morbid reversal of its formation in the womb's amniotic darkness, it will eventually come apart. The extremities first: fingers, hands and feet. Then arms and legs, and finally the head, all falling away until only the torso is left. When the last of the decompositional gases have seeped out, the torso too will slowly sink a second, and final, time.

But water can also cause another transformation to take place. As the soft tissues decompose, the layer of subcutaneous fat begins to break down, encasing a once living human body in a thick, greasy layer. Known as adipocere, or 'grave-wax' to give it its more colourful title, this pallid substance also goes by a less macabre name.

Soap.

Cocooned in its dirty white shroud, the internal organs are preserved as the body floats on its last, solitary journey.

Unless chance brings it once more into the light of day.

The skull was a young female's, the gender hinted at by its more gracile structure. The frontal bone was high and smooth, lacking any bulge of eyebrow ridges, while the small bump of the mastoid process beneath the opening of the ear looked too delicate for a male. Not that such things were definitive, but taken together they left me in little doubt. The adult teeth had all broken through by the time of death, which indicated she was older than twelve, though not by much. Although two molars and an upper incisor were missing, probably dislodged post-mortem, the remaining teeth were hardly worn. It confirmed the story told by the rest of her skeleton, that she'd died before reaching her late teens.

The cause of death was all too obvious. At the back of the skull, a jagged hole about an inch long and half that wide sat almost dead centre of the occipital bone. There was no sign of healing and the edges of the wound were splintered, suggesting the bone was living when the injury occurred. That wouldn't have been the case if the damage had been inflicted after death, when the bone dries out and becomes brittle. The first time I'd picked up the skull I'd been surprised to hear an almost musical rattle from inside. At first I'd thought it must be bone fragments, forced into the brain cavity by whatever object had killed the young victim. But it sounded too large and solid for that. The X-ray confirmed what I'd guessed: loose inside the girl's skull was a slender, symmetrical shape.

An arrowhead.

It was impossible to say exactly how old the skull was, or how long it had lain in the ground on the windswept Northumberland moors. All that could be said with any certainty was that she'd been dead over five hundred years, long enough for the arrow shaft to disintegrate and the bone to darken to a caramel colour. Nothing would ever be known about her; not who she was nor why she'd died. I liked to think whoever had killed her – as she was either turned or running away – had received some sort of punishment for the crime. But there was no way of knowing that either.

The arrowhead shifted with a soft percussive noise as I packed away the skull, carefully wrapping it in tissue paper before replacing it in its box. Like the other historical skeletons in the university's anthropology department, it was used to train undergraduates, a morbid curio sufficiently ancient as to be largely devoid of shock. I was used to it – God knows, I'd seen worse – but that particular *memento mori* always struck me as particularly poignant. Perhaps it was because of the victim's youth, or the brutal manner of her death. Whoever she was, she'd once been someone's daughter. Now, centuries later, all that remained of the nameless girl was stored in a cardboard box in a lab.

I put the box back in the steel cupboard with the rest. Rubbing a stiffness from my neck, I went into my office and logged on to my computer. There was the familiar Pavlovian expectation as the emails loaded. As usual, it was replaced by disappointment. There was only the everyday minutiae of academic life: queries from students, memos from colleagues and the occasional appeal the spam filter had failed to catch. Nothing else.

It had been like that for months.

One of the emails was from Professor Harris, the new head of anthropology, reminding me to schedule a meeting with his secretary. *To review options regarding your position*, as he delicately phrased it. My heart sank when I read that, but it was hardly a surprise. And it was a problem for the following week anyway. Turning off the computer, I hung up my lab coat and pulled on my jacket. A postgraduate student passed me in the corridor as I left.

''Night, Dr Hunter. Have a good holiday,' she said.

'Thanks, Jamila, you too.'

The thought of the long bank holiday weekend lowered my spirits even further. I'd foolishly accepted an invitation to spend it with friends at their house in the Cotswolds. That had been weeks ago, when it had seemed distant enough not to worry about. Now it was here I was less sanguine, not least since there would be a lot of other guests there I didn't know.

Too late now. I unlocked my car, swiping my pass against the scanner and waiting for the barrier to rise. I knew it was stupid driving in to the university each day, contending with London traffic and congestion charges rather than catching the Tube, but the habit was hard to break. As a police consultant I'd grown used to being called out to different parts of the country when a body was found, often at short notice. It had made sense to be able to leave quickly, but that was before I'd been unofficially blacklisted. Now taking my car in to work was beginning to seem less like a necessary routine and more like wishful thinking.

On the way home I stopped off at a supermarket to buy the sorts of things I remembered a house guest ought to take. I wasn't setting off until morning, so I needed something for dinner that evening as well, and wandered the shelves without any great enthusiasm. I'd been feeling vaguely under the weather for a few days now, but put it down to boredom and apathy. When I realized I was browsing the ready meals section I gave myself a mental slap and moved on.

Spring was late arriving this year, the winter winds and rain lingering well into April. The overcast skies did little to lengthen the days, and it was already growing dark by the time I pulled on to the road where I lived. I found a parking space and carried the shopping bags back to my flat. It occupied the ground floor of a large Victorian house, with a small entrance hall shared with another flat upstairs. As I drew nearer I saw there was a man in overalls working on the front door.

'Evening, chief,' he greeted me cheerily. He was holding a plane, assorted tools spilling out of the open bag at his feet.

'What's going on?' I asked, taking in the raw timber around the lock and wood shavings littering the floor.

'You live here? Someone tried to break in. Your neighbour called us out to repair it.' He blew sawdust off the door edge and set the plane back on it again. 'You don't want to be leaving the place unlocked in this neighbourhood.'

I stepped over his toolbag and went to speak to my neighbour. She'd only been living in the upstairs flat for a few weeks, a flamboyantly attractive Russian who, as far as I could tell, worked as a travel agent. We'd rarely spoken beyond the odd pleasantry, and she didn't invite me over the doorstep now.

'It was broken when I came home,' she said. A wave of musky perfume radiated from her as she tossed her head angrily. 'Probably some junkie, trying to get in. They steal anything.'

The neighbourhood wasn't exactly high-rent, but it didn't have any more of a drug problem than anywhere else. 'Was the front door open?'

I'd checked my own flat but its door was intact. There was no sign that anyone had tried to force their way in. My neighbour shook her head, setting the thick, dark hair bouncing. 'No, only broken. The scumbag got frightened or gave up.'

'Did you call the police?'

'Police?' She gave a *phhf* of disdain. 'Yes, but they don't care. They take fingerprints, they shrug, they go. Better to get a new lock. A strong one this time.'

It was said pointedly, as though the old lock's failings were my fault. The locksmith was finishing up when I went back downstairs.

'All done, chief. It'll need a new lick of paint, stop the planed wood from swelling when it rains.' He raised his eyebrows, holding up two sets of keys. 'So, who wants the bill?'

I looked back upstairs at my neighbour's door. It remained closed. I sighed. 'Do you take cheques?'

After the locksmith had gone, I fetched a pan and brush to sweep up the sawdust in the hallway. A curl of shaved wood had wedged itself in the corner. I crouched down to brush it up, and as I saw my hand against the black and white tiles I had a dizzying rush of déjà vu. *Lying in the hallway, a knife sticking obscenely from my stomach, blood spreading across the chequerboard floor . . .*

It was so vivid it took my breath. I stood up, heart racing as I forced myself to breathe deeply. But the moment was already passing. I opened the front door, drawing in the cool night air. *Christ. Where did that come from?* It was a long time since I'd had a flashback to the attack, and this one had come out of nowhere. I rarely even thought about it any more. I'd done my best to put it behind me, and while the physical scars remained, I'd thought the psychological wounds had healed.

Obviously not.

Recovering, I emptied the sawdust into the bin and went back into my flat. The familiar space was just as I'd left it that morning: inoffensive furniture in a decent-sized lounge, with a kitchen and a small, private garden out back. It was a perfectly good place to live, but now, with the flashback still fresh in my mind, I realized how few of the memories I had of this place were happy ones. Like taking my car to work, the only thing that had kept me here was habit.

Perhaps it was time for a change.

Feeling listless, I unpacked my shopping and then took a beer from the fridge. The fact was I was in a rut. And change was coming whether I wanted it or not. Although I was employed by the university, most of my work came from police consultancy. As a forensic anthropologist, I was called in when human remains were found that were too badly decomposed or degraded for a pathologist to deal with. It was a highly specialized field populated largely by freelancers like myself, who would help police identify remains and provide as much information as possible regarding the time and manner of their dying. I'd become intimate with death in all its gory excess, fluent in the languages of bone, putrefaction and decay. By most people's standards it was a gruesome occupation, and there were times when I struggled with it myself. Years before, I'd lost my wife and daughter in a car accident, their lives snuffed out in an instant by a drunk driver who'd walked away unscathed. Haunted by what had happened to them, I'd abandoned my work and returned to my original career as a GP, tending to the concerns of the living rather than the dead. I'd buried myself away in a small Norfolk village, trying to escape any connection to my old life and the memories that came with it.

But the attempt had been short-lived. The realities of death and its consequences had found me anyway, and I'd come close to losing someone else I loved before accepting that I couldn't run away from who I was. For better or worse, this was what I did. What I was good at.

Or at least it had been. The previous autumn I'd become involved with a brutal investigation on Dartmoor. By the end of it two of the police's own were dead and a senior ranking officer had been forced to resign. While I wasn't to blame, I'd been an unwitting catalyst for the scandal that ensued, and no one likes a trouble-maker. Least of all the police.

And suddenly the consultancy work had dried up.

Inevitably, there was a knock-on effect at the university. Technically, I was only an associate, on a rolling contract rather than tenure. The arrangement gave me the freedom to carry on with my police consultancy and allowed the department to benefit by association. But an associate who worked on high-profile murder investigations was a far cry from one who'd suddenly become *persona non grata* with every police force in the country. My contract only had a few more weeks to run, and the new head of anthropology had indicated that the department wouldn't carry any dead weight.

It was clear that was how he saw me.

With a sigh I flopped back into an armchair and took a drink of beer. The last thing I felt like was a weekend house party, but Jason and Anja were old friends. I'd known Jason since medical school, and met my wife at one of their parties. Along with every-thing else, I'd let the friendship slide when I left London after Kara and Alice died, and never quite got around to re-establishing it when I moved back.

But Jason had got in touch just before Christmas, after seeing my name in news reports about the fouled-up Dartmoor investigation. I'd met up with them several times since, and been relieved there'd been none of the awkwardness I'd expected. They'd moved home since we'd lost touch, so at least I was spared the bittersweet memories their old house would have brought. They now lived in an eye-wateringly expensive house in Belsize Park, and had a second home in the Cotswolds.

That was where I'd be driving to tomorrow. It was only after I accepted the invitation that I learned there was a catch.

'We're inviting a few other people,' Jason told me. 'And there's someone Anja would like you to meet. She's a criminal lawyer, so you should have plenty in common. Police stuff and all that. Plus she's single. Well, divorced, but same thing.'

'That's what this is about? You're trying to set me up with someone?'

'I'm not, Anja is,' he explained with exaggerated patience. 'Come on, it's not going to kill you to meet an attractive woman, is it? If you hit it off, great. And if not what's the harm? Just come along and see what happens.'

In the end I'd agreed. I knew he and Anja meant well, and it wasn't as though my social calendar was exactly full these days. Now, though, the prospect of spending a bank holiday weekend with strangers seemed like a terrible idea. *Can't cry off now. Better make the best of it.*

Wearily, I got up and began making myself something to eat. When the phone rang I thought it would be Jason, calling to check I was still going. The possibility of making a last-minute excuse crossed my mind, until I saw the number on the caller display was withheld. I almost didn't answer, thinking it must be a marketing call. Then old habits kicked in again, and I picked up anyway.

'Is that Dr Hunter?'

The speaker was male, and sounded too old for a telemarketing call. 'Yes, who's this?'

'I'm DI Bob Lundy, Essex Police.' The voice was unrushed, almost slow, its accent northern rather than estuary. Lancashire, I thought. 'Have I caught you at a bad time?'

'No, not at all.' I set down my beer, thoughts of food forgotten.

'Sorry to disturb your weekend, but I was given your name by DCI Andy Mackenzie. You worked with him on a murder inquiry a while back?'

His tone made it a question, but I remembered Mackenzie well enough. It had been the first case I'd been involved in after I lost my family, and hearing his name so soon after I'd been thinking back to that time was strangely apt. He'd been a DI back then, and it hadn't always been an easy relationship. My fault more than his, so I appreciated his putting a word in for me.

'That's right,' I said, trying not to raise my hopes. 'How can I help?'

'We've got a reported sighting of a body in the Saltmere estuary, a few miles up the coast from Mersea Island. We can't do much tonight but there's a low tide just after dawn. We've got a pretty good idea where it might have grounded, so we'll be carrying out a search and recovery as soon as light permits. I know it's short notice, but can you meet us out there first thing tomorrow morning?'

Jason and Anja's party flashed across my mind, but only for a second. They'd understand. 'You want me there for the recovery?'

I'd worked on water deaths before, but normally I was called in once the body had been retrieved. A forensic anthropologist was generally only needed if there were skeletal remains or if a body was badly decomposed. If this was a recent drowning, and the body was still in reasonably good condition, there'd be nothing for me to do. And this wouldn't be the first false alarm sparked by a floating bin-liner or bundle of clothes.

'If you can make it, yes,' Lundy said. 'A couple of weekend yachtsmen spotted the body late this afternoon. They were planning to drag it aboard until they got close enough to smell it and changed their minds.'

That was just as well. If the body had begun to smell that suggested decomposition had set in. Manhandling it on to a boat would likely have caused more damage, and although it was possible to distinguish post-mortem injuries from those caused before death, it was better to avoid them.

'Any idea who it might be?' I asked, hunting around for a pen and paper.

'A local man went missing about six weeks ago,' Lundy told me, and if I hadn't been so distracted I might have made more of his hesitation. 'We think there's a good chance this is him.'

'Six weeks is a long time for a body to be drifting in an estuary without being found,' I said.

No wonder the yachtsmen had noticed the smell. It wasn't unheard of for human remains to stay afloat for weeks or even months, but that was usually in deeper water or out at sea. In an estuary, where the body would be left stranded and exposed at low tide twice a day, I'd have expected it to have been noticed before now.

'Not this one,' Lundy said. 'You don't get many boats on it these days, and there's a rat's nest of creeks and saltmarshes feeding into it. The body could have been drifting in there for weeks.'

I scribbled on the notepad, trying to make the pen work. 'And the missing man, anything suspicious about his disappearance?'

There was another hesitation. 'We've no reason to think anyone else was involved.'

I lowered the pen, picking up on the DI's caution. If no one else was involved that left either natural causes, accident or suicide, and Lundy's manner suggested this wasn't either of the first two. Still, that didn't explain why he was being so cagey.

'Is there something sensitive about this?' I asked.

'I wouldn't call it *sensitive*, exactly.' Lundy spoke with the air of someone choosing his words. 'Let's just say we're under pressure to find out if it's who we think. I'll tell you more tomorrow. We're mustering from an old oyster fishery but it can be tricky to find. I'll email the directions, but you'll need to allow plenty of time to get there. Satnavs aren't much use in that neck of the woods.'

After he'd ended the call I sat staring into space. There was obviously more to this than the DI wanted to go into over the phone, although I couldn't think what. A suicide might require tactful handling, especially when dealing with the family. But police officers weren't usually so coy.

Well, I'd find out soon enough. Including why they wanted me present for the recovery. Even if they were right and the body had been in the estuary for weeks, the police didn't usually need a forensic anthropologist's help to remove it from the water. I wouldn't normally expect to be involved until the remains were back at the mortuary.

But I wasn't about to argue. This was the first consultancy work I'd been offered in an age, and hopefully a sign official attitudes towards me had thawed. *Please God*. Suddenly even the thought of Jason and Anja's dinner party didn't seem so bad. I'd have a longer drive to the Cotswolds, but the recovery shouldn't take all day. They'd understand if I was a little late.

Feeling brighter than I had in months, I went to get my things together.

2

IT WAS STILL dark next morning when I set off. There was traffic even at that time, the headlights of lorries and early commuters snaking along the roads. But they grew sparser as I drove out of London and headed east. Soon the roads were unlit, and the stars brightened as the crowded suburbs were left behind. The muted glow of the satnav gave the illusion of warmth, but that early in the morning I still needed to turn on the heater. It had been a long, cold winter, and despite the calendar the promised spring was still no more than a technicality.

I'd woken feeling sluggish and aching. I'd have put it down to a low-grade hangover if I'd had more than a single beer the night before. But I felt better after a hot shower and a quick breakfast, too preoccupied with the day ahead to worry about anything else.

It was peaceful on the early morning roads. The Essex coastal marshes weren't too far from London; flat, low-lying towns and countryside that fought a perpetual, and often losing, battle with the sea. I wasn't familiar with that stretch of the south-east coast, though, and in his emailed directions Lundy had again warned to allow plenty of time. I thought he was being over-cautious until I'd looked up maps of the Saltmere estuary online. The 'rat's nest' of creeks and saltmarshes the DI had mentioned was an area called the Backwaters, a tidal labyrinth of waterways and ditches that bordered one of the estuary's flanks. On satellite photographs it resembled capillaries feeding into an artery, most of it only accessible by boat. And not even then at low tide, when it drained to become a barren plain of mudflats. The route I'd be taking only skirted its edges, but even so the roads looked small and tortuous.

The glow from the satnav dimmed as the sky directly ahead continued to lighten. Off to one side, the refineries of Canvey Island were silhouetted against it, fractal black shapes sparkling with lights. There were more cars on the road now, but then I turned off on to a side road and the traffic thinned down. Soon I was on my own again, heading into an overcast dawn.

I switched off the satnav not long afterwards, relying solely on Lundy's directions. All around, the landscape was flat as a stretched sheet, scribbled over by thickets of hawthorn with only the occasional house or barn. The DI's directions took me through a small, dismal-looking town called Cruckhaven that lay close to the neck of the estuary. I drove past pebble-dashed bungalows and stone cottages to a harbour front, where a few dirty-hulled trawlers and fishing boats slumped at angles on the mud, waiting for the returning tide to give them grace and reason.

It looked an unprepossessing place, and I wasn't sorry to leave it behind. The road continued alongside the estuary, the tarmac eroded in places where the tide had overflowed the banks. Recently, by the look of things. It had been another bad winter for flooding, but wrapped up in my own problems in London I hadn't paid much attention to news reports of coastal storms. Judging by the sea-wrack stranded on the road and surrounding fields, they would be harder to ignore here. Global warming was more than an academic debate when you were this exposed to the results of it.

I followed the road out towards the mouth of the estuary. With the tide out all that was left was a muddy plain dappled with pools and runnels of water. I began to wonder if I'd missed a turn-off, but then up ahead on the shoreline I saw a row of low buildings.

There was an assortment of police vehicles parked outside, and if I was in any doubt the wooden sign a little further along confirmed it: *Saltmere Oyster Co.*

A PC stood by the gate. He spoke into his radio before letting me through. I pulled on to a crumbling patch of tarmac, alongside where the other cars and a police trailer were parked behind the derelict oyster sheds. After the warmth of the car the cold morning was as bracing as a shower when I climbed out, stiff from the drive. The air carried the mournful cry of gulls along with a smell of rotting seaweed and the salty, earthier scent of exposed seabed. I took a deep breath, looking out over the tidal landscape. The drained estuary looked as though a giant had gouged a long scoop out of the ground, leaving behind only a muddy plain dappled with trapped pools. There was a lunar bleakness about it, but the tide was already beginning its return: I could see rivulets snaking back along channels etched into the estuary bottom, filling them up even as I watched.

A change in the wind brought the rhythmic thrum of a police or coastguard helicopter. I could see the distant speck tracking back and forth across the water. It would be making the most of daylight and the low tide to carry out a visual search of the estuary. A floating body wouldn't ordinarily give off enough heat to be detected by infrared and would be hard to spot from the air, especially if it was drifting below the surface. There wouldn't be much time to find the remains before the tide returned and carried them off again.

So don't stand about daydreaming. A policewoman at the trailer told me DI Lundy was on the quayside. Skirting the shuttered oyster sheds, I walked around to the front. The tubular hull of a police RHIB – a rigid-hulled inflatable boat – was on a trailer at the top of a concrete slipway, and I saw now why the search was being carried out from here. The slipway ran down to a deep channel in the mud immediately in front of the quay. The returning tide would fill it first, allowing a boat to be launched without waiting for the estuary to flood completely. The water wasn't high enough yet, but from the swirls and eddies ruffling its surface it wouldn't be much longer.

A group of men and women stood by the RHIB, talking in low voices as they held steaming plastic cups. Several wore almost paramilitary-looking outfits, dark blue trousers and shirts under bulky lifejackets that identified them as marine unit, but the others were in plain clothes.

'I'm looking for DI Lundy,' I said.

'That's me,' one of the group responded, turning towards me. 'Dr Hunter, is it?'

It's hard to gauge how someone looks from their voice, but Lundy suited his perfectly. He was early fifties and built like an aging wrestler running to fat; out of shape but with bulk and muscle still there. A bristling moustache gave him the look of an affable walrus, while behind the metal-framed glasses the round face managed to look good-humoured and lugubrious at the same time.

'You're early. Find us all right?' he asked, shaking my hand.

'I was glad of the directions,' I admitted. 'You were right about the satnav.'

'They don't call it the Backwaters for nothing. Come on, let's get you a cup of tea.'

I thought we'd go to the trailer, but Lundy led me back behind the sheds to his car, a battered Vauxhall that looked as durable as its owner. Opening the boot he took out a large thermos flask and poured steaming tea into its two plastic cups.

'Better than the stuff from the trailer, trust me,' he said, screwing back on the lid. 'Unless you don't take sugar? I've got a bit of a sweet tooth.'

I didn't, but it was welcome all the same. And I was keen to hear more about the case. 'Any luck yet?' I asked, blowing on the hot tea.

'Not yet, but the helicopter's been up since dawn. The SIO – that's DCI Pam Clarke – is on her way with the pathologist, but we've been given the OK to recover the body as soon as we find it.'

I'd wondered where they were. The senior investigating officer and a pathologist always attended when remains were recovered on land, where the site where they were found was potentially a crime scene and had to be treated as such. But that wasn't always practical for sea recoveries, where the operation was at the whim of tides and currents. The priority in situations like this was usually to recover the remains as quickly as possible.

'You said you'd a good idea where the body might be?' I asked.

'We think so. It was spotted out in the estuary around five o'clock yesterday afternoon. The tide would have been ebbing, and it'd have carried the body out at a fair old lick. If it's made it out to sea then we're wasting our time, but we're betting it'll have grounded before then. See out there?'

He levelled a thick finger towards the mouth of the estuary, perhaps a mile distant. I could make out a series of long humps rising from the muddy bed like low brown hills.

'That's the Barrows,' Lundy went on. 'They're sandbanks, stretch right across the estuary. This whole region's been silting up ever since they put in sea defences further up the coast. Buggered up the currents so that now all the sand that gets washed down ends up dumped on our doorstep. Only small-draught boats can get in and out, even at high tide, so there's a good chance the body won't have made it past either.'

I studied the distant sandbanks. 'What's the plan for recovering it?'

I guessed that would be where I came in, advising on how best to handle the remains without damaging them if they were badly decomposed. I still couldn't see that my help would be strictly necessary, but I couldn't think why else they'd want me there. Lundy blew delicately on his steaming tea.

'Going to be a case of suck it and see once we know where it is. If it's in the Barrows we won't be able to winch it up to the chopper. The sandbanks are too soft to land on, and there's too big a risk of anyone lowered down getting stuck. A boat's the best bet, so we'll just have to hope we can get out to it before the tide

16

floats it off.' He gave a grin. 'Hope you've brought your wellies.'

I'd gone one better and brought waders, knowing from past experience what water recoveries could be like. From what I'd seen this promised to be worse than most. 'You said you'd an idea who it might be?'

Lundy took a slurp of tea and dabbed at his moustache. 'That's right. Thirty-one-year-old local man called Leo Villiers, reported missing a month ago. Father's Sir Stephen Villiers?'

He made it into a question, but the name meant nothing to me. I shook my head. 'I've not heard of him.'

'Well, the family's well known around here. All that land over there?' He gestured across to the far side of the estuary. It looked marginally higher than where we stood, and rather than salt-marshes and waterways there were cultivated fields clearly marked with dark lines of hedges. 'That's the Villiers estate. Some of it, at least. They own a lot of the land on this side as well. They're into farming, but Sir Stephen's got his fingers in all sorts. Shale oil, manufacturing. These oyster sheds belong to him as well. He bought the fishery out about a decade ago and then closed it six months later. Laid everyone off.'

'That must have gone down well.' I was beginning to under-stand where the pressure Lundy had mentioned over the phone was coming from.

'Not as badly as you'd expect. The plan is to develop it into a marina. He's talking about dredging channels in the estuary, building a hotel, transforming this whole area. It'd mean hundreds of local jobs, so that took the sting out of closing the oyster sheds. But there's a lot of opposition from environmentalists, so while the planning arguments go on he's just mothballed the place. He can afford to play the long game, and he's got enough political clout to win in the end.'

People like that usually did. I looked at the muddy bed of the estuary, where the tide was already returning. 'Where does his son come into this?'

'He doesn't. Not directly, anyway. Leo Villiers was what you might call the black sheep. Only child, mother died when he was a kid. Got himself booted out of private military school and then dropped out of university officer training corps in his final year. His father still managed to get him enrolled in the Royal Military Academy but he didn't finish. No official reason, so it looks like there was some scrape his father pulled strings to cover up. After that he went from one scandal to another. There was a trust fund from his mother so he didn't need to work, and he seemed to enjoy stirring things up. Good-looking bugger, like a fox in a coop with girls, but nasty with it. Broke off a couple of engagements and got into all sorts of trouble, everything from drunk driving to aggravated assault. His father's very protective about the Villiers name, so the family lawyers were kept busy. But even Sir Stephen couldn't cover everything up.' Lundy gave me a worried glance. 'Obviously, this is all off the record.'

I tried not to smile. 'I won't say a word.'

He nodded, satisfied. 'Anyway, long story short, for a time it seemed like he'd settled down. His father must have thought so, because he tried steering him into politics. There was talk of him standing for local MP, press interviews. All the usual fluff. Then all of a sudden it stopped. The local party found someone else to stand and Leo Villiers dropped out of sight. We still haven't been able to find out why.'

'And that was when he went missing?'

Lundy shook his head. 'No, this was a fair bit before then. But someone else did. A local woman he'd been having an affair with.'

I realized then I'd read this all wrong. This wasn't just about locating a missing man. I'd assumed that Leo Villiers was the victim, but he wasn't.

He was the suspect.

'This is strictly confidential,' Lundy said, lowering his voice even though there was no one around to hear. 'It doesn't have any direct bearing on today, but you might as well know the background.'

'You think Leo Villiers killed her?'

The DI hitched a shoulder in a shrug. 'We never found her body so we couldn't prove anything. But he was the only serious suspect. She was a photographer, moved out here from London two or three years back when she got married. Emma Derby – glamorous, very attractive. Not the type you'd expect to find somewhere like this. Villiers hired her to do his publicity photographs when he looked like going into politics, and then commissioned her to do some interior design for his house. Turns out that wasn't all she did, because his housekeeper and gardener both claim they saw a half-dressed woman fitting Derby's description in his bedroom.'

Pursing his mouth disapprovingly, Lundy patted his pockets and took out a packet of antacids. He popped a couple from the foil strip.

'Looks like they had a falling out, though,' he said, chomping the tablets. 'We've got several witnesses who heard her ranting and calling him an "arrogant prick" at some swanky political bash not long before she vanished.'

'Did you question him?'

'For all the good it did. He denied having an affair, reckoned she'd thrown herself at him but he'd turned her down. Hard to believe given his track record, especially when he didn't have an alibi for the day she went missing. Claimed he was away but wouldn't say where or offer anything to corroborate it. He was obviously hiding something, but the family's lawyers were throwing up every obstacle they could. Threatened to sue for harassment if we so much as looked askance at him, and without a body or evidence there wasn't much we could do. We searched the area around where Emma Derby and her husband lived, but it's mainly saltmarsh and mudflats you can't get to on foot. Ideal place to get rid of a body. Hellish to search, so finding anything in there was always going to be a tall order. And then Leo Villiers went missing himself, so that was pretty much that.'

I thought back to what Lundy had said on the phone the night before. 'You said his disappearance wasn't suspicious, but someone like that must have made enemies. What about Emma Derby's husband?'

'Oh, we took a good look at him. Bit of an unlikely match, to be honest. He was a good bit older than her, and it was no secret they were having difficulties even before she hooked up with Villiers. But he was out of the country when his wife went missing and then up in Scotland when her boyfriend disappeared. His alibis checked out both times.' Lundy turned down the corners of his mouth. 'You're right about Villiers having enemies, and I dare say not many people will shed a tear over him. But there's nothing to suggest any of them were involved, or that there was anything suspicious about it. There was a report that the gardener scared off a prowler from the grounds of his house not long before he disappeared, but that was more likely just local teenagers.'

I looked out beyond the oyster sheds to where the muddy estuary bed was disappearing under the returning water. 'So you think Villiers killed himself?'

The DI's caginess on the phone had made me think this was something more than an accident. Lundy shrugged. 'He'd been under a lot of pressure and we know he had at least one failed suicide attempt in his teens. Sir Stephen's lawyers have been blocking us from seeing his medical records, but going on verbal accounts from people who knew him there was obviously a history of depression. And there was a note.'

'A suicide note?'

He looked pained. 'We're not officially calling it that. Sir Stephen won't have anyone suggesting his son killed himself, so we're having to tread carefully. And the note was found in Leo's bin, so either it was a draft or he changed his mind about leaving it. But it was his handwriting, saying he couldn't carry on. Hated his life, that sort of thing. And the housekeeper who found the note told us his shotgun was missing as well. Handmade by Mowbry and Sons. You heard of them?'

I shook my head: I was more familiar with the effects of shotguns than with their manufacturers.

'They're up there with Purdeys when it comes to bespoke shotguns. Beautiful craftsmanship, if you like that sort of thing, and phenomenally expensive. Villiers' father bought it for him when he turned eighteen. Must have cost nearly as much as my house.'

A cheaper gun would have been just as lethal. But I was starting to understand why Lundy had been wary about saying too much earlier. Suicide was a difficult thing for any family to process, especially of a man suspected of murder. It would be a doubly hard blow for any parent to accept, so it was no wonder that Sir Stephen Villiers was in denial. What set him apart was that he had the money and power to enforce it.

That might be harder if this was his son's body.

The distant speck of the helicopter was still visible, although now the wind was carrying its sound away from us. It seemed to have stopped moving.

'What makes you think this is Villiers rather than Emma Derby?' I asked. I doubted the yachtsmen who'd seen the drifting body would have been able to tell its gender.

'Because she went missing seven months ago,' Lundy said. 'Can't see her body just turning up after all this time.'

He was right. Although a body would initially sink once any air trapped in its lungs had escaped, it would float back to the surface if the build-up of gases from decomposition made it buoyant again. When that happened it could drift for weeks, depending on the temperature and conditions. But seven months was too long, especially in the relatively shallow waters of an estuary. The combination of tides, marine scavengers and hungry seabirds would have taken its toll long before then.

Even so, there was still something about this I wasn't getting. I ran through what Lundy had said, trying to put it together. 'So Leo Villiers didn't go missing until six months after Emma Derby disappeared?'

'Around that, although we're not sure exactly when. There's a two-week gap between the last time anyone had any contact with him and when he was reported missing, but we're fairly sure that—'

The DI broke off as a whistle came from the direction of the quayside. One of the marine unit had emerged from behind the oyster sheds. He held up a thumb before turning and heading back.

Lundy shook the last few drops of tea from his cup. 'Hope you're ready to get your feet wet, Dr Hunter,' he said, screwing it back on to the thermos. 'Looks like the helicopter's found something.'

3

SALT SPRAY STUNG my face as the RHIB heeled over to one side. I wiped it from my eyes, gripping the edge of my seat as we skimmed over the water. The estuary wasn't particularly rough but we were heading against the tide and wind. The boat juddered as its bow smacked into successive waves, each one sending a curtain of cold spume into the open cockpit.

It was fully light now, although the sun was no more than a diffuse glow in the overcast sky. The smell of plastic from the boat's hull mixed with diesel fumes and salt-soaked rope. The marine unit sergeant stood at the controls, riding the waves easily as he gripped the small wheel. I sat behind him with Lundy and three other life-jacketed officers from the marine unit. The boat was cramped. The six of us shared it with a stretcher and two piles of aluminium stepping plates, set either side of the boat so as not to unbalance it.

I was jerked in my seat as the boat hit a wave head on. Lundy gave me a smile, his glasses flecked with water. 'You all right, there?' he shouted above the noise of the wind and engine. 'Shouldn't be much longer!'

I nodded. I'd sailed when I was younger, and normally the choppy ride wouldn't have bothered me. It wasn't helping the vaguely washed-out feeling I'd woken with, but I tried to put it from my mind. I'd been given a lifejacket to wear as well, this one bright orange rather than the dark blue of the marine unit's. My chest-high rubber waders were uncomfortable to sit in, as were the waterproof coveralls I wore underneath. Still, looking at the estuary's muddy banks on either side, I knew I'd be glad of them later.

The tide had returned with surprising speed. By the time I'd changed and collected my flight case of equipment from the car, the marine unit were already manhandling the boat down the slipway and off the trailer. The channel in front of the quayside was almost completely flooded, water slopping around the concrete ramp as the estuary's mud and shingle disappeared under the encroaching sea.

'We're not going to have much time,' Lundy had warned me as we'd stood by the slipway. 'The helicopter says the body's grounded partway up a sandbank, but it won't stay there long. The tide here comes in quicker than a man can run, so we'll need to work fast.'

Very fast, by the sound of it. This was going to be a race to recover the body before the returning tide floated it off again, which made me question even more why I was there. Although I preferred to examine remains *in situ* given the chance, there wasn't going to be much time to do that here. The priority would be to retrieve the body as quickly as possible, and Lundy and the marine unit were perfectly capable of doing that by themselves.

I stared over the RHIB's blunt bow as we reached the deeper water in the middle of the estuary and then headed out towards the Barrows. The sandbanks lay dead ahead, a natural barrier stretching almost from shore to shore. They'd been isolated by the rising tide but they were still exposed, smooth brown humps emerging from the water like a pod of beached whales. Beyond them, where the estuary met the open sea, I could see three strange-looking structures rising from the water. They were too far away to make out any detail, but from the pitching boat they looked like square boxes perched on pyramidal stilts. Oil derricks, perhaps, although they seemed too close to the shore for that.

Lundy saw me looking. 'It's a sea fort.'

'A what?'

We had to yell above the din of the engine. 'A Maunsell sea fort. The army and Navy built them along the coast during the Second World War to keep German ships out of the estuaries. This is an army one. It used to have seven towers all linked by walkways, but these three are all that's left.'

'Is it still in use?' I shouted. Lundy said something but it was lost in the wind and noise. I shook my head. He leaned closer.

'I said only by seagulls. None of the army forts are. A few of them were used by pirate radio stations back in the sixties, like the one here and at Red Sands in the Thames estuary. But most were either dismantled or fell down years ago. There was talk about turning this one into a hotel a while back, but nothing came of it.' Lundy shook his head at the thought of such folly. 'Can't say I'm surprised. I wouldn't want to stay there.'

Neither would I, but we were almost at the Barrows so I gave up attempting any more conversation after that. It became blessedly quieter as the RHIB throttled down, slowing to make its approach. It was possible to hear the chop of the helicopter now. It hovered ahead of us, lights winking as it held station above the body.

The marine unit sergeant eased the RHIB between the sand-banks. They rose up like small islands all around, waves lapping at their smooth sides. It wouldn't be much longer before the rising tide covered them, and I understood what Lundy had meant about the Barrows making the estuary all but impassable. It was hard enough negotiating them even when they could be seen above the surface. Hidden by the high tide they'd be treacherous.

We were almost directly under the helicopter now. The wash from its rotors was deafening, buffeting us and flattening the water's surface.

'There it is.'

Lundy pointed at something ahead of us, but I couldn't see past his bulky figure. Then the RHIB slowed and came around, and I had my first sight of the body. The tide had deposited it partway up the muddy slope of a sandbank, a sodden mess of clothing slumped in the stillness only the inanimate and the dead can achieve. It lay face down with its head nearest the water and its legs and feet trailing up the sandbank, angled away from us. As I watched, a gull landed nearby, but after hopping closer to examine the body it lost interest.

I knew then this was no recent drowning.

Lundy spoke into his radio, raising a hand in acknowledgement as the helicopter rose up and banked away. Our momentum carried us forward as the boat's engine was cut, and in the sudden silence there was a bump as we ran aground. Intent on the body, I began to climb out of the boat. The sandbank looked solid enough but it had the gelid, grainy consistency of wet mortar. I almost over-balanced as my leg sank in up to my knee.

'Careful there,' Lundy said, grabbing my arm. 'Best wait till we've got the stepping plates down. You've got to watch yourself on this stuff or you'll be in up to your waist.'

'Thanks,' I said, embarrassed. I tugged my foot free, glad of the waders. I could see now why the police hadn't wanted to winch anyone down from the helicopter. It would have been impossible to recover the body that way without getting stuck.

The marine unit officers began laying down stepping plates on the sandbank, making a path up to the body. The metal plates sank under our weight, water squeezing up around their edges. They were soon smeared and slippery, but it was better than trying to walk across the wet sand.

I stayed back while they worked, noting the haphazard arrangement of limbs. The tide had deposited the body face down, in the same position as it would have been floating. It wore a long, dark coat of waxed cotton or some similar stiff material, caked in mud and ballooned by the air still trapped inside. One arm was by its side while the other was draped across its head in apparent abandon.

Even from where I stood I could see that the hands and feet were missing.

'I'd like to take a look before we move it,' I said to Lundy when the officers finished laying the plates. He gave a nod.

'It'll have to be quick. Another few minutes and this is going to be underwater.'

He was right. Despite his earlier warning I was still surprised by how fast the tide was returning. Waves were already snapping at our heels; in the time it had taken to lay the stepping plates the water level had kept pace with us, rising more than halfway up the sandbank's slope.

Careful not to slip on the muddy plates, I picked my way up to the body. It looked a forlorn thing lying there, like something discarded and thrown away. Another gull hopped towards it, leaving arrowhead-shaped prints in the wet sand. It launched itself into the air and flapped away, cawing in protest as I approached. More of them wheeled above us in the zinc-coloured sky, but like the lone seabird I'd seen earlier, none paid any attention to what lay on the sandbank. That said a lot about its condition. If voracious scavengers like gulls weren't interested then it must be badly decomposed.

That was confirmed a moment later when the wind shifted, and the rank odour of rotting animal tissue polluted the salty tang. I stopped a few feet away and studied the body. Even lying crumpled as it was, in life this would have been a taller than average individual. That made it more likely to be male, although not certain: it could be an unusually tall woman. Most of the head was concealed by the long coat, which had bunched up over it like a hood, so only a few sparse strands of sand-clogged hair were visible above the collar.

I crouched down for a better look. Blunt stumps of pallid bone and gristle emerged from the trouser bottoms, while the forearms ended at the wrists. A gold watch was embedded in the swollen flesh of one of them. There were no signs of the missing hands or feet on any of the nearby sandbanks, but I'd have been surprised if there had been. Although this wouldn't be the first body I'd encountered where the hands had been removed to prevent

27

identification, I couldn't see any obvious damage to the bones of the wrists and ankles here to suggest they'd been severed. With no clothing to protect them, the hands and feet would have simply fallen away as the connective tissue of the joints decomposed.

I took my camera from the bib pocket of my waders and began taking photographs. I didn't hear Lundy approach until he spoke.

'You can have copies of our video.'

I glanced round: he moved lightly for a big man, even on the metal plates. 'Thanks, but I'll take a few of my own anyway.'

I usually did: that way I'd only have myself to blame if I missed anything. Lundy stood looking down at the body. 'Male, by the look of things. Must have been in the water a while to lose its hands and feet. Fits with how long Leo Villiers has been missing, wouldn't you say?'

I'd been waiting for him to ask. Normally, estimating a time-since-death was something of a speciality of mine. I'd trained at the original body farm in Tennessee, where human cadavers were used for controlled experiments into decomposition. I'd learned how to establish when an individual had died, assessing bacterial activity and the degree of putrefaction, using esoteric formulae to analyse the breakdown of a body's volatile fatty acids. I could say without conceit that I understood as well as most forensic entomologists the life cycle of blowflies, and the way different insects will colonize a rotting corpse. And while I still preferred to call it experience rather than instinct, over the years being able to accurately judge such things had become second nature.

But that was on land. On land a body would stay in one place, and nature cooperated by providing obligingly measurable criteria. Water was different. While there was no shortage of aquatic scavengers, there wasn't a water-based equivalent of a blowfly, whose life cycle provided a convenient stopwatch to gauge time-since-death. And a floating body would move, changing depths and therefore temperature as it was subjected to tides and currents. The situation was even more complex in an estuary like this, where river met sea and marine and freshwater ecosystems converged.

I looked down at the body. Except for the gnarled joints of the wrists and ankles the coat covered most of it. Still, I could see enough. 'In these conditions it wouldn't take long for the hands and feet to detach, even at this time of year. So probably, yes . . .'

At the last second I stopped myself from adding *but*. Four to six weeks was certainly long enough for the hands and feet to drop away in shallow tidal waters like this. That wasn't what bothered me, but I didn't want to say anything until I'd seen more.

Lundy looked at me for a moment, as though expecting me to go on. When I didn't he gave a nod. 'Right, let's get it in the boat.'

I moved aside as two marine officers clumped along the stepping plates, carrying the stretcher between them. The sergeant followed with a body bag and a folded plastic sheet.

'How're we going to do this?' one of them asked, setting down the stretcher and looking at the face-down body with distaste.

'Roll it over on to the sheet, then we can lift that into the body bag,' the sergeant instructed. He turned to Lundy, remembering at the last minute to include me as well. 'Unless you've any other ideas, sir?'

'Just so long as we get it back in one piece,' Lundy said equably. 'That sound OK to you, Dr Hunter?'

It wasn't as though there were a lot of options. I shrugged, knowing the question was a formality. 'Yes, fine. Just be careful with it.'

The marine unit sergeant exchanged a look with one of his team, passing silent comment on my advice. The tide was already lapping at the body's head as the plastic sheet was unfolded and spread out next to it. The officers all wore masks and thick rubber gauntlets as well as chest-high waders similar to mine. Now I'd finished with the camera, I put on a mask and gauntlets of my own, pulling them over the thin blue nitrile ones I'd been wearing.

'OK, nice and careful. Lift and turn on three. One, two . . .'

The body shifted sluggishly as it was eased on to the plastic sheet. A waft of foul, damp air was released as it sucked free of the wet sand and flopped on to its back. One of the marine officers turned away, raising an arm to cover his nose.

'Oh, nice.'

Wrapped in the long coat, the thing lying on the plastic sheet no longer looked human. There was no hint left of age, race or gender. Most of the skin and flesh was gone from the skull, and the eye sockets were empty holes. The vulnerable balls of jelly would have been one of the first targets of scavengers. There were even early signs of adipocere, a dirty white build-up as though a melted candle had been dripped on to the remaining features. It was a caricature of a face, hollow eye sockets clogged with sand, while the nose was a stub of gnawed gristle. That was only to be expected, given how long the body had been in water.

But the lower face was missing completely. Where the mouth should have been was a gaping maw that exposed the cartilaginous tissue at the back of the throat. The jawbone, or mandible, was completely gone and only a few shattered stumps of teeth remained in the upper jaw.

The head had tilted to one side as the body had been rolled on to the sheet. Now it wasn't covered by the coat collar I could see what looked like an exit wound at the rear of the skull, big enough to put my fist in.

Unperturbed, Lundy studied it, then turned to me. 'What do you think, Dr Hunter? Shotgun?'

I realized I was frowning. I roused myself. 'It looks like it,' I agreed. The damage to the lower face certainly suggested the more explosive violence of a shotgun rather than a rifle or handgun. 'There's something embedded at the back of the throat.'

Without touching the body I leaned closer for a better look. An object was buried in the mangled bone and tissue: a small brownish disc, too regular to be natural.

'It's the wad from a shotgun shell,' I said, making no attempt to remove it.

That would confirm the type of weapon. Not that there was any real question, but it was unlikely any of the pellets would have lodged in the body. Shotgun pellets begin to disperse the moment they leave the barrel. The further they travel, the larger their spread, and the bigger the resulting wound. From the relatively small size of this one the pellets had been closely bunched, and remained so as they punched a hole through the back of the skull. That suggested they'd been fired at close range.

Very close.

'Contact wound, by the look of it,' I said. A shotgun blast fired from one or two centimetres created a sort of tattooing effect, and that was evident here. 'There's blackening on what's left of the teeth and bone, quite a bit of searing still present on the soft tissue, too. The barrel was either inside the mouth or resting against it when it was fired. At that range I'm surprised the wad from the shell didn't go through as well.'

Lundy nodded agreement. 'So it could be self-inflicted.'

'It could, yes.'

A contact wound would be in keeping with a suicide, especially when a shotgun was used. The length of most shotgun barrels made it awkward to reverse them and still reach the trigger, so contact was usually unavoidable. Of course, that didn't rule out the possibility that someone else had shot him.

Lundy must have picked up on my tone. His eyes creased in a smile, although I couldn't see it because of his mask. 'Don't worry, I'm not jumping to any conclusions. But it looks like it's who we thought it would be.'

I couldn't argue with that. A potentially suicidal man had gone missing along with his shotgun, and now a body with a close-range gunshot wound had been found. There seemed little doubt this was Leo Villiers.

I said nothing.

Lundy beckoned to the waiting police officers. 'OK, let's get it on the boat.'

In the few minutes we'd been talking the tide was noticeably higher. The sea was already covering the lower edge of the plastic sheeting. As Lundy called in to report, I took hold of one corner while the marine unit officers took the others. Water streamed from the plastic as we lifted the dead weight and lowered it into the open body bag on the stretcher.

It seemed the least I could do; I hadn't been able to contribute much else.

After everything had been loaded on to the RHIB, I took the same seat as before as the engine roared to life. The tops of the sandbanks had been above our heads not so long ago: now we were almost on a level as the tide rose. As the RHIB pulled away I looked back to where we'd just been. The waves were already lapping over where the body had lain, smoothing over the sand and erasing any sign that anything had been there.

Lundy nudged my arm as the boat picked up speed. He pointed to a rocky promontory that jutted into the estuary on the seaward side of the Barrows.

'See over there? That's Willets Point, where Leo Villiers lived.'

Unlike most of the other places I'd seen around here, the promontory was thickly wooded. Almost hidden by the trees, a large white Victorian villa stood alone on the lonely outcrop of land. Its large bay windows faced out to sea over a small dock, their view only interrupted by the towers of the sea fort that guarded the estuary.

'Used to be the family's summer home, but it was mothballed until Villiers decided to move in a few years back,' Lundy said, raising his voice above the engine. 'His father splits his time between London and the main house near Cambridge, so he had it to himself. Not a bad bachelor pad, is it?'

It wasn't, but the family's wealth hadn't done Villiers much good in the end. I thought again about the condition of the body. 'You were saying earlier you weren't sure exactly when he disappeared,' I shouted. 'How come?'

Lundy leaned closer so he could speak without yelling. 'He wasn't reported missing until a month ago, but the last actual contact anyone had with him was a fortnight before. He called a vet out to his house to put his old dog down. She said he was pretty cut up over it, and no one saw or spoke to him after that. No phone calls or emails, no social media. Nothing. So whatever happened was sometime during that two-week window. We haven't narrowed it down beyond that, but the vet's fee was the last time his credit card was used. So the thinking is that whatever happened was probably closer to six weeks ago than four, but nobody realized until later.'

'No one missed him for two weeks?' That might be feasible if this was some lonely pensioner without friends or family, but it seemed a long time for someone like Leo Villiers. 'What about his father?'

'They weren't what you'd call close. Seems to have been a bit of tension there, so it wasn't unusual for them to go weeks without talking. It was his housekeeper who reported him missing. Villiers didn't have many staff, just her and a gardener who both came in once a week. She had her own key and it wasn't unusual to find no one at home, so she didn't bother at first. But then she turned up one week and the place was a mess. Bottles everywhere, dirty plates in the sink, half-eaten food. He'd thrown benders before, so she just tidied up and left. She noticed the Mowbry's cabinet was unlocked and empty, which she thought was strange because Villiers rarely took it out. Didn't like hunting, which is a surprise. But it wasn't till she went back the following week and found the house exactly as she'd left it that she thought something might be wrong. There was post filling up the mailbox, Villiers' car hadn't moved and neither had the dinghy he kept there. So she had a look round, found the note and that's when she called us.'

'She didn't call his father first?'

'I don't think Sir Stephen's the sort who takes phone calls from staff. Besides, I think she felt the news was better coming from us. Shooting the messenger, and all that.' Lundy looked sheepish as he realized what he'd said. 'Sorry. Bad choice of words.'

'What about the shotgun? Wasn't it at the house?' I asked. Even if the gun had fallen in the water it should have been found at low tide.

'No, which made us wonder at first if someone else might be involved. But given the note and everything else, suicide still seemed more likely, so we were working on the theory that he shot himself somewhere else. Probably the Backwaters, which is why it's taken so long for his body to turn up. Explains why we haven't found the Mowbry as well.'

He sat back, leaving me to think over what he'd said. Leo Villiers had been missing at least four weeks, but more likely nearer to six. I weighed up the decomposition I'd just seen, and the probable factors that might affect a body drifting in these estuarine waters. There was temperature and scavengers, both aquatic and avian. And then the effect of brackish water and tides that would leave it exposed to wind and weather twice a day.

My thoughts were interrupted by the sun breaking through a gap in the gauzy cloud. It gilded the estuary's choppy surface with points of light. There was a sudden glare from the shore as the sunlight glinted off something; a bottle or shard of glass. Then the sun was veiled again and it vanished.

4

A RECEPTION COMMITTEE WAS waiting by the oyster sheds. As we approached I could see several other people standing on the quayside, in addition to the police officers we'd left there. One of them wore heavy-duty blue coveralls, so I guessed he was the pathologist Lundy had mentioned earlier. Next to him was a tall woman in a pale mackintosh, who I supposed must be DCI Clarke, the senior investigating officer.

I didn't know who the other two men were. They stood apart from the rest, at the far side of the quay. Both wore dark overcoats, and as the RHIB drew closer I saw the peaked cap that marked one of them as a senior police officer.

'Oh, lord,' Lundy muttered, when he saw the people on the quayside.

'What is it?' I asked.

The DI had spent most of the trip back from the Barrows at the prow of the boat, mindless of the cold spray dousing him each time the RHIB slapped into a wave. The pitching and bouncing didn't seem to discomfort him at all. He showed every sign of enjoying himself, facing into the wind like a dog with its head out of the car window.

Now he gave a sigh, as though the brief boat journey had been an interlude all too soon over. He took off his glasses and began wiping the spray from them. 'That's Dryden, the Deputy Chief Constable. He's got Sir Stephen Villiers with him.'

I turned back towards the quayside, beginning to feel apprehensive myself. I'd never heard of a DCC attending a straightforward recovery, let alone the victim's parent. That was a bad idea, an unnecessary stress for both the relative and the police officers forced to work while they watched.

There was silence except for the marine unit sergeant's terse instructions as we approached the oyster sheds. The engine dropped to a low chunter and the RHIB slowed, settling in the water. Waves slopped against the tubular hull as momentum carried the boat the last few yards to the quay. The water in the estuary had risen enough to allow us to moor alongside rather than use the slipway. The boat bumped next to a flight of concrete steps that disappeared into the water. Clarke and the others watched in silence as one of the marine unit jumped out and secured the RHIB's line to a metal stanchion.

'You next, Dr Hunter,' Lundy said. 'We'll get the stretcher off last.'

Conscious of the solemn figures watching from the quayside, I caught hold of the steps and pulled myself from the unsteady boat, cumbersome in my waders and waterproofs. The steps were slippery and the sodden concrete was tinged green from algae. At the top I paused to wipe the slime from my hands, conscious of how muddy I was as the woman in the cream mac and the man in coveralls came over.

'Dr Hunter? I'm DCI Pam Clarke. This is Professor Frears, the home office pathologist.'

Clarke was tall and thin, with frizzy ginger hair that blew around her pale face despite being tied back in an attempt to tame it. It was hard to put an age on Frears. The wavy hair was silver but the face below it was sleek and unlined, so that he could have been in his forties or a well-preserved sixty. Together with the flushed cheeks of a *bon viveur*, it gave him the look of a debauched cherub.

'I won't shake hands,' he said cheerfully, holding up his to display his gloves. He looked thoughtful. 'Hunter, Hunter. Name's familiar. Have we met before?'

'I don't think so.'

'Well, it'll come to me.'

As he turned his attention to the activity on the boat, I glanced across at the two dark-coated men standing at the other end of the quay. They were out of earshot but it still felt uncomfortable having this discussion with the potential victim's father nearby. Sir Stephen Villiers looked in his sixties. He wore a charcoal overcoat I thought was probably cashmere over a pale-grey suit. The thinning hair that blew across his scalp was grey as well, making him appear colourless as he watched the progress of the stretcher. There was nothing outwardly imposing about him, yet somehow he seemed to radiate far more authority than the senior policeman he was with. Dryden, the Deputy Chief Constable, was lantern-jawed and had the build of a rugby player, with deep-set eyes beneath the shiny peaked cap. He towered over the man next to him, yet it was the smaller man who commanded attention.

Sir Stephen's face wore no expression as he stared at the body bag on the stretcher. Perhaps feeling my eyes on him, he suddenly looked straight at me. His gaze was incurious, without interest or acknowledgement. A moment later he resumed his study of the stretcher, leaving me with the sense that I'd been assessed and cursorily dismissed.

Lundy had clambered out of the boat and was hauling himself up the steps, puffing from the exertion. The stretcher was lifted out of the boat and carried up after him.

'Careful,' Clarke warned as it was hoisted on to the quay. 'All right, set it down there.'

Grunting with effort, the marine unit lowered the stretcher. Water trickled from it and pooled on the concrete as they stood back. Frears went to stand by it.

'Right, what do we have here?' He gestured to the sergeant. 'Let's take a quick look, shall we?'

Although Clarke didn't quite glance over at where Sir Stephen was standing, it was clear what she was thinking. 'Shouldn't we get it back to the mortuary?'

The pathologist gave a thin smile. 'I don't like working in front of an audience either, but since I'm here I'm going to do my job.'

His tone was affable but carried enough edge to deter any further interference. Clarke gave a curt nod to the marine unit sergeant.

'Open it up.'

The sickly odour of decomposition rolled across the quay as the bag was opened. The pallid body inside it looked even worse against the black plastic, like a melted waxwork dummy.

'I suspect matching dental records will be a challenge,' Frears commented, taking in the shattered remains of the mouth and lower jaw. 'Stature suggests a male, obviously been in the water for some time. Pull the bag open a little more, will you? There's a good man.'

The sergeant bent down to do as he was told, then stopped. He peered closer. 'Hang on, there's something – *Jesus!*'

He reared back at a sudden movement inside the exposed gullet. Something coiled in what was left of the mouth, then surged out from it like a silver tongue. Sliding free, the eel dropped into the body bag.

'Looks like we have a passenger,' Frears said drily, though I noticed he'd pulled back as well.

'Sorry,' the sergeant mumbled. Clarke made an impatient gesture, her face colouring.

'Don't just stand there, get rid of it.'

The eel must have been hidden further down the gullet when we'd recovered the body. With his expression showing what he thought of the task, the sergeant reached into the bag next to the body. The creature writhed sinuously, twining round his gloved hand and wrist as he brought it out. He stood there uncertainly, holding it at arm's length.

'What shall I do with it, sir?'

38

'Well, they're delicious smoked, but I suggest you throw it back,' Frears drawled. 'Unless you've any use for it, Dr Hunter?'

I hadn't. This wasn't like a land recovery, where information might be gleaned from the creatures infesting the remains. In all likelihood the eel had just colonized a convenient food source, feeding on either the decomposing tissue or the smaller creatures that were drawn to it.

With an expression of distaste, the marine unit sergeant shook the eel off his hand and let it splash back into the water. I tried not to look across at Sir Stephen Villiers as Frears resumed his study of the body. The dead man's father had obviously insisted on being here, and the presence of the senior police officer with him was a clear signal of his influence. But this wasn't something a family member should have to see.

'Well, the entry and exit wounds are fairly self-explanatory,' Frears went on. 'Judging from the amount of damage either a large calibre bullet or a shotgun fired from extremely close range.'

'Shotgun, I think,' I said. 'There's what looks like a wad from a shell embedded at the back of the throat.'

'So there is.' Frears peered into the wound. 'And there's something else underneath it. Metal . . . looks like a shotgun pellet.'

That hadn't been visible earlier: the wad covering it had probably been dislodged by the eel as it wriggled free. 'Can I take a look?'

'Be my guest.'

He leaned back so I could see into what had once been the mouth. A glint of something round and shiny was visible, lodged in the mess of cartilage and bone behind the brown cartridge wad.

'Seems a bit big for a shotgun pellet,' I commented. 'And it looks more like steel than lead.'

'Plenty of people use steel shot these days,' the pathologist said, clearly not appreciating being contradicted. 'Could be something like large bore buckshot. I'll have a better idea when I take it out.'

'You'd expect a pellet to pass straight through from that sort of range.'

'Yes, but steel pellets are a lot harder than lead. They're more prone to ricochet so perhaps this one got bounced around and lodged here. At this stage I don't really know,' he said with exaggerated patience. 'Anyway, moving on to something that's more your field, Dr Hunter, any thoughts on how long the body's been in the water? Six weeks seems about the right sort of time given its condition.'

The *more your field* was said pointedly. Taking the hint, I straightened and considered the soaking wet remains.

'Hard to say,' I hedged, trying to decide if I wanted to commit myself at this stage. 'It'll have been exposed to air temperatures twice a day at low tide, so it'll have decomposed faster than if it was submerged all the time. And the hands and feet would have trailed on the bottom, which would help dislodge them.'

Frears raised an eyebrow. 'True, but there's adipocere as well. That doesn't appear overnight.'

'No, but that'll have been accelerated by the clothes, especially the coat.' Not much research had been done into adipocere, but the crumbly deposit formed by the breakdown of subcutaneous fats seemed to build up more quickly when the body was covered. And natural fibres, like the cotton of the duster-style coat, enhanced the effect more than synthetic materials. 'I'm just not sure six weeks is realistic. Not somewhere as shallow and tidal as this.'

Clarke interrupted. 'What are you saying?'

'I think Dr Hunter might have doubts about the length of time the body's been in the water,' Frears told her.

That was met by silence. My doubts had been growing since Lundy told me about the two-week gap between when Villiers was last seen and when he was reported missing. Unless he'd somehow avoided all contact with everyone who knew him, then whatever happened probably occurred soon after the vet destroyed his dog. As Lundy had said, that placed the probable time-since-death at six weeks rather than four.

The problem was that I didn't think these remains could have been in the water that long. If the body had been drifting in this estuary for an additional two weeks it would be in an even worse condition than it already was. Which meant that either Leo Villiers had completely isolated himself for almost a fortnight before he shot himself, which was possible but unlikely . . .

Or this wasn't his body.

'I want *facts*, not doubts,' Clarke snapped, keeping her voice pitched low. 'How soon can we confirm an ID?'

'Well, I think we can safely rule out any help from dental records or fingerprints,' Frears said. 'I'll do what I can, but we'll probably have to wait for the DNA results. Although . . .'

He broke off as footsteps approached on the quayside. I looked around to see Sir Stephen Villiers approaching. Dryden, the Deputy Chief Constable, had come over as well, though he remained a few paces behind the older man and looked as though he'd rather be somewhere else. Clarke stepped towards them, placing herself in front of the stretcher lying on the quay's concrete floor.

'Sir Stephen, I don't think—'

'I'd like to see my son.' The man's voice was dry and inflection-less, yet carried an unshakable authority.

'I'm sorry, but we don't know yet if—'

But he was already moving past her. She shot a look of appeal towards Dryden, but the senior police officer's impassive face made it plain he wasn't going to intervene. Clarke reddened, her ginger hair and pale complexion a giveaway to her emotional state. Tight-lipped, she said nothing as Sir Stephen stood by the open body bag. For a few seconds, the silence was broken only by the gulls. The wind ruffled the grey man's hair as he gazed down at what lay on the concrete at his feet.

'I recognize the coat.' Sir Stephen sounded as unemotional as he appeared. 'It's an old one, from Collier's on Jermyn Street. My son had an account there.'

Clarke and Lundy exchanged a glance. Frears' attention was already back on the body. 'There's a label,' he said, carefully lifting the coat to see inside the lining. 'Collier's Bespoke Tailors.'

'The watch is his as well. You'll find an inscription on the inside. His mother bought it for him before she died.' Sir Stephen raised his head to stare at Clarke. His expression was cold. 'I told you all along that my son was dead. Perhaps now you'll believe me.'

'Sir Stephen, I—'

'My son was clearly the victim of a shooting accident. I fail to see what can be gained by protracting an already painful process.'

'I'm sure DCI Clarke will ensure that a formal identification is given full priority,' Dryden said, his bluff baritone no more subtle than his words. 'Isn't that right, Detective Chief Inspector?'

'Of course.' Clarke tried to keep her face neutral, but she didn't have the colouring for it. 'Dr Hunter, would you excuse us for a moment?'

I nodded, relieved. There wasn't anything else I could do until the body was back at the mortuary, and I'd no desire to be part of any dispute with the dead man's father. Sir Stephen Villiers' reluctance to accept that his son might have killed himself was understandable, but denial couldn't alter the facts. And while a close-range shotgun wound to the face could be called many things, 'accident' was rarely one of them.

But there was another reason I was glad to get away: I'd got it wrong. Unorthodox or not, Sir Stephen's recognition of his son's coat and watch pretty much ended any questions over the body's identity. So much for my doubts over how long it had been in the water. Perhaps I'd been trying too hard, I thought wearily. Clutching at complications that weren't there. And I knew now why I'd been asked to go on the recovery in the first place. The marine unit hadn't needed a forensic anthropologist with them. My presence had been little more than a tick-box exercise, so the dead man's powerful father couldn't accuse the police of overlooking anything.

They'd just been covering their backs.

My rubber waders whickered against each other as I left the quayside and walked behind the oyster sheds to where I'd left my car. There were more parked there now, one of them a muscular black Daimler with darkly tinted windows. I doubted the police budget or a pathologist's wages would stretch to that, so guessed it must belong to Sir Stephen. A man I took to be the driver was leaning against the bonnet, legs crossed at the ankles. He wore a smart but functional suit, close enough in colour to the dark-grey tie to look like a uniform. He'd quickly lowered his hands when I first came around the corner, but now he relaxed. I saw him take in my coveralls and muddy waders as he drew on the cigarette he'd just been about to let drop. Evidently Sir Stephen didn't like his employees smoking on the job.

'So is it him or her?'

I looked at him, surprised. 'I'm sorry?'

Smoke wreathed his head as he regarded me. Except for pock-marking on his cheeks, the legacy of old acne, he had the sort of face it's hard to recall afterwards. The same could be said for the rest of him. Average height, average build, neatly cut mid-brown hair. From a distance I'd thought he was around forty, but now I saw the signs of aging: a lightening of the hair around the temples and faint lines around the mouth and eyes. Nearer fifty, I thought.

He tapped ash from his cigarette. 'The body you've just brought back. Is it him or the woman?'

By *him* he'd mean his employer's son. He'd have to have been blind not to know what we were doing at the quayside, and it wasn't much of a leap for anyone to guess the body must be either Leo Villiers' or Emma Derby's.

But I wasn't about to fuel any gossip. 'Sorry, I can't help you.'

A smile played around his mouth. 'OK. Just making conversation.'

Paying me no more attention, he drew on his cigarette as he kept watch on the corner of the oyster sheds. I carried on to my own car, my mind returning to the scene on the quayside yet again.

But no matter how many times I replayed what had happened, or went over my reasoning about the time-since-death, I didn't come out of it feeling any better.

Opening the car boot, I perched on its edge as I tugged off the waders and then wrestled out of the heavy coveralls. Despite the cold, I was sweating underneath, more than I should have been. Now the recovery was over, I realized I was aching and feeling more out of sorts than ever. Hoping whatever I was coming down with would at least hold off until later, I towelled myself off and took a drink of cold water from one of the bottles I'd put in the cool-box. The Brie I'd bought to take to Jason and Anja's was in there as well, and I felt my spirits sink as the sight of it reminded me I still had to drive all the way across country to the Cotswolds.

Focus on the job and stop feeling sorry for yourself. Shivering in the chill air, I put the lid back on the water bottle. As I pulled on my jacket Sir Stephen and Dryden appeared from behind the sheds: whatever discussion Clarke had wanted to have in private was over. There was a brisk handshake, and then both men went to their separate cars. The Daimler's driver was now ramrod straight, his cigarette nowhere in sight as he went to open the rear door with practised efficiency. Sir Stephen climbed in without giving me a glance. Neither did the driver as he closed the door and then got in himself. The big car started with a low thrum, and then crunched across the broken tarmac to the gates.

By now more police officers were emerging from the quayside. Clarke headed straight for a VW, followed shortly afterwards by Frears. The pathologist had already stripped off his coveralls and looked sleek and well fed in a tailored pinstripe suit and tan brogues. The coveralls had disguised an unexpected plumpness, but he had the confidence and flamboyance to carry it off.

He gave an airy wave as he headed for a BMW that looked as polished as he did. 'See you at the post-mortem,' he called.

I raised my hand in return, feeling scruffy and unkempt in comparison. Now the stretcher appeared, carried by two marine unit officers. Lundy was with them, and peeled off to come over as they headed for a windowless black van.

'Sorry about that. I wasn't expecting Sir Stephen to be here,' he said.

'Everything OK?'

He smiled. 'I think it was what's called a frank exchange of views. Meaning he expressed his, and we listened. Didn't have much choice with the Deputy Chief Constable standing there.'

'Is he involved with the investigation?' I asked. A DCC didn't normally take such a hands-on approach, let alone attend a recovery in person. Dryden hadn't looked exactly happy about it himself.

'Not officially. But like I was saying earlier, Sir Stephen's got a lot of clout and no one wants to ruffle his feathers. Getting the DCC down here's meant to show how seriously we're taking this. Keeps us on our toes as well.'

It would do that, all right. 'What Sir Stephen said about his son's death being an accident. He can't still believe that, can he?'

Lundy absently rubbed his stomach with a look of faint discomfort. The DI was evidently having problems, I thought, remembering the antacids. 'Your guess is as good as mine. His lawyers have come down like a ton of bricks on any suggestion of suicide ever since Leo went missing, but that's one for the inquest. Let's get the post-mortem out of the way first. You clear on how to get to the mortuary for the briefing?'

I said I was. Before a post-mortem, the police team would meet with the pathologist, mortuary technicians and any forensic experts such as myself to brief on the case. The mortuary was in Chelmsford, a good hour's drive, although once I was away from the winding roads around the estuary it should be easy enough to get there.

When Lundy had gone I took a few moments to unwind the kinks from my neck. The feeling that I was coming down with something persisted, and a headache had started to form. Doing my best to ignore it, I put my muddy waders and coveralls into bin bags before cramming them at the back of the boot.

Closing it, I paused to look at the estuary. The returning tide had wrought a dramatic transformation. The barren mudflats had vanished, replaced with a broad stretch of choppy sea. The Barrows were all but hidden, the tips of the highest sandbanks only just breaking the surface, creating oily, flattened patches of water around them. Further out, the three towers of the derelict sea fort stood at the mouth of the estuary on stilt-like legs.

I looked round as an unmarked black funeral company van crunched past, on its way to the mortuary with the body. Following it came the marine unit Land Rover, bouncing over the potholes with the RHIB behind it on its trailer. Quiet settled again once they'd gone. I took a moment to enjoy the estuary's mud and saline air. Although it wasn't exactly picturesque, there was still something restful about this landscape. I would have liked to stay longer, but I was the last one there. The parking area was empty except for my car.

It took more of an effort than it should to rouse myself. I got in my car and drove through the open gateway, then pulled up while I shut the gate. There was no way to lock it, but perhaps there was no need. The oyster sheds had none of the broken windows or graffiti-covered walls you'd expect to find nearer a town or city, and I doubted there'd be anything left to steal. It would take a very bored or determined vandal to come all the way out here.

I backtracked the way I came earlier, passing through the same run-down town that if anything looked even more dismal in full daylight. After that, though, it was a different route. Now I was on the edge of what Lundy had called the Backwaters. The road itself wasn't quite single track, but it wasn't far off. It meandered and twisted back on itself, forced to follow the dictates of the water-logged landscape. High hawthorn hedges bordered it on either side, making it difficult to see what was around the bends. I took it steadily, checking Lundy's directions from time to time to make sure I was still heading the right way. It was hard to tell, but it wasn't as if there were many other roads to choose from.

Still, as one featureless field or marsh merged into another, I began to worry I'd somehow taken a wrong turn. I reached to switch on the satnav; even if it struggled to find a route, it might at least give me a better idea of where I was.

I tapped my fingers on the steering wheel, waiting for the spinning disc to be replaced by a map.

'Come on . . .' I muttered, reaching to tap the screen. I couldn't have taken my eyes from the road for more than a split second.

When I looked up again a man was right in front of me.

5

HE WAS WALKING in the middle of the road with his back to me. I stamped on the brake and swerved, wrenching the wheel as hard as I could. There was a teeth-grating squeal as the side of the car scraped against the hedgerow, and the car juddered as the off-side went onto the grass verge. As the man flashed by my window there was a dull bump of impact. I felt a sick, hollow sensation in my chest as I fought the car, branches snapping as it skidded to a halt on the gravel.

I was flung against the seatbelt, my head jolting as I rocked back in my seat. Oh, God, I thought numbly, heart thumping as I twisted to look behind me.

The man was still standing in the middle of the road.

I'd expected to see a bloodied body lying there, or thrown into the hedgerow. The sight of him still upright and apparently unhurt washed through me like an unexpected reprieve. Unsteady myself, I opened the car door and got out.

'Are you OK?' I asked.

He looked at me blankly, protruding eyes blinking from a long, gaunt face. He was tall and cadaverously thin, wearing a greasy old brown raincoat and wellington boots. The greying hair was matted and a ratty beard sprouted unevenly from a pallid face. He held something clasped to his chest in both hands, and it was only when it cocked its head towards me that I realized it was a seagull.

'Are you all right?' I repeated, and took a step towards him. He backed away, a look of panic and confusion in his eyes. Tall as he was, there was something vulnerable about him. I stopped and held up my hands. 'It's OK, I just want to make sure you're not hurt.'

His mouth worked as though he were going to say something, then his eyes slid away. Still hugging the seagull to him, he started walking along the road.

'No, hang on . . .' I began, but he took no notice. His wellingtons slapped loosely around the long stork-like legs as he trudged right past as though I weren't there. Only the seagull he was carrying paid me any attention, blinking with one angry eye as it turned its head to keep me in view.

OK . . . I watched him go, still shaken by the near miss. If I'd taken the bend any faster I'd have hit him. It had been a stupid place for him to walk, but his ragged state and manner suggested serious mental health issues. Unsure what to do, I stared after him. It went against the grain to just drive away, but I didn't see that I had much option. He wasn't hurt, and while walking in the road made him a danger to himself as well as drivers, I couldn't physically stop him. Besides, the stick-thin legs could cover a lot of ground: he was already out of sight around the next bend.

With a last glance at the empty road, I went back to my car. There was no serious damage, although the hawthorn branches scraped across the bodywork as I eased out of the hedgerow. I gritted my teeth at the sound, trying not to think about the paintwork.

I checked the dashboard clock as I pulled away. There was still time to get to the briefing, but I couldn't afford any more delays. My headache had grown worse, not helped by the jolting from the emergency stop. Opening my window for fresh air, I kept my speed down in case the ragged man had decided to stop on another blind bend. But there was no sign of him around the next, or the one after that. I began to relax, thinking he'd cut across one of the fields, and then I rounded another bend and saw him.

Walking down the middle of the road, right in front of me.

Oh, for crying out loud . . . Slowing, I drew up behind him. He didn't turn around or show any sign of getting out of the way. Just carried on walking at the same pace, arms cradling the seagull to his chest. My hand went instinctively to the horn, but I didn't press it. He was obviously in a fragile state, and I didn't want to frighten him.

Instead, with the car crawling along behind him, I wound the window the rest of the way down and called out.

'Do you want a lift?'

Providing he didn't live too far away I should have enough time to drop him off. That would get him out of the way and ease my conscience at the same time. *Very principled*, a small voice mocked. I silenced it by telling myself that I could always contact social services later. Right now there was somewhere I needed to be.

But the man walking in front of the car gave no response. Wondering if he might be deaf, I called again. This time a slight sideways jerk of his head said he'd heard me.

He just wasn't taking any notice.

Despite myself, I could feel my frustration growing. I tried a different tack. 'Can you let me pass?' I shouted.

Again, there was no response. I looked at the gap between him and the hedgerow, wondering if I could squeeze by, before abandoning the idea. The road was too narrow, and trying to push past a pedestrian with a car was never going to end well.

My car rumbled along in first gear behind the gangling figure in the filthy raincoat. He continued plodding along the road, still carrying the seagull. I considered getting out of the car and trying to persuade him to move, but I knew that would be asking for trouble. Although I'd only been a GP, not a psychiatrist, it was clear the man had problems. There was no telling how he'd react if he felt threatened, and I could already see signs that he was distressed. He'd started walking faster, his head twitching to the side as he cast glances over his shoulder. Whatever else might be wrong with him, he was vulnerable and scared, and right now I wasn't helping.

With a sigh, I dropped back, letting the car coast almost to a stop so he could pull ahead. *So now what?* I gnawed my lip, feeling clammy and out of sorts as I fretted over the lost time. For all I knew he might carry on like this for miles, and wouldn't that make a fine excuse when I showed up late for the briefing?

Or missed it altogether. The satnav had finally sorted itself out, the GPS kicking in to establish where I was. Lundy had warned against relying on it out here but I didn't need an alternative route. Only a detour so I could get past the man in front of me. There was a turning coming up that seemed to connect back to this road after a mile or so. It would take me right into the saltmarshes of the Backwaters, but only for a short while. One thing was certain: if I didn't do something I was going to be late.

The road ahead was clear. I set off again, watching the on-screen arrow marking my position draw closer to the turn-off. There was no sign of the walking man. I wondered again who he might be, what his story was. And why was he carrying a bloody seagull?

I almost missed the turning. It was little more than a gap in the tall hawthorn hedgerow, a single lane track that cut off at a right angle. Hoping I didn't meet another car, I set off down it. The tarmac was broken and overgrown with weeds and grasses, except for two parallel ruts made by previous vehicles. The tall hedge-rows funnelled me along, keeping me from seeing where I was going. I was forced to trust the satnav's map, which showed a T-junction with another road coming up. All I had to do was turn on to it and follow it for about a mile, then I'd be able to cut back on to the route I'd just left. There was still enough time to make the briefing, I told myself, and then the hedgerows ended and I saw what lay ahead.

The road ran into a river.

A broad swathe of water lay in my path, cutting me off from the road on the far side. Not a river, I realized, a tidal creek. It must feed into the estuary, and now it was being flooded by the returning tide as well. It was taking longer this far inland, but water already covered most of the muddy creek bed. The road promised by the satnav was no more than a thin causeway, a rough finger of built-up shingle. Crossing it wouldn't be a problem at low tide, but sections of it were already submerged and the rest soon would be.

I swore and stopped the car. There was no room to turn around, and I didn't relish trying to reverse all the way back up the winding lane. I told myself to stay calm as I stared at the rapidly flooding causeway. The creek wasn't very wide here, and over on its far side I could see the T-junction with the road I'd intended to take. It was agonizingly close. The water covering the causeway was still shallow, and I couldn't see that it would be any different from driving along a flooded road. But it wouldn't stay like that for long; if I was going to cross I'd have to go now.

So what's it to be? Go or stay here? There wasn't really any decision to make. Putting the car into gear, I drove down on to the causeway.

Shingle crunched under the tyres, then was muted by the hiss of spray. I kept my speed slow but steady, not taking my eyes off the barely visible strip in front of me. In places it disappeared altogether, and I had to keep the car straight and trust there were no bends. My knuckles whitened on the steering wheel as water sluiced up on either side like a bow wave. But the opposite bank was drawing closer, and as I passed halfway I allowed myself to relax. Almost there, I thought, and then the car jerked as a front wheel dropped into a submerged pothole.

It wasn't very big, but it didn't have to be. The car's front end dipped down, slapping deeper into the water, and as quickly as that the engine cut out.

'No!' I said, hurriedly reaching to restart it. 'No, no, no . . .'

The engine wheezed for long enough to give me hope, then died. I turned the key again, holding it as tight as I could as though that would make any difference.

'Come *on* . . . !'

The engine whined before dying once more. I tried it again, and then again, but there wasn't even a murmur. I sat in the sudden silence, stunned by this new disaster. The far bank couldn't be more than a few car lengths away. I stared at it, and then flung open the car door and jumped out. The water was bitingly cold and came almost to my knees. It poured over the sill, soaking through my boots and trousers. The pull of it surprised me, and I recalled Lundy telling me the tide came in faster than a man could run.

Not that I was running anywhere. The driver's window was still open, so I quickly closed the door on the water and reached inside to steer with one hand. Then, putting my shoulder into it, I began to push. The car shifted forward and then stopped. The wheel was still stuck in the pothole. Swearing, I dug my feet into the shingle and heaved against the car. Again, the wheel caught on the pothole, but this time I'd been expecting it. As the car rolled back I heaved again, using its own momentum to bump it free.

Yes! Sluggishly, the car began to move forward. I kept pushing, water sloshing up to my knees as I struggled to keep it going. The causeway was becoming difficult to see as the tide covered more and more of it, but I kept the bonnet aimed at where it emerged on to the far bank. The water tugged at my legs as the rising water flowed past. It was becoming harder to push the car as it deepened, but every yard I managed was that much closer to dry land. I was getting into a rhythm when the car suddenly lurched to a halt. I clutched on to it as I lost my balance, realizing straight away what had happened. The back wheel had caught in the same pothole.

'Don't do this,' I breathed, trying to rock the car free again.

This time I wasn't so lucky. I strained against the car, my feet skidding and sinking into the shingle, but it didn't budge. Gasping, I abandoned the attempt. The car wasn't going anywhere unless I could clear away some of the shingle. By now I was soaked to my thighs. Taking off my coat, I put it on the roof and pushed back my sleeves before reaching into the freezing water, groping for the hole the wheel had sunk into. Sharp stones and shells scratched at my hands, cutting into my bloodless fingers as I tried to scrabble them away.

It was a waste of time: the wheel was too firmly held. I banged the side of the car in frustration, trying to think of something in the boot I could use to dig with. The lid from the cool-box would make a poor shovel, but it was better than bare hands. Hugging the side of the car so as not to slip off the causeway, I splashed around to the back. But even as I did I knew it was no use. The water was rising too quickly. It was already so deep that I wasn't sure I'd even be able to push the car through it. It wouldn't be safe to stay out here much longer.

I wasn't ready to give up just yet, though. The water hadn't quite reached the boot. I opened it up, ignoring the bin bag containing the waders that I didn't have time to put on, and pulled the cool-box towards me. I was about to take the lid off when I heard a noise. Faint, but unmistakable: the sound of an engine. Looking out from behind the boot, I saw a flash of grey streaking behind the hedgerow that ran along the creekside road.

A car was coming.

6

I COULDN'T SEE IT clearly through the bushes but it was travelling fast. Water sloshed around my knees as I hurried to the front of my car. As the deep growl of a diesel engine grew louder, I frantically began waving.

'*Hey!* Over here!'

The car was close enough now to see it was some kind of 4x4. There was no way it could miss me: the road would take it within a stone's throw of where I was stranded. It was a Land Rover, a gunmetal-grey Defender, and as it drew nearer I saw a face inside turn my way. The car slowed.

Then it speeded up and carried on.

'*No!* What're you *doing*?'

I stared after the Land Rover in disbelief as it continued down the road. How the hell could the driver not have seen me? Then, just when I thought it was going to keep on going, it pulled up. For a few seconds it just sat there with its engine running, until with a rising whine it quickly reversed up the road. It went past the track leading down to the causeway, but only far enough so it could turn into it facing the creek. Then it bumped down the track and drove straight into the water. Spray shot up as it ploughed towards me, stopping a few yards away. Its engine chugged, exhaust venting from a vertical pipe by the cabin. A snorkel, I realized as the wind whipped the fumes away.

The door opened and a man jumped out into the creek. Indifferent to the water that darkened his jeans to the knees, he waded round to the back of the Land Rover and opened the rear door. Reaching inside, he took something out before returning to the front.

'Here.'

He threw a length of coiled-up rope to me, holding on to one end so it unravelled in the air. It slapped into the water a few feet away. I hurried to grab it as it began to sink and turned back to my car. Reaching into the cold water, I felt for the tow point under the bumper and tied the rope as best I could. By the time I straightened the man had already secured his end of the rope to the Defender's half-submerged tow hitch.

'Make sure you stay on the causeway when I start to back up,' he shouted. 'If you go off the edge I won't be able to pull you out.'

I looked at the rippling water; the pale strip of shingle underneath had all but vanished. 'I can't see it.'

'Just aim for me. I'll flash my lights before I start.'

He turned away and climbed back into the Land Rover. I reached through my car's open window and took hold of the steering wheel. It would have been easier to steer from the driver's seat, but if I opened the door now the inside of the car would be flooded.

The Land Rover's engine suddenly revved and its lights flashed twice. The rope came out of the water as it took up the slack, shedding droplets as it snapped taut. For a second nothing happened. Then the rope quivered and with a lurch my car started moving. I kept my eyes fixed on the Land Rover as it reversed slowly out of the creek. My hands hurt from gripping the steering wheel as the 4x4 backed up on to the bank.

And then my car was bumping up on to the track and off the causeway. The Land Rover carried on going, towing me well clear before it stopped. Water streamed from the car, and when I opened the door the footwells were a sodden mess. But the door seals had kept out the worst of it, and the seats were dry. I looked back at the flooded creek bed. The water completely covered it now, with no sign whatsoever of the causeway.

I turned at the sound of the Land Rover's door slamming. The man looked in his mid to late forties, the unkempt dark hair shot through with the same grey that stubbled his chin. There were deep lines running from his nose to the corners of his mouth, and the creases on the broad forehead suggested a disposition more inclined to scowl than smile. He wore thick-framed but stylish glasses and a brown leather jacket over a navy sweater and jeans. All were well worn, but the jacket looked expensive, and I noticed the discreet designer logo on the side of the glasses.

I held out my hand. 'Thanks. I thought I was—'

'What the hell were you doing?'

His vehemence took me aback. I lowered my hand, my face beginning to burn. 'The satnav showed this as a detour. There was somebody in the—'

'Are you blind or just stupid? See all that wet stuff? That's *water*. You don't try driving across a causeway when the bloody tide's in!'

'The tide wasn't in, and if I'd known there was a pothole I wouldn't have tried to cross. But I appreciate your help.'

I kept my own voice calm with an effort. I didn't need anyone telling me I'd been stupid, and even though I was in his debt I wasn't going to be yelled at by a complete stranger. And not one who'd clearly thought long and hard before deciding to come back.

He glared at me, and I could almost feel the desire to argue radiating from him. I couldn't believe it was just because he'd had to pull my car out of the creek. But I was aching, soaking wet and terminally late for the pathologist's briefing. Whatever his problem was, right then I didn't care. I stared levelly back at him, holding my own temper in check.

After a moment he looked away, breathing out as though audibly letting go of something. 'What are you doing here anyway? We don't get many people coming this far out.'

I hesitated. But by now Sir Stephen Villiers' driver wouldn't be the only person who knew a body had been found. And if this man was local he could hardly have missed the police helicopter that had been circling since first light.

'I was here for a police operation,' I said after a moment.

His gaze suddenly became more piercing. 'You mean the body? You're a police officer?'

Here we go again. My headache had never gone away, but now I became aware of its dull throbbing again. 'No, I'm not a police officer. And I'm not going to tell you what I've been doing, so there's no point asking.'

It came out sharper than I intended. Now it was his turn to look taken aback. 'Well, that's honest, at least. What are you, some sort of police consultant? Or can't I ask that either?'

That much was hardly a secret. 'I'm a forensic anthropologist.'

It wasn't giving much away but he nodded, apparently satisfied. 'Sorry for taking your head off. I'm Andrew Trask.'

He said it as though it should mean something. It didn't, and I was too on edge to pay much attention. I shook the offered hand. 'David. David Hunter.'

A gust of wind suddenly made me realize how cold and wet I was. It belatedly occurred to me that Trask wasn't much better. Water pooled round his boots, and the denim of his jeans was darkened up to the knee as he looked past me at my car. I could almost see some sort of internal debate going on.

'You're not going to be able to call a recovery service.'

'I've got breakdown cover,' I told him, misunderstanding. This wasn't the first isolated place my work had called me out to, so I'd made sure I wouldn't be stranded if I broke down.

'No, I meant you won't get a phone signal. Reception's patchy out here.' He paused, and again I got the impression of a decision being made. 'I'll give you a tow to my house. It's not too far and you can make the call from there.

'That'd be great. Thanks,' I said, surprised by the offer after his earlier hostility.

But I wasn't about to refuse. I'd need all the help I could get if I was going to even make the post-mortem itself, never mind the briefing.

He shrugged, looking as though he were already having second thoughts. 'I can't leave you out here. It'll be easier for directions and my son's good with engines. He might be able to help.'

'No, that's OK. I'm putting you to enough trouble already.'

That was true enough, but I didn't want an amateur mechanic making things worse, no matter how well intentioned.

Trask gave me an odd look. 'Hardly matters, does it?'

At another time I would have wondered what he meant, but I was too tired and dispirited to give it much thought. Some of the energy seemed to drain out of him as he looked down the creek, then he straightened.

'Come on, let's get back,' he said.

While Trask turned the Land Rover around so the rope could be retied to the rear tow bar, I tried my phone. As well as the recovery service, I needed to call Lundy to let him know I'd be late. I'd no idea what damage the salt water would have done to my car, or how long it would take to repair. But if I had to I'd leave it here and worry about that later. My priority now was getting to the mortuary.

Trask was right about the poor mobile reception. I tried wandering round, but my phone stubbornly refused to find a signal. Fretting over the delay, I put it away as Trask finished securing the rope to his Land Rover. I took a last look back at the creek before I climbed into my car again. It was completely flooded, seabirds bobbing on the small waves that ruffled its surface as they were swept along by an invisible current. There was no sign of the causeway at all, and from the erosion on the creek's soft banks from the normal high-water mark, the level was still rising. If Trask hadn't towed me out my car would have been completely submerged before much longer, and there was ample evidence that the tides sometimes rose even higher. A line of dead and bedraggled vegetation lined the creek's banks, detritus from what looked like a recent flood. With the land around here so low-lying, it wouldn't take much for it be overwhelmed.

The tow took fifteen uncomfortable minutes. My arms and legs were cold and soaked through, and my boots squelched whenever I moved. The road meandered, following a convoluted path through the wetlands. From what I could see there was more water than land, a maze of reedy channels and pools in the boggy-looking saltmarsh. The Backwaters were well named.

I saw a few small boats dotted around as I steered behind the Defender, but most of them looked either abandoned or were still battened down from the winter. There weren't many houses, and most of the buildings I saw were old ruins steadily crumbling back into the waterlogged landscape.

Even so, Trask wasn't the only person who lived out here. We passed a converted boathouse, an old stone building that jutted out into the creek's waters. A sign by the small parking area announced, *Holiday cottage to let*. It seemed a remote place for anyone to want to stay, but it was certainly peaceful. With the creeks and channels glinting in the muted sunlight, I couldn't deny the Backwaters had a desolate appeal. At another time I might have liked to stay there myself.

But this was no time to let my concentration wander. My head still ached, and I was starting to shiver. It was an effort to keep the car on the winding road behind the Land Rover, and I wasn't sorry when Trask pulled off on to a gravelled parking area. Behind it was a copse of young trees, and through their still-bare branches I could see a contemporary-looking house on the bank of the creek.

We'd arrived.

Making sure the handbrake was on, I stiffly climbed out. The cold air on my wet clothes sent a chill through me. Trying to disregard it, I looked around. There were two other cars there. One was a Mini convertible that had been covered by a plastic tarpaulin. It stood on a banked-up area of ground to keep it clear of flooding, and from the grime on the tarpaulin I guessed it hadn't been moved for some time. Nearby was another Defender, this one white and ancient, once again with the stovepipe of a snorkel sticking up from it. The young man working under the open bonnet straightened to stare at us.

Trask jumped out of the Land Rover. 'Jamie, run and fetch a towel, will you?'

The request was met with reluctance. 'Why, what's happened?'

'It doesn't matter, just get the towel.'

The younger man's expression made it clear what he thought. He was seventeen or eighteen, good-looking and nearly as tall as Trask. The resemblance was clearly that of father and son, and judging by the teenager's expression they shared a similar temperament as well as looks. Wiping his hands on a piece of cloth, he irritably tossed it down before heading for the house without another word.

If Trask was embarrassed he didn't show it. 'You should get a signal out here if you want to call a recovery service.'

'Thanks. Nice house,' I commented, looking over at the building visible through the copse. The cedar-clad walls were faded to a silver-grey that blended in with the trees, and the sloping roof was lined with solar panels. It faced out over a broad stretch of creek, and I saw now it sat on thick concrete pilings that raised it off the ground. It had obviously been designed to withstand floods, which said a lot about the sort of weather they must get out here.

Trask looked surprised. He glanced at the house as though it wasn't something he usually thought about. 'I built it for my wife.'

I expected him to say more, but that seemed to be as much information as I was going to get. He obviously wasn't one for small talk. 'What's the address? For the recovery service,' I added when that prompted a frown.

'It's Creek House, but the postcode won't help them out here. Tell them to take the road into the Backwaters, then follow the creek until they reach us. If they wind up at Willets Point they've gone too far.'

That was the promontory where Leo Villiers lived. Conscious

that Trask seemed to be watching me, I kept any reaction from my face. 'Thanks.'

His eyes went to my wet clothes. 'Do you want a hot drink while you're waiting?

'A coffee would be great.'

Trask gave a nod, already turning away. I couldn't blame him for not inviting a dripping wet stranger into his home, although I'd have appreciated the chance to dry off and change. I'd brought fresh clothes for my stay at Jason and Anja's, but I needed to sort out my car before I did anything else. Barring miracles, it wasn't just the pathologist's briefing I was going to miss.

Conscious of how time was ticking by, I phoned the recovery service. I didn't hold out much hope of getting a truck out here very soon, and what little I had was soon dashed. This was a bank holiday weekend and the roads were full of people going away. And breaking down, apparently. Priority was being given to lone women, medical emergencies and cases where the car might cause an accident, none of which applied to me. When I explained I was on my way to a post-mortem, the harried operator was less than sympathetic.

'Well, they'll still be dead when you get there, won't they?'

I was told they'd try to get a mechanic out in the next few hours, although even that couldn't be guaranteed. There was no use in arguing, so I gave details of my location as best I could and rang off. *Christ, what a balls-up.* My headache was getting worse. Rubbing my temples, I tried Lundy next. I wasn't looking forward to this call, and felt a sneaking relief when it went straight to voicemail. Without going into details, I left a message saying I'd be delayed because my car had broken down. Hopefully by the time he phoned me back I'd have better news.

The shivering had grown worse. I needed to get out of my wet clothes, so I went to the boot for my overnight bag. At least the water hadn't got in there, which was something. My trousers were soaked to mid-thigh, but I wasn't about to strip off outside Trask's house. Instead I settled for swapping my wet shirt for a thick sweater, and then pulled my only-slightly damp jacket back on.

That done, there was nothing to do but wait. Even though I knew it was clutching at straws, I tried the ignition again. The engine gave a dull, grinding noise and then stopped. The next time it sounded even weaker. I waited a while and then reached to try it again.

'You'll only make it worse.'

I hadn't heard Trask's son approach. 'I don't think it'll make much difference.'

'Maybe not, but it's not going to start again until it's dried out. Flooding the engine isn't going to help.'

The advice wasn't quite surly, but it wasn't exactly gracious either. He really did look like a younger version of Trask, loose-limbed and athletic in faded T-shirt and jeans. On his feet were some sort of neoprene surf shoes that had masked his footsteps. He held out a thickly folded towel.

'Coffee's on its way.'

'Thanks.' I took the towel, drying off my hands and forearms. 'Your dad said you know about engines.'

'A bit.' He glanced at my car, clearly unimpressed. 'If you've got salt water in it you'll need the whole thing stripped down and cleaned. The oil'll need changing, maybe the fuel. It's a big job.'

Fantastic. I'd been considering taking up his father's suggestion and asking if he could take a look after all. But aside from his obvious lack of enthusiasm, it sounded as though I'd need an experienced mechanic anyway.

'Is there a garage around here?' I asked.

He shook his head. 'None that'd be any use.'

'How about car hire? Or taxis?'

If there was any sort of transport available in the nearby town I'd at least be able to get to the mortuary. I could worry about my car later.

But he gave a snort. 'Have you seen Cruckhaven?'

I would have offered to pay him to drive me, but the truculent look on his face told me I'd be wasting my time. He clearly didn't want to get involved in a stranger's problems, and I couldn't blame him. Frustrated, I swore under my breath as he went back to the house. I considered asking his father to take me to the mortuary, but quickly gave up on the idea. Trask had come close to leaving me stranded in the creek, and his entire attitude made it plain he was helping me under sufferance. I could imagine his response if I suggested putting him to any more trouble.

I had to try something, though. The signal wasn't strong enough to go online, so I phoned a directory enquiry number and asked for nearby garages. There might not be anything locally, but Trask's son might only have meant the immediate area. Even if there was one a little further away it would be quicker than waiting for the recovery truck.

Given the way my luck had been running I wasn't optimistic, so I was surprised when the operator came up with a number. It was a boat and car repair business in Cruckhaven, the town I'd driven through earlier. Telling myself not to build up my hopes, I called the number. A man's gruff voice answered.

'Coker's Marine and Auto.'

'My car's broken down. Do you do recoveries?' I asked.

'Depends whereabouts you are.'

'In the Backwaters.' I explained about getting caught on the causeway. There was a snort.

'Bet you won't try that again in a hurry. OK, I should be able to sort you out. Hang on, let me get a pen.'

I offered up a silent prayer of thanks. Now there was an outside chance I could at least make the post-mortem. I checked my watch, gauging how much time I had left as the man came back on the phone.

'Right, fire away. Whereabouts in the Backwaters are you?'

'A place called Creek House. It's not far from an old boathouse. Do you need directions?'

For a heartbeat he didn't answer. 'Don't bother, I know it. You a friend of theirs?'

An edge had entered his voice, but I didn't think anything of it. 'No, they just gave me a tow. How soon can you get here?'

'Sorry, can't help you.'

For a second I thought I'd misheard. 'But you just said you could come out.'

'And now I'm saying I can't.'

'I don't understand. Is there a problem?'

'Yeah, you've got salt water in your engine.'

The line went dead.

What the hell . . . ? I stared at my phone, unable to believe he'd hung up. The suddenly hostility had come out of the blue, as soon as I mentioned Creek House. I hit the steering wheel and swore again. Whatever issue the garage owner had with Trask, it had just cost me my last chance of making the post-mortem.

The headache was throbbing all the way from the base of my neck. Massaging it, I closed my eyes and tried to think what to do next. A dog's excited barks made me open them again. A woman and a young girl were coming along the path through the copse, accompanied by a brown mongrel that pranced and yapped around them. The girl was precariously carrying a mug, holding it up as the dog bounced around.

'. . . *spill* it! Naughty girl, Cassie,' the girl was saying, but in a tone of voice that encouraged the dog even more. She was about eight or nine, with the same bone structure as her father and brother. Even though she was laughing, the thin arms and dark rings under her eyes suggested some underlying problem.

I assumed the woman must be her mother, although there was no obvious resemblance between them. She was slim and attractive, considerably younger than Trask. She had dark, honey-coloured skin and thick black hair tied casually back with a black band. Her jeans were faded and paint-stained, while the chunky sweater she wore looked at least two sizes too big. It made her look even younger, and I found it hard to believe she could have a teenage son.

'We've brought you a coffee,' the young girl said, carefully offering the mug she was carrying.

'Thanks. Here, let me.' I hurried to take it, giving her mother a smile. She returned it, but it was a token effort that vanished as soon as it came. She wasn't conventionally pretty, her features were too strong for that. But she was undeniably attractive, with striking green eyes that were all the more startling against the olive skin. I found myself thinking that Trask was a lucky man.

'Dad says you got stuck on the causeway,' the girl said, looking past me at my car.

'That's right. I was glad he was there to tow me off.'

'He says it was a bloody stupid thing to do.'

'Fay!' her mother admonished.

'Well, he did.'

'He was right,' I said, smiling ruefully. 'I won't do it again.'

Trask's daughter studied me. The dog had flopped down at her feet, grinning up at her with a lolling tongue. It was only young, hardly more than a puppy. 'Where are you from?' she asked me.

'London.'

'I know someone from London. That's where—'

'OK, Fay, let's leave the gentleman alone,' her mother cut in. She regarded me with a look that was cool rather than unfriendly. 'How long are you going to be here?'

'I don't know. It looks like I picked a really bad day to break down.' The weak attempt at a joke fell flat. I shrugged. 'The garage in Cruckhaven won't come out, so I'll just have to wait for the recovery service.'

I saw her react when I mentioned the garage, but she made no comment. 'When can they send someone?'

'They can't say. But I'll be out of your way as soon as I can.'

The green eyes considered me. 'I hope so. Come on, Fay.'

I watched them walk back to the house, Trask's wife slim and poised as she rested her hand protectively on her daughter's shoulder while the dog sprinted ahead. *Well, that was blunt.* I wondered if the inhabitants of the Backwaters were always this friendly, or if it was just me.

But I'd more to worry about than local hostility, so I soon put it from my mind.

7

THE SOFT BANKS of the creek had been eroded away. Tides and currents had conspired to carve a sweeping arc out of the sandy earth, like a giant bite-mark flanked with reeds and marsh grass. It formed a natural trap, in which a variety of flotsam bobbed on the slow-moving water. Driftwood and twigs bumped alongside man-made detritus: a muddy training shoe, a doll's head, plastic bottles and food containers, all caught in the circular eddy.

It was peaceful out here in the Backwaters. The world seemed ruled by gulls, marsh and water. And sky: the flatness of the landscape made it seem huge and vaulting. If I looked back the way I came, Trask's house was just visible behind the copse of trees a couple of hundred yards away. I'd headed out along the creek after I'd finished the coffee. There was a path of sorts, not much more than a ribbon of bare earth worming its way through the tough and wiry grasses. It soon petered out, though, and I found it wasn't possible to walk any distance without being diverted by another water-filled ditch or pool. It would be much easier in a boat, although even then I could imagine quickly becoming lost in this maze of saltmarsh and reeds.

I watched the swirling water nudge the trainer against a tennis ball without really noticing it. I'd been too restless to sit in my wet car while I waited for the recovery truck. I still hadn't spoken to

Lundy, but I knew the pathologist's briefing would have already started. That wouldn't take long, and then Frears would go ahead with the post-mortem whether I was there or not. Not that it would make any difference. I doubted I'd have been able to contribute much anyway. I was under no illusion about why I'd been included in the investigation, and my presence was even more redundant once Sir Stephen had identified his son's belongings. Decomposed or not, confirming the ID and probable cause of death seemed likely to be a formality after that. Just as everyone had thought – with the possible exception of his father – Leo Villiers had killed Emma Derby, his estranged lover, and then cracked under the pressure and shot himself.

So why did I still feel uneasy?

I looked out across the waterlogged landscape. Not far from where I stood, a derelict old boat lay stranded with its bow on the bank and its stern sunk into the water, crumbling and rotten. On the bank next to it was a dying willow tree. The bottom half of its thick trunk was stained, and strands of dead grass and weeds trailed from its lower branches as a reminder that the creek wasn't always so sedate. It wasn't hard to see how Leo Villiers' body could have remained hidden for several weeks out here, sunk to the bottom of some deeper hole until it refloated and was carried into the estuary by the tide. It was a perfectly plausible scenario.

Except I still felt six weeks was too long for it to have played out in. Four, perhaps, but not six. Even if the body had remained on the creek bed for much of the time, it would still have been susceptible to the twice daily tides. It would have been dragged and pulled across the sandy bottom, bumped against rocks and stones, all the while subject to the depredations of whatever scavengers happened upon it. And during all that time its own internal decay would have continued, accelerating the body's disintegration even more. I could tell myself that the cold water and air of the winter months would have preserved it, that estimating time-since-death wasn't an exact science at the best of times, let alone in an estuarine environment like this. It didn't matter.

Six weeks was too long.

Fine. Then Villiers locked himself away and drank himself into a stupor for the missing fortnight. And then came out here and shot himself. It was possible. Although I was sceptical that someone like Leo Villiers would cut himself off so completely, I hadn't known him. And people were unpredictable enough even when they weren't contemplating suicide.

Yet I couldn't believe that was the explanation either.

A shiver ran through me, reminding me that it was time to go back. Mobile reception was unreliable away from the house, and for all I knew Lundy might be trying to get hold of me. I needed to check on the situation with the recovery service as well, and I'd still to call Jason to let him know I wouldn't make it to the party. That was a silver lining of sorts, I supposed.

Turning away, I began retracing my steps to the house. I'd felt better after the hot coffee, and thought a walk would help my headache. Now I was belatedly starting to think it hadn't been such a good idea. Despite the cold breeze I was sweating heavily, and I couldn't stop shivering. The journey back seemed to take an age. I was forced to detour each time I found the way cut off by another water-filled ditch, and there seemed far more of them than I remembered. By the time I reached the house I felt worn out, my arms and legs leaden. Another car was parked near mine on the gravelled parking area, though unfortunately it wasn't from the recovery service. Not unless they'd sent an old white Ford Fiesta with a bright-red racing stripe across its top.

Trask's son was again busy under the bonnet of the old white Land Rover. A blond girl I guessed was the Fiesta's owner stood next to him, arms folded and lips clamped tight. She looked in her late teens, pretty but a little overweight. And overdressed: her tight skirt, high-heeled shoes and heavy make-up looked more suited for a Saturday night.

Neither of them noticed me approaching, and their voices carried clearly on the creekside path.

'. . . come on, Jamie, why not?' Her voice was pure Essex. Trask's son answered without breaking off what he was doing.

'You know why.'

'But that was ages ago. I came specially when I heard!'

'I didn't ask you to. If you can't—'

He stopped when he realized I was there. The girl turned to give me a glare, as though I were to blame for the argument. I mustered a tired smile as I continued past to my car. Disregarding me, she turned back to Trask's son. Her fingernails were a bright, blood red, and the toenails peeping from the open-fronted shoes were painted to match.

'Come on, Jamie, he won't know.'

'I don't care.'

'Then what's the problem?'

He didn't answer. I was trying hard not to listen but it was impossible not to.

'Jamie, why won't you talk to me?' Again there was no response. The girl's wheedling tone became accusing. 'You didn't use to be like this.'

'Stacey . . .'

'Well, you didn't. It's not my fault that—'

'Jesus, give it a *rest*!'

There was a bang as the Land Rover's bonnet was slammed shut. I looked round and saw Trask's son stalking back to the house, leaving the girl standing behind.

'Jamie? *Jamie!* Right, fuck off then!' the girl yelled after him. The slam of the front door came through the trees. 'Prick!'

She turned away, her face flushed and angry. She was close to tears, but then she saw me and her mouth twisted.

'The fuck are you looking at?'

Yanking open the Fiesta's door, she threw herself inside and started it up. Gravel scattered from its tyres as she pulled away, over-revving as she accelerated back towards the road.

I wasn't the only one having a bad day.

The noise from the car engine faded. The only sound was the

lapping of water from the creek and the calling of seabirds. I checked my phone for messages, but there was nothing from either Lundy or the recovery service. I was putting it away again when it rang.

It was the DI. 'Just got your message, Dr Hunter. I've been in the post-mortem. Had a spot of bother, did you?'

I looked at the flat expanse of fields and water, as if they might offer some last minute inspiration. 'You could say that.'

Without going into details, I explained that my car wasn't going anywhere, and that I'd no idea how long a repair would take. I'd expected annoyance, but Lundy seemed as amiable as ever.

'Well, there's not much point you coming to the mortuary now anyway,' he said when I'd finished. 'Frears was ready to wind things up when I came out. No major surprises. Probable cause of death a contact shotgun wound to the head. Body's male, and the X-rays didn't show any bone injuries that might make us think it's not Leo Villiers. The watch has an inscription on the back from his mother, and the rest of the clothes all match ones Villiers wore. We can't say for sure yet that they're his, but they're the same expensive brands he bought. So, pending DNA results, it's looking like a pretty solid ID.'

'What about the piece of metal stuck in the gullet?' I asked, glancing towards the house to make sure no one was nearby.

'Gone off to the lab with the cartridge wad. It's badly deformed, so we still can't say if it's a pellet or not, but you were right about it being steel rather than lead. Stainless, by the look of it.' I heard him sniff. 'That's about it. All fairly straightforward, so I don't think you missed much.'

Neither did I, but I still should have been there. 'I can take a look tomorrow. My car should be fixed by then.'

Even if it wasn't, I'd hire one. I might not be able to add much to Frears' findings, but I'd at least like to try. I heard the DI clear his throat.

'Thanks, but I don't think there's any need.'

I could hear the embarrassment in his voice. I bit back the

impulse to try to persuade him, knowing this would have come from Clarke. Nothing I said would make any difference.

'OK,' I said, masking my disappointment. 'Let me know if you need me.'

Lundy assured me he would and rang off. I lowered the phone. *Well, you did a great job today, Hunter. Congratulations.* Unlocking my car, I sank wearily onto the driver's seat and sat with my legs stretched outside. So that was that. It was hard to believe the day had started off with such promise.

I watched a seagull splash down into the creek. It was still full, small ripple-like waves lapping close to the top of the bank. Yet in another few hours the water-filled saltmarsh would drain and revert back to muddy ditches and channels. And then the whole cycle would repeat itself, again and again.

I was sure there was a healthy lesson in perspective there some-where, but right now I felt too dispirited to appreciate it. I pulled my jacket tighter as another shiver ran through me. It must be turning colder, I thought. I shivered again, and then, as though my body had been waiting for me to notice, it occurred to me that I wasn't feeling very good at all. I'd been so fixated on not missing the post-mortem that I'd shut out everything else. The shivers weren't just down to the cold, I realized. I was starting to feel feverish. My headache was worse, joined by a soreness in my joints and throat, and when I touched the glands in my neck they felt tight and swollen.

I sat up straighter, realizing how stupid I'd been. I'd been feeling out of sorts for days, had even woken up feeling as though I'd a hangover. Getting soaked in the creek hadn't helped, and even then I'd not had the sense to get out of all my wet clothes. And now, surprise, surprise, I was coming down with a chill. For most people that would be no big deal.

But I wasn't most people.

As well as a scar on my stomach, the knife attack at my flat had left me without a spleen. That weakened my immune system, which meant I had to take prophylactic antibiotics every day for the rest of my life. Most of the time it wasn't a problem: I'd recover from colds and bugs like anyone else. But there was always a risk that an infection could flare up into something called overwhelming post-splenectomy infection, or OPSI. It was rare, but when it happened it could happen fast.

And it could be fatal.

I got to my feet, the weakness in my legs another sign of my stupidity. I was supposed to be a GP, for God's sake, I should have known better than to ignore the warning signs. Now what had just been a frustrating day had turned into something very different.

I felt weak and unsteady as I went to open the car boot. My work often involved travelling – or at least it had – sometimes to places even more isolated than this, so I kept emergency antibiotics permanently packed. Amoxicillin was a broad-spectrum antibiotic, much stronger than the penicillin I took every day. Neither would be any use if this was a virus, but they'd help fight off a bacterial infection.

I swallowed the pills down with a bottle of water from the supply I also carried in the boot, then collapsed back on to the driver's seat again while I debated what to do. If this developed into OPSI then I needed to be in a hospital. On the other hand, it might still prove to be no more than an annoying virus I'd shake off with no ill-effects.

The problem was there was no way of knowing. At the moment I didn't feel ill enough to go to hospital, but that could soon change. Especially if I sat around for much longer in wet clothes. *All right, then.* I quickly ran through my options. Going back to London obviously wasn't an option, and neither was sitting around out here any longer. My head throbbed as I stood up. I waited for the light-headedness to pass and then set off along the gravel footpath running through the trees.

Up close, Trask's house was even more striking, angular and contemporary, with weathered cedar walls designed to blend in with the natural environment. The concrete pilings raising it off the floor might make it flood-proof, but they also meant I'd a flight of steps to climb up to the front door. I felt as weak as a baby as I hauled myself to the top, pausing to catch my breath before knocking on the oiled wood. I heard the dog barking from inside, and a moment later Trask opened the door.

He didn't seem overjoyed to see me. 'Is the recovery here?'

'No, I . . . there's been a change of plan. Is there a hotel nearby?'

'A hotel?' Trask sounded as though that were an alien concept. 'I've no idea. I don't think so.'

'What about a B and B? Or a pub?'

'No, not for miles. Why? Don't tell me you're turning this into a holiday?' Some of his irritation faded as he looked at me. His frown deepened. 'Are you all right? You look bloody awful.'

'I'm fine, it's . . . it's just a bug.' I played my last card: after this I was out of ideas. 'We passed a house on the way here, a holiday rental. Do you know who owns it?'

If the owners were local and prepared to let it out for a few nights then I could rest up until the antibiotics kicked in. Part of me knew I was being stupid, gambling that I wasn't going to get worse rather than make a fuss. But I'd deal with that if it happened.

Trask was looking at me uncertainly. 'The old boathouse, you mean?'

I nodded, relieved. 'Do you know whose it is?'

'It's ours.' He seemed taken aback. 'My wife was renovating it.'

At another time I might have picked up that something was wrong, but right now it took all my energy just keeping upright. 'I know this is an imposition, but can I stay there tonight? I'll pay for a full week,' I added, seeing his reluctance.

He looked away, running a hand through his hair. 'I'm not . . . it isn't really ready.'

'It doesn't matter. If there's a bed and some heating, that'll be enough.'

Trask still didn't seem happy. But then he looked at me again, and whatever he saw must have decided him.

74

'Wait here, I'll go and get Rachel. She knows more about it than I do.'

With that he closed the door, leaving me standing outside. I felt too wretched to care, assuming he didn't want me passing whatever I'd got on to his family. I leaned back against the wall, resting my head against the weathered timber. It seemed a long time before the door opened again. This time it was Trask's wife. The attractive features were set in unforgiving lines, and the green eyes were cold as she faced me.

'Andrew says you want to rent the boathouse.'

'Just for the night.'

'Bad case of man flu, is it?' She handed me a set of car keys. 'Here, go and wait in the car while I get some things together. You can put the heater on.'

Feeling too drained to be embarrassed, I trudged back through the copse to where the cars were parked. Trask's wife hadn't said which of them we were going in, but the keys had an electronic fob, so it wasn't the antiquated white Defender. I climbed into the newer grey Land Rover, feeling a touch of déjà vu at the memory of the car I used to drive as I started the engine. While I waited for the heater to warm up I took out my phone to cancel the recovery. I hated causing Trask and his family any more trouble, but it wasn't as though I had much choice.

I called Jason after the recovery service to let him know I wasn't going to be able to make it to the Cotswolds. He was sceptical at first, assuming it was just an excuse to duck the party, but something in my voice must have convinced him. Watch yourself, he told me, sounding concerned. I said I would, aware that I'd left it a little late for that. I was putting away my phone when Trask's wife reappeared. She was carrying a cardboard box and bags of what I guessed were towels and bedding. I got out of the car, a reflexive action to help, but she brusquely shook her head.

'I can manage.'

It was perhaps as well. While she bad-temperedly dumped her

parcels into the back of the Land Rover, I collected my laptop and travel bag from the car. My legs felt like water.

'That it?' she asked when I came back. 'Come on then.'

Despite the car heater I was still shivering as we set off. She didn't speak but communicated her disapproval every time she changed gear. The silence built until I had to say something.

'Sorry for putting you to all this trouble.'

'It's a holiday let. That's what it's for.'

Another emphatic gear change. I tried again. 'I honestly didn't know who owned the boathouse when I asked about it.'

'Would it have made any difference?'

'I'm just . . . I was hoping to get out of your way.'

'Yeah, that's worked out well, hasn't it?'

Her face in profile was angry and uncompromising. I'd no idea why she was so upset, but I'd had enough.

'Look, forget about the boathouse. Just . . . drop me off anywhere.'

'So now you've changed your mind?'

Jesus. 'Just pull over. I'll get out here.'

There was nothing except marshland and fields either side of the creek, but I didn't care. She frowned.

'Now you're being ridiculous. I can't leave you in the middle of nowhere.'

'Then drop me somewhere I can get a taxi. The town, anywhere, I don't care.'

She glanced across at me. I tried to stop shivering but couldn't. 'You don't look good,' she conceded.

'I'm fine,' I said, knowing I was being stupid as well as stubborn.

Trask's wife didn't respond. She carried on driving for a while before she spoke. 'This isn't just a cold, is it?'

I was going to say it didn't matter. But the more rational part of me recognized that I couldn't afford pride just now.

'There's a problem with my immune system,' I admitted.

'What sort of problem?'

76

'Nothing contagious,' I told her, guessing what she was thinking. I didn't want to have to explain, but I couldn't see a way round it. *Oh, hell.* 'I don't have a spleen.'

'Shit.' She sounded concerned as well as shocked. 'Shouldn't you see a doctor?'

'I am a doctor. I'm on antibiotics. I just need somewhere to rest up.'

That earned another glance, dubious this time. 'I thought you told Andrew you were a forensic expert?'

'I am.' I wished I'd never started this. 'I used to be a GP.'

'Not a very good one. What the hell were you thinking, sitting around in wet clothes? Why didn't you say something?'

In hindsight it wasn't one of my better ideas, but I didn't have the energy to argue. 'I'll be fine,' I repeated weakly.

Trask's wife gave me a look that told me what she thought of that. 'I hope so. We're there now.'

She bumped the Land Rover on to a cinder-covered parking area and put the handbrake on. The boathouse was a small stone building that jutted out from the bank of the creek. Its lower half stood in the water, stone walls stained with a line to show where the high tide came. The top half was a single storey built on a level with the creek bank. Two small windows were on either side of a door, like a child's drawing of a house.

Trask's wife went to it, balancing the box against the wall while she went through a large ring of jangling keys.

'Come on, where are you?' she muttered to herself.

Finally, she found the right key and nudged open the door with her hip. The inside was a surprise. There were no interior walls, just a single large room that had been decked out like a studio apartment. It was much brighter than I'd have thought from outside. The unplastered stone walls had been painted white, and light spilled through a large arched window facing out on to the creek. A small kitchen area had been built at one side, while a sofa and armchair stood either side of a wood-burning stove at the other. The furniture was sixties-style Scandinavian, plain lines and muted colours, and a deep-red rug covered most of the varnished floorboards.

Everything looked new and unused, and a faint smell of fresh paint still hung in the air. Small as it was, the place was bright and airy, the sort of thing that could feature in the pages of a glossy travel magazine. Trask had said his wife had renovated it, and she'd done a good job.

She dumped the box down on the kitchen worktop. 'We weren't expecting anyone to be staying here till the season starts,' she said, going round briskly flicking switches. Warm air began to waft from a heater mounted on one wall. 'It's not finished but you should be comfortable enough. The woodburner works if you need it. No wi-fi or TV, but you can generally pick up a mobile signal. Oh, and the bathroom's in there.'

She gestured towards a door in a small cubicle tucked away in one corner. I nodded, but I'd noticed something was missing. 'Where's the bed?'

I was hoping I wouldn't have to sleep on the small sofa, but Trask's wife went over to a section of wall panelled with rough-hewn planks. Taking hold of a leather strap, she heaved and the entire panel swung out to reveal a pull-down bed.

'I've brought bedding and towels in the car,' she said unenthusiastically. 'You might as well take it easy while I get everything made up.'

I didn't argue. An armchair was next to the arched window. I sank into it, light-headed and shivering despite the warm air from the heater. I was feeling feverish now, my whole body aching and weak. Outside, I saw that the water level in the creek looked much lower. For as far as I could see there were only fields, dunes and water. I wondered if I'd done the right thing, if I shouldn't have just found a hospital. If my condition deteriorated it would take a long time for any help to get out here. I'd be on my own.

But I was used to that.

I got to my feet when Trask's wife came back, but she brusquely waved aside my offer of help.

'It's OK.' She actually gave me a smile. A strained one, but still a smile. 'You should sit down before you fall down.'

She had a point. It didn't take her long to make up the bed. That done, she straightened and looked round.

'OK, I think that's everything. I've left tea, coffee, some soup and a few other things, so you shouldn't starve. Do you need anything else?'

'No thanks.' I just wanted her to leave so I could collapse onto the bed.

'I'll take your boots with me. We've got a drying room we can put them in. Someone can drop them off for you tomorrow.' She regarded me uncertainly. 'Are you sure you're going to be OK?'

'I'll be fine.'

'I'll write you my number down in case . . . Well, just in case.' She scribbled it down on a pad from one of the kitchen drawers and handed it to me. 'Is there anyone I can call to let them know? Your wife or someone?'

'No. But thanks anyway.'

She still looked unhappy as she went to the door. She reached out to open it then paused. 'Look, I'm sorry I gave you a hard time earlier. It's been . . . a strange day. Emotions have been running a bit high. For all of us.'

If I hadn't felt so wasted I'd have wondered what that meant. 'Don't worry about it. I appreciate what you and your husband have done.'

'My husband?' She looked puzzled, then her face blanked as she understood. 'You mean Andrew?'

Seeing her expression, I realized my mistake. 'I'm sorry, I thought . . .'

'Andrew's not my husband. He's my brother-in-law.'

Colour had risen to her cheeks. She went to the door while I floundered for something to say.

'Call if you need anything,' she said without looking at me, and went out.

The door closed behind her. I looked down at the notepad in my hand, already knowing what I'd see. In looping script above the phone number she'd written her name.

Rachel Derby.

8

THE CALL OF seagulls woke me next morning. Their raucous cries dragged me from a deep sleep, so loud it sounded as though they were in the room with me. There was a gentle light against my eyelids, which was strange because I slept with the curtains closed. I tried to ignore both, loath to rouse myself, but then opened my eyes. I stared up at the unfamiliar pointed ceiling, with its white-painted roof beams, with no idea where I was. Then I remembered.

Still alive, then.

I lay there for a while, comfortable and warm under the duvet. I felt no great urgency to move as I cautiously took stock of how I felt. Better, I decided. Much better.

And hungry.

That was a good sign. I'd hardly eaten anything the night before. After Rachel Derby had left I'd briefly entertained the idea of a shower, but didn't feel I had the strength. I took a couple of paracetamol to bring down my temperature, then opened a can of tomato soup, putting it to warm on the electric hob while I got out of the still-wet trousers. I ate what I could, shaking so much that the spoon rattled against the bowl.

I'd no appetite, though. Leaving most of the soup unfinished, I crawled into bed and pulled the duvet over me. I ached all over, and as fits of shuddering racked through me I wondered again if, in a day already littered with bad decisions, coming here rather than a hospital might be the worst one yet. For a few hours I'd dozed feverishly, but at some point I'd sunk into a proper sleep.

Now, looking at my watch, I saw it was after ten. I stared at the wooden beams above me, listening to the scrabble of birds' feet on the roof. No wonder it sounded as though they were in here with me: they practically were. There was another noise as well, one that it took me longer to identify. I was in the upper floor of what had been a boathouse, with the dock below. The tide must be in, and the sound I could hear was the gentle slap of water from under the floorboards.

I sat up carefully and swung my legs off the bed, taking a moment before I stood up. I still felt washed out, but nothing like the day before. The infection hadn't been the onset of OPSI after all, just some short-lived bug that either the antibiotics or my own immune system had fought off. Provided I didn't overdo things, in a day or two I should be fine.

Now I was famished. And badly in need of a shower, I realized, wrinkling my nose. Hungry as I was, I'd enjoy it more once I'd cleaned myself up. The bathroom was compact but as well designed as the rest of the studio flat. I stood for a long time under the hot needles of water, relishing the sting of it. Clean and shaved, I dressed in clothes I'd brought for my stay at Jason and Anja's. Then I went to see about breakfast.

There was milk, butter and eggs in the fridge, plus a half loaf and an unopened jar of marmalade on the kitchen worktop. I toasted two slices of bread and scrambled a couple of eggs while the kettle boiled for coffee. I ate ravenously at the small dining table, then made more toast which I slathered with butter and marmalade.

When I'd finished I felt better than I had in days. Making myself another coffee, I took it over to the arched window, watching sea-birds bobbing on the half-full creek as I finally allowed myself to consider the situation I'd put myself in.

It was a clumsy mistake by any standards. Lundy had told me that Emma Derby, the supposed victim of Leo Villiers, was married. It just never occurred to me that she might have a different surname from her husband. Even when Trask had mentioned his wife I'd failed to make the connection, assuming he must be referring to Rachel.

Emma Derby's sister.

The scale of my gaffe appalled me. No wonder they'd all seemed so on edge. Trask and his family would have been going through all sorts of torture yesterday. If they hadn't been told by police, they would have heard rumours about what had been found in the estuary. Even though Emma Derby had been missing too long for the floating remains to be hers, her family would still have wondered. And they'd be aware that, if not hers, the body probably belonged to the man who'd killed her.

Rachel had practically said as much the evening before: *It's been a strange day. Emotions have been running a bit high. For all of us.* I winced to think how insensitive I must have seemed. As a police consultant, they'd have assumed I'd know who they were. Instead, blinded by my own problems, I'd had to have it literally spelled out for me. And then only after I'd blundered into the middle of a grieving family's lives.

But I couldn't change what had happened. All I could do now was apologize and leave them in peace as quickly as possible. Although, with my car still broken down outside Trask's house on a bank holiday Sunday, that would be easier said than done.

Finishing my coffee, I called the recovery service. As Rachel had said, there was a signal in the boathouse, if only a weak one. I found a spot by the window where it seemed stronger, but when I rang the number and the 'non-emergency' option from the menu I found myself held in a queue. While I waited to speak to someone I looked around the studio flat. It was simple but well done, the sort of place I'd like to stay for longer under different circumstances. Trask's wife had evidently had a knack for design, and as I thought about her my eye fell on the framed photographs stacked against the wall. I recalled Lundy's saying something about her being a photographer. Curious, I started to go over, only to lose the signal as soon as I stepped away from the window.

I redialled and found myself at the back of the queue again. *Great.* Turning the phone's speaker on, I set it down on the windowsill and went over to the photographs. They were obviously waiting to be hung on the boathouse walls, so I didn't think anyone would mind if I took a look. There were about a dozen, various sizes but all black and white. At the bottom of each photograph was the same flamboyant signature: *Emma Derby.*

They were mostly still-lifes or landscapes. There was a study of the boathouse and creek, all moody shadows and dark, reflective water. Another showed the sea fort, sun glinting off the waves as it was artfully silhouetted by a monochrome sunset. I was no expert, but they seemed competent enough, if slightly clichéd. One in particular, a shot of a gleaming chrome motorbike on a sand-bank, was so obviously staged it practically shouted 'poster art'.

There was only one portrait. It was of an attractive woman, long dark hair framing her face as she smiled at the camera, naked except for a tastefully draped white sheet. The title, written in the same handwriting as the signature, was simply *Me.*

It was the first photograph of Emma Derby I'd seen. Even allow-ing for the flattering nature of the self-portrait, she was very good-looking. And evidently knew it. It took a lot of self-assurance – or vanity – to pose like that. There was a knowing, self-satisfied look in the eyes that stared back at the camera, a suggestion of arrogance in the tilt of her chin. I knew it was unfair to make a snap judgement, but it was hard to imagine the confident woman in the photograph settling in a remote place like this. Or being married to Trask, I thought, an older man with a teenage son and young daughter. Lundy had told me Emma Derby had moved here two or three years ago when she'd got married, so she wasn't Fay and Jamie's mother. The DI had also said that her marriage was in difficulties even before her affair with Leo Villiers. Now I was beginning to understand why.

I found myself studying the photograph, looking for any resemblance between the sisters. There was a little around the eyes, and in the luxuriant dark hair, but if I hadn't known their relationship I wouldn't have guessed. Rachel Derby wasn't as obviously attractive, but I didn't think she'd rely as heavily on make-up and lighting, either.

And there's another snap judgement. The recorded voice from my phone's speaker continued to ask me to hold as I went through the rest of the framed photographs. I'd just leaned them back against the wall when a knock came on the door.

I gave a guilty start, as though I'd been caught out. Making sure the photographs weren't going to slide over, I went to see who it was.

I felt a brief disappointment when I opened the door to find Trask outside. He was wearing the same battered leather jacket as before, although the stern face was clean-shaven today. He was carrying my boots in one hand, and what looked like the cool-box from my car in the other.

'Can I come in?'

I stood back to let him inside. He glanced around the studio as though unfamiliar with it.

'Can I get you a coffee?' I offered.

'No, I'm not staying. Thought I'd see how you were.'

'Better, thanks.'

'Glad to hear it. Here, I brought you these.' He handed me my boots, setting the cool-box on the floor. 'Rachel dried them out overnight but you'll probably want to get them cleaned. The salt'll rot them if not.'

'Thanks.' I appreciated the gesture, but I thought the real reason he'd come was to make sure their lodger had survived the night. Not that I could blame him. 'Look, I need to apologize for yesterday. I'd no idea who you or your family were. I wouldn't have put you in that position if I had.'

'Yes, I heard about that.' He shrugged. 'You weren't to know. I shouldn't have assumed you did.'

85

He looked down at the cool-box, the lines on his face deepening. It was either mine or one just like it, and I thought he was about to explain why he'd brought it.

'Jamie took it on himself to start working on your car,' he said instead. 'The salt water would have wrecked the engine if it was left any longer. Ordinarily I'd have checked with you first, but I assumed you'd be wanting to get away so I told him to go ahead. Hope that's OK.'

I could understand why they'd want to see the back of me, but I wasn't entirely happy about Trask's son tackling the repair. He hadn't seemed inclined to help the day before. And while I didn't want to appear ungrateful, if the job was as complicated as Jamie had said I had mixed feelings about a teenager working on it anyway.

I picked my words carefully. 'I thought it needed to go into a garage. Can he do it here?'

'Provided the salt's not corroded the engine too badly, he says he should be able to. Don't worry, Jamie knows what he's doing. He rebuilt his Land Rover, the old white one, from scratch. Saved up and bought it himself when he was fifteen, repairing what he could and buying spares from scrap yards and online. He's perfectly capable of stripping and cleaning an engine.'

It sounded more a statement of fact than a boast. I couldn't help wishing the offer had been made yesterday, but they'd had enough to deal with without having to bail me out as well.

'I can still get a breakdown call-out,' I said. 'I don't expect your son to give up his bank holiday.'

'He won't mind, it's his hobby. If you're happy with what he does you can always pay him. He's going to university next year, so he can use the money.' Trask tipped his head at my phone, which was now playing tinny music. 'Doesn't sound like your breakdown service is coming any time soon.'

He had a point. If his son could repair it I'd probably be out of their hair a lot sooner than if I waited for a recovery truck to arrive. But something else had occurred to me. I looked over at where my car keys lay on the kitchen worktop.

'How did he open the bonnet?'

'Same way we got in the boot. You left the car unlocked.'

I'd been more out of it than I'd thought. I could remember fetching my travel bag from the boot while Rachel loaded the Land Rover, but for the life of me I couldn't recall locking the car again afterwards. I hurriedly tried to think what was in the boot: muddy coveralls and waders, plus the flight case containing my forensic equipment. Nothing confidential or sensitive, but I was normally more careful than that.

'That's why I brought this.' Trask made as if to nudge the coolbox with his foot, but stopped short of touching it. His frown had deepened into something like distaste. 'Jamie noticed the smell. We didn't open it, but I didn't really want it outside my house.'

Now he'd mentioned it I could smell it myself: a pungent, ammoniac odour coming from the box. I bent down and unfastened it. The stink suddenly became stronger. Trask took a quick step back as I opened the lid.

'I was supposed to be staying with friends yesterday,' I told him, letting him see the cheese and wine inside. The ice packs that had been in with them had long since thawed. The wine would be fine, but the lack of chilling hadn't done the already ripe Brie any favours.

Trask looked startled, then gave a laugh. 'Jesus, I thought . . . you know.'

I did. Given my work, he'd assumed the box must hold some grisly piece of evidence. Trask's face settled back into its habitual severe lines as his amusement faded.

'I had a call from DI Lundy earlier,' he said, trying to sound businesslike. 'Not an official one, just . . . a courtesy. He told me the body in the estuary was almost certainly Leo Villiers.'

I was surprised, but of course Lundy would know the Trasks from when Emma Derby went missing. Putting their minds at rest so soon might not have been standard protocol, but it was a humane thing to do. The DI went up in my estimation because of it.

But I wasn't going to comment either way. I gave a non-committal nod. Trask frowned down at the floor.

'Look, yesterday was . . . well, wires got crossed. Jamie's hoping to get your car done by this afternoon, but he won't be sure until he knows what the damage is. If it takes longer . . .' He seemed to be struggling for words. 'What I'm saying is this place is supposed to be for renting out. If you need to stay for another night you can.'

It wasn't the most gracious of offers, but I could understand why he'd be conflicted. 'Thanks, but I'd prefer to get back.'

He nodded, brusqueness covering what I guessed was relief. 'Up to you. The offer's there if you change your mind.'

I gave him my car keys and phone number, so Jamie could run the engine, and let me know when the car was ready. After Trask had gone I took the ruined cheese from the cool-box, tentatively sniffing it before deciding it was too far gone. Wrapping it in a plastic bag I found on a roll in a kitchen cupboard, I threw it in the bin outside. The cool-box still stank, so I washed it out to get rid of the smell. Even that exertion left me feeling shaky, so I made a mug of tea and sat down by the window. The thought of Trask's misunderstanding made me smile again. It was understandable, I supposed. And I couldn't blame him for not wanting a body part left outside his house.

I knew from experience what that was like.

Something was pricking at my subconscious, but it slipped away again almost straight away. I felt better after the short rest, so after I'd finished the tea and washed out the mug I went to examine the boots Trask had returned. They weren't meant to be soaked in seawater, but despite being a little stiff they were still wearable. I was about to set them down when the feeling of unease returned. Stronger this time. I stared at the boots, trying to think what was bothering me. And then I realized.

'Oh, you bloody idiot,' I breathed.

9

THERE WAS LESS water in the creek than when I'd walked along its bank the day before. Although I'd no way of checking, from the look of it high tide was still an hour or two away.

I hoped it would be long enough.

Before I set out from the boathouse I tried to think through what I might need. My camera had been in my overnight bag, so luckily I had that with me. But even if I found what I was looking for, there was no way of knowing how easy it would be to reach. My waders were still in my car over at Trask's, and after yesterday I didn't plan on getting wet again. There was nothing in the studio that would help me, but I tore off several plastic bin-liners from a roll under the sink and put them in the freshly cleaned cool-box. Leaving the ice packs in the fridge's small freezer to chill, I went outside to see what I could find.

A flight of steps led down to a jetty at the front of the boat-house. Halfway up the wall was a line where the high tide would reach; the stones dry and pale above, dark and damp below. The water level was lower than that at the moment, well below the top of the jetty. The entrance to the boathouse dock was at the far side, a large square opening that faced directly on to the creek. It was barred by a waterlogged timber gate that was secured by a rusty but solid-looking padlock. I wasn't going to get in that way, but partway down the steps there was a small platform next to a hatchway in the wall. The rough wooden board covering it was only held shut by a loop of rope hooked over a rusty nail, so I didn't think anyone would object if I looked inside.

The hinges protested as I pushed it open. A musty, cellar smell of water and damp stone greeted me. The opening was low and I had to duck to get through. I was almost caught out by the drop on the other side, where the floor level was lower. It was cold and dark inside as I paused to let my eyes adjust. Bars of light came through the gate in the front wall, enough to see by once I'd blocked the hatch open as well.

The makeover that had transformed upstairs into a studio flat hadn't extended to down here. I was standing on a narrow walkway – too small to be considered a jetty – that ran along one wall. At high tide this lower level would be flooded with water, but right now the muddy creek bed was visible below the dock. The walkway's timbers were slick and rotten, and held an assortment of old boating junk. A canoe with a gaping hole in its bottom lay on its side, half buried by cork buoys, disintegrating lifejackets and torn sections of wicker fishing baskets.

I'd been hoping there'd be a boathook or something similar, but the nearest thing I could find was a short oar with a broken shaft. Not ideal, but better than nothing. Taking it back outside with me, I hooked the rope back around the nail to hold the hatch shut, then went back up the steps to where I'd left the cool-box.

Just that small exertion had been enough to tire me. I rested for a few moments, catching my breath while considering the creek winding through the expanse of sandbanks and saltmarsh. I wondered if I was up to doing this. Less than twenty-four hours ago I'd been worried I might end up in hospital: now here I was about to set off hiking across tidal marshland on what was probably a wild goose chase.

But it was my own fault. Ill or not, I should have recognized what was right in front of me yesterday. I might have missed my chance already, and if I left it any longer I certainly would.

Picking up the cool-box, I struck out along the bank of the creek. The afternoon was brighter than the day before, but there was still a blanketing layer of clouds that turned the sky the colour of spoiled milk. There wasn't much of a path to start with, just a narrow ribbon of muddy ground where the marsh grasses and plants weren't quite so thick. Before long even that had disappeared. I tried to keep my eyes on the creek as I walked by the water's edge, but it wasn't easy when I had to constantly pay attention to where I was treading.

If anything the going grew even worse. The tides had carved an intricate network of waterways through the soft sandy soil of the marsh. The creek was like a giant root, from which smaller roots branched off, and then smaller ones from those. I found my way blocked by murky pools and partly flooded ditches. Some of them were small enough to step or jump over; others I had no choice but to detour round and hope I could eventually negotiate my way back to the creek. After following one channel for what seemed an age without finding a way across, I stopped to rest and get my bearings. The flat landscape was devoid of features other than sandy hummocks topped with spiky grass. Banks of rushes blurred the line between land and water, and looking back I could only just make out the boathouse.

Setting down the cool-box, I debated what to do. I'd hoped that by following the creek inland I'd eventually come to the same stretch I'd reached the day before, when I'd walked along it in the opposite direction from Trask's house. But I'd no idea how far it was, and now I'd wandered so far off course it was hard to distinguish the creek from the numerous channels and ditches that also carved their way through here. The tide was already spreading back through the saltmarsh, and at this rate I was either going to get lost or break an ankle.

I was reluctantly considering turning back when I saw a figure some way off across the marsh. I was too far away to make out any details, but as it drew closer I saw it was a woman. I felt an odd sort of tension when I realized who it was.

Rachel Derby walked towards me on the other bank of the flooded channel I'd been trying to get round. She had a canvas holdall slung across one shoulder, more satchel than handbag. The thick dark hair was tied back in a loose plait, and she managed to make even the wellingtons, old jeans and red waterproof jacket look good.

She stopped opposite me, her expression bemused. 'I didn't expect to see you out here.'

'I was . . . I thought I'd take a walk.' Conscious of how bizarre I must appear, I raised the broken oar. 'I borrowed this from the boathouse.'

'So I see.' Her gaze went to the cool-box. 'Off on a picnic?'

'Uh, no. I know it looks a bit strange . . .'

'Not at all. I'm sure a broken oar's going to come in very useful.' She didn't smile, which made me feel even more ridiculous. 'I'm not going to ask why you're out here. It's none of my business and I'm sure you've got a good reason. But are you sure you're up to it? You looked terrible last time I saw you.'

'I'm feeling much better,' I told her.

The green eyes were sceptical. 'So long as you know what you're doing. It's going to be high tide in an hour or so, and I wouldn't advise you to be wandering out here then. If you think this place is bad now, it'll be a lot worse when it's flooded.'

I looked at her wellingtons and satchel, unsure whether the idea that had come to me was good or bad.

'How well do you know your way around here?'

'Well enough to know which parts to avoid.' She frowned. 'Why?'

'I'm trying to find my way back to the stretch of creek I reached yesterday. It wasn't far from your house, so I thought if I followed the creek it'd bring me back to it.' I gave a shrug. 'It hasn't been that easy.'

'Welcome to the Backwaters,' she said. I thought there was the hint of a smile, but I could have imagined it. 'Whereabouts is it you want to get to?'

'I don't know exactly. The bank had crumbled away, and there was an old boat sunk in the mud—'

'Near a dead willow? I know it. It's not far, but if you don't know how to get there it's easy to get lost, and that really isn't good when the tide's flooding back. If you can get to it from Creek House can't you wait until later and then try again from there?'

'Not really.' If I waited then whatever chance I had of finding what I was looking for would be gone. 'Can you give me directions?'

'Out here?' Her tone made it clear what she thought of that. 'This isn't the sort of place you can just go for a stroll. I'd have thought you'd learned that after yesterday.'

'It's important.'

She shook her head, either resigned or marvelling at my stupidity. 'Does it have something to do with my sister?'

It was a good question, and I took a second or two to answer. 'Not as far as I know.'

I could tell her that much. For all I knew this could be a huge waste of time. But I had to know one way or the other.

Rachel looked off across the saltmarsh, brushing away a strand of hair that blew across her face.

'OK,' she said after a moment. 'I'll take you.'

We walked on opposite sides of the flooded channel until we came to a point where it narrowed. It was still too wide to jump, but thick weathered planks had been laid across to make a rudimentary bridge. Once I'd joined her on the other side, Rachel set off confidently back towards the creek. There was no obvious path, but she seemed to have no problem finding her way through the tough vegetation that covered this part of the marsh like a green mat.

We walked in silence at first. It wasn't awkward exactly, more a case of feeling a way towards a safe territory for conversation. Rachel broke it first.

'So . . . How was the boathouse?'

'Good. I like it, it's a nice place.'

'Thanks. It isn't quite finished. I've still got some odd jobs left before it's let out for the summer.'

'You're doing the work yourself?'

'It's kept me busy. Most of it was done before . . . before I came here.' She continued past the stumble. 'Andrew's an architect, so he did all the structural stuff and my sister was in charge of the interior design. They got contractors in to do the major work, so it's just a matter of finishing off. A few bits of paint to touch up, pictures to hang. That sort of thing.'

Trask had said he'd built Creek House for his wife, but I hadn't realized he was an architect. 'I looked at your sister's photographs. Hope that was OK.'

'That's what they're there for. Or will be, once I've put them up. Except for a couple of the older ones, like the motorbike and the self-portrait, they were all taken round here. The idea was to sell them to people who stay at the boathouse, so they're all for sale. Well, except for the self-portrait. I've been meaning to take that one away.' A sour note entered her voice. 'Not that Emma would mind.'

The disapproval seemed unconscious. But the mention of her sister gave me an opening for what I'd been wanting to bring up.

'Look, about yesterday. I'm sorry, I should have realized.'

'Don't worry about it. Anyway, I should apologize for giving you such a hard time. I felt like a real cow when I found out you weren't . . . you know.'

'Malingering?'

Her wince was only partly feigned. 'Yeah, something like that. Seriously, though, are you sure you're all right? We can stop if you need to rest.'

'No, I'm fine.'

I tried to say it with more conviction than I felt. The slog across the marsh was taking a toll. I could feel my leg muscles beginning to ache, and I would have liked to put the cool-box down for a few minutes. But I wouldn't have admitted that even if we'd had the time. I'd made a bad enough impression the day before.

'So you used to be a GP? What made you change?' she asked.

That wasn't something I wanted to go into. 'Long story. Let's just say I realized I was better at doing this.'

'OK, I can take a hint. Can I at least ask how you lost your spleen? Was it a car accident or something?'

I'd rather have avoided talking about that as well, but if I kept ducking her questions it'd look like I was snubbing her. I didn't want that. I tried to think of a less dramatic way to explain before deciding it was best to just say it.

'I was stabbed.'

'Yeah, right.' Rachel's wry look changed when she saw my face. 'God, you're not kidding, are you?'

She seemed genuinely shocked. I hadn't intended to go into any details, but I found myself telling her about Grace Strachan. How I'd become involved when she'd left a trail of carnage on a tiny island in the Outer Hebrides, and almost became a victim myself when she'd attacked me on my own doorstep back in London. Rachel's frown deepened as she listened.

'She just turned up at your home and *stabbed* you?' she exclaimed when I'd finished. 'God, what a bitch!'

I started to say that Grace had been mentally ill, that she'd been the victim of abuse, but it didn't seem worth the effort. 'You could say that.'

'What happened to her? Is she still in prison?'

'No. They never caught her.'

'You mean she's still *out* there?'

'The police think she's probably dead.' It wasn't a subject I liked to dwell on. 'How about you? You don't sound like a local.'

'I'm from Bristol originally, but I was living in Australia before I came here.'

'Doing what?' I asked, intrigued.

She gave a dismissive shrug. 'I'm a marine biologist. I was researching how plastic contaminants affect the Great Barrier Reef but I'm on sort of indefinite sabbatical now.'

I paused to tug my boot free from a muddy tangle of marsh grass. 'Must be quite a change coming here.'

'No more so than switching from being a doctor to a forensic anthropologist,' she countered. 'The Backwaters isn't so bad. I like the peace and quiet, and from a marine biology point of view it's actually pretty cool. Not as exotic as the Reef, obviously, and I'd be a liar if I said I didn't miss the sun. But there's still something about this place. The ecosystems are just as complex as anything you find on the Reef, they're just a bit . . .'

'Muddier?' I offered.

She smiled. It was the first real one I'd seen, and it lit up her face.

'Definitely. But the overlap between fresh and saltwater ecology is really fascinating. And it's not all about crabs and shellfish. We often get seals coming from the estuary, sometimes all the way up to Creek House. Did you hear them last night?'

I couldn't remember hearing anything once I'd gone to bed. 'I don't think so.'

'You'd know if you had. They're rowdy devils; you can't miss them. Sound like drunken Labradors. And then there's eels.'

'Eels . . .'

She glanced back at me, amused. 'I know, they get a bad press. But they're really unique, and we still don't know much about them. You know they all swim back to the Sargasso Sea to spawn?'

I looked at her, trying to tell if she was serious.

'It's true!' she protested. 'Every single eel you'll find here was born in the Sargasso Sea in the North Atlantic. Once they've hatched, the young migrate all over the planet. They live in estuaries or fresh water until they're mature, and then they swim all the way back to the Sargasso Sea to mate so the cycle can begin again. They're remarkable creatures, but thanks to overfishing they're an endangered species. Their population's dropped by ninety-five per cent, but no one . . .'

She stopped, shrugging self-consciously.

'See what happens when you get me started? God, eels and DIY. What a hedonist.'

'So are you out eel watching today?' I asked, pushing away a sudden image of the eel slipping from Leo Villiers' ruined face.

'No. I wanted to get out for a bit, so I thought I'd do some foraging.' She opened the bag to show me a few strands of glistening wet plants. 'It's a bit early for samphire but you can sometimes find it if you know where to look. There's all sorts of sea vegetables grow here, as well as mussels, shellfish, crabs . . . That's one thing about the Backwaters, you need never starve.'

She halted, looking around.

'Anyway, I'd better stop boring you. We're here.'

I'd been so engrossed in talking to her I'd not paid any attention to where we were. A little way ahead of us, the rotting hull of the old boat emerged from the creek like a giant ribcage. Beyond it was the gnarled trunk of the willow tree, its dead branches trailing desolately in the water.

'Was this where you meant?' Rachel asked.

I nodded. 'Thanks for the help. I'll be OK now.'

She didn't seem to have expected that. 'How are you going to find your way back?'

'I'll manage.'

It shouldn't be hard to find my way to Trask's house from here, and then I could follow the road to the boathouse. Or even take my car if Jamie had finished repairing it. I was beginning to feel washed out again, but it was better if I was on my own for what I had to do next. And if I found what I was looking for I didn't think Rachel would want to be there anyway.

But she had other ideas. 'You do know that just because something was here yesterday it doesn't mean it'll still be here today, don't you? Whatever you're looking for, if it can float it's probably been carried off God knows where by now.'

I didn't need reminding. 'I know.'

Rachel was looking at me with exasperation. 'This is silly. If you tell me what you're looking for I might be able to help you find it. I'm not an idiot; I know it's going to be something gruesome. But I've seen shark attacks so you needn't worry that I'm going to throw up or faint. And I'm guessing since you're here by yourself instead of with the police you're still not sure if it's anything or not.'

'No, but—'

'Look, I've spent the last few months going mad because I can't *do* anything. You've already said this doesn't have anything to do with Emma, so chances are it's about Leo Villiers. And if you think I'm going to get upset at finding one of that bastard's body parts you really don't know me.'

Patches of colour had risen on her cheeks, as they had when she'd been angry the day before. I seemed to have that effect on her.

'It's a training shoe,' I said.

She stared at me for a few moments. 'Well, that's an anticlimax.'

I hoped that was all it was. Just the thought of it made me annoyed at my own stupidity. I'd been standing on the bankside right next to the shoe the previous afternoon, watching it bob around with the other flotsam snagged by the creek's tide. At the time I'd been too busy worrying about missing the post-mortem to realize what might be staring me in the face.

For all I knew it might be nothing more sinister than an old trainer. But unless I found it I'd never know one way or the other. Rachel was right: I didn't know the Backwaters the way she did, and if the shoe had drifted off I'd need her help to find it again.

'So what's special about it?' she asked, as we made our way to the section of bank I'd been to yesterday. 'Or do you just go around collecting old trainers?'

'Not from choice. There was a case a while back in British Columbia,' I told her. 'Shoes were being washed up along a stretch of coastline. A lot of them, about a dozen over five years or so. There were boots and other shoes as well, but it was mainly trainers. And they'd all still got feet inside them.'

Rachel grimaced but didn't look shocked. 'Nice. What was it, a serial killer?'

'That's what the police thought at first. Or that it might be victims of the Asian tsunami. But it turned out that most of the shoes belonged to people who'd jumped or fallen from a particular bridge in Vancouver. Their bodies got washed out to sea, and . . .'

'And the feet fell off.' Rachel nodded. As a marine biologist she'd know about the effects of water better than most people. 'How come they didn't sink?'

'Because they'd got air-filled rubber soles.' I paused to wipe my forehead. My body was letting me know I was overdoing it, but we were almost there. 'The soles kept them afloat, and the shoes stopped scavengers from getting at them. They drifted hundreds of miles before the sea currents washed them up on the same stretch of coast.'

'And you think this shoe might still have got Leo Villiers' foot in it?'

I'd been careful to avoid any mention of either Villiers or her sister, but Rachel was no fool. 'I don't know,' I admitted. 'It could just be an old training shoe someone threw away. But it looked like a man's size.'

Ordinarily I wouldn't have jumped to that sort of conclusion: women's feet could be every bit as large as men's. But that was rare, and even though I hadn't taken much notice of it at the time, I could remember the shoe was a sizable one. Unless Emma Derby had abnormally large feet then it wasn't hers, and I wanted to set Rachel's mind at ease without being obvious about it.

She saw through my coded comment, though. 'Don't worry, my little sister wasn't the training-shoe type. Emma was a swimmer, but if she'd gone running she'd probably have done even that in high heels.'

There was another note of disapproval in her voice, but I didn't have time to reflect on any tensions between her and her sister. We'd reached the side of the creek. The water was lower than the last time I'd been here, but the crescent-shaped bite from the sandy bank was otherwise the same. Bits of wood, plastic bottles and other debris floated in it, and I saw the same doll's head as the day before.

There was no training shoe.

'Are you sure it was here?' Rachel asked doubtfully.

'Certain.'

I looked up and down the muddy water's edge. Even though I'd known there was only a slim chance that the shoe would still be here, that the fast-moving tide had probably carried it off by now, it was still a bitter disappointment. A wave of fatigue washed through me, and if Rachel hadn't been there I'd have flopped down on to the cool-box to rest.

'The tide probably carried it towards the estuary rather than further inland,' she said, her brow furrowing. 'There's a section where the bank's collapsed down that way. It might have got caught there.'

We didn't talk as we walked along the creek bank. I was beginning to feel shaky now. The sensible thing to do would be to call it a day, but I'd no intention of doing that. After about ten minutes we reached a section of bank that had crumbled, forming a partial dam. Rachel slowed.

'This is it,' she said. 'If it's not here it could be anywhere by now.'

My optimism was flagging along with my energy. I was already berating myself for missing what could well have been my only opportunity to examine the shoe when Rachel pointed.

'What's that over there?'

A small bush had fallen into the creek when the bank collapsed. The tangle of dead branches was draped with grasses and weeds, and now I saw something pale had snagged there as well.

Floating on its side was a training shoe.

'Is that it?' There was excitement in Rachel's voice.

'I think so.'

Unless there were two of them, which was possible but not likely. When we drew closer I could see that it was a right shoe. It was only a few feet from the side, caught on the straggly branches with its sole facing towards us. If I'd got my waders on I could have easily retrieved it, but I wasn't going to paddle out in my boots. I set down the cool-box and carefully stepped on to the crumbled bank. My boots sank into the sandy mud as I tried to snag the shoe with the oar blade. It splashed into the water a few inches short. I leaned further out.

'Here, grab hold.'

Rachel offered her hand. It was warm and dry when I took it, her grip strong as she pulled backwards to counterbalance me. I reached out with the oar and missed again, but only just. Next time the blade caught the trainer, knocking it clear of the branches and nearer the side.

I nudged the shoe closer, then used the oar to steer it through the water towards me. Rachel let go of my hand, and I tried not to notice the sudden absence of warmth against my skin.

'I hate to rain on your parade, but that doesn't look like something Leo Villiers would be seen dead in,' she said.

I'd been thinking the same thing myself. Beneath its coating of mud, the training shoe looked cheap and chunky, designed with high street fashion rather than sport in mind. It didn't fit my image of Villiers, a man who bought bespoke outdoor clothes from his tailors in St James's and had a custom-built shotgun worth a small fortune.

'Is that a purple sock?' Rachel asked, leaning over my shoulder for a better look. '*Definitely* not Leo Villiers'.'

She was right. Although I'd known all along it was probably nothing, I felt a sense of anticlimax take what little energy I had left. I was about to let the shoe drift away again when I realized a discarded shoe wouldn't still have a sock in it. And then I noticed something else.

The sodden laces were still tied.

'You might want to move away,' I warned. But it was too late. The trainer had turned in the water as I'd nudged it closer, presenting its open top towards us.

Nestling inside the training shoe, and half hidden by the lurid sock, was the pale bone and gristle of an ankle.

10

'YOU SHOULD HAVE called me.'

Lundy sounded more reproachful than annoyed. We stood in the kitchen area of the boathouse, mugs of untouched tea cooling on the worktop. He was dressed more smartly than before, and I wondered if my call had interrupted his own bank holiday plans.

'And what would you have said?' I asked wearily. 'For all I knew it was just some old trainer. I only went to set my mind at rest. And there wasn't enough time before the next high tide to organize a search anyway.'

That earned a grudging sniff. 'Pity you didn't think to take a look when you saw it yesterday.'

Tell me about it. Once I'd seen what the training shoe contained, I'd been faced with a tough choice. Although I was loath to handle it myself – that was a CSI's job – the tide was flooding back into the creek at an alarming rate. If I didn't move it soon the water would, and I didn't want to risk losing it again.

So, after taking photographs, I'd used a bin-liner to pick up the shoe, then reversed the plastic bag so it was wrapped inside. There was no mobile service out there, and it wasn't until we were back at the boathouse that I could phone Lundy.

The DI had been surprised to hear from me, especially when I told him where I was staying. Trask obviously hadn't mentioned it when they'd spoken earlier, but Lundy didn't pass any comment beyond an exasperated sigh. He'd be right out, he told me, adding that I should stay put.

I wasn't planning on going anywhere. The trek across the marsh had taken a lot out of me, and by the time Rachel and I had walked back to the boathouse I felt done in. While she made tea, I put the ice packs I'd frozen earlier into a plastic bag and slipped them into the cool-box with the foot before gratefully sinking on to a chair. I could see Rachel wanted to ask me about it, but she restrained herself. Just as well: I couldn't have told her anything anyway.

I'd more questions than answers myself.

Lundy arrived sooner than I expected, with a pair of CSIs in tow. He stayed with me while Rachel took them to where we'd found the training shoe. I didn't offer to go with them, knowing I'd already pushed myself more than I should, and in any case the high tide prevented walking along the creek. Rachel said there was a small road bridge that wasn't too far from where we'd found the trainer, so they could take their car and go on foot from there. The three of them left, the CSIs taking the cool-box and its contents with them. Lundy barely waited until the door was closed before turning to me.

'Right, Dr Hunter,' he'd said, folding thick arms across his chest. 'Care to tell me what's been going on?'

Now he let out a long breath. 'I don't have to tell you how awkward this is, do I? Emma Derby's family have been through enough without getting dragged into this.'

'And if I'd known her husband's name was Trask I might have made a better job of avoiding them,' I shot back. 'OK, I cocked up, I admit it. But what else could I do?'

Lundy pushed his glasses up on his forehead and kneaded the bridge of his nose. 'Well, what's done is done. At least we've got the foot. You say you've got photographs?'

I'd not had a chance to transfer the shots I'd taken at the creek to my laptop, so I found them on my camera and passed it over.

'I'll need emails of these,' Lundy said as he studied the images on the small screen. 'Doesn't look like it was severed, does it?'

'Not from what I saw.'

Although I'd known better than to examine the actual foot, by expanding the photographs on the camera's screen I'd been able to view it in better detail. The curved sculpture of the talus – the ankle bone – was visible inside the filthy purple sock. Fish, crabs and seabirds had picked clean as much of the soft tissue as they could get to, but a few tattered vestiges still clung to the ankle's exposed surface. Except for the tiny pitting caused by scavengers, the contoured face of the ankle bone itself was smooth, with no obvious evidence of cuts or splintering. Even from the little I'd seen, I felt certain that the foot had separated naturally when its connective tissues decomposed.

That was all I was certain about.

'Looks too big to be a woman's,' Lundy said, flicking to another photograph. 'Don't suppose you saw what size it was?'

'No, I thought I'd better bag it up and get it in the cool-box. It looked around a ten, but that's only a guess.'

If that meant anything one way or the other he gave no sign. 'Any thoughts on how long it might have been in the water?'

'Not beyond the obvious. Long enough to detach from the leg, so at this time of year let's say a few weeks. Beyond that I can't say without examining it.'

'So roughly the same length of time as the body we found yesterday.'

'The foot will have been protected inside the shoe, so it could be longer. But possibly, yes.'

'And there was no sign of the other foot?' I just looked at him. He sighed. 'All right, stupid question.'

If there had been I'd have already said so. But the feet and hands wouldn't have fallen away at the same time. It would be sheer fluke if they'd ended up in the same place.

Lundy flicked back through the photographs to one that showed the entire training shoe. His lips pursed as he studied it.

'Are you going to say it or shall I?' I asked.

He smiled. 'Say what?'

'From what I've heard about him, that doesn't look like something Leo Villiers would wear.'

'Doesn't mean he didn't. People have all sorts of surprising things tucked away in their wardrobes.'

'Purple socks?'

'I grant you, it's not the sort of thing I'd imagine Villiers wearing, but stranger things happen. We're still trying to persuade his father to let us see his medical records, so until that happens for all I know he might be colour blind. It's not as if anyone knew what clothes he had on when he went missing. We weren't allowed to search his house, so we can't say what sort of stuff he might have had there.'

'You weren't *allowed*?' I asked, surprised. Withholding access to medical records before someone was officially declared dead was one thing, but I couldn't see how anyone could prevent the police from carrying out a search, no matter who they were. 'What about when Emma Derby disappeared?'

'We didn't have enough evidence to get a warrant.' He shook his head, annoyed at the memory. 'His father's lawyers were all over us. We carried out a cursory search when he was reported missing, to make sure he wasn't dead in a spare room or something. They couldn't stop us from doing that. But somebody had obviously been through the place already by then. The housekeeper said she'd tidied it before she realized he'd disappeared, but this had been cleaned top to bottom.'

'Wasn't that obstruction?'

Lundy took a new packet of antacids from his pocket and began stripping off the plastic. 'Nothing we could successfully argue. It wasn't as if we knew what we were looking for, except perhaps Emma Derby's body, so we couldn't accuse anyone of destroying evidence. But the point I was making is that we don't know enough about Leo Villiers to say he didn't own cheap trainers and purple socks. If he was planning to blow his brains out with a shotgun he probably wasn't too bothered about what he had on his feet anyway.'

He sounded as if he was trying to convince himself.

'You're not happy about this either, are you?' I said.

'It doesn't matter what I am.' He crunched down on two antacids as though taking it out on them. 'Frankly, I'd rather believe that Villiers Junior had dodgy taste in footwear than the alternative, which is that we've got another dead body missing its feet somewhere.'

There was another possibility, but now wasn't the time to go into that. Besides, I felt sure that Lundy would be aware of it already.

'Do you know when Frears is planning on examining the foot?' I asked. 'I'd like to be there.'

Lundy suddenly seemed uncomfortable. 'Thanks for the offer, but I don't think that'll be necessary.'

I tried to hide my disappointment. An individual foot might not tell us very much, but I'd assumed the police would want me to take a look anyway. And while I was there I'd thought I could examine the body from the estuary as well. I was still annoyed with myself for missing the post-mortem, and even if I couldn't add to the pathologist's findings I'd at least like to know I'd done what I could.

Now I wouldn't get the chance. 'So Clarke's mad at me,' I said.

Lundy sighed. 'There are enough complications with this case as it is. The chief doesn't want any more.'

'How is letting me examine the foot complicating things?'

'Well, apart from missing the post-mortem, you've ended up being house guest with the family of a missing woman, and taken her sister on a hunt for a misplaced body part. Not bad going for twenty-four hours, is it?'

Put like that it didn't sound good, but we both knew that wasn't a fair picture. 'Aside from the fact that I didn't know who they were, you'd already told me I was off the investigation before I even thought about renting this place.'

'I know. And we wouldn't have found the foot if not for you, I'm not disputing that. But the chief's decided, so . . .' He spread his hands. 'I dare say she'll come round once she's calmed down. There'll be other investigations in future. The best thing you can do now is keep a low profile.'

If my profile was any lower it wouldn't exist. But Lundy was right, and antagonizing his SIO wasn't going to help.

The DI took a drink of tea, closing the subject. 'So how much longer are you planning on staying?' he asked, setting down his mug.

'Only until my car's ready.' I raised an eyebrow at him. 'Was that a hint?'

He chuckled. 'No, I'm just making polite chit-chat. To be honest, I'm surprised Trask let you stay here in the first place. Has he tried to discuss the case at all?'

Now we were getting to it. 'No, and I made it clear I wasn't going to talk about it.'

'He did ask about it, then?'

'Wouldn't you if it was your wife?'

I hadn't meant to snap. Recovering the foot had left me feeling irritable as well as washed out, but Lundy didn't seem offended.

'Fair enough, but I'm not convinced that wasn't part of the reason he's been so obliging. You know this boathouse was Emma Derby's pet project? And getting his son to fix your car as well. Sounds like a bit of a charm offensive to me. Perhaps he reckons it can't hurt to have a friendly police consultant on his side.'

I didn't think 'charm' really applied to Trask's manner. 'That's not the impression I got. If anything he seemed reluctant to let me stay, so I doubt he'll be sorry to see me go.'

'I dare say, but I wonder if he'd have been so amenable if you weren't involved in the police inquiry.'

'He didn't know about that when he towed me out of the creek,' I said. But I also remembered how I'd thought the Land Rover wasn't going to stop, how its driver seemed to deliberate before coming back. And the offer of a tow to Creek House was only made after Trask found out why I was there. Even then he'd seemed torn. 'It sounds as though you don't like him much.'

'It's not a case of liking him or not. He can be an abrasive bugger but you've got to feel for him and his family. They've had a rough time of it this last year. Bad enough for his wife to go missing, but for it to come out that she'd been having an affair as well . . .' Lundy shook his head, frowning into his tea. 'The family's had rotten luck. Trask's first wife died not long after his daughter was born, some sort of complication after the birth. He had to bring up a baby and young lad by himself, which can't have been easy. Then he meets this glamorous younger woman, London type who's on the rebound herself, marries her and brings her out to the arse end of nowhere, if you'll pardon my French. Christ knows what either of them were thinking, but it's hard to see how it was ever going to work.'

'Did he know about the affair with Leo Villiers before she went missing?' I belatedly realized I'd no right to quiz him when I wasn't on the investigation any more. But Lundy only shrugged.

'He says he guessed she was seeing somebody, but not who it was. That came out later, when we pulled her phone records. There were a lot of recent calls to Villiers' number, ending a few days before she disappeared. After that, everything pretty much pointed one way.'

'You said yesterday that you'd suspected Trask at one point?'

Lundy's smile was humourless. 'He's the husband; of course we did. But he was in Denmark for an architectural conference when she disappeared. Several witnesses saw or spoke to her after he'd gone, then two days later she dropped off the radar. His son and daughter were both away as well, the girl on a school trip and the lad staying with a friend from sixth form, so the alarm wasn't raised until he got back later that week.'

I thought about the beautiful and assured woman in the framed photograph. Barring some unexpected stroke of luck, with Leo Villiers dead no one would ever know what had happened to her. Death was bad enough for a family to cope with, but for a loved one to simply vanish was even worse. And if her killer had disposed of her body in the Backwaters, as seemed likely, then there would be little left to recognize by now. The vitality, vanity, ambition and everything else that had made Emma Derby who she was would be long gone. Even though I hadn't known her, I felt a familiar hollowness at how that could happen. The gulf between life and death is a mystery I couldn't reconcile now any more than when I lost my own family.

'Dr Hunter?' Lundy said. 'You all right?'

I pulled myself together. I'd been drifting: I was more tired than I'd realized. 'Sorry. Just thinking.'

He drained his tea and put the mug down. 'Well, I'd better get off. I'm supposed to be at my granddaughter's birthday party this afternoon. She's promised to save me a piece of cake, though I'm not holding my breath.'

'No, I wouldn't.' I smiled at the bittersweet memory of my own daughter's birthday parties. 'How old is she?'

'Four. Proper little madam, Kelly is. Already knows how to wrap me round her little finger.'

'Have you any other grandkids?'

'Not yet, but one's on the way. My daughter Lee – that's Kelly's mum – is expecting her second.' He shook his head. 'Doesn't seem two minutes since she was blowing out birthday candles herself. How about you? Do you . . . ah, do you have any plans for when you get back?'

He'd recovered well, but I knew what he'd been about to ask. *Do you have any kids?* He'd caught himself in time, so either he'd done his homework on me or someone had told him about my past. I'd grown adept at fielding the question by now, and while it would always be painful it rarely caught me off guard any more. But Lundy looked mortified, his already ruddy face blooming an even deeper red.

'No, no plans,' I said, brushing over it to spare his awkwardness.

'Right. Well, thanks again.' He stuck out a meaty hand for me to shake. 'Safe journey, Dr Hunter.'

After Lundy had gone I poured my cold tea away and made another mug. Although I still felt wrung out, I couldn't detect any chills or feverishness that might indicate the infection was flaring up. But the DI's visit had left me feeling flat and depressed. I couldn't really blame Clarke for not wanting me back on the investigation – I'd hardly covered myself with glory so far – but it was still a disappointment. Still, dubious circumstances or not, I'd redeemed myself to some extent by finding the foot. Going out on the marsh might have been ill-advised but at least I could return to London knowing I'd done something useful.

And it had been worth it to get to know Rachel better. We seemed to get on well now we'd cleared the air, and despite everything I'd enjoyed spending time with her. I'd got the impression she felt the same way. *Yes, because nothing helps hit it off with someone like finding a rotting foot.*

I drank the tea sitting in the chair by the arched window, looking at birds paddling on the full creek outside. I told myself I should call to find out what was happening with my car, but decided it could wait a few more minutes. Trask had said they'd let me know when it was ready, and hassling them wouldn't get it done any faster.

Besides, I wasn't in any hurry to get back to London. The prospect of spending the tail end of the bank holiday on my own in an empty flat settled on me like a pall. I could always head over to Jason and Anja's, but it was a long drive and by the time I got there it would hardly be worth it.

I shifted to a more comfortable position in the armchair, stretching my feet out as I watched the afternoon slipping by outside. I'd only seen a little of the Backwaters, but I liked it here. The low-lying saltmarshes under the high sky had a restful, meditative quality. It seemed a long way from the noise and clamour of London, where the only green spaces were parks hemmed in by arterial roads. I'd not realized how tightly wound I'd become, how wrapped up in the grind of commuting and traffic. And the boathouse was a good place to stay: basic but with everything I needed. I'd be sorry to leave the peace and quiet.

Is that all you'll be sorry to leave?

I didn't know I'd dozed off until the sound of an engine outside woke me. I sat up, rubbing my eyes as I checked the time: I'd been out for over an hour. I felt better for it, though, still tired but clear-headed again. Thinking it must be Jamie with my car, I got up from the chair and almost tripped as I stubbed my foot on something under the rug. I swore, hobbling over to open the door just as someone knocked on it.

Rachel stood on the doorstep, hand raised. 'Oh,' she said, startled.

'Sorry, I thought it was Jamie,' I said, then felt like an idiot as I realized that didn't make much sense.

'What's wrong with your foot?' she asked, seeing me favouring it.

I straightened, trying to ignore the throbbing of my stubbed toes. 'Nothing. I just caught it on something under the rug.'

'That's my fault, I should have warned you,' she said, looking pained herself. 'There's an old trapdoor in the floor. The handle sticks up, so it's a bit of a trip hazard. That's another of those last-minute jobs I still need to do. Please tell me you haven't broken it?'

'I can't vouch for the handle, but my foot's OK.' I smiled. Even if it wasn't there was no way I was going to admit it. 'How did it go with the CSIs?'

She shrugged. 'There wasn't much for them to do. They just took a few photographs of the creek where we found the shoe and then gave me a lift back to the house.'

She'd changed out of her wellingtons but wore the same red waterproof jacket as before. It was open to reveal a chunky Aran sweater that went well with her jeans.

'Do you want to come in?' I asked, standing back.

But she shook her head. 'I'm not staying. I'm on my way to pick up Fay from a friend's, but I told Jamie I'd drop by. The good news is that your car's nearly ready. He's changed the oil and stripped and cleaned everything, so it should be OK. He says you're lucky it's not a new car, because they've got more complicated electrical systems and he wouldn't have been able to fix them.'

I tried to muster up some enthusiasm. 'That's great.'

'Don't build your hopes up. The *bad* news is it needs new spark plugs. Jamie doesn't have any, so you've two options. There's a big car spares store about twenty-five miles away that's open on a bank holiday. He's offered to pick some up from there. He says it shouldn't take him long to get the car running again once he's got them. I think he feels bad he hasn't managed to finish it yet.'

That wasn't his fault, and what he was suggesting would involve a fifty mile round trip for him, on a bank holiday Sunday afternoon. There was bound to be traffic once he hit the busier roads, and he'd still have to fit the replacement spark plugs when he got back.

'What's the other option?' I asked.

'There's a petrol station at Cruckhaven that should have them. It's only a local one, so it'll be closed now. But it'll be open tomorrow morning, if you don't mind staying another night.'

I'd been so resigned to leaving that evening I didn't know how to respond. God knows, I didn't feel up to driving back to London after trekking across the marsh: I'd pushed my luck enough for one day. The sensible thing to do would be to rest up until tomorrow, and Trask had already said that would be OK. But even if Clarke wasn't already annoyed that I'd involved Emma Derby's family, there was another potential drawback.

'This petrol station isn't called Coker's, is it?' I asked, remembering my attempt to call out a mechanic.

Rachel gave me a wary look. 'No. Why?'

'It doesn't matter.'

For a moment I thought she was going to pursue it, then she evidently decided against. 'It's up to you, but I've got to go into Cruckhaven in the morning anyway. I can pick up the spark plugs then and you'll be on your way by lunchtime. It just depends how much of a hurry you're in.'

No hurry at all, I thought, thinking about the empty flat waiting for me. I felt my resolve wavering.

'What does your brother-in-law say?'

'Andrew doesn't mind either way.' She pushed a hank of dark hair from her forehead, and for an instant I saw a resemblance to her sister. 'It's not as if you're getting in anybody's way out here.'

Again, I thought back to my conversation with Lundy. I'd told him I'd only stay until my car was repaired, but I didn't say when that would be. One more night couldn't make much difference, not if Trask didn't object.

Besides, I'd already been thrown off the investigation.

'Can I walk to Cruckhaven from here?' I asked, stalling. I'd put on the family enough as it was without Rachel's having to fetch sparks plug for me as well.

'You can but it's the best part of an hour, depending on the tide. And there's not much point when I'm going there anyway.' She gave me a sudden smile that carried a shade of embarrassment. 'If it makes you feel any better why don't you come with me?'

There were still any number of reasons why I shouldn't. I felt a brief, internal tug of war.

'I'd like that,' I said.

11

IT WAS THE best night's sleep I'd had in months. I'd slept on my first night in the boathouse but that had been more like exhaustion, as my body fought off the infection. This was a deep, restful sleep of a kind I'd almost forgotten.

After promising to pick me up at ten next morning, Rachel had left, leaving me to wonder if I'd done the right thing. It was still only late afternoon, and I'd no idea what I'd do to pass the rest of the time. There was no internet or TV, or even any music or books. Or work. Usually when I was working on an investigation I'd spend any downtime going through reports and case notes. That didn't apply now, and although I had my laptop I couldn't even go online to check emails.

But for once the need to work, to *do* something, didn't nag as loudly as usual. Rachel had offered to bring more groceries, but – providing I didn't mind soup or eggs again – I'd enough food left to see me through till morning. There was no pressing need to go anywhere if I didn't want to, so I didn't. Instead I kept station in the armchair, staring through the window at the slowly ebbing tide and trying not to read too much into an innocent offer of a lift.

Prodded by a rumbling stomach, I made an early supper from what was left of the tomato soup with an omelette and toast. Not exactly haute cuisine but I enjoyed every mouthful. As the last of the light faded from the sky, I took an after-dinner walk along the bank of the muddy creek, this time heading out to where it fed into the estuary. The going was much easier than when I'd headed into the Backwaters that morning. There was no path as such, but the ground was drier and firmer underfoot, the marsh giving way to low sand dunes covered in tough, spiky reeds. After a while I came to an overgrown shingle embankment, part of an old tidal defence that had been allowed to crumble so the tides could reclaim the land. Climbing up on to it, I looked out at the exposed mudflats of the estuary. Further inland was a cluster of lights I thought must be Cruckhaven, while out to sea I could see the lights of container ships making their slow way across the darkening horizon.

I would have liked to go further, but it would soon be dark. I turned back, feeling an odd and unwelcome restlessness I couldn't identify at first. It wasn't until I was almost back at the boathouse that I realized seeing the estuary had reminded me of the Barrows, which had in turn jogged loose thoughts of the body we'd recovered from the sandbanks.

I tried to put it from my mind, telling myself it was no longer anything to do with me. It didn't work. Even though I was now off the case, that didn't stop me thinking about it. Besides, I hadn't entirely finished yet: Lundy had asked me to email him the photographs I'd taken of the training shoe. I couldn't send them to him from the boathouse, but I could at least transfer them onto my laptop, along with the ones I'd taken out at the Barrows.

And if I happened to take another look as I did, then where was the harm in that?

Back at the boathouse, I put the kettle on and connected the camera to my laptop. With a mug of tea next to me, I studied the images of the training shoe again. They were a lot more detailed on the laptop's bigger screen, but with the foot largely hidden inside the shoe they didn't tell me much I didn't already know. I spent a while studying the gaudy purple sock, enlarging it to better see the fabric. Although it wasn't my field, I was pretty sure the muddy cloth was man-made rather than natural, either polyester or some other synthetic.

I was only guessing about that, but there was no doubt about what else I saw. On the shoe's sole, obscured by the coating of mud, were printed words I hadn't noticed before. They'd been too small to see on the camera screen, but they were more clearly visible on the laptop. Again, I magnified the image, zooming in and playing with the contrast until I could clearly make them out. Three words, stamped or moulded into the sole's rubber base: *Made in China.*

Cheap training shoes and colourful synthetic socks didn't fit with the image I'd formed of Leo Villiers, but that was Lundy's problem now. Even so, I still opened the photographs I'd taken of the body itself as it lay on the sandbank. The right ankle joint protruded from the sodden leg of the jeans, but not enough to see anything one way or the other. I went to the images of the head. The horrendous injury was as bad as I remembered. Opening another photograph to view alongside, I considered what I could see of the exit wound, trying to gauge the shot's trajectory.

But it was pointless speculating. And I wasn't going to see anything in a few photographs that the police wouldn't find out for themselves. I made myself close the laptop before I could become too engrossed, knowing it would only frustrate me. Instead, I made myself another mug of tea and sat with the light off, watching night settle over the creek before going to bed.

I woke once, roused by a series of grunts and weird, mournful howling from outside. Seals, I realized drowsily. Rachel was right, I thought as I drifted back off to sleep. They did sound like rowdy Labradors.

The alarm on my phone pulled me from a deep, dreamless sleep. I felt more rested than I had in a long time. The only aftermath from whatever bug I'd had was a lingering ache in my joints, and a ravenous appetite. I showered and shaved, then toasted what was left of the bread for breakfast and ate it with the last of the eggs. I didn't know if I'd be coming back to the boathouse after I'd got the spark plugs from Cruckhaven, so once I'd washed the dishes I packed what few things I had with me in my bag.

That done, there was nothing left to do but wait. I sat by the window again, trying not to glance at my watch or acknowledge how nervous I was beginning to feel. *She's giving you a lift to buy car parts. Stop acting like a schoolboy.* When I heard a car crunching over the cinders I jumped up, narrowly avoiding stubbing my toe again on the trapdoor handle hidden under the rug. I took a final look around the boathouse, feeling a touch of regret that this would be the last time I'd see it.

Then I grabbed my jacket and bag and hurried outside.

Rachel was leaning through the open rear door of the old white Defender, making room in the back. I could see a mess of sports equipment and what looked like a wetsuit thrown inside.

'Morning,' she said, pushing aside a box full of coiled rope. 'I swear I don't know where Jamie gets half this stuff from. You should see the state of his room – I looked in once and slammed the door as quick as I could. Here, do you want to put your bag in? There's space now.'

She was wearing a tan suede jacket today, open to reveal a black sweater over her jeans. If she wore any make-up it was too subtly applied for me to notice, but her hair looked more carefully tied back than usual, exposing more of her smooth forehead and strong features. I found myself wondering if any of that might be for my benefit, before telling myself not to be stupid.

I crammed my bag on the floor under a seat, then got in the front passenger side next to Rachel.

'I locked the door,' I told her, handing her the key. 'Force of habit. I've just had a failed break-in at my flat, but I don't suppose you need to bother too much out here.'

'You'd be surprised,' she said, starting the engine. 'There was a spate of burglaries not long after I arrived. Creek House was broken into.'

'Did they take much?' I was surprised thieves would go to the trouble of coming all this way.

'Nothing that couldn't be replaced, just computers and the usual stuff. But the timing wasn't exactly ideal.' Her face set at the memory as we pulled away. 'Makes you wonder about people, doesn't it?'

Rachel looked small behind the wheel of the big old car, but she handled it well enough. She was a confident driver, manoeuvring the reluctant gearstick into place with obvious familiarity. And less forcefully than the last time she'd driven me.

'I used to drive one of these,' I told her, trying to lighten the mood. 'I thought that was pretty ancient but it wasn't as old as this.'

'Yeah, Jamie says this is one of the first models. He found it at a scrap yard and rebuilt it from spare parts.' Trask had told me as much, but I'd not really appreciated what a good job his son had done. For all its age, the old Land Rover was beautifully restored. Rachel forcibly changed gear as we approached a bend. 'What did you think of it?'

'I liked it,' I said. Being back in a Defender brought back associations for me, not all of them pleasant. But that wasn't the fault of the car.

'Yeah, they're real workhorses. No power steering, so it's a bit like driving a tank. On these roads they're good fun, though.'

'I imagine the snorkel comes in handy as well.'

She gave an arch smile. 'Especially when some townie gets caught by the tide.'

'Ouch.'

'Don't worry. You weren't the first, and I doubt you'll be the last.' Her grin faded as she saw something up ahead. 'Oh, great.'

A tall, thin figure was shambling down the middle of the road, heading away from us. Even from the back I recognized the man I'd almost run down on my way to the mortuary. He seemed oblivious of the Land Rover's approach.

118

'Come on, Edgar, get out of the way,' Rachel said with a sigh, slowing almost to a stop.

'You know him?' I asked.

'Everybody round here knows him. He does this all the time.'

'I know. I nearly knocked him down the other day.' I shrugged when she glanced at me. 'That's why I tried to take the causeway.'

'Bet it seemed a good idea at the time.' She wound down the window and leaned her head out. 'Edgar? Edgar, can you get off the road, please?'

It was like a replay of two days ago. The man trudged on unhurriedly without looking around. The baggy raincoat flapped around his knees as the muddy wellingtons slapped rhythmically on the road.

'What's that he's carrying?' I asked. His arms were crooked, clutching something to his chest, but from behind him I couldn't see what it was.

'God knows. He's always rescuing things, even if they don't need it.' Rachel leaned out of the window again. 'Come on, Edgar. *Edgar!*'

The gaunt figure continued along the road, giving no indication that he'd heard.

'Bloody hell,' Rachel muttered, and stopped the car. She got out, and after a second I did as well. The man hadn't seemed violent, but cadaverous or not he still dwarfed Rachel. Me too, if it came to that.

She fell into step alongside him. 'It's me, Edgar. Rachel.'

Only now did he seem to register her presence. He spoke without looking at her or breaking stride.

'I'm in a hurry.'

'I know, but you need to walk at the side of the road, not in the middle. I've told you before.' Rachel's tone was firm but friendly. 'What've you got there?'

'It's hurt.'

His voice was low and hushed, as though he was distracted. But at least he was responding, which was more than he'd done the last

119

time I'd encountered him. I'd hung back so as not to unsettle him, but I was close enough to see the bundle of spines cradled against his chest. A hedgehog, limp and unmoving. I remembered the seagull he'd been carrying before.

'It's dead, Edgar,' Rachel told him gently. 'You can't help it.'

'It's hurt,' he repeated.

She gave me a what-can-you-do glance. 'OK, Edgar. But you need to walk on the side of the road. The *side*, OK? Not the middle. You'll get knocked down, like you nearly did a couple of days ago. Do you remember Dr Hunter?'

The man's protuberant eyes passed over me. 'Hello, Edgar,' I said.

His Adam's apple bobbed, but that was the only indication he knew I was there. Rachel motioned for me to drop back and lowered her voice. 'It might be better if you stayed here. He doesn't like anything new.'

I looked uncertainly at the scarecrow-like figure. 'Are you sure you'll be OK?'

'Don't worry, he's harmless.'

I stayed back while she hurried to catch him up, although I kept close enough in case he proved her wrong. I still didn't feel any sense of threat from him, but fear makes people unpredictable. Gangly or not, if he grew agitated he might hurt someone without meaning to.

But Rachel was already steering him to the side of the road, her hand on his grubby arm. She spoke to him in a reassuring voice too low for me to catch, but whatever she said seemed to do the trick. Watching him to make sure he kept to the edge of the road, she came back.

'OK, let's go before he changes his mind.'

We got back in the car. Rachel pulled away, driving slowly and giving the gaunt figure a wide berth until we were past him.

'Will he be OK?' I asked.

'There aren't many cars out here. Anyway, if we took him home he'd only come straight back out again.'

'Have you any idea what's wrong with him?'

'Not medically. He just doesn't seem aware of much that's going on. I've wondered if he might be autistic or something, but no one seems to know. He's got a thing about injured animals, though. Always rescuing something or other. God knows what he does with them all.'

I was no expert, but even if he did place somewhere on the autistic spectrum, I thought it likely he had other mental health issues as well. 'Where does he live?'

'In a run-down cottage in the Backwaters. I've been past a few times, and it's pretty grim. If you think we're isolated you should see that.'

'He lives by himself?' From what I'd seen, Edgar didn't seem capable of functioning independently.

'He does now. The story is that he was some kind of academic or naturalist. He used to be married with a young daughter, but then the little girl disappeared. Went out to play one day and never came back. Everyone thought she must have drowned, but Edgar never recovered. His wife left him, so now he spends his time searching the Backwaters for his daughter. If you believe the locals, anyway,' she added.

'The police never found her?' I asked, struck by the eerie echoes to Rachel's sister. If the story was true then Emma Derby wasn't the Backwaters' first victim.

'No, but there's no connection with Emma, if that's what you're wondering.' Rachel kept her voice neutral as she spoke. 'It was twenty-odd years ago, and it's probably mostly gossip anyway. You even get some people saying Edgar murdered his own daughter, or that he rescues birds and animals because he couldn't save her. It's best to take it all with a pinch of salt.'

We'd reached the outskirts of town. Rachel fell silent as we passed a weather-beaten road sign that proclaimed *Welcome to Cruckhaven.* Below it someone had spray-painted *Now fuck off.*

'Catchy slogan,' I said, to change the subject.

'Wait till you see the town.'

We passed a scattering of small bungalows and then came to a main street of brick and pebble-dash shops. She pulled up next to a concrete quay, stubby metal mooring posts sprouting from its edge like fossilized tree stumps.

'Jamie wrote down what sort of spark plugs you need,' Rachel said, handing me a piece of paper with scrawled handwriting on it. 'The petrol station's a bit further along this road. You can't miss it. I've just got a few groceries to buy, so shall I meet you back here in, oh, half an hour?'

I said that was OK, trying not to show the unexpected disappointment I felt. *What did you expect? Her to come along and hold your hand?* 'While I'm here is there anything worth seeing?' I asked.

'Depends how much you like closed shops and mud.'

'I'll take that as a no, shall I?' I said, looking out of the car window at the tired seaside town.

'Afraid so. Whatever Cruckhaven used to have going for it went belly-up long before I got here. There's a fish and chip van that might be open, and a coffee shop on the quayside that's making an effort. If you get bored with the sights they make a decent latte.'

'Why don't you meet me there?'

I said it before I'd even thought. Rachel looked surprised and I cursed myself for putting her on the spot. I was about to try to dig my way out of it when she surprised me in return.

'Are you offering cake as well?'

I pretended to consider. 'I might.'

She grinned. 'See you there.'

12

THERE ARE FEW sights sadder than a working town that doesn't work any more. Cruckhaven had that look. On a bank holiday, any normal seaside resort should have been bustling. Here the main road was all but deserted and half of the businesses on the small harbour front were closed. There was an old souvenir shop that looked as though it hadn't been open in years. Its window was lined with yellow cellophane to protect the display from the sun, but its corners had come away and now drooped forlornly. Dead flies lay in the window bottom along with crab-lines, seashell trinkets and bleached-out postcards, as though the owner had locked up one day and never come back.

There were a few people about, though not many. Harassed young mothers wore thousand-yard stares as they pushed prams, and a gang of teenagers sulked on a street bench, eyeing passers-by like potential prey. I'd not taken much notice of the town when I'd driven through it before, more concerned with getting to the recovery operation. Now I saw what a drab place it was.

I walked to the edge of the harbour and looked out. Where there should have been lapping water there was only oily mud, even though it wasn't yet low tide. The harbour was almost completely silted up, so much so that weeds and wiry-looking grass were growing in it. An unsafe-looking wooden jetty extended out to the few small boats moored in what sluggish water there was, but it had the look of a makeshift, temporary measure.

I watched a black and white bird picking through the mud on delicate, stilt-like legs. Lundy had told me the estuary had been silting up for years, and the problem was obviously worse this much further inland. In a few more years the harbour would choke up altogether, and then Cruckhaven would have lost any remaining reason for its existence.

No wonder there was local support for Sir Stephen Villiers' plans to build a marina. Having met the man, I couldn't see him letting much get in his way, certainly not the concerns of environmentalists. And for the people trying to scrape a living here, the prospect of new jobs and regeneration must seem like a lifeline. But I could also remember the almost casual manner in which Sir Stephen had regarded the remains of his son, and was glad I didn't have to entrust my future to that cold and indifferent gaze. Any pact with him was likely to be a Faustian one.

I'd dawdled long enough. Turning from the harbour, I set off along the road in the direction Rachel had indicated for the petrol station. The estuary was less clogged with silt out here, the mud mostly covered by small waves. At the water's edge I passed the body of a gull, eyes pecked out of a head that rolled loosely back and forth. The sight reminded me of Edgar, scuffling along on his search for injured animals. Or dead ones, I thought, recalling the hedgehog he'd been carrying; he evidently couldn't tell the difference.

I hoped the story Rachel had told me about his missing daughter was just a local myth, but I doubted it could all be made up. Even if the details had become blurred or exaggerated over time, the disappearance of a little girl from a small community like this wasn't something people would forget, even twenty-odd years later. And perhaps it wasn't so far-fetched after all that her father was still trying to find her. Looking back on my own behaviour, I wasn't sure I'd been entirely sane myself after Kara and Alice died. Grief is devastating even for those with family and friends to support them. For someone living alone in an isolated place like the Backwaters, it wasn't difficult to imagine how their mental health could disintegrate.

There but for the grace of God . . .

Whatever had happened to Edgar, I'd feel happier knowing that social services were aware of him. Making a mental note to check into it when I got back, I looked up and saw a sign for the petrol station up ahead. But before that, on the estuary side of the road, was another sign, this one large and hand-painted on peeling timber.

Coker's Marine and Auto.

In smaller lettering under it were the words *Salvage, Spares and Repairs.* Not so good on the repairs, evidently.

The sign was suspended above a single-storey prefabricated building set on a small quay. Small boats of varying degrees of decrepitude were moored in cramped berths and lined up on the muddy bank by the quayside, exposing algae-smeared hulls. A muddy pick-up truck was parked in front of the prefab, along with several other cars in various states of disrepair.

I'd stopped when I realized what the place was. It crossed my mind to go and find whoever I'd spoken to – Coker, presumably – but there was no point getting into an argument. He'd evidently got some grudge against Trask, and a pretty weighty one if he was prepared to turn down work. From the look of things the yard wasn't exactly thriving.

But before I could walk away a man stepped out from behind one of the boats. He was middle-aged, with oil-stained blue overalls stretched tight over a big frame. An equally grimy baseball cap was tilted back on the dirty blond hair. He held some sort of engine part in his hands, wiping it on a greasy rag. Shrewd eyes regarded me from a heavy-featured face running to fat as he tilted his chin in enquiry.

'Help you?'

The gravelly voice was the same one I'd spoken to on the phone. 'No thanks.'

'Then what's so interesting about my yard?' He wore a smile but there was nothing friendly about it. 'Just admiring the view?'

'Something like that.'

'Yeah, people are always doing that. How's the car? Still fucked?' His smile broadened at my surprise. A crooked incisor gave him a faintly wolfish look. 'I've got an ear for accents. And we don't get that many visitors.'

'I wonder why.'

The smile slipped a notch but stayed in place. 'Trask's son got it running, did he?'

'Yes, he did.' I wondered if I should just walk away. But for some reason this felt like a confrontation, and I knew better than to turn my back.

The man nodded. His hands carried on wiping the engine part, slowly turning it in the rag. 'Thought as much. So you staying out there with 'em?'

'Why?'

'Because you can give him a message.' His face twisted, all pretence dropped. 'Tell that wanker—'

Before he could finish the prefab door opened and a girl came out. 'Dad, I can't find the—'

It was the girl I'd seen with Jamie two days before. She wasn't dressed quite as skimpily today, but her red jeans and tight sweater still looked out of place in the salvage yard. She broke off when she saw me, recognition blanking her face. Then she hurriedly went on.

'I, uh, I can't find the petty cash tin. Do you know where it is?'

It was a good attempt but didn't fool her father. His eyes narrowed as they went from one of us to the other.

'You know him?'

'No, course not!' the girl said quickly.

'Then why'd it look like you did?' His daughter blinked, her mouth opening as though she hoped an excuse would form by itself. He turned to me. 'Well?'

Behind him, the girl gave me an imploring look that seemed close to panic.

'Well what?' I asked.

'Don't get smart. How do you know each other?'

'We don't.' It wasn't quite a lie: I might have seen her before but I didn't know her.

'I'm not fucking stupid. She's seen you somewhere.'

I guessed then what was going on, and bit back the impulse to say he should ask his daughter. The girl looked terrified. Whatever issue her father had with Trask, it was enough to make her scared he'd find out she'd visited his son.

'I came through here the other day,' I said. 'She might have seen me then.'

'What are you doing out here?'

'That's none of your business,' I said easily.

It was my turn to stare him down. I could see the doubt forming as he wondered who I was. His daughter stood by, anxiously worrying at a glossy red thumbnail. It was a good time to leave.

'Nice meeting you,' I said, vaguely enough to mean either of them.

Leaving them there, I turned and walked away.

The petrol station was only a little way along the road. It was small, with two pumps that offered an obscure brand of fuel I'd never heard of. But as well as the spark plugs I needed it sold a few basic groceries as well, so I was able to buy replacements for the food Rachel had brought to the boathouse.

As I walked past the salvage yard I half expected to be accosted again, but there was no sign of anyone there.

Back at the quayside, I found a cashpoint machine and drew out what I hoped would be enough to pay Jamie. If it wasn't I'd have to send the rest once I got back to London. The thought of returning was depressing, so I put it from my mind and went to meet Rachel.

The coffee shop was actually called just that, the words capitalized in case anyone wasn't sure. It was more like an old-fashioned tea room than a café, with cakes and sandwiches behind a glass counter and red-and-white checked cloths on the cramped tables. There was even a bell that tinkled merrily when I went inside.

There was no Rachel, though. Or anyone else: I was the only customer. A tired-looking woman with a warm smile was serving behind the counter. I ordered a coffee and went to a table in the window. Even though I was feeling much better I was glad to sit down after the walk. Outside, the harbour didn't look quite so grim now I couldn't see the oil-stained estuary bed. Once upon a time I could imagine Cruckhaven might have been a nice place, before the estuary silted up and the water abandoned it.

I tried not to glance at my watch as I waited, but as soon as I stopped making a conscious effort not to I did anyway. Rachel was ten minutes late. Not long, but I found myself worrying that she'd changed her mind, or even forgotten we were meeting. And then I looked up and saw her hurrying along the harbour front.

She was carrying a shopping bag and looked distracted. Her expression cleared when she glanced through the window and saw me. The bell over the door chimed again as she came in.

'Sorry I'm late,' she said breathlessly. 'Hi, Debbie, how're you doing?'

'Oh, surviving.' The woman behind the counter seemed pleased to see her. 'We've got some freshly baked orange and cinnamon muffins. Or there's a coffee and walnut cake I made yesterday.'

Rachel looked mock-pained. 'You're a bad influence, you know that? What are you having?'

She looked at me expectantly as she sat down, but I didn't have much of a sweet tooth. 'I'll stick with coffee, thanks.'

'He'll have the cake,' Rachel told the woman with a grin. 'I'll have a muffin and a latte, please.'

I raised my hands in surrender. 'Coffee cake it is.'

'You can't let me eat alone.' Rachel glanced across at the counter as the woman began making the latte, masking our conversation beneath a chug of steam. 'I always try and stop off here when I

128

come into town. Debbie lost her husband last year and she's got two kids, so she needs all the support she can get. Plus everything's homemade and she's seriously good at cakes.'

'It's OK, I'm sold. Did you get everything you came for?'

'Yeah, it was just a few things we were running short of. Someone finished off all our eggs and milk.'

'Just as well I bought some,' I said, lifting up my carrier bag.

She laughed. 'That'll teach me. Seriously, you didn't have to do that. I wanted an excuse to get away from the house for an hour or two. Doesn't hurt to give everyone a bit of space sometimes.'

It was the first real hint she'd given of the strain the family must be under, but it seemed more of a slip than an invitation. She quickly carried on.

'So did you get the spark plugs?'

'I did, yes. I had a fun encounter at the marine salvage yard as well.'

Her face fell. 'What happened?'

I told her about trying to hire Coker to repair my car, and his subsequent antagonism. 'There doesn't seem to be any love lost between him and your brother-in-law.'

'You could say that.' Rachel stopped as the woman brought over the coffee and cake. She gave her a smile. 'Thanks, Debbie. That looks evil.'

She was right. Looking at the slab of cake on my plate I wondered if I'd be able to finish it. Rachel's smile faded as the woman went back to the counter. With a sigh she turned to me.

'I'd no idea you'd had a run-in with him or I'd have warned you to steer clear. He's got sort of a vendetta against Andrew and Jamie. Well, all of us really. It's a long story, but I didn't think you'd get caught up in it.'

'You don't need to explain. I just hope I haven't caused any trouble.'

She smiled grimly as she stirred her coffee. 'Believe me, when it comes to Darren Coker you can't make things any worse.'

I wasn't so sure about that. 'His daughter was there as well.'

'Stacey?' Rachel looked up, the coffee forgotten. 'How do you know about her?'

'I saw her at the house the other day. She recognized me and her father picked up on it.'

'Oh, God, she's been out to see Jamie *again*?'

I had the feeling I was getting into murkier waters than I'd intended. 'I didn't say anything, and she denied it to Coker. But I don't think he believed her.'

Rachel closed her eyes and sighed. 'No, he wouldn't. You probably gathered that Jamie's got a history with Stacey. They were only kids but things got messy and . . . well, it caused problems. Her father's banned her from seeing him, and to be honest Jamie's not interested any more anyway. He hasn't been for a while, but Stacey's not the sort to take no for an answer.'

'I sort of guessed that.'

That earned a smile, but it was strained. She prodded at the muffin with her fork. 'I can't blame her father for being protective. She's his only daughter and Andrew isn't exactly tactful when he loses his temper. But Coker's gone way overboard, turning it into this ridiculous feud. It's like the Montagues and Capulets, except it's all one-sided and Stacey's no Juliet.'

She looked surprised when I gave a laugh.

'I know, that sounds biased. But this happened before I came here, so it wasn't anything to do with me. The first I knew about it was about a month after . . . after I arrived and I bumped into Coker in town. I'd no idea who he was but he launched into this *rant*, going on about how it served Andrew right that Emma had gone missing, calling her a "stuck-up bitch" and worse. I mean, who says something like that? And to someone he's never even *met* before?'

Her face had flushed, but I wasn't sure if she was more upset or angry. 'What did you do?'

'I told him to fuck off.' She picked up her fork and stabbed it into the muffin. 'Seemed to work.'

I tried to imagine the slim woman in front of me facing down the loudmouth owner of the boat yard, and decided it wasn't so difficult a stretch. 'Did you tell the police?'

'About that? No, but they'd questioned Coker when Emma disappeared, because of the trouble over his daughter and Jamie. More routine than anything else. He's an arsehole, but that's all.' She tilted her chin at my plate, mouth quirking in a smile. 'You should eat your cake.'

I took the hint and let the subject drop. We kept the conversation lighter after that, avoiding anything personal. She told me how Cruckhaven used to be a thriving little harbour town, benefiting from the nearby oyster fishery and home to a small fleet of fishing boats. But dwindling fish stocks and the silting up of the estuary had changed all that.

'I don't think anybody realized the silt was such a problem at first,' she said, hands cradling her coffee cup over the remains of the muffin. 'Because it didn't happen overnight people tended to ignore it. They were more concerned with the fishing drying up than the harbour, and by the time everyone woke up to what was going on it was too late.'

'Can't it still be dredged?'

'It could, but it's so bad now it'd be prohibitively expensive. Give it another decade and this whole area will be like the Backwaters, either mudflats or saltmarsh. Which is no bad thing from an environmental point of view, but it's like a slow motion disaster for the people who live here. In some ways it's worse than a flood. At least once a flood's over people can rebuild, even after something like the big North Sea one. Have you heard about that?'

I hadn't. My grasp of history was sketchy at the best of times, and it seemed that every year brought depressing news of more communities hit by flooding. Though apparently that was nothing new.

'It was a huge disaster in the 1950s,' Rachel went on, setting down her cup. 'There was a storm tide that swamped here and northern Europe. It killed hundreds of people on the east coast, and the south-east was really badly hit. Canvey Island was inundated, and Cruckhaven was nearly wiped out. The town survived that, but this is different. Without the harbour it's hard to see how it's ever going to recover.'

'What about the marina development? Wouldn't that turn things round?' It was only after I'd said it that I realized anything connected with the Villiers family probably wasn't the best topic of conversation.

She gave a huff. 'Don't get me started. OK, if it was done properly you could probably limit the damage. I'm not a tree-hugger; I know there have to be compromises. But this scheme is basically about taking a wrecking ball to the whole area, burying the marshes under concrete and tarmac and turning the estuary into a glorified waterpark. And because they know people are desperate, they're dangling the prospect of jobs and prosperity to try and bulldoze any objections. God, every time I hear the name Villiers I could . . .'

She stopped herself, smiling self-consciously.

'Well. Never mind. We should be getting back. I promised Fay I'd take her out later, and she doesn't do waiting.'

She smiled as she spoke, her fondness for Trask's daughter obvious. I wondered if that was why she'd stayed with the family as long as she had. But I hadn't realized it was so late either: the wall clock behind the counter showed we'd been sitting there for well over an hour. Reluctantly, I stood up as we prepared to go. I insisted on paying, complimenting the coffee shop owner on her cake, even though my teeth still felt coated with sugar.

'What are your plans now? I suppose the police want you to take a look at the foot from yesterday?' Rachel asked as we went back to the Land Rover. She pulled a face. 'That sounded weird. And don't worry, I was just asking. I *really* don't want to hear any details.'

'You're safe enough. I won't be working on it anyway.'

She looked surprised. 'How come? I thought you were an expert on that sort of thing.'

'I think the police feel I've done enough.'

'But if not for you they wouldn't even have found it.'

I shrugged, not wanting to get into it. 'That's how it goes sometimes.'

'So you're heading straight off back to London then?'

'Soon as my car's ready.'

Rachel was quiet as we walked along the harbour front. I'd been surprised how easy talking to her was, and thought she felt the same way. Now a tension seemed to have come between us. She looked preoccupied as we reached the Land Rover. Taking out her keys, she unlocked it and then paused.

'Don't take this the wrong way, but—'

Her phone interrupted whatever she was going to say. Don't take *what* the wrong way, I wondered uneasily? I tried to think if I'd done something else wrong as she answered her phone.

'Hi, Andrew. I was just . . . No, why?'

I saw the change come over her expression. Whatever this was, it wasn't good.

'When?' She listened. 'OK, I'm on my way.'

'Everything all right?' I asked as she thrust the phone in her pocket and threw the shopping bag into the back of the Land Rover.

'We need to go.'

She was already climbing in and starting the engine. I'd barely managed to get into the passenger side before she was turning the car round.

'What's happened?'

Rachel's face was pale and intent, but the grinding as she crashed the gears betrayed her emotion.

'Fay's missing.'

13

RACHEL DROVE IN silence most of the way back to Creek House. She couldn't tell me much more, only that Trask's daughter had walked off after an argument with her brother an hour before, and not been seen since. Neither had her dog.

'Have you any idea where she might have gone?' I asked.

She slowed to take a narrow bend, then quickly accelerated again. We'd come a different way back, making better time now the tide was low enough to permit the old Defender to bump across still-flooded crossings. 'Probably into the Backwaters. Apparently she got bored of waiting for me and wanted Jamie to go out in the boat with her. He was busy so she went off in a strop.'

I could hear the self-recrimination in her voice, and felt some of my own. If I hadn't asked Rachel for coffee she'd have been back home by now. And Jamie had probably been busy working on my car.

'Has she done anything like this before?'

'Once or twice. Andrew's forbidden her to go off by herself, but it hasn't always worked.'

I felt a little less worried when I heard that. The young girl's disappearance sounded more like a tantrum than anything more serious.

We'd reached a causeway I recognized as the one where my car had been caught by the tide. It was still partially covered by water, visible only as a pale strip below the surface, but Rachel didn't hesitate. Dropping to a low gear she drove out on to it, sending a surge of water up around the wheels. I stiffened reflexively, then relaxed. It obviously wasn't the first time she'd done this, and with its drainpipe-like snorkel the old Land Rover made the crossing seem easy.

Reaching the other bank, she accelerated away again. She drove straight past the boathouse, and in much less time than it had taken Trask to tow me we were at Creek House. Jamie was already running towards us as we pulled on to the gravelled parking area. My own car stood nearby, untended but with its bonnet still open. Rachel wrenched on the handbrake and jumped out.

'Is she back yet?'

'No.' Trask's son looked pale and worried. He barely spared me a glance. 'Dad's getting the boat out.'

'What happened?' Rachel asked as they headed back towards the house. Not knowing what else to do, I went as well.

'Nothing, but you know Fay. She kicked off on one when I wouldn't drop everything and take her out in the boat.'

'Did you see her go?'

'No, but not long after that Dad couldn't find her. She wasn't in the house and Cassie's gone as well. They're not around here, so she must have taken herself off into the Backwaters. God, she is *such* a spoiled little—'

'That's enough.' Trask had appeared from around the side of the house as we emerged from the copse, coiling a nylon rope in his hands. 'If you had more patience with her she might not keep acting like this.'

'Not just me, is it?' Jamie muttered under his breath. His father turned on him, jaw muscles clenched.

'What was that?'

'Nothing.'

I was beginning to feel more like an intruder than ever. This was a family spat: I'd no business being there. I certainly wasn't needed.

Still, since I was there I could at least offer. 'Can I help?' I asked, more to break the tension than anything else.

With a last hard look at his son, Trask turned to me. 'No, it's all right. You might as well—'

We all heard the dog at the same time. There was a low whine from off down the path, and a moment later the girl's pet appeared through the trees. Its coat was wet and muddy, as though it had been in the creek, and it was limping as it hobbled along the path. I looked past it, but there was no sign of Trask's daughter. The animal whined again and as it drew closer I saw its fur was clogged with something darker than mud.

'She's bleeding!' Rachel exclaimed, rushing over. 'Oh, she's cut all over!'

The little mongrel yelped, wagging its tail as Rachel tried to examine it. It was shivering miserably, the bloody patches on its muddy coat all too visible now.

'They look like bites. Something must have attacked her,' Jamie said.

'Can I see?' I asked.

He moved aside. The dog whimpered when I smoothed the thick fur back to get a better look at its wounds. They were mostly superficial, either ragged cuts or small punctures.

'They aren't bites,' I said. Teeth or claws would have torn the flesh much more. I was more relieved that they weren't clean-edged enough to be from a knife. 'They look more like tears. Like she's been caught up on something.'

'Like what?' Jamie asked, as though it were my fault.

I'd no answer. Trask had lost interest in the dog anyway. He strode into the copse in the direction the dog had come from and cupped his hands round his mouth.

'Fay! *Fay!*'

There was no answer. He stared at the empty landscape, then came back.

'I'm going to take the boat up into the Backwaters. Jamie, you head along the creek bank towards the boathouse. Take your phone and call me the minute you find anything.'

'What if there's no—'

'Just do it!'

'What about me?' Rachel asked as Jamie broke into a run.

'You stay here. If Fay comes back let me know.'

'But—'

'I'm not arguing.'

He was already striding towards the corner of the house. I went after him. 'I'll go with you.'

'I don't need any help.'

'You might if she's hurt.'

He glared at me, as though furious I'd voiced his fear. But Rachel had followed us, and broke in before he could respond.

'He's a doctor, Andrew. You saw Cassie.'

Trask hesitated, then gave a terse nod. We'd reached the front of the house. This side was nearly all glass, huge windows facing directly out on to the creek. A floating jetty sat on top of the water, a small fibreglass boat with an outboard motor moored to it. The jetty swayed as Trask hurried out and climbed in.

'Untie the line.'

I cast off and got in, green water sloshing around the algae-coated bottom as the boat rocked. I sat in the bow as Trask started the outboard with a *blat* of blue exhaust. Then he was gunning the motor and taking us upstream.

Looking back, I saw Rachel crouching down by the dog, staring after us.

Trask didn't speak as the boat roared up the creek, heading deeper into the Backwaters. The receding tide had exposed the drying banks on either side, but there was still enough water in the middle for the boat's shallow draught.

I watched gulls swoop and dive over something in the mud, but it was only a plastic bag. 'Does your daughter have a phone?'

'No.' I thought that was all I was going to get. He stared ahead of us at the creek. 'I told her she was too young.'

There was no point saying anything to that. The only thing that would make him feel any better was finding his daughter safe. I could imagine all too well what would be going through his mind right now. 'Are there many places she could have gone?'

He steered around a patch of ripples on the water, the only indication of a sandbank just under the surface. 'A few, but it's tricky on foot. We can cover more ground by boat.'

Saltmarsh gave way to tall banks of rushes. In places they reached above our heads now the tide was falling, so that the boat seemed channelled along between them. Every now and then Trask would shout his daughter's name as the boat droned along. It produced a raucous response from disturbed birds, but that was all. We passed gaps in the banks that looked like secondary channels branching off the main creek, until we drew close enough to see they led to dead ends. No wonder few boats bothered to come here: it would be easy to become lost in this labyrinth of reeds and water.

The tide had fallen noticeably in the short time since we'd set out: now the creek's banks rose above us on either side like miniature canyons. Even though we kept to the very centre of the channel, it was obvious we wouldn't be able to go much further before we ran aground. When we came to a point where the creek was split by a long sandbank, Trask let the boat idle, gnawing at his lip as he studied the diverging waterways.

'What is it?'

'I don't know which way she'll have gone from here, and the tide's getting too low to search them all.' Abruptly, he killed the motor. The boat rocked as he stood up and shouted into the sudden silence. '*Fay!*'

There was no answer. Water slopped against the hull as the boat drifted backwards. Grim-faced, Trask yelled her name again before reaching to restart the engine.

'Hang on,' I told him.

I thought I'd heard something just as he'd moved. He stopped, listening.

'I can't—'

And then it came again. A young girl's terrified voice. *'Daddy!'*

This time Trask heard it. *'All right, Fay, I'm coming!'* he yelled, firing up the engine.

His knuckles were white on the tiller as he aimed the boat up the left hand fork. Rotten wooden posts lined the banks, sticking out of the mud like broken teeth. We passed the tumbledown remains of an old corrugated metal shack, and then the boat rounded a bend and we saw Trask's daughter.

She was lying half in, half out of the creek, sobbing and covered with mud. All around her the surface was broken by what at first I thought was some kind of weed, exposed by the falling tide. Then we drew closer and I realized what it was.

The creek was full of barbed wire.

'It *hurts*, Daddy!' Fay sobbed as we jumped out of the boat and splashed through the cold water towards her.

'I know. It's all right, sweetheart, don't try to move.'

She couldn't have anyway. Only one of her arms was free; the other was caught on the rusty wire. The barbs had bitten into skin and clothing alike, and the mud that coated her was streaked with blood. Only her upper body was visible, but the wire obviously snared her underwater as well.

Her face was pale and blotched with tears. 'Cassie jumped in the water and then just started *screaming*! I tried to help her but she got free and I fell in, and . . . and . . .'

'Shh, it's OK. Cassie's fine, she came back home.'

Trask crouched beside her, carefully feeling the wire. This was a different man from the one I'd seen so far, tender and patient. But there was fear in his eyes as he turned to me.

'I need you to hold the wire still,' he said in a low voice.

'We should call the emergency services . . .' I began, but he shook his head.

'It'll take them too long to get out here. I'm not leaving her like this.'

I understood how he felt: if it had been my daughter I wouldn't have wanted to wait either. I just wasn't sure the two of us could free her without making her injuries worse.

But I could see Trask's mind was made up. Fay began to panic when she saw what we were about to do. 'Nonono, don't!'

'Shh, I need you to be brave. Come on, be a big girl.'

She squeezed her eyes shut, turning her face away as her father set to work. Knowing it would be needed later, I took my jacket off and flung it on the dry bank before joining him. Getting soaked again so soon after I'd recovered was asking for trouble but there was nothing else for it. Trask's face was grim and intent as he crouched chest deep in the water, groping for the barbs below the murky surface. The mud sucked at my feet as I took hold of the wire strands, trying to keep them still. It wasn't easy. Although I'd pulled my shirt sleeves down to protect my hands, both Trask and I were soon bleeding from where the sharp metal had ripped our skin like paper.

Even so, I knew we'd been lucky. If the tide had been coming in rather than going out this could have been a very different story. Watching Trask with his daughter I felt relieved for them both, but there was also a keen ache as I was reminded of my own loss.

But I couldn't afford to let myself be distracted. Forcibly pushing the thoughts aside, I examined the barbed wire more closely. The creek here was partially dammed by a sandbank, forming a pool that looked deep enough to retain water even at low tide. Only a few strands of barbed wire broke the surface, disturbed by the girl's struggles. Ordinarily it would be completely submerged, and it made me angry to think that some idiot had dumped it here.

Trask grimaced with effort as he groped below the water.

'Good girl. Only one more,' he told his daughter. He gave me a glance. 'Get ready to pull the wire away.'

His shoulders tensed, and the young girl yelled in pain. Then Trask was lifting her out, water dripping from them as he straightened. The wire was heavier than I'd expected, moving slowly as I dragged it clear so Trask could carry his daughter up the muddy bank. Fay was sobbing, clinging to her father as he murmured reassurances. She was shivering and bleeding, but none of her wounds seemed serious. Thank God, I thought, letting go of the wire.

But then she stared past me and her eyes widened in shock. I looked back to see a disturbance in the middle of the creek. The water swirled as though a huge fish was turning underneath, and then something broke the surface.

Caught on the barbed wire, the body emerged slowly into the air, arms and legs hanging like a broken puppet. As Fay's screams rang out, a pale head turned empty eye sockets to the sky.

Then, as though retreating from the daylight, it sank down again and the water closed over it once more.

14

THE BLACK-HEADED GULL had found something. It stood with its head cocked, eye levelled at the mud, then stabbed down with its beak. There was a brief, uneven tug of war before the bird plucked a small brown crab from the creek bed. The crab's legs wriggled as it was dropped on its back, the instinct to survive continuing even in the last moments of life. Then the yellow beak came down again, tearing at the vulnerable underbelly, and the crab became another part of the food chain.

I looked away as the gull went about its meal. Beside me on the bank, Lundy stared down at the waterlogged torso suspended on the barbed wire.

'So this is what you call keeping a low profile, is it?'

It was said without any real heat. But we both knew this was different from when I'd found the training shoe.

This changed everything.

The body was strung out on the barbed wire like so much dirty washing. The water level in the creek hadn't yet dropped enough to expose all of it, but from the waist up the torso was now revealed in all its decaying glory. Police officers and CSIs stood around in coveralls on the bank, waiting for the water to sink low enough for the unenviable task of recovery to begin. At least the tide meant there was no need for police divers: by the time they could have got here the creek would have drained enough not to need them.

Right now, though, it seemed like a long wait.

I'd gone back to Creek House after Trask and I had freed his daughter from the barbed wire. There was no point in staying with the body until the police arrived. For one thing it had sunk under the water again; it wouldn't be going anywhere. For another, I needed to change out of my wet clothes. I'd only just shaken off one chill after standing around soaking wet, and I'd pushed my luck enough as it was.

I steered the boat while Trask huddled with his daughter. The sight of them together made me feel more of an outsider than ever, and stirred something that was uncomfortably like envy. Although Fay was older than my own daughter had been when she'd died, she was still younger than Alice would be now. The realization lay heavily on me as the boat droned along the creek.

Telling myself it was probably cold and fatigue talking, I focused on more immediate problems. We couldn't do much for Fay's wounds out there, but although she'd need stitches none of the cuts looked deep enough to have caused serious blood loss. More worrying was the risk of infection from the contaminated water. A decomposing corpse was host to all manner of bacteria, some of them potentially deadly. I'd received shots for most of them because of my work, and I was on antibiotics anyway. But the girl would need a full course of inoculations, and so would her father. We'd both gashed our hands on the barbed wire, and Trask's cuts were much worse than mine.

Still, I didn't think there was any great danger. They hadn't come into direct contact with the body, and the creek's saline waters were kept fresh by the constantly flowing tides. The most immediate threat to Fay was shock and hypothermia. Although the water temperature wasn't as low as it could have been, we were only just coming into spring and it was still cold. I'd given Trask my dry jacket to wrap her in, but other than that there wasn't much I could do. Except one, small thing.

Trask had looked stunned, his face bloodless as I started the engine and set us back on course for the house, keeping to the deeper water in the middle of the creek. He said nothing, but it wasn't hard to guess what he was thinking.

He jerked, startled, when I touched his shoulder to get his attention. 'It was male,' I told him quietly. 'OK? It was male.'

He seemed to sag, then made a visible effort to pull himself together. Giving a nod, he hugged his daughter to him while I opened up the motor and sent the boat roaring back down the creek.

I hoped I'd done the right thing.

The truth was that it was impossible to guess the corpse's gender, and certainly not from the brief glimpse I'd had. Under normal circumstances I would never have committed myself like that. But the young girl needed her father, and Trask looked like a man close to the edge. Small wonder. Only two days ago the body of his wife's suspected killer had been found. That was enough for anyone to deal with without having to agonize over whether we'd just found his missing wife's remains as well.

And so I'd spoken as a doctor rather than a forensic anthropologist. If I was right, then it would spare the family days of tortured waiting. If I was wrong . . . well, I'd made mistakes before, and for worse reasons.

Back at the house, I'd called Lundy to let him know what had happened and agreed to meet him out at the creek. With Trask's hands badly cut from the barbed wire, Jamie had driven his father and sister to hospital. I'd changed into dry clothes from my bag and patched up my own cuts as best I could. My jacket was no longer needed – Fay had been wrapped in a blanket – but it was wet and muddy. Leaving it there, I'd accepted Rachel's offer of an old one of Trask's, and also a pair of wellingtons to replace my waterlogged boots. The melancholy that had gripped me on the way back had faded now I had something to do. All things considered, physically at least I didn't feel too bad. A little shaky, but that was more adrenalin than anything else. When I found out that Rachel was taking the injured dog to an emergency vet, I asked her to drop me off as close as possible to the stretch of creek where we'd seen the body.

It was easier reaching the place on foot than I'd thought. The road crossed a small bridge that was only fifty yards from where Fay had been caught on the barbed wire. It made a convenient landmark for the police to assemble at, and there was also a trail of sorts – a dirt path that ran from the bridge to the creek itself. From there, it took only a few minutes to walk along the bank to the trapped pool of water where we'd seen the body.

First to arrive were a pair of uniformed PCs. One of them waited at the bridge while I took the other to the creek, and shortly afterwards the rest of the orderly circus that attends a crime scene began to troop up as well. By the time Lundy and Frears got there the creek's level had dropped as though a plug had been pulled, exposing loops of barbed wire that coiled from the water like rusty brambles.

Inch by inch, the body emerged. The head first, its crown breaking through the surface like the dome of a jellyfish. Then the shoulders, chest and arms. It wore a heavy leather jacket that could have been either black or brown, although it was too filthy and waterlogged to be sure. The body was suspended face down. One elbow was bent the wrong way, and the hands had fallen away to reveal stubs of bone and gristle inside the jacket cuffs. Tilted at a sideways angle, the head also looked on the verge of coming loose, supported more by the barbed wire than any remaining connective tissue.

Frears had waited until the water level was low enough for him to get a look at the body and then headed back to the mortuary. It was obvious that freeing the fragile remains from the barbed wire without damaging them was going to be a slow process, and the pathologist didn't strike me as the patient sort. Not that there was much point in his staying. Clarke was tied up in court, but Lundy was more than capable of overseeing the recovery until she got there.

There was no reason for me to stay either: as a witness I'd

technically no right to even be there. But no one suggested I leave, so I sat down on a convenient hummock with a plastic cup of coffee Lundy had provided and watched as the tide slowly revealed its secret.

'Not something you'd want a kid to see, is it?' the DI commented as the CSIs began to wade into the creek. 'Bad place for her dog to go for a swim. You reckon it could smell it?'

'Probably.'

I'd had time to think it over as I'd been waiting. A dog's sense of smell would be sensitive enough to detect a badly decomposed corpse when the ebbing tide brought it closer to the surface. Rachel had told me that Trask had only bought his daughter's pet after his wife disappeared, so they'd owned it less than seven months. It had been a long, wet winter that would have discouraged walks in the Backwaters. It was possible – likely, even – that the excitable young animal hadn't had a chance to discover the intriguing scent coming from the water until today.

The CSIs began negotiating the barbed wire to get closer to the body. They were wearing heavy duty gauntlets and chest-high waders, but I still didn't envy them the task. Lundy continued to watch them as he spoke.

'I spoke to Trask on my way here. He said you'd told him it's male.' His tone made it a question as well as a reproach.

'I thought he'd got enough to worry about without wondering if this was his wife.'

'And if you're wrong?'

'Then I'll apologize. But even if this is a woman I don't think it's Emma Derby.'

Lundy gave a sigh. 'No, me neither.'

The lower half of the body was still under the water, so it was hard to gauge its height. But, even allowing for bloating and the thick leather jacket, there was no mistaking the broadness of chest and shoulders. Whoever this was, it had been a heavy-framed individual.

That didn't necessarily mean it was male. Determining the

146

gender of a body, particularly a badly decomposed one like this, wasn't always as clear-cut as it might seem. While male and female skeletal characteristics did exist, the line between them was often blurred. The skeleton of a juvenile male might superficially resemble an adult female, for instance. And not all fully grown men conformed to the traditional stereotype of large-boned masculinity, any more than every woman was petite.

I'd once worked on a case involving a skeleton over six foot tall. The skull had a heavy, square jawbone and thickly pronounced eye ridges, all strong male indicators. The police thought it could be a missing father of two who'd disappeared eighteen months before, until the oval-shaped pelvic inlet and width of the greater sciatic notch revealed the body to be female. Dental records eventually identified her as a forty-seven-year-old teacher from Sussex.

As far as I know, the missing man was never found.

Even so, from what little I could see of the body hanging on the barbed wire, one thing was clear. It was much too big to belong to the slender woman whose self-portrait I'd seen in the boathouse.

The level in the creek had fallen about as low as it was going to. The sandbank formed an effective dam on this side, trapping a pool of water perhaps twenty yards long and several feet deep. The efforts of the CSIs had exposed the body to its hips, but both legs were still hidden beneath the surface.

There was a debate between Lundy, the CSIs and the crime scene manager about the best way to get the body off the wire. 'Can you drag the whole thing out?' Lundy asked as the CSIs sloshed through the murky water.

One of them, a young woman rendered sexless and unrecognizable under the protective gear, shook her head. 'Too heavy. I think the wire's caught on the bottom. We're going to have to try and get the body off.'

'OK, but watch out for those barbs. I don't want to have to fill out any accident forms.'

That merited a snorted laugh. Lundy stared at the body

contemplatively. 'How long would you say it's been here?' he asked me.

I'd been wondering that myself. Until Trask and I disturbed it, the body would have been submerged in the deeper water dammed by the sandbank even at low tide. That would make it decompose at a slower rate than if it had been exposed to sunlight and air, and with the barbed wire holding it in place it wouldn't have suffered the wear and tear of being dragged around by tidal currents.

Still, there were too many unknowns to offer anything better than a rough guess. 'It's started to come apart and there's quite a build-up of adipocere. That's slow to form, so several months at least.'

'But we're talking months, not years?'

'I'd say so.' Any longer than that and the head would have fallen away. Submerged or not, the creek's waters were relatively shallow and warm, and constantly moving with the in-and-out of tides. 'Has anyone else local been reported missing?'

'Only Emma Derby, and we can rule her out. But just so I'm clear, you think this has been in the water longer than the body from the Barrows?'

Lundy's face gave nothing away, but I knew what he was thinking. Finding a second body so soon after the first was a potential – and unwelcome – complication, especially if the evidence suggested they'd died around the same time.

I could reassure him about that much, at least. 'A lot longer for it to be in this condition. It'll have decomposed more slowly underwater than on the surface, but a lot depends on how long it was drifting before it got caught up.'

'If it was drifting.'

I looked at him. 'You don't think it was?'

He made a see-sawing motion with his head. 'Not sure yet. Looks a bit too well trussed to me.'

I'd been focusing on the body rather than what it was caught on, assuming it had been deposited here by the tide. Now I paid more attention to the wire coils. Tatters of grass and torn plastic trailed from them like tired party streamers. The barbs were buried as deep as fishhooks, gouging indiscriminately into clothes and flesh. That could have happened as the creek rose and fell, the body's own weight progressively working the rusty points deeper. But would that have snared it in so many places? Or entangled it quite so much? There were even strands of wire caught on the back of the remains, apparently by chance. That could have been caused by the natural motion of the water in the creek: as well as twice daily tides, storms and tidal surges which would have caused both body and wire to shift around.

Yet now Lundy had planted the doubt, I saw what he meant. Earlier, I'd been angry at whoever had casually dumped barbed wire in the creek.

Perhaps there hadn't been anything casual about it at all.

Moving the body from the creek proved even harder than anyone had expected. It was too badly decomposed for the barbs to be removed while it was still in the water, so a decision was made to leave them embedded while the wire was snipped with cutters. Lundy had told me of the plan rather than ask my advice, but I'd agreed that sounded the best approach. Only then did he turn to the CSIs and give them the go ahead to start.

Each time a wire parted, the body would sag and cause the whole mass of coils to flex, vibrating like a strummed guitar. It took more than half an hour, but eventually the last strand parted with a twang. Still sprouting stubs of clipped wire like coarse hairs, the remains were eased on to a stretcher and brought to the side. I moved aside as the body was set down on the bank. Up close there was the familiar reek of putrefaction. A few flies darted around, but this was too far gone even for their rarefied tastes.

This was the first chance I'd had to take a good look at it, and nothing I saw contradicted the instinctive reassurance I'd given Trask that it was male. This had been a big individual, not a giant but well over six feet tall. The jacket was biker-style, made from thick dark leather, with a rusted metal zip. A black shirt, now filthy and torn, hung loosely over black jeans. The right leg was at a strange angle, with something protruding under the denim below the knee, making me think the tibia and fibula of the shin were probably broken as well as the left elbow. I'd expected the feet to have fallen away like the hands, and it had crossed my mind that the right foot I'd found inside the training shoe before might be from these remains rather than Leo Villiers'. Lundy hadn't said anything else about that, and the idea of the cheap trainers belonging to the wealthy failed politician still bothered me.

When the body emerged from the water, though, I saw it still wore a pair of calf-high leather boots. They would have protected the vulnerable ankle joint, preventing the feet from detaching as they otherwise would. I looked at them and then back to the jacket, on the verge of grasping a half-formed thought.

But whatever it was slipped away. There was more than enough here to consider anyway. The eyes had been picked away by scavengers, and most of the hair had sloughed off the scalp, leaving only a few lank strands of indeterminate colour. A dirty-white coating of adipocere had formed over the whole head and neck, giving it a waxy, mannequin-like appearance. Not even that could disguise the damage that had been inflicted on the face. From the forehead down, it was striped with raw, parallel slashes that had gone through both flesh and bone. The nasal area was all but obliterated, and a series of cuts had taken away most of the teeth and shattered those that were left. They extended across the throat and on to the chest, slicing through the thick leather to expose the underlying ribs before petering out.

I looked at Lundy, to see if he was thinking the same thing as me. This was the second body we'd found in the waters around the estuary that had its identifying facial features destroyed. Not by a shotgun this time, but the damage was every bit as bad.

'I know,' Lundy said, answering my unspoken query. 'Doesn't necessarily mean anything.'

'Boat propeller,' one of the CSIs asserted, a big man red-faced from exertion. 'I've seen that sort of thing before. Body's

150

floating along just below the surface, boat comes along and bam!'

He slapped his fist into his palm. Lundy gave him a reproving look before turning to me.

'What do you think, Dr Hunter?'

'It's possible,' I admitted. The wounds could have been caused post-mortem, and at first glance they seemed consistent with the parallel slashes caused by a small boat propeller. Or, at least, what I could see of them under the adipocere. But there was a flaw in that theory.

'I'm not sure how a propeller could have struck the face,' I said. 'Not to that extent. The body would have been floating face down, not on its back.'

'I know how bodies float,' the big CSI snapped. 'The boat could have rolled it over first. It's got a busted arm and leg, so that'd explain them as well.'

I still didn't like it, but there was no point in arguing. Until the body could be examined at the mortuary it was all speculation anyway. And it would be someone else doing that, I reminded myself. Lundy had done me a favour by letting me stay for the recovery, but I was under no illusions that Clarke would suddenly change her mind and allow me back on the investigation. She'd been annoyed enough with me even before this.

The DCI still hadn't appeared, but Lundy got a call from her as the remains were being carefully lowered into a body bag. He moved off down the bank to take it, looking at the body as he spoke. He listened, nodding, then ended the call and headed back.

'That was the chief. She's been held up in court so she's going straight to the mortuary.'

It was a convenient opening for what had been on my mind. 'You're going to need a forensic anthropologist for this.'

I'd been thinking it through while he'd been on his phone, realizing this could be the last chance I'd have to press my case. Lundy just nodded.

'You're probably right. How are the hands?'

I'd forgotten about the cuts from the barbed wire. I flexed my plaster-covered fingers, only becoming aware of the soreness now he'd mentioned it.

'They're OK,' I said, not really caring just then. 'Look, since I'm here don't you think it's stupid for me not to take a look?'

'That's up to the chief.' He seemed amused. 'If I were you I wouldn't call her stupid, though.'

I was letting my frustration get the better of me. 'I'd still like to talk to her.'

'Fair enough. You can ask her about it at the mortuary.'

'At the mortuary . . . ?' His easy agreement took me by surprise. 'So Clarke wants me to examine the body?'

'I don't know, she's not said anything about that.' Lundy grew serious. 'There's something else we'd like your opinion on.'

15

THE MORTUARY WAS an unobtrusive building situated not far from the hospital. I signed in and was told which examination room to go to before being pointed to the changing room. Putting my own clothes into a locker, I pulled on a set of clean scrubs, replacing the old wellingtons of Trask's that Rachel had lent me with a new pair of white surgical ones.

I still didn't know what I was doing there. Lundy hadn't told me very much at all, only that Clarke would meet me here. 'She'll explain then,' he'd said. 'Best you go in with an open mind.'

I always tried to anyway, but I could see I wasn't going to get anything more from him. The DI hadn't come with me to the mortuary, saying he wanted to stay while the rest of the barbed wire was recovered from the creek. He arranged for me to be given a lift by a talkative young PC, since my car was still waiting to have its spark plugs fitted at Trask's house. I didn't know now when that would happen.

Clarke was waiting for me in the examination room. With her pale colouring, the DCI's thin face looked bleached out under the harsh lights. Frears was with her and already scrubbed up, although the policewoman had made do with a lab coat. They broke off talking when I went in. The chilled air conditioning wrapped around me like a cold blanket as the door eased shut.

'Ah, Hunter. Glad you could make it,' Frears greeted me cheerfully. The cherubic face looked incongruous under the surgical cap. 'Safely negotiated the water hazards this time?'

'I wasn't driving,' I told him.

He gave a barking laugh. 'If it's any consolation, same thing happened to me once. Made a complete mess of the old Jag I used to have.'

I gave an obligatory smile as I took in the room. It was well equipped and modern. There were two stainless-steel examination tables, spaced well apart from each other. A body lay on one, partly obscured behind the pathologist and DCI.

Sitting in a stainless-steel tray on the other was a decomposed foot.

Clarke's mood didn't seem to have improved since I'd seen her on the quay of the oyster factory, but perhaps that was her normal manner. 'Thanks for coming, Dr Hunter.'

'That's OK. Although I still don't know why I'm here.'

But I was starting to have a good idea. Clarke turned to Frears, leaving the explanation to him. He went to where the foot stood on the examination table.

'Recognize this?'

'It was in a boot the last time I saw it, but I'm guessing it's the one from the creek.'

'Care to tell me what you make of it?'

Puzzled, I pulled a pair of nitrile gloves from a dispenser, easing them over the plasters on my hands as I went across. Despite the cool of the air conditioning, there was a sour smell underlying the more stringent scent of antiseptic. The foot was large, pale and swollen, and wrinkled with the distinctive 'washerwoman's skin' characteristic of immersion. The dirty-white adipocere had been given a faint, almost violet hue where it had absorbed the dye from the garish purple sock. The toes were like puffy albino radishes in which the yellow nails were embedded. They had bent under themselves, in a painful condition known as 'hammertoe'. The exposed surface of the ankle joint was a gnarled mess of cartilaginous tissue

154

and bone. This was the only part that had been exposed to the elements and scavengers, and what should have been the smooth surface of the talus – the uppermost bone of the ankle that connected to the tibia and fibula of the lower leg – was pitted and scratched.

'Well?' Frears prompted.

'I can't really tell you anything you won't already know. Right foot, size ten or eleven by the look of it. Probably an adult male's, although I can't rule out a female with large feet. You don't normally see hammertoes like that on younger people, which suggests it belongs to someone older.' I paused, trying to think what else there was to say. I shrugged. 'That's about it, except that the build-up of adipocere and the fact it's detached suggest it's been in the water a considerable time.'

'How long?' Clarke asked.

'Impossible to say just by looking at it.' The shoe would have protected it, and perhaps accelerated adipocere formation. 'If I had to guess I'd say a minimum of, oh, four weeks. But it could be much longer.'

'Go on.'

'There's no sign of trauma, and only superficial pitting of the talus that's consistent with weathering and scavengers. I can't see any of the cut marks or damage I'd expect if it had been chopped or sawn off. So it looks as though it detached naturally. Can I take a look at the X-rays?'

Frears nodded. 'Before that, would you mind measuring the ankle joint?'

I turned to him, puzzled. This was all basic stuff. 'Why? Haven't you done that already?'

'Just humour me, will you?'

The pathologist wasn't smiling now. Neither was Clarke. They both watched as I picked up a pair of sliding calipers from a second steel tray. 'It'd be better to strip off the soft tissue first. I could—'

'Just measure the joint as it is, please. There's enough bone exposed.'

This was beginning to seem bizarre. I opened the calipers wide enough to fit over the talus, then carefully slid them shut until they were just touching the bone at either side.

'I make the width 4.96 centimetres,' I said, reading from the instrument's ruled shaft. Removing the calipers, I opened them wider to measure the bone's length.

'You don't need to bother with that,' Frears said. He went to stand by the body on the other examination table. 'Now, if you wouldn't mind, I'd like you to measure the joint of the tibia and fibula. Right leg, obviously.'

Even if I hadn't already guessed, the shotgun injury to the lower face would have confirmed this as the man's body from the estuary. The clothing had been removed, and the remains lay naked on the table. Like the foot I'd just examined, they were badly swollen and well into the bloating stage of decomposition, the limbs with a stubby, unfinished appearance without any hands or feet. Exposed to the elements and scavengers, the skull was a bleached mess, and the damage caused by the shotgun blast was all the more evident now the estuary mud had been cleaned off. The chest and torso bore the Y-shaped incision from the post-mortem, although I thought the internal organs would have been too decomposed to offer much information. In deeper, colder water, they could sometimes be preserved by adipocere, but I doubted that would have been the case here. The genitals were still more or less intact, protected from insects and scavengers by the clothing, which at least simplified determination of biological sex. But with the remains in the condition they were, I doubted that the post-mortem would have established very much else.

'Any time you're ready,' Frears said with a thin smile.

Leaving the first set of calipers on the first table, I exchanged my gloves for a fresh pair so as not to transfer any genetic material from the foot to the body. It was unlikely, since I'd only touched the calipers rather than the foot itself, but it was better not to risk cross-contamination.

Especially if this was shaping up the way I thought.

The heads of the tibia and fibula had been cleaned of any remaining shreds of tissue, exposing the ends of both bones. The heavier tibia, or shin bone, would have rested on the upper surface of the talus, with the slimmer fibula extending down the outside. Selecting another pair of calipers from the instrument tray, these designed for internal surfaces, I carefully measured the joint of the tibia and fibula as I had with the talus. Then, just to be sure, I measured them again.

I turned to Frears. '4.97 centimetres.'

He turned to Clarke. 'As I told you. And it'll stay the same no matter how many times we measure it.'

'They're not exactly the same size. The ankle's slightly smaller,' the DCI said doggedly.

Frears clamped his mouth shut, folding his arms as though they'd already been through this. He raised his eyebrows at me, all but saying *you try*.

'There's always going to be a slight variation,' I told her. 'It's the same between left and right sides, they're never going to be identical. If the difference was more than a few millimetres then yes, it'd probably mean it was from a different body. But one millimetre is a very close match.'

'So in your opinion the foot definitely belongs to this body?'

'I can't say "definitely" without more tests. Going by what I've seen so far, though, it seems likely.' Even though the possibility of two different people having ankle joints the same width couldn't be entirely ruled out, the odds of them both being found dead in the same stretch of water were remote, to say the least. I looked down at the foot. 'I'm guessing there's a reason you think this isn't Leo Villiers' foot?'

'We don't have his actual measurements, but he took a size eight shoe. This one's nearly twenty-eight centimetres long, which makes it a size ten.' She made it sound like a personal insult.

'Shoe sizes vary,' I said, playing devil's advocate. There was obviously more going on here than a discrepancy in shoe size.

Clarke didn't seem inclined to answer, so Frears spoke instead.

'True, but Leo Villiers broke his right foot playing rugby when he was nineteen. We've been allowed to see the original X-rays, which show the second and third metatarsals were badly damaged. They healed crookedly, but on the X-rays we took of this foot they're perfectly intact. No old breaks, no calluses. Nothing.'

'All right, Julian, I'm sure Dr Hunter doesn't need it spelling out,' Clarke told him irritably.

I didn't. And now I understood the reason for her bad mood. The difference in shoe size might not be definitive, but bones didn't lie. A break forms a callus where the two surfaces fuse together. That could remain for years, and if the bone healed in the wrong position the old break would be clearly visible on X-rays. So if this foot *was* from the remains recovered from the Barrows it could mean only one thing.

This wasn't Leo Villiers' body.

'Did the post-mortem turn up anything?' I asked, forgetting for the moment my embarrassment over missing it.

'No smoking gun, if that's what you mean. Except for the one that blew off the back of his skull, obviously.' Frears seemed to have recovered his sense of humour. 'No evidence of foam in the airways or lungs to suggest drowning, but I think we can safely assume he was dead when he hit the water anyway. The entry wound was contact or near as damn it. There's searing from powder burns on what's left of the jaw, and the wounds show the pellets were very tightly bunched. None of them remained in the body, and at that range there'd be no difference in spread, so I can't say if it was birdshot or buckshot.'

'But the barrel wasn't actually inside the mouth?' I asked.

The pathologist's smile was cool. 'No, it wasn't. There'd be less of the skull left intact if it were, as I'm sure you're aware.'

I was: if the shotgun had been behind the teeth when it was fired, the explosive expansion of hot gases would have virtually blown the cranium apart.

'Is that relevant?' Clarke asked.

'That depends,' Frears said. 'I believe Dr Hunter is entertaining doubts about the wound being self-inflicted. A question of reach, isn't that right, Dr Hunter?'

'He'd have to reverse the gun and still reach the trigger,' I explained to Clarke. 'If the barrel was pressed against the outside of his mouth it would've meant he'd have to stretch further than if it was inside.'

'We're waiting to get the barrel length from the gunsmith,' she said impatiently. 'The missing shotgun's a bespoke Mowbry, so they'll have his arm measurements as well.'

'What about the trajectory?' I asked. It was even more apparent now how flat that was. The exit wound was in the lower part of the cranium rather than the crown, which suggested the shotgun had been held horizontally in front of the face. Not with its stock propped on the floor and its barrel pointing upward.

'All that shows is that the gun was extended out in front of him,' Frears countered. 'It suggests he was standing rather than kneeling or sitting when the gun was fired.'

'Or else someone else shot him,' I said.

Suicide was only a workable theory as long as we thought the body was Leo Villiers, a disgraced and depressed suspect in a murder investigation. If this wasn't him then we were looking at something else entirely.

'I said the wound *could* be self-inflicted, not that it was,' Frears said, his annoyance showing. 'It's inconclusive, as I made clear in my post-mortem report. Which you'd know if you'd been here.'

'All right, let's move on,' Clarke said impatiently. 'What else have we got?'

'What about the piece of metal lodged at the back of the mouth?' I asked Frears. 'You said there were no pellets left in the body, so what was that?'

'Ah, yes.' He glanced at Clarke, who gave a nod. Going to the bench, he picked up an evidence bag and brought it over. 'Know what it is?'

I'd not been convinced at the time that it was a piece of shot, and now I could see it wasn't. Inside the bag was a small steel ball, about five millimetres in diameter and slightly deformed on one side. No, not deformed, I saw, holding it up to the light. Something had been broken off it.

'It's a stainless-steel tongue stud,' I said, handing it back. I'd done some work with body piercings before, analysing how steel rings, bars and studs moved in buried bodies as the soft tissue decomposed.

Frears looked disappointed. 'Technically, a "tongue barbell". Part of one, at least,' he added. 'The rest of it must have been blown out with the pellets. Not the sort of thing one would normally imagine an aspiring politician like Leo Villiers to sport, is it?'

'For all we know he could have decided to turn punk before he shot himself,' Clarke said, exasperated. 'We don't even know for sure the stud was *in* the tongue. It could have got wedged in the mouth along with other debris while the body was in the water.'

'That's highly unlikely,' Frears began, but Clarke was having none of it.

'I don't care whether it's unlikely or not, I need to know for certain. And I mean *absolutely* certain. I've got Sir Stephen Villiers already convinced that this is his son and pushing for official confirmation. If I'm going to tell him otherwise I better be bloody right this time.'

'Is there anything else in his medical records?' I asked. Lundy had told me they still hadn't been allowed access the day before, but they'd obviously seen the X-ray of the broken foot. If Sir Stephen Villiers had finally released his son's records they might contain something else to help with identification.

Clarke blew out an irritated breath. 'We don't know. Sir Stephen only agreed to let us look at the X-ray and even that was like getting blood from a stone. We'll need a court order for the full records, and if this isn't his son's body I'm not sure we'd have grounds for one anyway.'

'That's ridiculous,' I said. 'What's going to be in them that's more important than helping identify his son?'

'I've no idea, but whatever it is, it isn't going to help us now. Sir Stephen's made it clear he's going to fight tooth and nail to stop them being released.'

'Then you'll have to wait for the DNA results.' Frears shrugged. 'Sorry, but there's not much more I can do.'

That was met by silence. I turned back to consider the foot, thinking something through. Clarke must have noticed.

'Dr Hunter?'

I thought for a moment longer. 'I'm assuming you've taken DNA samples from the foot as well as the body?'

She turned to Frears. The pathologist looked irritated. 'Of course, but we won't get any test results back for another few days. I rather think DCI Clarke would like something sooner than that.'

There were new DNA testing systems being developed that claimed to produce a profile from samples in a matter of hours. That would revolutionize the job of identification, but until they became more widely available we'd have to rely on the old, slower method of analysis.

Or something even less high-tech.

'There's always the Cinderella test,' I said.

Clarke just stared at me. Frears frowned. 'I don't follow.'

I looked down at the blunt protuberances of the tibia and fibula.

'Do you have any cling film?'

It took a while for the cling film to materialize. It wasn't the sort of thing there was normally much use for in a mortuary, even one as modern and well equipped as this. In the end Frears dispatched a young APT – an anatomical pathology technologist whose job was to assist at post-mortems – to find a roll from somewhere.

'I don't care if you have steal it from the hospital canteen, just find one and get it back here, will you?' Frears instructed.

We'd gone into the briefing room while we waited. Soon afterwards Frears had excused himself to attend to some unconnected query, but by then Lundy had arrived. He'd finished overseeing the removal of the barbed wire from the creek, and cups of tea from a vending machine steamed on the table in front of us as he briefed his SIO.

'The end of it was stuck in a lump of concrete. An old fence-post, by the look of it,' he told her.

'Could it have been just dumped there?' Clarke asked.

'It could, although it begs the question of who'd take it all that way. There aren't any fences nearby, and there're a lot more convenient places for fly-tipping.'

'So you think someone used it to deliberately weigh down the body?'

I'd been wondering about that myself, ever since Lundy's comment about the remains being surprisingly well trussed to say they'd supposedly drifted onto the wire. The DI absently stroked his moustache with a thumb and forefinger.

'I don't think we should rule it out,' he said at last. 'Look at where it was. The creek's partially dammed by a sandbank there, so it never fully drains. And it's not far from the road. Someone could have taken the body there in a car and carried it from the bridge. Tangle it up in the barbed wire to weigh it down, so even if it was found it'd look like it got caught up by accident. And a place like that, you could reasonably hope it'd stay hidden for years. Pure fluke we found it when we did.'

Fluke and bad luck for Trask's young daughter. Clarke pinched the bridge of her nose with her thumb and forefinger. I could almost see her headache. 'Dr Hunter, you said it'd probably been in the water for several months?'

'Going on its condition and what I could see, yes.'

'So it can't be Leo Villiers?'

'I don't see how it can be,' I said. Villiers had been missing for six weeks at most, and the advanced state of decay of the remains from the barbed wire told me they'd been in the water much longer than that.

162

A knock on the door announced the APT's return. Frears re-joined us as we filed back to the examination room.

'I take it this isn't routine procedure?' Lundy commented, pulling on a pair of surgical gloves. They made his thick fingers look like blue sausages.

'Not really. It wouldn't hold up in court, but it should give us a pretty good indication of whether the foot's from this body or not.'

Lundy stared down at the naked remains. 'If it's a match that's really going to put the cat among the pigeons.'

He was right, but there was nothing I could do about that. The APT, a young Asian woman called Lan, handed me the cling film.

'I could only get a twelve-metre roll. Will that be enough?'

'That'll be plenty,' I told her.

Forensic science was becoming increasingly sophisticated, with technology steadily overtaking the more hands-on approach I'd been trained in. The old plaster of Paris used to make casts had been replaced by silicon-based alternatives, more efficient and less likely to damage the bone. And scanners were now being developed that would eventually make even that obsolete, allowing a perfect replica of any bone to be created on a 3D printer.

But we didn't have a scanner or 3D printer, and even if we had, both that and casts required the bones to be properly cleaned. That would take time, and Clarke wanted a quick answer. So I'd make do with less sophisticated resources.

In this case, a roll of cheap cling film and a steady hand.

The APT hovered behind Clarke, Frears and Lundy, clearly curious as to what I was going to do. The group of them watched in silence as I tore off a length of the transparent plastic, carefully smoothing it over the exposed surface of the ankle bone.

'Somewhat unconventional, I have to say. Hope you didn't try anything like this on the Jerome Monk inquiry last year.' Frears looked amused at my surprise. 'Knew I'd heard your name before. Turned into quite the debacle, as I recall. Hardly your fault, of course, but not the sort of career move you'd want to repeat.'

'No, it wasn't,' I said without looking up. What had happened on Dartmoor was a matter of public record, and I didn't need reminding. I glanced at Clarke, but the DCI wasn't paying any attention. She'd have known all about my history before hiring me, and was clearly more concerned with what I was doing now.

'Are you sure about this?' she asked sceptically. 'There won't be any cross-contamination?'

'There shouldn't be,' I told her, spreading the cling film over the rest of the foot and making sure there were no wrinkles. The transparent plastic would minimize any risk, and DNA samples had already been taken from both the foot and the body. If any more were needed, they could be extracted from deep inside bones well away from the exposed surfaces.

But I didn't think cross-contamination was going to be an issue anyway. The wrapped foot resembled an off-cut of meat from a butcher's counter as I set it aside and turned to the body. Stripping off my dirty gloves and replacing them with a fresh pair, I tore another section of cling film off the roll and smoothed it over the ends of the right leg's tibia and fibula, making sure it fitted smoothly on to the surfaces of the exposed bones.

I stood back and considered my handiwork for a moment, then picked up the cling-film-wrapped foot again.

'OK, let's see what we've got.'

Without a cushioning layer of cartilage, the ankle joint was never going to fit together as snugly as it had in life. Yet even though the cling film was a poor substitute, the foot and lower leg came together like old friends. I gently rotated the foot, exploring the full range of movement, but there wasn't really any doubt. Not even twins would have identical joint surfaces. Subtle differences would develop over time, variations caused by wear and tear. Yet there were no ill-fitting bumps of bone here to disrupt the smooth motion. The fit was near perfect.

I set the foot back down. There was silence before Clarke spoke.

'Shit.'

Everyone there understood the seriousness of what had just happened. If this wasn't Leo Villiers' foot, then it couldn't be his body either. Which potentially meant there were now two unknown male bodies to identify, neither of them his. And Emma Derby's remains were still out there somewhere, waiting to be found.

'Well, I think it's safe to say this undermines the suicide theory somewhat,' Frears said. The pathologist's blue eyes twinkled. 'Still, looking on the bright side, we don't have far to look for a suspect.'

16

I CAUGHT A TAXI back to Willets Point. Lundy told me he could arrange for me to be given a lift but I preferred to make my own way. One thing I hadn't thought through was having to give the taxi driver directions. He was a young man, and grew increasingly unhappy as civilization gave way to the Gordian knot of waterways that carved their way through the flat marshland.

'You sure you know where we're going, mate? There's nothing out here,' he said nervously, as the single lane road doubled back on itself before passing over a small, hump-backed bridge.

I hoped I did. I recognized some parts, but this was a different route from the one I'd taken from London, and I'd not been paying much attention when the police officers had driven me earlier. The light was failing now besides, and with the creeks and channels swollen with the returning tide the landscape looked completely different.

In the end I decided it would be easier for me to make my own way for the last half-mile or so and told the driver I'd walk. His mood improved even more after a healthy tip. He gave me a cheery wave as he turned the cab around awkwardly in the cramped lane before disappearing back the way we came. I stood for a moment as the sound of the car's engine faded, listening to the gentle lapping of the waters in the marsh, then set off along the empty road.

Clarke had asked me to stay at the mortuary after I'd established that the detached foot belonged to the remains from the Barrows.

'If this isn't Leo Villiers then I want to know who the hell it is,' she'd said before she and Lundy left. 'Age, ancestry, anything to help us narrow down the ID or time-since-death. Can you help with that, Dr Hunter?'

'I'll do what I can,' I told her, and turned to Frears. 'Did you find any blowfly pupae or casings trapped in the clothes?'

'No, but if it's been in water I wouldn't expect any.'

Neither would I, but that was the point. Blowflies are incredibly persistent. Even in winter, a small amount of sunshine can raise the temperature enough to bring them out. But they can't lay eggs underwater, and although the body had been exposed during low tide, no eggs laid then would have survived the subsequent immersion. So if there had been any sign of blowfly activity, it would have meant the remains had been on the surface for longer than the interval between tides. That would significantly skew the rate of decomposition, and therefore the length of time-since-death.

If there were no blowflies, at least we could rule that out.

While Frears went to carry out the post-mortem on the remains from the barbed wire, I set about the grisly task of my own. I don't think any of us seriously doubted any more that Villiers had faked his own death. What had started out looking like a suicide had suddenly turned into a murder inquiry, and this time there was a body tying him to it.

Not even his father's lawyers could argue that away.

I was optimistic that I'd be able to provide Clarke with more information about the unknown man found in Leo Villiers' clothes. I started by looking at the X-rays taken before the post-mortem. The hammertoes of the foot from the training shoe had suggested this was an older individual, but what I could see of the body's joints on the X-rays told a different story. They looked in good condition, with virtually no age-related degradation.

I thought about that as I studied the X-ray of the foot. The second toe in particular was badly deformed, and if age wasn't a factor that meant the cause must be either congenital or occupational. Looking at that second toe, I thought it was probably the latter. But to find out more would involve examining the bones themselves, and there was only one way of doing that.

Denuding a decaying human body of any remaining soft tissue was never pleasant. Wearing a rubber apron and thick rubber gloves, I removed as much of it as I could with a knife and scissors, cutting it away as close to the bone as I could without touching it. It would be stored with the organs and rest of the body for later burial or cremation, once we'd extracted as much information as we could.

What remained on the examination table was a grisly stick-figure, more anatomical caricature than human being. Even then I hadn't finished. I carefully cut through the cartilage at the joints, gradually disassembling the remains like the carcass of a chicken. The disarticulated body parts went into large pans of weak detergent solution, which I left to simmer overnight in a fume cupboard. Sometimes stripping the skeleton in this way could be a time-consuming business, involving repeated soakings in warm detergent and then a degreasing agent before it was ready to be examined. But that wasn't necessary when the remains were as decomposed as these had been, especially since their long immersion in the creek had started the process anyway. By morning the bones should be clean enough for me to examine, and hopefully give Clarke more information.

Once the pans were gently simmering away, there was nothing more I could do. I'd gone to find Frears but Lan, the young APT, told me he'd already left. Evidently the post-mortem hadn't taken long, but that was no surprise. A pathologist would struggle to learn much from a body as badly decomposed as the one from the creek had been.

That was my job.

I'd been disappointed not to have a chance to hear what Frears had found. Even though the circumstances were different this time, it was the second post-mortem I'd missed. But the day's events caught up with me as I stripped off my scrubs and cleaned up in the changing room. It didn't seem possible it was only that morning I'd had coffee with Rachel in Cruckhaven. It had been a long day, and the leadenness of my limbs as I trudged along the empty road reminded me I still wasn't entirely recovered from the infection.

I was glad when I reached the turn-off for Creek House, although the thought of seeing Rachel again brought nervousness as well as anticipation. I told myself there was no call for either as I approached the house. The battered white Defender was parked by the copse of trees, but there was no sign of Trask's grey Land Rover. My own car stood a little way off to one side, an odd note of familiarity in that setting.

I made my way through the trees and up the steps to the front door. I could see a light through the frosted glass panel, a warm, homely glow I knew was illusory given what the family had been through. Then the door was opened and Rachel was standing in front of me.

She looked tired herself but gave me a smile. 'Hi.'

Without asking, she stood back to let me in. I'd been inside the house earlier to change out of my wet clothes, but I'd not taken much notice then. It was a reverse-level design, with a family bathroom on the ground floor. Other doors led to what I presumed were bedrooms off the hallway. The place had a Scandinavian feel, though it was too lived in to call minimalist. The white walls were scuffed with marks from boots and bike tyres, and an assortment of shoes and wellingtons was clustered untidily on the polished floorboards. A flight of wooden stairs ran up to the first floor, from which I could hear music playing quietly in the background.

'How's Fay?' I asked as Rachel closed the door behind me. I could smell a faint scent of sandalwood. Too light to be perfume, more likely soap or shampoo.

'Protesting about the injections, which is a good sign,' she said with a smile. 'They're keeping her in overnight as a precaution.

None of the cuts are serious but they gave her a blood transfusion, and she had mild hypothermia as well. But Andrew thinks she'll be home tomorrow. Can I get you a coffee or something?'

'That's OK, I only came to collect my things. And to return these.'

I indicated Trask's jacket, and also the old wellingtons I was still wearing. Rachel saw them and laughed. 'Yeah, I can see why you'd want to get rid of them. Look, why don't you take them off and come upstairs for a drink? Andrew's still at the hospital and Jamie's gone to a friend's so there's no one else here. I'd be glad of the company.'

The hallway was lit only by the glow from upstairs. Rachel wore a short black T-shirt that just came to the top of her jeans, displaying slim, toned arms. There was a tentative smile on her mouth, and her eyes held a trace of uncertainty that mirrored my own. The tension I'd been feeling vanished.

'Sounds good,' I said.

I'd expected the living area of the house to be impressive, but Trask had excelled himself. The whole of the upstairs looked to be open plan, sections of it partitioned off with bookshelves to create an illusion of privacy. The slate floor was dotted with an assortment of rugs, and comfortable-looking sofas and chairs were arranged around a wood-burning stove. The largest part of the room was taken up by a sleekly modern kitchen, a low wooden cabinet dividing it from a rosewood dining table with bentwood chairs.

But the most impressive feature was the glass wall that ran along the entire front. Dwarfing the arched window in the cabin, it faced directly over the creek, with floor-to-ceiling panels opening on to a long balcony. Beyond that there was nothing except the darkening sky above a marsh and creek almost lost in twilight.

'That's some view,' I said.

Rachel gave it a cursory glance, as though the huge curtain wall were something she no longer noticed.

'Andrew wanted it to be the main feature of the house. He

designed it all himself, when he first met Emma. I don't think she was quite as keen as he was, though.' She seemed to regret the admission. 'So how are you? No ill-effects from getting soaked again?'

'No, I'm fine.'

'I washed your clothes, by the way. Your jacket's still damp, so you might as well hang on to Andrew's until it dries out.'

'Thanks,' I said, surprised. 'You didn't need to do that.'

'You didn't need to go with Andrew, but you did.' She gave a quick smile. 'You might have to invest in a new pair of boots. I cleaned them as best I could but they've seen better days.'

That was hardly surprising: this was their second soaking in the space of three days. 'Is Fay's dog OK?' I asked, realizing I hadn't seen the little mongrel.

'Cassie? She should be. The vet had to knock her out to sew her up, so she's being kept overnight as well.' Rachel went to a large island in the middle of the kitchen. 'Oh, and before I forget, your car's ready. Jamie's replaced the spark plugs.'

'When?' With everything that had happened I was surprised he'd found the time.

'This afternoon after he came back from the hospital. I think he was glad of something to do, to be honest.'

I supposed it was good news, but there was none of the relief I'd have expected. The journey would take longer, but there was no longer any reason to stay in the Backwaters.

'What would you like to drink? Tea, coffee, or something stronger?' Rachel asked.

'Hmm? Oh, just coffee, thanks.'

'Have you eaten? I could make you a sandwich,' she offered. I hadn't had anything since that morning, and the reminder made me aware of my empty stomach. Rachel smiled when I hesitated. 'I'll take that as a yes.'

I sat down on a stool at the island. On the wall opposite was a photograph, of Emma Trask with Fay and Jamie. The London Eye was in the background, and Fay and Jamie appeared much younger.

The two of them were laughing, Jamie looking across at their step-mother as she smiled at the camera. It seemed to be a natural moment, but Emma's smile had the same posed quality as it did in the self-portrait in the boathouse.

Rachel had busied herself filling the kettle and taking food from the fridge. There was a tension about her as she cut slices from a loaf of bread. Abruptly, she stopped and set down the bread knife.

'I've got to ask. Andrew said you told him that . . . that it was a man you found today. Not a woman. Is that true?'

'Yes, it is.'

'So it's definitely not Emma?'

'No, it's definitely not.'

She breathed out, her shoulders losing some of their rigidity. 'OK. Sorry, I didn't mean to put you on the spot. It's just . . . I mean, now they've found *two* bodies? What the hell's going on?'

'I don't know,' I said. Which was also true.

Rachel nodded, then gave a rueful smile. 'Screw it, I'm having a glass of wine. How about you? It'd be rude to make me drink on my own.'

I thought about the antibiotics, but only briefly. 'Well, I'd hate to be rude.'

She laughed, a good, full-throated chuckle that sounded like a release. I poured the wine while she buttered the bread. We chinked glasses before taking a drink.

'God, that's welcome,' she said with a sigh. Setting her glass down on the granite-topped island, she went back to making the sandwiches. 'So will you go back to London now?'

'I expect so.'

'But you're still working with the police? Out here, I mean?'

'Probably more in Chelmsford, but yes.'

She kept her attention on the sandwiches. 'You could still stay at the boathouse, if you like.'

That was so unexpected I didn't know how to respond. 'Uh, I don't . . .'

'No, of course,' she rushed on. 'I'm sure you'll want to get home. I just thought, you know, it'd save you time. Seems pointless having to drive all that way.'

It did. I thought of all the reasons I shouldn't, not least of which would be what Clarke and Lundy would say. But we'd gone past the stage where it could really matter any more. And it *would* make more sense for me to stay somewhere local. I knew I was rationalizing a decision that I'd already made, but all the arguments against seemed less compelling than the flush I could see spreading up Rachel's throat.

'Are you sure it'll be OK?'

'Of course. Why wouldn't it be?' She gave me a quick smile, and I felt something tighten in my chest. Rachel busied herself setting out plates. 'Anyway, tell me a bit about yourself. You didn't want me to call anyone when you were ill, so I know you're not married. Are you separated, divorced . . . ?'

I felt I'd walked off a too-high step. 'Widowed. My wife and daughter died in a car accident a few years ago.'

I kept my voice even. The words had lost much of their impact by now, repetition numbing the old wound. Surprise widened Rachel's eyes, then she reached out and rested her hand on my arm.

'I'm sorry.' There was sympathy but none of the awkwardness or embarrassment I'd come to expect. She left her hand where it was for a second longer, then let it fall. 'How old was your daughter?'

'She was six. Alice.' I smiled.

'That's a nice name.'

We thought so. I nodded, suddenly not trusting my voice. Rachel's face had softened.

'Is that why you try so hard?'

'I'm not with you.'

'Your work. It's not just a job for you, is it? You really care.'

I struggled for a moment, then shrugged. 'No, it's not just a job.'

There was a silence, but not an uncomfortable one. Rachel slid the plate of sandwiches across to me. 'You should eat,' she smiled.

The sky was still darkening outside, giving the room a dusky, intimate feel. It would soon be time to turn on the lights, but Rachel seemed content to sit in the gathering twilight. She looked younger, more relaxed, and I didn't think that was just the light.

She glanced up and caught me looking. 'What?' she asked, smiling quizzically.

'Nothing. I was just wondering about you. Are you planning to stay over here or will you be going back to Australia?'

It was the wrong thing to ask. She lowered her sandwich.

'I don't know. I was at a bit of a crossroads, I suppose, even before Emma disappeared. I'd just broken up from a seven-year relationship. He was a marine biologist as well. And my boss, which made things . . . awkward.'

'What happened?'

'Oh, the usual. A twenty-two-year-old post-grad who looked better in a bikini.'

'I doubt that,' I said without thinking.

I could see the white teeth of her smile in the dim light. 'Thanks, but I'd have to give her that. I've met squid with more morals, but she did look good in a two-piece. Anyway, I'd come back to the UK to think things through. Clear my head, work out what I was going to do. The only good thing that came of it, if you could call it that, was that it meant I was here when Emma went missing.'

The mood changed as though a cold draught had brushed over us. 'You were staying with them?'

'No, I was over for a wedding in Poole. An old friend from uni, hadn't seen her for years, but at least it meant I was back in the country. Our parents are dead, so there wasn't any reason to come back very often. Emma and I had talked about meeting up while I was over, but we never got round to it. We'd both got our own lives, and there didn't seem to be any rush.'

There never does. 'You said she was younger than you?'

'By five years. We were never that close, to be honest. Too

different. She was always the confident and outgoing one. And Emma had this knack of making people like her. When she paid anyone attention she'd make it feel like the sun was shining on them. It just didn't tend to last very long.'

She gave a self-conscious laugh.

'Wow. I don't know where that came from. I must sound like a real cow.'

'You sound like a sister.'

'Now you're being diplomatic.' She reached for the wine bottle and topped up our glasses. 'Don't get the wrong idea. Emma could be lovely. She was great with Fay, even though she wasn't what you'd call the maternal type. She didn't really "do" kids, so she treated Fay more like a teenager. A kid sister. Fay worshipped her. That's why this past year's been so hard on her. Probably harder on her than anyone.'

I thought about the shadows under the little girl's eyes, the too-thin arms. Trask's daughter would have been too young to remember her mother, but at her age losing her stepmother as well must have been a cruel blow. 'Is that why you stayed?'

I thought I'd overstepped. Rachel didn't answer at first, watching her fingers slowly twirl the stem of her wine glass.

'One of the reasons, yeah,' she said at last. 'To start with it didn't seem *right* to leave, not without knowing what had happened to Emma. We all thought there'd be news fairly soon. Every day you expect the police to call and say they've found something, but they never did. And the longer it went on, the harder it was to just say, OK, I've waited long enough, I'm leaving. I know Emma was only their stepmum, and that Fay and Jamie aren't really my family. Except they sort of are now. Does that make sense?'

She was looking at me for reassurance. The light had faded so that her green eyes looked luminous in the dim room. 'I think so,' I said.

'It's not Andrew and Jamie so much, although God knows it's bad enough for them. I didn't know either of them very well before, but by all accounts Jamie used to be cheerful and outgoing before

175

all this. You wouldn't know it now, and between him and Andrew it can be like walking on eggshells at times. But they're old enough to cope. It's Fay who worries me. Maybe if they lived in a city, where there were other people and she had friends around, it'd be different. But out here . . . there's nothing for her.'

I looked out through the huge windows at the shadowed landscape. The sky had lost most of its light, and only the rippling glints of the water distinguished the black creek from the surrounding marsh.

'It doesn't seem like your sister's sort of place either,' I said.

She gave a lopsided smile. 'That's an understatement.'

'How did they meet?' I waved the question away. 'Sorry, I'm prying.'

'No, that's all right. To be honest it's good to be able to talk about it.' Rachel stared down at her glass. 'A friend of hers was building a new house, and Andrew was the architect. Emma used to dabble in interior design as well as photography, so she wound up doing the interiors. She was always good at that sort of thing, and this wasn't long after she'd split up with her long-term boyfriend. One of those uber-confident types, into martial arts and self-help. Fancied himself as a musician and a film-maker because he used to make pretentious music videos. He was a real dickhead.'

'You liked him, then?'

'Can you tell?' Her smile quickly faded. 'In a lot of ways they were very alike. Both extroverted, full of big schemes that never happened. It was always an on-off relationship, and she met Andrew during one of the off times. Six months later they got married.'

Rachel looked over at the photograph of her sister with Jamie and Fay, as though still trying to work out what had happened.

'I could have dropped when I got the wedding invitation. Not so much that she was getting married, because Emma was always impulsive. But Andrew didn't seem her type, and as for coming out here . . .' She shook her head. 'Emma needed *people* around her, she liked galleries and parties. Not mudflats and marshes.'

'Did you talk to her about it?'

'I'm her big sister, of course I did.' There was a smile in her voice. 'She told me I was too frightened of change, and that she'd wasted enough of her life on "bastards". Which I couldn't argue with. She claimed she was ready to settle down, that this house was going to be a showroom for both her and Andrew. He'd design houses, and she'd do the interior design and fill in with a spot of photography. Everything was going to be perfect. And then Leo Villiers came along.'

She broke off, taking a drink of wine. I waited. The dim room had developed the atmosphere of a confessional, and I sensed Rachel was glad to have someone to talk to.

'Villiers hired Andrew to do some work,' she went on. 'He's got this lovely old house on the estuary, I think Emma has photographs of it somewhere. Villiers wanted it ripping apart and remodelling, so she persuaded Andrew to let her design the interiors.'

I remembered Lundy pointing out Villiers' house on the mouth of the estuary. A big Victorian place, with bay windows looking out to sea. 'Did she tell you she was having an affair?'

'No, but I knew something was going on. She told me there were problems between her and Andrew, and that she was thinking of leaving him. I guessed she was seeing someone else, but she wouldn't say who it was. I even wondered if . . .' She shook her head abruptly, dismissing some unpalatable thought. 'Anyway, things got a bit heated. I was having my own relationship problems around that time, so I might have overdone the big sister bit. Emma told me to mind my own business and put the phone down on me. That was the last time I spoke to her.'

I could better understand now why Rachel had felt obliged to stay out here with an extended family she barely knew. Guilt was a powerful motive, particularly when grief was added to the mix.

'Did Andrew suspect anything?' I asked. 'About the affair, I mean?'

'It's not something he talks about, least of all to me. He

admitted once that he thought Emma was seeing someone else, because she'd been making a lot of trips to London. But it was only afterwards, when the police told him she'd been seen half dressed in Villiers' bedroom and all the rest of it, that he realized who it was. God, that was awful. Andrew went storming out to Villiers' house to confront him. There was no one there, thankfully, but it was still a stupid thing to do.'

'When was this?'

'Oh, it was well before Villiers went missing. And yes, the police do know about it.' There was a wry note to Rachel's voice that said she knew what I was thinking. 'Andrew and Jamie had a big row over it. Jamie accused him of being selfish, and that he needed to think about Fay. He was right, and God knows what would've happened if Villiers had been home. But it was weeks before they'd even speak to each other again.'

'This is none of my business,' I said carefully. 'But if Emma was talking about leaving anyway, she couldn't have just *left*, could she?'

Rachel shook her head.

'That was my first thought. But somebody would have heard from her by now. Like I said, Emma needed people, and it wasn't her style to leave quietly. She was a serial door-slammer; she wouldn't just pack up and leave, not without scenes and tantrums. And no *way* would she have left all her things behind. All she had with her was her bag and camera. She left her clothes and passport, even her car. It's the Mini convertible covered up outside. The police found it abandoned at an old oyster factory not far from here. None of us have liked to drive it since.'

I was glad it had grown dark enough to mask my surprise. There was no reason why Lundy should have mentioned it, but that had to be the same quayside where the estuary recovery operation had been launched from.

Rachel absently toyed with her almost-empty glass. 'Nobody'll say so officially, but they think she must have gone there to meet Villiers. After that, no one knows. And now we probably never will, because that . . . that fucking *coward* killed himself rather than tell us.'

No, I thought, no, he didn't. He'd killed someone else to make it look that way.

The intimacy I'd felt between us earlier was slipping away. The last of it vanished as a car door slammed outside.

'That'll be Andrew,' Rachel said. She straightened, looking around as though remembering where she was. 'It's getting dark in here.'

She got up and switched on the lights. The twilight outside turned black, creek and marsh vanishing as the window's glass expanse became a mirror that reflected the room back at us. There was the sound of the front door opening, and then Trask's heavy tread came up the stairs.

He looked worn out. The skin of his face was bloodless, the lines in it etched more deeply than ever. With his clothes still crumpled and mud-stained, he seemed ten years older than he had that morning. He paused when he saw me, as though struggling to register why I might be there.

'How is she?' Rachel asked as he crossed to the sink.

'Sleeping. The doctors say she should be OK to come home tomorrow.' Running the tap, he filled a mug. His Adam's apple worked as he drained it thirstily, then set it down with a sigh. 'Where's Jamie?'

'Out with Liam and some of the others. He didn't say where they were going.'

A look of annoyance crossed Trask's face, but he didn't seem to have the energy to sustain it. I saw him take in the wine glasses and sandwiches still left on the plate. So did Rachel. I expected her to ask if he wanted a glass, but she didn't.

'Do you want me to make you something to eat?' she asked quickly.

'I'll get something later. So is this a social visit, Dr Hunter?'

'No, I called to collect my things,' I said, getting to my feet. The last thing Trask looked as though he needed was guests. 'I'm glad Fay's all right.'

179

'So am I.'

'David's going to be here for a few more days,' Rachel told him. 'I said it'd be OK for him to stay at the boathouse.'

Something like interest kindled in the bloodshot eyes. 'Are you working with the police?'

'Just routine lab work.'

I hoped that was vague enough to put him off. He nodded, his interest already waning. 'Stay as long as you like.'

There was an awkward moment. 'Well, I'd better be going.'

'I'll see you out,' Rachel said as I headed for the stairs. We'd started down them when Trask called.

'Dr Hunter.' He came to the top of the stairs as we paused. 'If you're around tomorrow evening you can join us for dinner. We eat around seven thirty.'

I could see Rachel was as surprised as I was. I hesitated, quickly weighing up whether or not to accept. But after everything else that had happened I couldn't see any reason not to. 'I'll look forward to it.'

My boots had stiffened from their second soaking but they were still serviceable. Rachel gave me my freshly laundered clothes and still-damp jacket as I shucked on Trask's old one again, insisting I take the replacement groceries I'd bought that morning as well. But she seemed subdued, and as the door closed behind me I hoped she wasn't regretting opening up as much as she had.

Night was settling on the Backwaters as I set off through the copse of silver birch. The white trunks looked ghostly in the near-dark, and their branches stirred in the wind that carried the faint lapping of the creek. I was halfway back to my car when I realized I didn't have my key. I turned to head back to the house, but stopped when the front door opened and Rachel emerged.

'Looking for this?' she asked, coming down the steps and holding out my car key.

'It might help. Thanks.'

'I've still got the one for the boathouse, as well. You gave it back to me this morning.'

I'd forgotten all about that. Glad I hadn't driven there before I'd found out, I waited as Rachel began going through the assortment of keys on the heavy ring.

'Sorry, it's on here somewhere. I've been using Emma's spare set, and I still don't know what half of them are,' she said, struggling to see in the poor light. 'OK, here it is.'

Her fingers brushed against mine as she gave me the boathouse key. The contact was fleeting, but I felt a tingle like a tiny electric shock. Rachel stood on the path, looking uneasy.

'Look, what I was telling you earlier . . .'

'Don't worry, I won't say anything,' I reassured her, disappointed she felt she had to ask.

'Oh, no, I didn't mean that,' she said quickly, reaching out to touch my arm. 'I just . . . well, I wanted to say thanks. I don't usually moan on like that, but there's no one out here I can talk to.'

'You weren't moaning. And I was glad to listen.'

She was standing close enough for me to feel her body heat in the evening's chill. The moment stretched on.

'OK, then,' she said, giving a quick smile as she stepped away. 'I'll see you tomorrow.'

OK, then. I watched her go back to the house, waiting until I heard the door close before carrying on to my car. It was still damp inside, with a musty smell I knew would take for ever to fade, but I barely noticed. I realized I was still smiling. The engine started first time, and if anything the car handled more smoothly than it had before. Jamie had done a good job, and I made a note to thank – and pay – him when I came for dinner tomorrow evening.

But it was Rachel I was thinking about as I drove back to the boathouse. *She touched your arm a couple of times; let's not read too much into it.* I should be focusing on what I had to do tomorrow at the mortuary. I'd a busy day ahead of me.

As it turned out it was busier than I expected. Next morning the police found a grave at Leo Villiers' house.

17

I GOT THE CALL from Lundy just before lunchtime. I'd spent the morning rinsing the disarticulated skeleton from the Barrows, which had been simmering in detergent solution overnight. Even though the bones had been inside a fume cupboard the air still smelled disconcertingly of beef stew. The next step would be to reassemble them, a time-consuming process that involved laying out all two hundred and six individual bones in the correct anatomical position, until the full skeleton was re-formed. That would take even 'longer here, with the cranium shattered by the shotgun blast. So, since Clarke was impatient for information, I'd been examining the surfaces of certain key bones as I'd removed them from the pans. I hoped to be able to give her at least a preliminary summary by the end of the day.

Lan tapped on the examination room door as I was rinsing off the pelvis. 'Detective Inspector Lundy's on the phone, Dr Hunter.'

I'd left my own phone in the locker with the rest of my things, not wanting to take it into the examination room while I was working. Putting the pelvis on to a stainless-steel tray, I stripped off my gloves and went to take the call.

'How soon can you be at Leo Villiers' house?' Lundy said, without preamble.

'How soon do you need me?'

'Now would be good.'

Clarke hadn't wasted any time in obtaining a warrant. Once it was known that the body found in Villiers' clothes wasn't him, there was ample justification for a full search of his property. First thing that morning, the police had arrived at the big house on the mouth of the estuary, and a cadaver dog had found what looked very much like a grave hidden away in a secluded part of the grounds.

'Something's obviously been buried there,' Lundy said. 'The dog gave a positive response, and you can clearly see the outline of the hole. There's been a half-arsed attempt to replace the turf, but the soil hasn't had a chance to settle, and there's a clear mound. We've started excavating, but we'd like you out here when we find anything.'

By the sound of it the grave was relatively recent. It could take years for a buried body to rot away enough for the displaced soil above it to settle and sink level with the surrounding ground, but a lot less time for grass and vegetation to grow back. There was often still a visible difference, not least because plants fed on the nutrients released by the body into the earth. But if the replaced sod showed no sign of growth, then that suggested the grave had been dug sometime over the winter, after the last growing season had ended.

I glanced towards the examination room where the cleaned bones of the skeleton were waiting. I'd only taken around half of them out of the solution, but it wouldn't hurt the rest to stay where they were for a while longer.

'Give me an hour,' I told him.

A young PC stood in front of the gateway to the private road at Willets Point, making me wait until he'd called in to check before letting me through. The road ran along the promontory, passing through woods before the trees gave way to landscaped lawns. Someone had been maintaining them, because the grass looked newly mown, probably the first cut of the spring. Specimen trees dotted the lawn; redwoods, cedars and others I didn't recognize, while a beautiful magnolia tree was close to flowering, cream-tipped buds bursting from its branches like candles.

The road curved around a thicket of rhododendrons, and hidden away behind them was Leo Villiers' house. If 'house' was the right word: it wasn't quite a mansion, but the Victorian building was still imposing enough. The drive approached the house from the rear, and beyond it I had a clear view of the estuary and open sea. It was a lovely spot, marred now by the jumble of police vehicles parked outside.

I saw Lundy waiting as I pulled up. The DI strolled over, looking at his watch as I climbed out.

'Dr Hunter. You made good time.'

'There weren't any causeways on this side.'

He chuckled. 'There is that. Protective gear's over here. We can talk while you're getting ready.'

We went over to a trailer containing disposable coveralls and the other paraphernalia that were integral to any police crime scene.

'Is Clarke here?' I asked, selecting what I needed.

'She was, but she was called away. Sorry to interrupt what you're doing at the mortuary, but we'd rather have you here for the excavation.'

I sat down on the open rear of the police truck to pull on a pair of white coveralls. 'Any sign of what's in there?'

'Not so far, but they've not gone very deep.'

'What about the house?'

'Funnily enough, it looks as though somebody's been doing some tidying up.' His tone was jocular, but his eyes weren't amused. 'The place had been cleaned when Villiers went missing; we saw that much before the lawyers booted us out. But this is more recent. It's not just been wiped down; the whole house stinks of bleach. Someone's really gone to town.'

I paused to look at him, a plastic overshoe half on my foot. 'If it had already been cleaned after Villiers disappeared, why do it again now?'

'Why indeed?' Lundy gave a wry smile. 'No law against it, but the place is supposed to have been shut up since he went missing. His normal cleaner was laid off, but somebody's obviously been in. Recently, too. If I were a cynical type I'd say someone anticipated we'd be out to search the house once we found the body in the estuary, and decided not to leave anything to chance.'

'Sir Stephen?' I asked, lowering my voice as I zipped up my coveralls.

'I think that's more likely than Leo popping back to do his own spring cleaning.' Lundy looked back at the house. 'I doubt Sir Stephen got the mops out personally, but it's a safe bet it was done on his instructions.'

I tore the plastic wrapper off a new mask and pulled on a pair of gloves. 'Do you think he knew the body wasn't his son's?'

'I think he knows more than he's saying. As to what that is, your guess is as good as mine.' Lundy beckoned with his head. 'Come on, the grave's round the front.'

The cry of gulls accompanied us as we followed a stone-flagged path around the house. It faced out over the mouth of the estuary, with only a sloping lawn and wooden jetty separating it from the open water. A little dinghy with an outboard motor was moored at one end of the dock, where the water was still deep enough for it to float. The low tide had exposed rock pools and a little crescent of sandy beach, but in bad weather the waves must break right over the jetty. The wind blew straight off the sea, strong enough even today to tug at my baggy coveralls. The only thing visible between here and the distant horizon was the sea fort. It was perhaps a quarter of a mile out, its three ungainly towers standing in the waves like rotting derricks.

I was surprised Villiers hadn't had it torn down for spoiling his view.

Large bay windows stood either side of a porticoed front entrance. Instead of individual panes sitting inside timber or stone frames, the glass itself was rounded, an impressive piece of crafts-manship that gave the windows the slightly magnifying curvature of a goldfish bowl. Through them I could see the ghostly white figures of the police forensic team moving silently inside.

'Used to be the family's summer residence,' Lundy told me as we walked across the lawn towards a clump of rhododendron bushes. 'It was shuttered up for years until Leo decided he was going to move in. Course, the first thing he decided to do was rip half of it out and "modernize" it. You should see inside. Like something from a magazine.'

'Is that what Trask and Emma Derby worked on?'

He nodded. 'It'd have saved everybody a lot of grief if they'd turned the job down. Right, here we go.'

He stopped a few yards from where a group of CSIs in soil-caked coveralls knelt around a rectangular hole next to the bushes, scraping at the earth with trowels. Under a grid of orange string, the hole was perhaps four feet long and three wide, and about eighteen inches deep. It looked small for an adult's grave, but that didn't mean it wasn't. I'd encountered more than one murder where the killer had bent their victim double to bury them, indis-criminately snapping bones and tearing joints in the process.

'Any luck?' Lundy asked.

One of the CSIs broke off to answer. 'Not yet, but I don't think we've far to go. We're close enough to smell something.'

The speaker was anonymous under the hooded coveralls and mask, but I recognized the voice from the creek. It was the big CSI who'd said the facial injuries to the body on the barbed wire had been caused by a boat propeller.

'You remember Dr Hunter from the other day,' Lundy told them. 'He's going to lend a hand.'

'Hallelujah,' the big CSI muttered, but he still shuffled to one side to make room for me.

I'd been doing this for too long to waste energy butting heads. I knelt down beside them. 'The soil looks pretty soft. How long ago would you say it was dug?'

The big CSI sniffed under his mask. 'A few months, tops. Probably less. The turf had been put back on top but it hadn't had time to root properly. And there wasn't—'

'Got something.'

The atmosphere changed as another CSI spoke. Everyone watched as she scraped delicately at the soil with the point of her trowel. She peered at something protruding above the dark earth.

'It's some sort of fabric. Could be a coat.'

I glanced at Lundy. He raised his eyebrows but said nothing as more of the object emerged. A section of dark cloth was revealed, and with it came a noticeable smell of decomposition.

'Something's wrapped in it,' the same female CSI said. 'Hang on . . . Oh.'

'What is it?' Lundy asked, trying to peer past her into the grave.

'Fur. It's an animal,' she said, sounding disappointed. 'Looks like a dog.'

The tension was snuffed out as though a switch had been thrown. Lundy's sigh could have been disappointment or relief. 'Right, well, let's have a look at the rest of it. And make sure there's nothing hidden underneath. I've known some crafty buggers try to pull that before now.'

So had I. The DI motioned with his head for me to go over. Pulling off my mask, I went and stood with him a few paces away from the grave.

'Villiers' beagle,' he said, looking back at the dirty coat of tan and white fur the CSIs were uncovering. 'He had it put down just before he disappeared.'

I nodded, remembering him telling me that the vet had been the last person to see Leo Villiers. At least that we knew of.

'He must have been fond of the dog if he buried it himself,' I said. Most people let the vet dispose of their pet's remains.

'He'd had it since he was a teenager, by all accounts. The vet said he was "visibly distressed" when it was destroyed. Even she was surprised, but it seemed to fit in with the suicide theory. Final

187

straw, sort of thing.' Lundy looked back at the grave again, his moustache turning down in disapproval. 'That's one death he didn't fake, at least.'

'Do you want me to stick around until they've made sure there's nothing else buried in there?'

He shook his head. 'No, I think we've found all we're going to. Sorry for the false alarm. You might as well get back to the mortuary. The sooner we know who we fished out of the estuary, the better idea we'll have of what's going on.'

I pulled off my gloves, careful not to strip the sticking plasters off with them. I'd got changed for nothing, but that was how it went sometimes. 'Could it be someone else local?'

'Not that we're aware of. The only two people reported missing from round here are Emma Derby and Leo Villiers, and we know it's neither of them.'

'Whoever he was, he was probably still in his twenties,' I said. 'The hammertoes on the foot are misleading. Whatever caused them wasn't age related. He was an adult, but from the condition of the bones I've seen so far I'd say he was almost certainly under thirty.'

I'd been deliberately selective in which bones I'd taken from the detergent, concentrating first on those I thought would yield the most information. The ends of the sternal ribs change with age and so does the auricular surface of the ilium on the pelvis, both becoming rougher and more porous over time. I'd found some coarsening but no porosity in any of the bones I'd seen, and while I'd still need to carry out a much more thorough examination, I was confident my estimate wasn't far out.

'A fair bit younger than Leo Villiers, then,' Lundy said. 'That helps, but have you got anything else? As things stand we don't even know if who we're looking for was white or black.'

I'd been trying to determine that myself, without much success. People are every bit as complicated in death as they are in life, and determining ancestry was notoriously tricky even in intact remains. Skin colour can be misleading, and changes anyway once a body begins to decompose. Death is the great leveller, turning pale skin darker and vice versa. There are some skeletal characteristics that point to one genetic background or another, but even these can't always be relied on.

These remains were a case in point. When everyone thought the body was that of Leo Villiers, the assumption was that it must be white. Now even that couldn't be taken for granted. There was also another problem. Most ancestral characteristics are found in the skull, but the one belonging to the body recovered from the Barrows had been damaged by the shotgun blast. Not only was the mandible missing, but the upper jaw bone below the nasal cavity, which would once have housed the front teeth, had been broken off in a splintered arch. Only broken stumps of back molars and empty sockets remained, not enough for even a forensic dentist to help with.

'What's left of the nasal bridge doesn't project very far, which suggests possible black or Asian ancestry,' I told Lundy. 'But the eye orbits are more angular than rectangular or rounded, which is more of a white characteristic.'

'So he could be mixed race?'

'Possibly. Or he might just have had distinctive facial features.' I shrugged. 'Sorry I can't be more help.'

Lundy puffed out his cheeks. 'Well, it gives us a bit more to go on. Although if he *was* mixed race . . .'

'What?' I prompted.

But he shook his head. 'Just thinking out loud. Come on, I'll see you back to your car.'

We'd only gone a few steps when Lundy's phone rang. He stopped to answer it, and I saw his expression change.

'Here now, you mean?' Whatever was said at the other end didn't reassure him. The heavy shoulders slumped. 'Christ. OK, then.'

He put his phone away.

'We've got company.'

*

189

Sir Stephen Villiers wasn't on his own. There was no senior police-man with him this time, but to make up for it he was accompanied by three lawyers, two of them middle-aged men in expensive but conservative suits and the third a woman whose matt-black hair betrayed a bad attempt to dye it. All three walked slightly behind him in unconscious order of deference, the eldest lawyer just by his shoulder, with the other man and the woman each a half-step further back. As they advanced towards us over the lawn the effect was like watching a mother duck trailed by her brood. Albeit much more predatory.

I'd told Lundy I'd go back to the mortuary, expecting he'd want to speak to Leo Villiers' father by himself. The DI nodded, distracted, but then called me back.

'On second thoughts, Dr Hunter, can you stick around for a bit? If you don't mind, it might help to have you here.' He arranged his features into an affable smile as the group bore down on us. 'Can I help you, Sir Stephen?'

'Where's your senior officer?'

The voice was like ice. Leo Villiers' father was dressed as impeccably as before, a mid-grey cashmere coat over a darker grey suit. Everything about him was precise, from the closely trimmed fingernails to the parting in the slightly thinning hair. But the hair was already being ruffled by the stiff breeze blowing from the sea, and underneath the controlled demeanour was a sense of fury barely held in check.

'Not here at the moment,' Lundy told him. 'Was she expecting you? If she knew you were coming, I'm sure she'd have—'

'I want you off my property.'

Lundy's eyebrows went up. 'I was under the impression that this was your son's house. Have I got that wrong?'

The most senior lawyer hurriedly cut in. 'The house and its grounds are part of the Villiers estate. I suggest you leave straight away or you'll be facing charges of harassment and illegal damage.'

'Well, we wouldn't want that,' Lundy said equably. 'We do have a warrant to search the property, though. I thought you'd seen it, but if you like I can—'

'We don't recognize the warrant's validity. It's been issued on entirely spurious grounds, for no other reason that I can see but to cause unnecessary emotional suffering to a bereaved father.'

The lawyer spoke with considerably more bluster than his employer, who continued to regard Lundy coldly. Lundy seemed unperturbed.

'Well, I don't know about "spurious". I'd have thought finding a body with half its face blown away was grounds enough. What with it wearing Leo Villiers' clothes and all.' The DI raised his eyebrows at Sir Stephen. 'You remember, the ones you identified?'

Sir Stephen stared at him. 'Are you accusing me of lying?'

'Perish the thought.' From anyone else it might have sounded insincere. 'We're not disputing that the clothes were your son's, just the body. As his father I'd have thought you'd be keen to find out what's going on.'

'There's nothing to find. My son died in a tragic accident, and his body was discovered three days ago. I saw it for myself, and until now the police seemed convinced as well. Now I'm to believe your earlier assertions were wrong? That smacks of incompetence.'

'No, it's just allowing for new facts. Dr Hunter here's a forensic anthropologist. He expressed doubts at the time that the body had been in the water long enough to be your son, as I believe DCI Clarke informed you. Now we've found more evidence that suggests it wasn't.'

Sir Stephen's head turned so the frosty eyes were fixed on me. All three of his lawyers did the same. Thanks, Lundy, I thought.

'What evidence?'

I glanced at Lundy but he kept his expression bland. *All right, then*. 'As far as we can tell, the right foot found in the creek belongs to the body from the estuary. But your son broke his foot playing rugby, so if this was his it would still have the healed breaks. It doesn't. And if the foot isn't his, the body can't be either.'

Sir Stephen considered me. His expression didn't quite change, but somehow his disdain was made plain. 'You say this foot was found in the creek.'

'Yes, that's—'

'So it wasn't anywhere near where my son was found. It wasn't even in the estuary.'

'No, but—'

'Then why would you think it was his? I assume there must be DNA evidence to support your theory?'

He knew full well there wasn't: Clarke would have told him we were still waiting for the test results. 'Not yet, but the measurements I took showed—'

'Measurements.' The word dripped with scorn. Sir Stephen turned back to Lundy. 'And this is your evidence?'

'Once we get the DNA results—'

'I'm confident they'll confirm my son is dead. But you don't have them, do you? So all this . . .' A hand gestured contemptuously at the house. '. . . is based on the opinion of a disgraced forensic expert with a reputation as a troublemaker.'

I wasn't sure if I was stunned more by the insult or that he'd gone to the effort of finding out who I was. He'd barely seemed to notice me at the body recovery. Blood rushed to my face as I started to respond, but Lundy beat me to it.

'Dr Hunter's reputation isn't the issue here, Sir Stephen. He didn't invent your son's broken foot, he just confirmed discrepancies between the remains and the X-rays you yourself provided. Of course, if you really want to move the identification along you could always let us see the rest of his medical records. That'd help no end.'

Lundy sounded as amiable as ever, but no one there could have been fooled. The senior lawyer hurried to fill the silence.

'Sir Stephen has already made his position very clear. Medical records are, and should remain, private. In the interests of cooperation an exception was made for the X-rays, but—'

'There is nothing in my son's medical records that would help this investigation.' Sir Stephen spoke over his lawyer as though the man weren't there. 'If you have grounds to believe otherwise, then please share them. If not then I'm sure there are more productive ways of spending police time than wasting it here. As I'll be sure to mention to your superiors.'

'I'm sure you will,' Lundy said pleasantly. 'In fact, here's one of them now.'

DCI Clarke was hurrying across the lawn past the house, face set and mackintosh slapping around her legs. Lundy pursed his lips when he saw her expression.

'You might as well head on back,' he murmured to me as Sir Stephen and his entourage turned towards Clarke. 'I'll call you later.'

The DCI didn't acknowledge me as we passed each other, but I wasn't in the mood for pleasantries either. My face was still burning as I followed the path round to the rear of the house to where the cars were parked, still fuming over the run-in with Sir Stephen. *Of all the smug, arrogant* . . . Christ, what sort of man didn't even bother to ask who the police thought the body might belong to?

Or why it had been found in his son's clothes?

At the plastic bins set out for the used protective clothing, I yanked at the zipper on my coveralls so hard it jammed. I wrenched at it bad-temperedly, swearing under my breath when the paper fabric ripped.

'Bad day at the office?'

I hadn't noticed anyone nearby. The man who'd spoken was leaning against a sleek black Daimler, and it was more the car than his face that jogged my memory. Then I took in the pock-marked cheeks and recognized Sir Stephen's driver from the oyster factory.

He was smoking again, a thin plume rising from the half-smoked cigarette he held by his side. From where he stood he had a good view of the path at the side of the house, and he flicked another glance towards it now.

'You're OK, they're still talking,' I said, still struggling with the partially zipped coveralls.

He smiled, giving a nod of acknowledgement as he took another drag on the cigarette. He looked older than I'd thought, definitely closer to fifty than forty. If he hadn't been standing by the car again I doubt I'd have remembered him. Even with the acne scarring, he wasn't the sort of man who would stand out in a crowd. His features were pleasant but nondescript, and the neatly trimmed hair was the sort of non-colour that lightened rather than greyed with age. Now I looked at him I saw a compactness about his slim build that belied his sedentary job, but it wasn't immediately obvious. In his navy-blue suit – a durable synthetic blend – he could have been an accountant or a civil servant. He could have been anything.

'Not another one, is it?' he asked, lifting his chin towards the activity at the house.

'Another what?'

He smiled, acknowledging the evasion. 'A body. First the one in the estuary, then one yesterday. Seems like there's quite a glut of them.'

'If you say so.'

As far as I knew, the police hadn't announced that a second body had been found. Word was bound to get out, but the remoteness of the Backwaters had worked better than any attempt to restrict publicity.

But Sir Stephen's driver clearly knew something. He shrugged and took a drag of his cigarette. 'Suit yourself. I'm not asking you to tell me anything, just saying what I've heard.'

'And what's that?'

'Well, if you're not going to tell me why should I tell you?'

He smiled, as though we were sharing a private joke. But his eyes remained watchful and shrewd in their nest of laughter lines. He blew a stream of smoke off to one side, away from me.

'Only kidding. All I know is another body turned up yesterday. One of the perks of a job like mine. People think you're part of the furniture and forget you've got a pair of ears.'

So someone had told his employer, and he had overheard. I

wondered if the information had come officially or courtesy of Sir Stephen's friends in high places. I didn't respond, busying myself shucking out of the ruined coveralls.

'He's never been any different.'

I looked up, not sure what that was supposed to mean. The driver took another pull on the cigarette.

'The old man's son,' he said, smiling through the smoke. 'Always was a wanker. Some people don't know when they're well off.'

I was saved from having to answer. I nodded towards the house as I wadded up the coveralls and dumped them in a bin.

'I think your boss has finished.'

His head snapped round as Sir Stephen and his lawyers appeared from around the front of the house. Evidently the discussion with Clarke had been a short one. Without seeming to hurry, the driver came to attention, the cigarette vanishing as though by sleight of hand.

Not wanting anything more to do with any of them, I turned and walked away.

18

I WORKED AT THE mortuary until after six. I would have stayed later but I was mindful of Trask's dinner invitation and wanted to get back to the boathouse to change. There wasn't much more I could have done by then anyway.

I'd spent the afternoon taking the rest of the cleaned bones of the estuary body out of the stew formed by the detergent, rinsing them off before setting them out in their correct position on a table to air dry. Cleaned of any soft tissue, the individual bones were creamy-white and smooth, from the elegant curve of the ribs to the intricate discs of the vertebrae. This was a human being reduced to its most basic mechanical components, biological sculptures that gave no sense of the person they'd once been. It was a final indignity imposed on what had not so long ago been a living individual. But it was a necessary one, and to my mind far less of an affront than the act that had ended this man's life.

With luck it would tell us more about who he was.

Reassembling a skeleton becomes easier with practice. Essentially, it's repeating variations on the same jigsaw puzzle, where the pieces are familiar yet different each time. With the obvious exception of the cranium, the skeleton was in good condition. Not only was there an absence of any other violent trauma, but there were no old injuries, deformations or signs of degradation due to disease or age. The most remarkable thing about it was how unremarkable it was.

If time wasn't such an issue I'd have waited until the skeleton was fully reassembled before examining it. I would do that again anyway before I wrote my report. But I'd been able to get a good idea of the condition and characteristics of the bones as I'd been handling them, and a picture was already beginning to form. With the quiet hum of the fume hood as accompaniment, I let the lingering anger over Sir Stephen slough away and lost myself in what I was doing. It was straightforward, repetitive work, the sort of thing I'd done so many times before that it had acquired a meditative quality. When an APT came to tell me Lundy was on the phone, I was surprised by how quickly the afternoon had gone.

Leaving the chemical and cooked-meat smell of the examination room, I went to take the call. Lundy began by apologizing.

'I shouldn't have put you in that position with Sir Stephen,' he said. 'I thought it might help to hear it from the horse's mouth, but I should have realized he'd take aim at you as well.'

'I've had worse,' I told him. 'I was just surprised he'd bothered to do a background check.'

'You don't get to be where he is by leaving anything to chance. I dare say he knows what we all have for breakfast. Including the chief.'

'How did that go?' I asked, remembering Clarke's expression as she'd gone to speak to Sir Stephen.

'Oh, I'd call it a draw. Diplomacy isn't her strong point, but not even Sir Stephen's lawyers can argue away hard evidence.'

I'd had time to think about that as I'd driven back to the mortuary from Leo Villiers' house. However I looked at it, Sir Stephen's entire attitude seemed out of kilter. Not so much the lack of emotion: people displayed grief in different ways, not all of them publicly. But his insistence that his son was dead seemed perverse. I'd known people who were in denial, who refused to accept a loved one's death, but never the other way around.

'Why do you think he's so insistent it's his son's body? He must realize the DNA results will prove it one way or the other, so what's the point?'

I heard Lundy let out a long breath. 'Maybe it's wishful thinking. He knows full well that if the body isn't Leo's, that puts his son in the frame for murder. This isn't like it was with Emma Derby: this time we've a dead victim and evidence pointing directly to Leo Villiers. That's not going to do his reputation any favours at all. Could be Sir Stephen would rather have a dead son than a live embarrassment.'

That seemed incomprehensible to me. Whatever Leo Villiers' flaws, however bad he'd turned out, I couldn't conceive how a father could feel that way about his own flesh and blood. But remembering the cold, immaculately dressed man I'd met earlier, I thought Lundy could be right.

'You still there, Dr Hunter?'

'Yes.' I brought my mind back to the here and now. 'Did you find anything else at the house?'

'Not really. The grave only had the dog in it, and the house might as well have been sterilized. Wardrobes nice and orderly, no dirty laundry left in the basket. The only thing that did emerge was that there might be another shotgun missing as well as the Mowbry.'

'Might?'

'We're still trying to get to the bottom of it. The Mowbry had its own locker in Villiers' study. His housekeeper said that was open and empty when she reported him missing, so we knew straight away it was gone. But when he had the house remodelled last year he changed the gun room into a gym. The original gun cabinet was moved into the cellar with other stuff he didn't want.'

'Villiers had his own gun room?' I'd thought he hadn't liked shooting.

'It came with the house. Sir Stephen was a keen shot by all accounts, used to have shooting parties when the family came to stay here. Except for the Mowbry, all the guns there were old ones dating from then. The cabinet should hold six of them, but there are only five there now. No one we've spoken to seems to know when or why one went missing. Or if they do they're not saying.'

'Was the cabinet locked?'

I heard a rustling, and when Lundy spoke I could hear him chomping what I guessed was another of his antacids. 'It was. Far as we know only Leo Villiers and his father had keys. His house-keeper told us there was a spare one in his desk drawer, but that's still there.'

'So what do you think happened to the other shotgun?'

'Good question.' There was a pause while he chewed and swallowed. 'Might be nothing, so until it turns up we'll just have to keep an open mind. Anyway, how've you been getting on? Any more clues about who we found in the estuary?'

'Everything I've seen confirms he was in his mid-twenties. No obvious congenital bone defects, very little wear of any kind to the joints. The skeleton's exceptionally well proportioned, too. Wide clavicles and scapulae, well-formed ribs, narrow hips. I can't say for certain that he was athletic, but he had a classic V-shaped upper body. And he'd probably have had a good musculature to support the bones.'

'So he was well built?'

A good bone structure didn't always translate to a good physique. An individual could have an athlete's skeleton and still be obese or unfit, and the body we'd brought back from the estuary had been too decomposed and bloated to say either way. But he was only a young man, and therefore more likely to be active. And from the size of the clothes he was wearing he didn't appear to have been overweight.

'I think he would have been, yes,' I said. 'The only skeletal deformity was the hammertoes, but in someone his age I'm start-ing to think they could be down to some sort of repetitive injury. Or even badly fitting shoes when he was younger, although it seems severe for that.'

199

I could almost hear Lundy thinking. 'You said there was a chance the victim was mixed race. Do you still think so?'

'I only know what I told you before, and that was only based on the eye orbits and nasal bridge. It isn't something I can say with any certainty one way or the other.' I recalled Lundy had also picked up on the possibility the dead man was of mixed race at Leo Villiers' house, though he hadn't said why. 'Do you have an idea who it could be?'

'Not really. It's probably nothing, but it put me in mind of the prowler the gardener reported seeing outside the house before Villiers disappeared. He only got a glimpse but he said it was a male, youngish and dark-skinned. "Like a migrant or refugee" was how he put it. Got me thinking how there isn't much of an immigrant population in the immediate area. No jobs, no housing, and if you're looking to illegally land a boat there're a lot better places further along the coast. So what would a refugee be doing here?'

'You're thinking it might have been someone mixed race?'

'It's not impossible. The tabloids have got everybody stirred up about migrants, and Cruckhaven's not exactly what you'd call multi-racial. Maybe the gardener just leapt to conclusions about the refugee part.'

Remembering the desperate town I'd visited the day before, with its closed shops and feral-looking teenagers, I thought Lundy might have a point. Still, it seemed like a long shot. 'It doesn't mean this is the same person. Or explain what he was doing at Leo Villiers' house.'

'No, it doesn't,' he agreed. 'There'd been a spate of burglaries at isolated houses not long before, so the assumption was it was probably someone checking the place out. He had a decent alarm system and there weren't any more break-ins reported, so it didn't seem relevant at the time. Not when we thought Villiers had killed himself. But I'm starting to wonder now if there might be more to it.'

So was I, though I'd no idea what. But Lundy had reminded me of something else. 'Rachel told me they were burgled as well. Not long after her sister disappeared.'

'That's right, they were,' he said thoughtfully. 'That was pretty much the first one, now you mention it.'

'Do you think there's a connection?'

There was a pause. A rustling noise came down the phone: I thought it was a bad connection until I realized he was rubbing his moustache. 'Hard to see how, but it's starting to seem like there's an awful lot of coincidences.'

It was. I could sense that Lundy was ready to wind up, but there was one more thing he needed to know.

'I spoke to Sir Stephen's driver at the house earlier,' I told him, and outlined the conversation I'd had. 'He didn't come right out and say how he knew about a second body, but he made out it was something he'd overheard.'

'There's a surprise,' Lundy said sourly. 'Given the names Sir Stephen must have in his address book it wouldn't surprise me if he knows what's going on before we do. Could his driver just have been nosy, or was he trying to pump you for information?'

'I don't know, but I didn't tell him anything. You think he was hoping to report back to Sir Stephen?'

There was a snort. 'Let's say I can't see anyone working for the Villiers if they don't know which side their bread's buttered on.'

'So why did he badmouth Leo Villiers?' I couldn't imagine Sir Stephen being happy about an employee talking about his son like that.

'Dunno. You're right, seems odd.' I could almost hear Lundy frowning on the other end. 'OK, leave it with me.'

Before he ended the call he told me Clarke wanted me to examine the remains from the barbed wire as well. He hadn't spoken to Frears and so didn't know the post-mortem findings, but promised to email me the report as soon as he could. As I hung up I reflected that only the day before I'd thought I was off the investigation for good.

I didn't intend to mess up a second time.

It was dusk by the time I pulled up outside the boathouse. I switched the engine off and sat for a moment, savouring the quiet. The old stone building on the creek's bank looked as much a part of the landscape as the dunes and marsh grass. This was my favourite time of day, the long moment when the day is paused between afternoon and evening. I felt tired, but it was the sort that came from a good day's work rather than illness.

Climbing out of the car, I stretched, then went to get my things out of the car boot. I'd called into a supermarket for groceries on the way: if I was going to be here for a few more days I'd need more than toast and eggs. Lifting out the carrier bags, I stepped back to close the boot and was almost hit by a car as it sped past.

'Jesus!'

I staggered, buffeted by its slipstream. The car was an old white hatchback with a red racing stripe. I caught a glimpse of the driver's blond hair and then it was gone, the yellow glow of its headlights swallowed up by the tunnel of hawthorns that formed an arch above the road. *Christ!* I stared after it, shaken by the near miss but not so much that I hadn't recognized Stacey Coker. I don't think she'd even noticed I was there, and as my heart rate subsided I realized she'd been coming from the direction of Trask's house.

That might explain the way she'd been driving.

Letting myself into the boathouse, I unpacked the groceries and put the kettle on to boil. Kicking off my shoes, I went across to the sofa where I'd left my overnight bag and swore as I stubbed my foot on the trapdoor handle under the rug again. Belatedly remembering Rachel's warning, I rubbed my toes and swore some more, then threw back the rug to take a look.

A heavy iron ring was set into the wooden trapdoor. It was partly recessed, but still raised enough to trip over. It was obviously a loading hatch for the small dock below, back when this must have been a working boathouse rather than a bijou holiday flat. I tried lifting it but it caught with a rattle, locked or bolted on the underside. The ring stubbornly refused to lie flat, and I considered

202

dragging the heavy pine trunk that doubled as a coffee table on top of it. But the ring protruded too far to stand anything on, so in the end I gave up and covered it over again with the rug.

The kettle had boiled. Checking the time, I went to make myself a mug of tea before I changed for dinner.

I parked on the gravelled area just off the track leading to Creek House. Out here, away from the light pollution of any towns, the darkness seemed to have a physical weight. The glow from an external light was visible through the copse of silver birch, but this far away it only served to enhance the blackness all around. I used the torch on my phone to guide me along the footpath through the trees, until I was close enough to the house not to need it. I turned it off as I emerged from the copse, and as I did Jamie appeared around the corner of the house. He seemed miles away, a distracted frown on his face. I stepped out of the shadows.

'Hi,' I said.

He flinched back, head jerking towards me in surprise. 'Fuck!'

'Sorry, I didn't mean to make you jump.'

'Yeah, no, I was just . . .' He looked flustered and embarrassed.

'Your dad invited me for dinner . . . ?'

'Oh. Well, he's in the house.'

He started walking past. 'Before you go, I've not had a chance to thank you for repairing my car,' I said. 'You did a really good job.'

He shrugged, uncomfortable again. 'That's OK.'

He obviously didn't want to talk, so I took the envelope from my pocket containing the money I'd withdrawn for him earlier. I held it out.

'Here. I hope that's enough to cover it.'

Jamie frowned down at the envelope without touching it. 'What's that?'

'What I owe you.'

'I don't want paying.'

'It's only what a garage would charge. Probably less,' I added, thinking of Coker. 'If you're going to university later this year you'll probably need it.'

His mouth set in a firm line. Even in the dim glow from the light above the front door, the resemblance to his father was unmistakable. 'Who told you that?'

'I thought . . .' I stopped myself from saying I'd heard it from both Rachel and his father. Evidently there was some dispute over his future, but that was one argument I wasn't going to get involved in. 'Well, I must have got it wrong. Put it towards a gap year, then.'

'I'm not taking a gap year either. I'm not going anywhere, not when—'

He broke off, looking away. I was still holding out the envelope, wondering how trying to pay someone could have become so complicated. 'OK, well, take it anyway. It's not a lot, but—'

'I told you, I don't want paying,' he said, his voice suddenly harsh, and before I could say anything else he walked away towards the cars.

I lowered the envelope, regretting inadvertently touching a raw nerve. A lot of teenagers would have been glad to get away after what had happened, but Rachel had told me how protective Jamie was. Still, throwing away his own future wouldn't help anyone.

As I put the money away – I'd have to give it to either Rachel or Trask for him – I was tempted to go back to my car and leave. But it was too late to back out now. Taking a deep breath, I went up the steps to knock on the door.

Trask opened it. He stared blankly, and I guessed he'd forgotten inviting me.

'I'm not too early, am I?' I said, giving him a hint.

'No. No, of course not. Come in.' He closed the door when I stepped inside. The hallway was unlit, but light spilled down the stairs from the kitchen. 'I'm just finishing something off, but Rachel's upstairs. I'll be with you in a minute.'

He headed off down the hallway towards a partly open door, through which I could see a drawing board picked out by lamp-light. Wondering if coming here was a mistake after all, I started up the stairs. The smell of cooking became stronger, a casserole scent of cooked meat that brought unwelcome associations with the vat of simmering bones at the mortuary.

Rachel was busy at the cooker while Fay sat on a bar stool at the granite-topped island, desultorily stirring something in a bowl with a long spoon. Her dog lay at her feet, looking sorry for itself. Large patches of its fur had been shaved away to reveal islands of bare skin and dressings, and there was a protective cone around its head to keep it from gnawing them.

It lifted its head when it saw me, briefly thumping its tail on the floor before slumping back down again with a tragic sigh. Rachel turned from the bubbling pans and gave me a determinedly bright smile.

'Hi. I didn't hear the door. Dinner'll be about fifteen minutes.'

'Can I do anything?'

She blew a strand of hair from her face, looking hot and bothered. 'No, thanks. Just make yourself comfortable.'

I looked over at Trask's daughter. She was pale, with shadows under her eyes. There were adhesive dressings on her hands and wrists, and I could see the outline of bulkier dressings underneath her long-sleeved top.

'Hi, Fay. How are you feeling?'

She hitched a shoulder in an indifferent shrug. 'OK.'

'OK, *thank you*,' Rachel told her, and received a deadpan stare. 'We tried to get the doctors to put a collar like Cassie's on her as well. But they said no, for some reason.'

Fay favoured her with a withering look before going back to stirring the bowl. Rachel looked at me over the girl's head and raised her eyes skyward. I held up the bottle of wine I'd brought. It was the white Bordeaux I'd planned to take to Jason and Anja's, still chilled from the boathouse fridge.

'Shall I open this?'

'Yes, please.' She silently mouthed *Thank God*.

'Dad doesn't drink wine,' Fay said without looking up.

'No, but I do,' Rachel said. 'And Dr Hunter might like a glass as well.'

Her niece gave her an arch look. 'Why? It's not a special occasion.'

'It doesn't have to be. Sometimes people like to drink wine with their food.'

'Alcoholics, you mean?'

'No, I don't mean that,' Rachel said, with exaggerated patience. 'Come on, Fay, don't start.'

'Start what?'

'You know what.'

'No I don't.'

The girl stared back at her with calculated insolence. Rachel shook her head, exasperated. 'OK, fine. Can you leave the dog food cake for now and set the table?'

'I'm tired,' Fay said, unceremoniously dumping the bowl down on the island and stomping downstairs.

Rachel gave a sigh as the girl's footsteps receded. 'And she isn't even a teenager.'

'She's bound to be upset after yesterday.'

'Oh, I know. But the little-madam routine is nothing new, she just knows she can get away with more at the minute.' She gave a grim smile. 'Glad you came?'

I had been when I saw her, but this was seeming more and more like a bad idea. Invitation or not, there was enough tension in the house already without my presence adding to it.

'I forgot to bring the jacket back you lent me,' I said, deciding to move on to safer ground.

'It doesn't matter, it's only an old one. Just leave it at the boat-house.' She nodded pointedly at the bottle of wine. 'Corkscrew's in the top drawer.'

'You don't have to open it on my account.'

'I'm not. Don't pay any attention to Fay, she's just . . . being Fay.

Andrew doesn't drink any more, but he doesn't mind anyone else doing it. Emma certainly did, and I'd really, really like a glass.' She winced. 'God, now I *do* sound like an alcoholic. But it's been one of those days.'

I found a corkscrew and opened the wine, pouring it into glasses Rachel set out for me. 'You're sure I can't help?' I asked as she drained pans.

'No, it's about ready, thanks. Although you can put the dog food cake in the freezer. There's a baking tray to scrape it into on the island.'

She gestured at the mixing bowl that Fay had been half-heartedly stirring. It contained a brownish mess, and a non-stick baking tray stood nearby. 'So this is, uh, a treat for Cassie?' I asked uncertainly, spooning it into the baking tray.

Rachel burst out laughing. 'No, it's pudding. Modged-up biscuits, raisins and melted chocolate, sort of like tiffin. That's just a family nickname for it because it looks like, well . . .'

'Dog food?'

I was pleased to see her laugh again. 'It tastes better than it looks. Honestly.'

Footsteps on the stairs announced Trask's arrival. In the bright lights of the kitchen I saw he looked better than he had yesterday, though not by much. The ratty sweater had been replaced by a faded black denim shirt and jeans, and the unshaven, greying stubble was beginning to look more like a beard. The glasses were pushed up on top of his head.

He took in the glasses of wine. 'That looks like a good idea.'

Rachel looked startled as he went to the cupboard and took down another glass. 'Sorry, I didn't think you'd be having one.'

'Well, I am.'

She turned away as he sloshed the wine into his glass, though not before I caught the unease on her face. They kept wine in the house, and Trask evidently didn't mind other people drinking. But there was obviously some sort of issue going on here, and I hoped I hadn't unknowingly triggered any kind of lapse.

Trask nodded approvingly as he took a drink. 'You didn't buy that in Cruckhaven.'

'No, Tesco.'

'Ah, thought I recognized the *terroir*.'

He was making an effort to be sociable. They wouldn't have had many dinner guests recently, I realized. 'Thanks for asking me over. I appreciate it.'

'Don't be ridiculous, it's the least we can do after yesterday,' he said, but not as though his heart were in it. He took another drink of wine, then picked up the bottle and topped up all of our glasses. Mine included, before I could stop him. 'Where is Fay anyway? I thought she was supposed to be helping.'

'She was. She just needed to go to the bathroom.' Rachel lifted a pan to the sink and drained it. Perhaps it was only because I knew about the white lie that I could detect it in her voice. Trask didn't seem to notice.

'And Jamie?'

'I bumped into him outside,' I said.

Trask's face hardened. 'Doing what?'

'I don't know,' I said, hoping I'd not spoken out of turn. Christ, Rachel was right: this was like walking on eggshells.

He shot Rachel a look. 'I told him he was eating with us tonight. He'd better not have taken himself off again.'

'He won't, he knows.' She kept her voice inflectionless, clearly used to this sort of mediating. 'Can someone set the table, please?'

I got up to do it but Trask waved me back down. 'I'll do it. I dare say you've been busy enough as it is, Dr Hunter.'

'Call me David,' I said, sidestepping the question. It might have been innocent or not, but I wasn't going to be drawn into discussing work.

Trask took cutlery and cane place mats from a drawer and went to set the rosewood dining table. 'So, do you know how much longer you're going to be here?'

'Perhaps a couple more days. But if staying at the boathouse is a problem, I can find somewhere else.'

'If it was a problem you wouldn't be staying there.' He finished laying the table and took another drink of wine. Glancing at the almost-empty bottle, he went to the wine cooler and selected another. I saw Rachel give him a nervous glance. 'How's the investigation going?'

'It's progressing.'

'Progressing.' Taking a corkscrew from the drawer he used the spike to strip off the foil from the bottle neck. 'What about that thing in the creek? Any idea yet who it was?'

'Andrew, I'm sure David doesn't—'

'I'm sure David can answer for himself.' He wound the corkscrew into place. 'I'm being a good boy, I've not asked anything about Villiers. And I think I'm within my rights to wonder about the corpse my daughter was sharing the barbed wire with.'

The cork came free with a *pop*. Trask set the opened bottle down, regarding me with a hint of challenge.

'Sorry, there's not much I can tell you,' I said, which was true however you looked at it.

'You're telling me the police haven't said anything else about it?'

'Not about who it is, no.'

My ignorance was genuine: I hadn't even had time to read the post-mortem report Lundy had emailed earlier. Trask didn't look satisfied, but before he could ask anything else the sound of the front door opening came from downstairs.

'That'll be Jamie.' Rachel sounded relieved at the distraction. She went to the top of the stairs and called down. 'Jamie, can you tell Fay to come up? Dinner's ready.'

Trask fell quiet as we went to the table, pouring the last of the wine I'd brought into mine and Rachel's glasses and refilling his own from the bottle he'd just opened. Rachel watched uneasily, but said nothing.

I should never have accepted Trask's invitation, I realized. Renting the boathouse was one thing, but sharing a dinner table with the man was another. It was asking too much to expect him to avoid any talk of the investigation. And I should have had enough sense to see what sort of position I'd be putting myself in. Everyone outside the inquiry still believed that Leo Villiers was dead, and that the body the police had recovered from the estuary was his. So now I was about to sit down to dinner with the family of a missing woman, pretending I didn't know her suspected killer was still alive.

What had I been thinking?

I became aware of Rachel looking at me as she brought dishes to the table. I forced myself to smile. I was here now: I'd just have to make the best of it.

Fay trudged up the stairs, a martyred expression of boredom on her face. 'Where's Jamie?' Trask asked.

His daughter scraped a chair across the floor and slumped down in it. 'He says he's not hungry.'

'I'll go and fetch him,' Rachel said quickly, but Trask was already getting to his feet. The same tight-lipped expression as I'd seen on his son's face earlier was now on his.

'No, you carry on.'

She watched him stride downstairs, anxiously. While Fay was preoccupied stroking and talking to the dog, which had come over to flop at her feet, I left the table and went over to where Rachel was taking the casserole out of the oven.

'I should go,' I said quietly.

With a glance over at Fay, she put the casserole down and turned to me. 'It'll be worse if you leave now.'

I didn't see how it could be. 'Sorry, I shouldn't have come.'

'I'm glad you did,' she said softly.

I felt something unravel as the green eyes looked at me, a knot that had been there for so long I no longer noticed it. Rachel held my gaze as footsteps on the stairs announced the return of Trask and his son. Then, picking up a stack of dinner plates from the worktop, she offered them to me.

'Please?'

Oh, hell. Wondering what I thought I was doing, I took the plates from her. Trask and Jamie came up as I set them out at the table. Neither of them looked happy as they took their places in silence. Jamie sighed ostentatiously as he sat down, watching his sister as she bent to stroke the dog.

'It looks like you're having a contest for who can have the most bandages.'

'Shut up.'

'I think Cassie wins. We should start calling her Frankencassie from now on.'

'No we shouldn't.'

'It's *alive*, master! It barks!'

'Stop it! You're the one who looks like Frankenstein!'

'And I haf created a dog! Rise, Frankencassie, rise!'

'Shut *up*!' his sister told him, but they were both laughing.

'All right, quieten down,' Trask said, and the brief moment ended. There was silence again as Rachel brought the casserole over to the table.

The scrape of the serving spoon sounded too loud as the food was dished out. I looked out of the long window and saw that night had once again turned it into a dark mirror. The creek had disappeared behind a smoky reflection of the room, where another five people sat around an identical table to ours. They didn't look to be enjoying it any more than we did.

'Help yourselves to jacket potatoes and broccoli,' Rachel said, ladling steaming chicken casserole on to plates and passing them round.

Fay scowled. 'I *hate* broccoli.'

'That's because it's brain food and you don't have a brain.' Her brother's tone was still jocular, but this time his sister scowled.

'I'm cleverer than you!'

'Yeah, in your dreams.'

'I am! If you're so clever how come you failed your mock exams?'

'That's enough,' Trask snapped. 'Fay, eat your broccoli and stop showing off.'

'I'm not—'

'I said that's enough!'

The musical chink of cutlery seemed to emphasize the silence. 'This is delicious,' I said, taking up another forkful of food.

Rachel smiled, more grateful for the attempt at conversation than the compliment. 'Thanks. The recipe calls it chicken stroganoff, but that's just a fancy name for chicken and mushroom casserole.'

'It's very good,' Trask said dutifully. He reached to pour himself more wine. I saw Rachel watching him. So did Jamie.

'Can I have a glass?'

'No.'

'Why not?'

'Let's just have dinner, shall we?'

'I don't see why I can't have a glass of wine as well. I'm eighteen, I drink when I go out.'

'But not in this house. Once you go to university you can please yourself, but until then you'll do as I say.'

My stomach sank: after the conversation I'd had with Jamie I knew what was coming. Jamie's expression hardened. 'I told you, I'm not going to university.'

Trask paused, then resumed eating. 'Don't start that again.'

'I'm not. You brought it up.'

'Then let it drop. We're not having this conversation now.'

'Fine. There's nothing to talk about anyway. It's my decision, and I've already made it.'

Fay had been chewing slowly, watching them both wide-eyed. 'I don't want Jamie to leave home.'

Her brother gave her a strained smile. 'It's OK, I'm not going anywhere.'

'Stay out of this, Fay,' Trask told her. 'And Jamie, don't make your sister promises you can't keep. It isn't fair to build her hopes up.'

'What's fair got to do with it?' Jamie demanded. 'It's my life, I can do what I want.'

'Jamie . . .' Rachel said, but neither he nor his father paid any attention.

'Not if you're going to be a bloody idiot!' Trask snapped. 'I'm not letting you throw everything away on some juvenile whim!'

'Right, because you're such an expert.'

'What's that supposed to mean?'

'You know what it means. You're really lecturing *me* about bad decisions?'

'That's enough. Go to your room.'

'Why? It's true, we all know it! If you hadn't insisted on dragging us all out here, she wouldn't be— '

Trask's chair screeched on the wooden floor as he jumped to his feet. I tried to think of a way to defuse the situation and came up with nothing.

'What're you going to do? Hit me?' Jamie's face was flushed and angry, making the twin patches that remained on his cheeks all the more livid. 'Go on then, you've been dying to for ages! You might as well—'

'*Stop* it!' Rachel's shout cut through the anger in the room. 'For Christ's sake, both of you, just . . . *stop*!'

Everyone looked at her. She stared down at the table, her chest rising and falling. The tension stretched out. Trask drew breath to speak, but as he did there was a loud hammering from downstairs.

Someone was at the front door.

19

IT WAS AS though a bubble had burst. For a second or two no one reacted, then Trask recovered.

'Who the hell's that?' he said, turning towards the stairs. Whoever it was, they wanted to attract our attention. I could feel the floor vibrate as the banging continued. The dog started barking, adding to the din.

'I'll go. Shush, Cassie,' Rachel said, starting to rise. Trask waved her back, a look of annoyance on his face.

'No, you stay here.' I got the impression he was glad of the excuse as he hurried downstairs. 'All right, all *right!*'

The banging didn't let up. Rachel turned to Jamie. 'You OK?'

He nodded, but his colour still hadn't returned to normal. 'Yeah.'

'They're going to break the *door*,' Fay said, sounding both indignant and scared as the hammering grew even louder.

'Jesus, I said all *right!*' Trask's voice carried up from the hallway. The noise stopped as the front door was unlocked. 'OK, what's the—'

'*Where is the little fucker?*'

There was a sudden commotion. I jumped up as heavy footsteps pounded up the stairs, and then Coker appeared at the top of them.

The oil-stained overalls and cap had been replaced by jeans and a short-sleeved shirt pulled tight over biceps and gut. The burly owner of the marine salvage yard came straight at Jamie, his face savage.

'You little shit, I fucking warned you!'

I stepped in front of Coker, intending to try and calm him down. I wasn't given the chance. He barged me aside, and whether by accident or design his hand caught me in the face. A flashbulb went off in my vision as I grabbed on to him, trying to pull him back. It was like trying to slow a bull. There was solid bulk under the fat, but instead of knocking me away he abruptly stopped. Blinking my eyes to clear them, I saw that Rachel had an arm around Fay, her other hand gripping the barking dog's collar. Jamie stood in front of them, his face now pale but determined.

In his hand was the long-bladed bread knife.

'What you going to do with that?' Coker sneered, but he didn't go any nearer. I still had hold of his arm, breathing in his odour of oil and sweat. As I wondered what to do next Rachel thrust the dog's collar into Fay's hand and advanced on him.

'What the hell's *wrong* with you?'

Coker seemed taken aback by her outrage. He jerked his chin at Jamie.

'Ask him!'

Jamie looked confused, then he stared past Coker and his expression changed. 'Dad? Are you OK?'

Trask had emerged at the top of the stairs, shaken and dishevelled but unhurt. His fists were clenched tight as he took in the scene.

'You've got five seconds to get out before I call the police.'

Coker jerked his arm away from me. 'Fine! Call them. Tell them what your fucking son did!'

'And what did he do?'

'He tried to rape Stacey!'

Jamie gaped at him, then his face suddenly coloured. '*What?* That's bollocks!'

'She phoned me up, terrified!' Coker snarled. 'She said you've been pestering her for weeks, wouldn't take no for an answer! And when she wouldn't change her mind you tried to force her!'

'Me, force *her*? You're joking, she's been *begging* me to—'

Trask's voice was like a whip. 'Enough!'

'But Dad—'

'I said that's *enough*. And for God's sake put that bloody knife down!' He turned to Coker. 'When's this supposed to have happened?'

'There's no *supposed*, it was after she left work this afternoon!' Coker spat. 'She called me in tears. Made me promise not to tell the police, didn't want to get the little bastard into trouble!'

Jamie threw his arms up. 'Oh, come *on*! She came out here wanting me to go to some crappy party tomorrow, and when I said no she slapped me and drove off! She's just causing trouble!'

'She should have ripped your balls off, never mind slap you!' Coker's fists were clenched, but he managed to restrain himself. 'Stacey wouldn't come here again, she knows better than that! You called her pretending there was something important you had to say, got her to meet you outside town and then you were all over her! Nearly ripped her top off!'

'Dad, this is bullshit!'

'Jamie was home all day,' Trask said stonily. 'I can't say what your daughter did, but I can tell you he hasn't been anywhere.'

'How do you know? Been watching him all the time, have you?' Coker sneered. 'You stuck up for him before and you're doing it now!'

This wasn't my argument, but I couldn't keep quiet when I knew something they didn't. 'What time was this?' I asked.

Coker glared at me. 'The fuck's it to do with you?'

'A white Fiesta with racing stripes nearly ran me over outside the boathouse about an hour ago,' I said. 'It was heading away from here, going back towards town.'

Coker's mouth worked as he processed the information. 'Fuck off! Stacey wouldn't be seen dead in this place!'

I hesitated, then decided it was better to tell him. 'She was here at the weekend as well. I saw her when I was waiting for my car to be repaired.'

If he'd taken the job he might have seen her himself, but I knew better than to mention that. Trask looked angrily at his son.

'Stacey was here?'

Coker didn't give Jamie a chance to answer. Now his full anger was focused on me. 'You're lying! You're covering up for them!'

'Oh, for God's sake, why would a complete bloody stranger *care* enough to make it up?' Trask demanded. 'And how about you show some consideration for *my* daughter? She only got out of hospital this morning, and now you come bursting in her home making threats?'

I don't think Coker had even noticed Fay until then. There was an uncertainty about him as he looked down at the frightened girl huddled behind Rachel, and I saw him take in the dressings on her thin arms.

But he still wasn't ready to back down. He confronted Jamie again.

'Stacey wouldn't make it up for no reason. I know you've done something to her, you little bastard!'

That earned a bitter laugh. 'Oh yeah, because she's such a—'

'Jamie!' Trask stared at his son, then turned back to Coker. 'You've had your say. Now get out or I'm calling the police.'

Coker had been looking cornered; now the anger was back. He levelled a thick finger at Jamie.

'Go near my daughter again and I'll kill you.'

He pushed past me and thumped down the stairs. A moment later the front door banged. For a few seconds no one moved or spoke, then Trask turned to his son.

'What did you do?'

'I didn't do anything! You know what she's like!'

'Yes, I do, and I'm asking what you did to make her tell her father something like that. What did you say to her?'

'Nothing, I just . . .' He seemed to slump. 'I called her a fat sow and told her to fuck off and die, all right? She wouldn't leave me *alone*! I mean, why can't she just take a hint and—'

'In my study.'

'Dad, I swear—'

'Now.'

Jamie's shoulders slumped as he followed his father downstairs. As he passed the table he slapped down the knife he'd been holding.

It clattered on the wood, spinning in a slow circle to a stop.

Rachel walked me back to my car. This time she didn't even attempt to persuade me to stay. We pretended not to hear the raised voices coming from Trask's study as she packed up some food to take with me. Watching her spoon casserole into a dish, I felt sorry for her, forced by circumstances and conscience into staying with a family whose only connection to her was through a shared tragedy. I wondered if she'd have stayed as long if she'd had a better relationship with her sister, or whether guilt over their final row had kept her here.

The night had turned cold, the air damp and smelling of marsh. 'How's the nose?' she asked as we walked along the footpath through the trees.

I touched it experimentally. It was still sore from where Coker had caught it, but wasn't bleeding. 'I'll live.'

'Glad to hear it.' Her smile faded. 'Not exactly a relaxing dinner, was it?'

'It was different.'

She gave a tired laugh. 'We seem to keep dragging you into our problems, don't we? You remember I said that Jamie and Stacey had a history? Well, it was a bit more complicated than that.'

I'd already guessed that much. 'Did she get pregnant?'

Rachel nodded. 'It was before I came here. Jamie had broken up with her, which was bad enough for Coker. Then Stacey announced she was pregnant and claimed it was Jamie's. It could have been but . . . she's a bit older than him so let's say he wasn't the only candidate. Anyway, Coker went ballistic and blamed everything on Jamie. There was an almighty row, and knowing Emma I can't imagine she would have been a calming influence. In the end Stacey had an abortion, but it left a lot of bad feeling. As you may have noticed.'

'What do you think she'll do now?'

'Hopefully let it drop. I'm just glad you saw her, because if it just had been her word against Jamie's . . .' Rachel let that hang, then gave a weary shrug. 'Anyway, it's not all her fault. Jamie shouldn't have said what he did. "Sow" was one of Emma's pet insults, so no prizes for guessing where he got that from. God, what an evening.'

'I'm sorry if bringing the wine made things awkward,' I said.

'You mean because of Andrew?' She shrugged. 'It isn't normally an issue. Like I said before, he's not an alcoholic or anything. He just started drinking more after Emma disappeared, and stopped when he realized things were getting a bit out of hand.'

'Like going to confront Leo Villiers, you mean?'

'That didn't help, no. And you saw how it can get between him and Jamie. They're very alike so they tend to rub anyway. It's worse if Andrew's been drinking'

We'd emerged from the copse and now stopped by my car. Rachel looked back at the house, a dark rectangle with yellow windows visible through the shadowy trees.

'Are you OK?' I asked.

'Me?' She shrugged. 'Yeah, I'm fine.'

She didn't sound it. A tension had been building up in me, and I spoke without thinking. 'Look, if you're not doing anything tomorrow night, how about going out for dinner? Or a drink, or something?'

She looked taken aback, and I felt my stomach lurch. *Where did that come from?* Less than an hour ago I'd been regretting accepting Trask's invitation: now here I was asking Rachel out. If I could have snatched the words back I would.

Then she smiled. 'I'd like that. But there aren't exactly many places to go around here.'

'It's OK. It was a bad idea anyway.'

'No, I'd love to. It just means driving for miles.' She hesitated. 'If you like, I could cook something at the boathouse?'

'Uh . . . Yes, if you're sure . . .'

'Great. How about seven?'

I said seven was fine.

Driving back to the boathouse, I swung between euphoria and apprehension. I told myself not to read anything into it, that Rachel was probably glad of the chance to get away from Creek House for an evening. Still, I knew I was potentially complicating things, involving myself even deeper in the Trask family's problems.

It didn't matter. Regardless of the circumstances, I couldn't remember feeling like this in . . .

Well. A long time.

I'd only been in one serious relationship since Kara had died. I'd been a GP at the time, and it hadn't survived the transition from my working with the living to the dead. But it meant I'd long ago resolved any guilt over becoming involved with someone else. I was glad for that much, at least, though it didn't make me feel any less nervous. I smiled ruefully as I caught myself. It was only dinner, after all. *Don't get carried away.*

Back at the boathouse I turned on the heater to counter the night's chill and took the still-warm casserole over to the table. With the soft whirr of the blown air as a background, I turned on my laptop and ate as I opened the files Lundy had emailed earlier. As well as the post-mortem report on the remains from the barbed wire, the DI had also sent a photograph of the custom-made shotgun that had disappeared along with Leo Villiers. I didn't like guns and had never been a fan of shooting as a sport, but even I had to admit that it was a beautiful piece of craftsmanship. The Mowbry was double-barrelled, with an over-and-under configuration rather than side-by-side. The stock was a burnished mahogany, while the barrels themselves were a smoky blue-black that seemed to glow. Most distinctive of all were the silver side plates, intricately whorled and engraved with the letters *LV*.

Leo Villiers.

I wondered if the man lying in the mortuary had appreciated the aesthetics of the weapon that killed him.

Lundy had attached a short note with the image: *FYI – barrel 32 inches. Frears says too long for estuary body to reverse and reach trigger.* Assuming the shot had come from Leo Villiers' missing Mowbry, as seemed likely, that ruled out any lingering question of suicide. Not that there had been any serious doubt once we knew the body wasn't his.

I went to the file containing the post-mortem report. It wasn't ideal reading material to accompany food, but my work had long since cured me of being squeamish. Even so, for once I found it hard to concentrate. My mind kept drifting to Rachel, until the words on the glowing screen finally snared my attention. I lowered the fork, a piece of chicken still speared on it, as what I was reading began to sink in. The broken arm and leg I'd noticed when the body was on the barbed wire weren't the only damage it had sustained. There were more injuries. A *lot* more, I realized, reaching for a pen and paper. I'd noticed that the head seemed to hang unusually loose, even for the length of time the remains had been submerged. With its thick layers of muscles and tendons, it's usually the last extremity to fall away. Now I saw that two of the vertebrae in the neck were broken, with what was obviously extreme force. And the right tibia and fibula weren't only snapped mid-shin, they'd been fractured at the knee as well. That same leg also had a dislocated hip, the ball-like head of the femur wrenched completely from its socket.

I tapped my pen against my chin. It was possible the multiple trauma could have been caused by the drifting body being struck by a boat, which might also explain the propeller-like wounds to the face. But it would have to have been a very forceful impact. Probably more than one, I thought, considering the extent of the injuries.

Then I saw something that really made me sit up.

I re-read it, then opened the file containing the mortuary X-rays. The extent of the sharp trauma injuries to the facial bones were evident even from the ghostly 2D images. The boat propeller – if that's what it was – had inflicted massive damage, making any potential reconstruction a complicated task.

But that wasn't what interested me. The world shrank around me, ceasing to exist outside the glow of my laptop screen as I enlarged the X-ray of the cranium. I zoomed in on one particular area of damage, chafing at the restricted views the flat X-rays provided. Then, like a pattern emerging from a puzzle, I saw it.

'And how did you get there?' I murmured, the half-eaten casserole forgotten as I stared at the screen.

I was too wired to relax after that. My mind was still buzzing when I went to bed, thoughts of Rachel flitting around with ideas about the case. For the first time I felt as though a chink of light was beginning to break through, that things were falling into place for my own life as well as the investigation. I should have known better.

Stacey Coker never came home that evening.

20

As LUNDY RELATED it later, Coker had gone back home to confront his daughter after storming out of Creek House. His wife had divorced him years before, so now he and Stacey lived alone in a bungalow not far from the marine salvage yard. When he found his daughter wasn't there, he'd tried calling her without success. Then, opening a pack of beer, he sat fuming while he waited for her to come home.

Except Stacey never arrived.

To begin with Coker wasn't worried. Even when phone calls to her friends failed to locate her, he was angry rather than concerned. It wouldn't be the first time his daughter had persuaded friends to lie for her. Only later, as their repeated denials began to ring true, did he start to realize this was different. Even so, convinced his daughter was simply putting off facing him, it wasn't until the early hours of the morning that he went out looking for her.

After banging on the doors of the friends most likely to be harbouring her, Coker remembered I'd seen Stacey driving past the boathouse. There were two ways back to Cruckhaven from there. One was what passed for the main road, which Coker had taken himself earlier. Not having seen any sign of his daughter then, he now took the other route. This cut further into the Backwaters,

223

less accessible but better for anyone who didn't want to risk their distinctive car being seen. About a mile before he reached the boathouse, Coker's headlights picked out a gap in the hawthorn hedgerow by the roadside. Even then he almost drove past, but some instinct made him pull over. Leaving his engine running so his headlights shone on the gap, he got out and found fresh breaks in the branches. The creek beyond was full and dark, but he made out a paler shape sticking from the black water.

It was the rear bumper and one back wheel of a car.

By the time the police arrived the tide was ebbing, and enough of the car was visible to see that it was small and white, with a red racing stripe. Tyre marks showed where it had left the road on the bend, before tipping over as it went down the shallow bank. It had come to rest upside down in the creek, on its roof but canted at an angle. The driver's door was open, but – as Coker had already established after plunging into the water himself – there was no sign of its occupant. Only a handbag remained inside the car, containing Stacey Coker's purse and driving licence.

'It looks like she took the bend too fast, lost control and then rolled it down the bank,' Lundy told me.

It was the following afternoon and we were in the hospital cafeteria, at an isolated table set away from any other diners. Not that there were many: it was after the lunchtime rush and half the tables were empty. Lundy had dropped into the mortuary unannounced to tell me what had happened. He'd seemed ill at ease as he'd stood by the examination table, rattling the loose coins in his pocket as I'd cut away the decomposed soft tissue from the second body and begun to cut through the connective tendons and cartilage of the major joints. It was unusual for a police officer to be bothered about such things, and he'd showed no such qualms when either of the bodies were being recovered. But he'd seemed relieved when I suggested we take a break for lunch, so we'd headed for the cafeteria.

'The seat belt was unfastened, so it's possible she managed to undo it and crawl out,' he went on, emptying a second sachet of sugar into his polystyrene cup of tea. 'Or she didn't bother fastening it and got thrown through the door as the car flipped. Either way, we've got to assume she got carried out by the tide or we'd have found her by now.'

I was still trying to absorb this new tragedy. I'd taken the more direct route to the mortuary that morning, and so missed the cordoned-off area of the Backwaters where Stacey Coker's car had been found. So I'd been unaware of what had happened until Lundy arrived, wanting to hear my version of events the previous evening. Coker had told the police about his daughter speeding past the boathouse, which made me the last person to have seen her before the accident. And, quite possibly, the last to see her alive.

'How fast was she going?' Lundy asked.

I remembered the tug of air as the car flashed past, almost clipping me. 'She was gone in a second, so it's hard to say. But fast.'

Lundy nodded, morosely. He looked tired, his eyes more pouched than normal and an unhealthy colour to his face. But then he'd had a late night. 'Figures. She's a bit hot-headed by all accounts, and she'd just had a row with Jamie Trask. She's already got points on her licence for speeding.'

'So what's happening now?'

He stirred his tea with a plastic spoon. 'We've got the helicopter and marine unit out, and foot patrols searching where we can in the Backwaters. But you've seen yourself what it's like in there. The tide was already going out by the time her dad found her car, so she could have wound up anywhere. Best chance is if the tide took her as far as the estuary, because then sooner or later she'll wash up on the Barrows.'

He was talking about a body, not an injured survivor. 'You don't think there's a chance she could still be alive?'

'There's always a chance.'

His tone made it clear how unlikely he thought that was. Even if Stacey had managed to crawl from the car rather than being

225

thrown out, she'd have still had to fight against the tidal current in the cold water. I'd felt how strong its pull was when my car stalled on the causeway. That had only been knee deep, and I hadn't been involved in a crash. Stunned and possibly injured, weighted down by waterlogged clothes and probably disorientated in the darkness, it wouldn't have been easy for her to reach the bank.

The fact that we were having this conversation suggested she hadn't.

'How's Coker taking it?' I asked.

Lundy turned down his mouth, moustache bristling as he took a sip of tea. 'As you'd expect. If he's any sense, Jamie Trask should steer well clear of him.'

I hadn't thought about that, but Lundy was right. Jamie hadn't been directly responsible for the accident, but I didn't think Coker would see it that way.

We fell silent in the echoing clatter of the cafeteria. I dutifully chewed my way through a limp cheese sandwich while Lundy tore the cellophane wrapper from a pre-packaged slice of fruitcake. He'd already eaten lunch but had decided he had room for a piece of cake. To keep me company, he'd said, smiling sheepishly.

'Funny places, these,' he said out of the blue, looking around the half-empty room. 'Hospital cafés, I mean. Always the same, wherever you go. Everything seems normal, but nothing is, if you get my drift.'

I hadn't really thought about it before, but then I'd once worked and trained in a hospital. That gave you a different perspective. 'People have to eat.'

'I suppose.' He'd finished the cake, and now absently began snapping off pieces of polystyrene from the rim of his cup. 'I'm here again myself tomorrow. The hospital, not this place.'

I looked across at him, wondering if this explained his odd mood. 'Is everything OK?'

The DI looked embarrassed, as though he regretted saying as much as he had. 'Oh, it's just routine stuff. Endoscopy. They think

I might have an ulcer. Lot about nothing, but you know what doctors are like.'

'Pesky bunch, aren't we?'

I'd noticed Lundy taking antacids but put it down to indigestion. He gave me a smile, acknowledging that he'd forgotten I'd been a GP myself.

'How are you getting on with the body from the creek?' he asked, moving off the topic. 'Did you manage to look at the post-mortem report?'

'I did, yes.' The news about Stacey Coker had dominated our conversation until now, so I hadn't had a chance to broach anything else. 'There are a lot more broken bones than I'd expect.'

'Couldn't they be from being hit by a boat?'

'They could, but it would have to have been travelling fast or be pretty big to do that much damage. Hard to see that happening in the Backwaters.'

'We don't know where the body came from. It could have been carried in from the estuary, or even further out.'

'And then stayed afloat long enough to get tangled up in the barbed wire like it was?'

Lundy watched himself break more pieces from the top of the polystyrene cup. 'I know. Doesn't seem likely, does it? Hard to see anything other than a boat prop that could have caused those injuries to the face, though.'

'Perhaps.'

His eyebrows went up. 'Have you found something?'

'I might have,' I admitted. 'It's hard to see enough detail from the X-rays. I won't know for sure until I've examined the actual skull.'

'Well, keep me posted.' Lundy already seemed distracted again. 'I checked into Sir Stephen's driver, by the way. His name's Brendan Porter. Forty-nine years old, been driving for the Villiers for over twenty years. Bit of a bad lad when he was younger, but then joined the army at eighteen and straightened himself out. Got taken on as a stand-in when the normal driver was ill and wound up replacing him. Seems like an odd fit, but if he's been there all this time he must have found a niche for himself.'

'Why do you think he was quizzing me? Trying to ingratiate himself with his boss?'

'Sir Stephen hardly needs his driver to tell him what's going on,' Lundy said drily. 'I dare say he'd have reported back if he'd learned anything juicy but my guess is he was just fishing. Maybe he hoped you'd open up more if he badmouthed Leo.'

I thought about the man's knowing smile as he'd insulted his employer's son. Watching to see how I'd react. 'Taking a chance, wasn't he? What if it got back to Sir Stephen?'

Lundy snorted. 'Would you tell him something like that?'

No, I had to concede I probably wouldn't. Still, this Porter must be either very blasé or confident of his position to risk it. 'What about him knowing we'd found a second body?'

'Not much we can do about that. People are always going to talk, and the local press have picked up on it now anyway, which was always going to happen after Trask took his daughter to hospital. The official line is that the body's an unknown male and pre-dates Leo Villiers' disappearance, so they're running with the idea it's an accidental death unconnected to any other investigation. Which it still might be.'

I gave him a look. He smiled.

'I know, I don't believe in coincidences either. But it's better not to make too many waves at this stage. Except for Sir Stephen, who's still refusing to believe us anyway, everyone still assumes the body from the estuary is Leo Villiers'. We'd rather keep it that way, at least until we get confirmation from the DNA results. If Villiers is still alive, we've got more chance of finding him if he believes he's safe.'

'You think he could still be in the area?'

Lundy had gone back to snapping chunks off the edge of his cup. 'I doubt it, but it's possible. We've got the National Crime Agency looking into the possibility he's abroad, but there haven't been any hits on his passport. So if he's left the country he didn't cross any checkpoints. Not under his own name, anyway.'

That didn't necessarily mean anything. Someone with Leo Villiers' money and resources could always forge a new identity, and there was no shortage of isolated creeks and coves along this coast where boats could come and go unobserved.

But there was something else that had been bothering me.

'If Villiers staged all this to make it look like he'd killed himself, he was taking a hell of a risk,' I said. 'He couldn't know how long it would take for the body to be found, or even that it would be. It might have washed up in the first few days, when it still had fingerprints or before it lost its feet. We'd have known straight away it wasn't him.'

'We would,' Lundy agreed, nodding slowly. 'But we don't know enough about the circumstances. Maybe Villiers wasn't thinking clearly. Not many people do when they've just killed someone.'

That was true enough, and something I'd seen for myself before now. Few murderers have enough presence of mind – let alone the know-how – to plan for everything. In that heightened, adrenalin-stoked state even obvious details are overlooked.

I just wasn't convinced that was the case here. Although I disliked the whole notion of 'instinct', I'd come to realize that experience created its own form of muscle memory. Our minds are constantly processing information that we aren't conscious of. Even though we might not recognize it as such, on a subliminal level an awareness can still filter through. I felt that now. I couldn't say why, not yet, but something about this didn't sit right.

'Is that what you really think?' I asked.

'Me? Doesn't matter what I think, I'm just a DI.' Lundy scraped the mound of broken polystyrene into his hand and pushed himself to his feet. 'For what it's worth, though, I reckon we've only just scratched the surface.'

It had started to rain when I left the mortuary for the day. I stopped off at a supermarket on the way back, and spent longer than I should deciding what wine to buy. Rachel hadn't said what she planned to cook, so in the end I bought both red and white, hoping that wouldn't make it look as though I were trying to get her drunk.

By the time I reached the Backwaters the rain had increased and a stiff wind was blowing in off the sea. Unhindered by the flat landscape, it whipped across the sand dunes and marshes, making the long grasses thrash bad-temperedly. Parking outside the boathouse, I grabbed my bags and hurried inside. I showered and changed, doing my best to ignore the nerves gnawing at my stomach. When I set the little table by the window and realized the boathouse didn't have any wine glasses, I actually considered going back out to buy some before I caught myself. *So use tumblers. For God's sake, relax.*

I managed to for a while, but the nervousness began creeping back as the time ticked by. I began to wonder if I should have checked to make sure Rachel was still coming. The news about Stacey Coker would have hit them all hard – the police would certainly have spoken to Jamie about their argument, as well as to Trask about Coker's barging in the evening before. But I'd decided against phoning, wanting to give them space and reasoning that Rachel would call me if she'd changed her mind.

Now I wasn't so sure. I'd just resolved to give it another ten minutes when I heard a car pull up outside. I opened the door in time to see Rachel hurrying from Jamie's white Land Rover, carrier bags in one hand and her coat held over her head against the rain with the other. I stood back to let her in.

'Hi. Sorry I'm late,' she said breathlessly, shaking off her coat outside before closing the door. She was still wearing jeans but these were newer and less faded, and her V-neck top revealed a thin gold chain lying on her skin. I caught a faint hint of perfume, something light and subtle.

'Don't worry about it,' I told her, taking her coat.

'I just wanted to make sure Fay was OK before I left, and then Andrew . . . Anyway, it took longer than I thought.'

I hung up her coat, wondering what she'd been about to say about Trask. 'How is everyone?'

'You mean because of Stacey?' She sighed. 'Still in shock, if I'm honest. The police came round earlier to take a statement from Jamie. He blames himself, which is pointless. But there's not a lot you can say when something like this happens.'

Nothing that would do any good, I knew that well enough myself. 'Would you like a glass of wine? There's Pinot Noir or a Sauvignon Blanc.'

'I'll have the Sauvignon, please.' Rachel's smile was tired and grateful. She began unpacking the bags. 'I made crab cakes, so I hope you like shellfish. Dessert's only dog food cake, but what with one thing and another I didn't have a chance to make anything else. And you didn't get to have any last night, so you can try some now.'

'I can't wait.'

Her laugh was strained but sounded genuine. 'OK, just for that, you don't get to have any.'

'I meant it!' I protested, opening the wine.

'Sure you did.' She accepted the glass I offered and took a drink. Her shoulders relaxed as she sighed. 'God, that's welcome.'

There was still a tension about her, and I didn't think it was all down to Coker's daughter. But I knew not to press: she'd tell me – or not – in her own time. Whatever was bothering her, she seemed to push it from her mind as she cooked the food she'd brought. Rain drummed against the window as we ate at the small table, but in the warm glow from the lamp the boathouse felt snug and warm. We talked about trivialities, not so much avoiding the topic of Stacey Coker, or Rachel's sister and the investigation, as postponing any need to discuss them. She told me more about her previous life, about the sun and outdoor lifestyle she'd lived while diving on the Great Barrier Reef. Without self-consciousness, she told me a little more about how her relationship with the marine biologist had ended when he slept with a post-grad student.

'Looking back, it was almost funny. The same morning I confronted him, we had a submersible camera get stuck on rocks forty feet down. Rick was so keen to avoid me he volunteered to dive for it, even though we'd sighted a tiger shark nearby.' She grinned evilly, cupping the wine in her hand as she remembered. 'Normally we'd have waited, but I think he thought that was the lesser of two evils rather than stay on the boat with me.'

'Are you that scary?'

'I have my moments. And I was pretty mad at him. Just before he went over the side I brought a bucket of fish guts on deck and told him I was going to chum the water while he was down there.'

'That's mean.' I hesitated. 'You didn't, did you?'

'No, but it wiped the smug look off his face.'

We cleared away the dishes and I made coffee while Rachel unpacked the dessert. I eyed the dog food cake as she offered me a piece.

'Remind me again what's in it?'

'Basically processed sugar and saturated fats. Here.'

She cut a small piece and held it out. I bit into it warily. 'God, that's delicious.'

'Told you,' she smiled.

I couldn't remember the last time I'd felt this comfortable with anyone. It wasn't even the wine, because we hadn't drunk very much. But then she paused, and I could feel the subtle change in mood. I knew what was coming before she spoke.

'Sorry if I was a bit tense earlier,' she said. 'You know, when I first got here.'

'I didn't notice.'

She gave me a wry smile. 'Yeah, right. It's just that today's been a nightmare. And I keep thinking about last night, that if Coker had come the other way to the house he might have found Stacey in time. Can you imagine what he must *feel* like, knowing his daughter might still be alive if he'd gone a different route?'

I could, only too well. 'It's no good trying to make sense of things like that. It's like being struck by lightning. Sometimes it just happens.'

'I know, but that doesn't make it any better. And then this afternoon I ended up having a row with Andrew. I said he should get

Fay away from here, take her somewhere where there are kids her own age. Where there's some *life*, for God's sake! I want to know what happened to Emma too, but we might *never* know. And there's Jamie as well. You heard him last night, saying he isn't going to university now. He thinks he needs to stay to look after Fay. And his dad as well, although he wouldn't admit it. In some ways he's more protective than Andrew, but him staying here won't do *any* of them any good. You can't put your life on hold indefinitely, waiting for something that might not happen. Sooner or later you've got to move on.'

'Are you talking about them or you?' I asked.

'I don't know. Both, I expect.' Rachel stared into her wine glass. 'Andrew told me it was none of my business, and that any time I wanted to leave I could. We were both angry and upset, but maybe he's right. Maybe it's time I left. I don't know how much good I'm doing here any more. Maybe I'm just another reminder of Emma, and God knows there are enough of those around.'

She didn't sound bitter, just resigned. The wind blew a gust of rain against the boathouse. It sounded like handfuls of gravel hitting the roof. I found myself looking at her sister's framed photographs leaning against the wall. The one of silhouetted geese against a Backwaters' sunset was uppermost.

'I rest my case.' Rachel said, seeing what I was looking at. She got up and went over to the pictures. 'I don't know if these are any good or not, but it seems a shame to just hide them away. Do you know much about photography?'

'Not really.'

'Me neither. Emma was the arty one, but she was always impatient. She liked things to look spontaneous, and if the shot wasn't right she'd just stage it. This one, with the geese flying into the sunset? She told me she set up her camera and then threw a stone into the water to startle them. And this one.' She pulled out the photograph of a motorbike on a beach, the gleaming machine incongruous in that setting. 'Somehow I don't think it just happened to be parked on a sand dune like that.'

Something stirred at the back of my mind. I hadn't given the photographs much thought since I'd gone through them on my first morning. I got up and went over to where Rachel was continuing to flick through the stack.

'Can I take another look?'

'Sure.' Rachel moved to one side to make room. 'I wasn't hinting, you know. You needn't buy one.'

I smiled, but distractedly. I went back to the motorbike photograph. 'When was this taken?'

'I don't know. It must be one of her older ones because I think that's her ex-boyfriend's bike. You know, the poser I told you about? He used to have a macho boy's toy like that. A Harley-Davidson or something.'

'So it wasn't taken around here?'

'No, it must be some other beach. Emma hadn't been here until she came with Andrew, and she'd already split with her ex by then. Why?'

'No reason.'

I'd been thinking about the sodden leather biker jacket and boots on the body recovered from the barbed wire. But if this were an old photograph taken somewhere else, it couldn't have anything to do with the remains we'd found in the Backwaters. I started to put it back but Rachel put her hand on my shoulder to stop me.

'Hang on a second.'

She was frowning as she stared down at the photograph. I looked back at it but couldn't see what had caught her attention. 'What is it?'

'Probably nothing,' she said, but didn't sound convinced. 'It sounds stupid, but I've never really *looked* at any of these before. Not properly. They're just . . . Emma's pictures.'

I waited. Almost reluctantly, she pointed at something in the background of the motorbike photograph.

'I'm not sure, but . . . doesn't that look like the sea fort? The one by the estuary?'

I took a closer look. There was something there, an angular silhouette rising from the sea, but it was too out of focus to make out. 'It might be. Or it could be an oil rig or derrick?'

Rachel didn't answer. She began flipping through the other framed photographs until she stopped at one. She started struggling to pull it out. I took the weight of the stack to make it easier for her. The second photograph was of a seagull, imperiously glaring at the camera from a tuft of spiky grass on a sandy ridge.

'There.'

She tapped the glass. What looked like the same structure could again be seen in the background. It was still in the distance, but clearer this time.

The distinctive towers of the Maunsell sea fort.

'This was shot from a slightly different angle, but I recognize where it is now,' Rachel said. 'It's the sand dunes out by the end of the sea wall. You get a good view of the fort from there.'

'Are you sure?'

Lundy had told me the old Second World War forts were dotted along the entire south-east coast. But Rachel was emphatic.

'Positive. I've walked there often enough. And look, you can see there are only three towers left, and one of those has partially collapsed. It's the same fort, I'm certain of it. Shit, I can't believe I never noticed before. When I saw the bike I just thought it must be one of her old photographs!'

She sounded upset, and I couldn't blame her. Rachel had already known her sister was having an affair with Leo Villiers. Now, if she was right about the motorbike, it looked as though Emma Derby had also continued to see her ex-boyfriend after she'd married Trask. That had all sorts of unpleasant implications, and not only for the family. It meant there might be someone else involved in all of this, someone the police knew nothing about. A man who owned a motorbike and might well have worn biker leathers.

Like the remains on the barbed wire.

Rachel didn't know anything about that, though. And this

235

could still be a false alarm. 'Did your sister use digital or film?'

A few photographers still used film, but if Emma Derby wasn't one of them then the original jpeg should show the date when the photograph was taken. Rachel shook her head.

'Digital, but we lost most of Emma's photographs when the computers were stolen in the burglary. The only reason we've got these is because she had enlargements made before she disappeared, and the print shop still had them on their system.'

'Even if the photo was taken here it might not be her ex-boyfriend's bike,' I said, not really believing it myself. 'Would you know it well enough to recognize it?'

'No, but how many other people could she have known with a stupid bike like that? Let alone who'd want its picture taken on a bloody sand dune!' Rachel seemed angry now. 'That's exactly the sort of thing Mark would do. He'd love having his bloody status symbol photographed and framed.'

'Mark?'

'Emma's ex. God, what was his surname? Something religious, Vickers or Church.' She shook her head. 'No, Chapel, that's it. Mark Chapel.'

I made a mental note of the name. 'It's probably nothing, but you still need to tell Lundy about this,' I said gently.

'God, I suppose so. *Shit!* Just when you think things can't get any worse.'

She looked so unhappy that I reached out and put my arm around her. She leaned against me, resting her head on my shoulder. I was very aware of the scent and warmth of her body. She lifted her face to look at me. Neither of us spoke, and then a gust of wind suddenly buffeted the boathouse. The structure shifted and creaked, and as quickly as that the moment was gone.

Rachel sighed and moved away. 'It's getting late. I'd better be going.'

I didn't trust myself to speak as she put on her jacket. The smile she gave me was both wry and regretful.

'Thanks for the wine and . . . you know. Listening.'

'Anytime.'

A blast of wind pushed the door back when she opened it, sending a cold spray of rain inside. She grimaced. 'They got the weather report right for once.'

'Hang on, I'll get my coat.'

'It's OK, there's no point us both getting wet.'

I didn't insist, knowing she didn't want me to. Framed in the pitch black of the open doorway, she gave me another smile. Slanting rain bounced down behind her.

'Well. Goodnight.'

Then she was gone. I heard her crunch across the cinders, but it was too dark to see. I closed the door, feeling the wind fighting me before it clicked shut. I stood in the sudden quiet, unable to decide if I was angry at myself for being tempted or because I hadn't done anything.

With a sigh, I picked up the coffee mugs and took them to the sink. As the water splashed on to the metal bowl I thought I heard something outside. I turned off the tap to listen. There was only the blustering wind. Then, as I reached for the tap, there was another noise, this one unmistakable. A short scream, quickly cut off.

It was Rachel.

21

IRAN AND TORE open the door. Rain beat against me, plastering my shirt to my skin as I rushed outside. In the spill of light that came from the doorway I could make out the pale shape of the white Land Rover. The driver's door was open, but no lights were on.

'Rachel?' I called, straining to see into the darkness.

'I'm here, it's—'

There was a scuffle and a gasp from the direction of the road. My eyes had started to adjust, and as I ran towards the sound I could make out two figures struggling in the shadows. Before I reached them the larger of the two broke away. I made a grab for it as it lurched past, but my fingers closed on oily, wet cloth. I caught a glimpse of wild eyes in a cadaverous face and then the figure pulled free. I slipped and went down on one knee on the mud as slapping footsteps disappeared into the rain.

'David?'

I climbed to my feet as Rachel hurried over. 'I'm here. Are you hurt?'

'No, I'm . . . I'm fine, just . . .' Her voice was unsteady. 'That was Edgar.'

'I know,' I said, wiping mud off my hands. I'd recognized the gangling man even in the dark, and been close enough to smell his rank, animal odour. *So much for him being harmless.* 'What happened?'

'He just appeared when I was getting into the car. I yelled, so perhaps that startled him, because he grabbed hold of me and started gabbling nonsense. I tried to pull away, and that was when you came out.'

She sounded almost normal now. 'You sure you're OK?' I asked.

'Yeah, I'm fine, just a bit shaken. I don't think he was trying to hurt me. He seemed more scared than anything.'

He wasn't the only one, I thought, as my heart-rate began to slow. There was no sign of Edgar, but it was so dark he could have been standing ten feet away and I wouldn't have known it. The rain drowned out any sound he might have made.

'I've never seen him like that before. Do you think he's all right?' Rachel asked.

Edgar's well-being hadn't been my main concern until then, but she had a point. Whether he'd meant to hurt her or not, he wasn't fit to be wandering around on a night like this. There had been enough tragedy already. I stared off into the darkness where he'd disappeared.

'Have you any idea where he was heading?'

'No, but it's the wrong way for his house. And it's high tide, so if he blunders off into the marshes it could be really bad.'

That settled it. It was hard enough trying to negotiate the Backwaters in daylight, and with the tide out. At night, with the creeks and ditches swollen and full, it didn't bear thinking about. I sighed. 'OK, I'll go and look for him.'

'I'll come with you.'

'There's no need, I'll find him.'

'And then what? Drive into the creek again? You don't know your way around here.' She gave my chest a little push, but she was smiling. 'You're soaking. Go and get your coat while I start the car.'

I didn't argue. Hurrying back into the boathouse, I took off

239

my wet shirt and pulled on a sweater, then grabbed my jacket and went back outside. Rachel was already backing up the Land Rover, the beam of its headlights turning the rain into fine silver wire.

'Does he often wander around at night?' I asked as we pulled away.

Rachel slowed as she came to a bend, only accelerating when she saw there was no one in the road ahead. 'Not as far as I know. I've come across him once or twice at dusk, but not this late. I don't think even Edgar would go into the Backwaters in the dark.'

Yet here he was. And now an idea had started to form, something that should have occurred to me before if I hadn't been so distracted by everything else that had been going on.

'People around here know about Edgar, don't they?' I asked. 'That he wanders around on the roads?'

'Everyone around here knows everything about everybody,' she said drily. 'Edgar's practically part of the scenery, nobody really notices him any more. But people generally know to watch out for him if they come over here. Unless they're strangers like you, or . . .'

She trailed off as she made the connection. It had taken me long enough, and it was only a few days since I'd had to swerve to avoid knocking down Edgar myself.

If I'd been going faster I might not have been so lucky.

Rachel eased off the accelerator. 'God, you don't think that's what happened to Stacey, do you? That she nearly hit Edgar?'

'I don't know,' I admitted.

But now it had occurred to me the idea was hard to shake. Lundy had said tyre marks showed the car had swerved on a bend, so the assumption was that Coker's daughter been going too fast and lost control. Which was entirely possible. Or she could have taken the bend and suddenly found Edgar in front of her. At the speed she had been going when I'd seen her, there would have been no time to think, only react. The instinct to swerve would be automatic.

'You said he was gabbling something. Could you tell what it was?'

'Not really. It sounded like something about lights on the water. Or in the water. I couldn't make much sense of it.'

I knew Edgar's words might not mean anything. They were probably just the ramblings of a disturbed mind, and it would be a mistake to read too much into them. Except that something else had occurred to me by now. I thought back to the previous evening, when the little white car had buffeted me with its slipstream as it tore past. As it disappeared into the dusk, I'd seen a yellow glow lighting up the overhanging hawthorn tunnel ahead of it.

The car's headlights had been on.

There was no more time to worry about that now, though. Up ahead of us, Edgar's shambling figure was caught in the Land Rover's full beam.

He was in the middle of the road, scurrying along with his head down. He must have noticed the headlights but his only concession was to hunch his head deeper into his shoulders. The Land Rover grumbled as Rachel slowed, winding down her window as she eased up behind him.

'Edgar? Edgar, can you stop, please?' There was no response; if anything he seemed to hurry his pace. Rachel breathed out. 'Bloody hell. Now what?'

'Let me out.'

She stopped but left the engine running. I got out of the car, blinking in the cold wind and rain as I hurried after the retreating figure picked out in the headlights.

'Hello, Edgar.' I kept my tone easy and conversational as I caught up with him. 'Are you OK?'

Nothing. He kept his eyes averted as he carried on walking, his breath steaming in the headlights' cold glare. The lank hair was plastered over his skull and water streamed down his face. Despite the rain, his long coat was unbuttoned, the greasy oilskin flapping like a loose sail in the wind.

I moved in front of him until I was walking backwards. Now I was facing into the headlights as Rachel crawled along behind us in the Land Rover. Squinting against the glare, I spread out my hands in a gesture I hoped was calming as I blocked his path.

'It's late to be out. Where are you going?'

The frightened eyes flicked to me then darted away again. He'd slowed but tried to move around me. I backed up, trying to keep the same distance between us without seeming threatening.

'Rachel's in the car,' I said. 'You remember talking to her earlier? She'd like to talk to you some more. About the lights you saw.'

That got a response. He slowed to a halt, and now I could see what Rachel meant about him being agitated. I didn't feel any threat from him but he looked like a skittish animal, on the verge of bolting.

'What lights were they, Edgar?'

His mouth worked noiselessly. He seemed calmer but still avoided eye contact, looking around as though searching for a way out. Behind him, I saw Rachel get out of the car. She came over, leaving the engine running.

'Hi, Edgar,' she said easily. 'Can you tell us where you saw the lights?'

His eyes darted to the side. 'In the water.'

'*In* the water? Do you mean they were *on* the water, like a boat?'

'In the water.'

Rachel glanced at me, and again I knew we were thinking the same thing. 'Were they car headlights, Edgar? Was it a car you saw?'

The pallid head bobbled in a nod.

'When did you see them?' I asked. Headlights wouldn't last long underwater without shorting out. If he'd seen Stacey Coker's car, he must have been there when it went into the creek, or very soon after.

Edgar didn't answer. His eyes darted around again. Rachel briefly touched my arm, indicating that I should let her question him.

'It's all right, Edgar. Nobody's cross, we just want to hear about the lights. Who was in the car?'

He pressed his bony hands together, clasping them flat between his legs as though in inverted prayer. 'I saw her hair.'

Rachel hesitated, confused. 'Whose hair?'

'Like sunshine.'

I looked to see if Rachel was making any sense of this. She gave a helpless shrug. 'Was there a girl in the car, Edgar? A blond girl, is that what you mean?'

'It wasn't her.' His agitation was growing. He started shuffling forward. 'Got to go.'

Rachel gently reached out her hand. 'Please, Edgar, it's important. There was a girl in the car, wasn't there? Tell us what happened to her.'

'No, I didn't . . .'

He stumbled forward again but Rachel didn't move. 'Was she hurt?'

Edgar was rocking from foot to foot, misery and tension written all over him. 'She's asleep. I've got to go . . .'

'Asleep where? Where is she, Edgar? At your house? Did you take her to your house?'

But Edgar had done talking. Rain dripped from the end of his nose as he stood with his head bowed. He was soaked through, and Rachel and I weren't much better.

'Come on, let's get him home,' I said.

I thought we might have difficulty getting him into the car, but after a moment's resistance he came along meekly enough. The inside of the Land Rover filled with Edgar's smell as he huddled in the back seat, dripping wet and hunched over like a living question mark.

'I don't know what to think,' Rachel said, putting the car into gear. She switched on the radio, letting incongruous beat-heavy music mask our voices from the man behind. She turned a knob on the dashboard until it was replaced by a calming piano. 'When he said "It wasn't her." It didn't sound like he was talking about Stacey.'

I glanced into the back seat, trying to decipher some meaning from Edgar's words. 'Was his daughter blond as well?'

'You mean what he said about hair like sunshine? I've no idea, I just know she's supposed to have gone missing. But that was years ago, and she'd have been a little girl. He can't have thought Stacey was her, could he?'

I was at a loss, but something about this made the hairs on the back of my neck stand on end. I'd seen enough of Edgar to know he was acting strangely, even by his standards. He wasn't just upset, he was frightened. Frightened enough to be heading *away* from his house on a filthy night like this.

Whatever had happened, it was bad.

The windscreen wipers beat across the glass with a metronomic squeak as I took out my phone. Rachel looked across as I dialled.

'Who are you calling?'

'Lundy.'

Or trying to, at least. The signal fluttered teasingly and then died. I kept trying as Rachel drove through the dark Backwaters, slowing to bump over a timbered bridge, then accelerating through muddy puddles that filled the road. I was glad Rachel had insisted on coming with me. The Land Rover was built for these sorts of conditions, and I'd never have found my way around here on my own.

I still hadn't managed to get through to Lundy by the time Rachel turned off the lane. We drove down a rutted track flanked by overgrown brambles. It ended at a ramshackle old house, and when I saw it the sense of foreboding I'd been feeling intensified. It was in darkness, a tall but ill-proportioned brick cottage with cracked and boarded-up windows. Large old trees surrounded it, hemming it in behind gnarled trunks and dead branches.

Rachel turned off the engine. For a few moments only the sound of rain on the car roof broke the silence, then she turned round in her seat to face Edgar. He hadn't moved during the journey, and showed no sign of wanting to do so now.

'Here we are, Edgar. Home.' There was no response. 'Come on, don't you want to go inside?'

He shook his head, wrapping his arms around himself. Rachel gave me a worried glance before turning back to him.

'Why not? What's wrong?'

Edgar hugged himself tighter, burrowing his chin on to his neck to avoid looking at the darkened house.

'I think he should stay here,' I said quietly, looking at the dark house. 'Do you have a torch?'

There was one on my phone but it wasn't very bright, and I'd feel happier keeping my phone free anyway. Rachel rummaged in the cluttered storage compartment and produced a heavy rubberized flashlight. I didn't say anything when she got out of the car with me. I knew I'd be wasting my breath, and I didn't want to leave her alone with Edgar anyway. I was going to suggest locking the Land Rover while we went inside, but she didn't need to be told. If Edgar noticed the *clunk* of the doors locking, or realized what it meant, he gave no sign.

Without the car headlights, it was pitch black outside. The rain had almost stopped but the wind still gusted petulantly, making the unseen leaves and grasses whisper all around. When I turned on the torch, its beam threw a shaft of light across a tangle of briars and weeds. Rachel shivered as I shone it on to the dark house.

'God, I really don't want to go in there. Do you think we should?'

I didn't want to either, but I didn't see that there was any choice. Something had scared Edgar out of his house, and if there was even a small chance that Stacey Coker was inside I couldn't ignore it. Or wait until the police arrived. If he'd brought her back here she must be seriously hurt, or she'd have contacted someone by now. And Edgar's words still rang in my head.

She's asleep.

'Wait here. I'm going to take a look inside,' I told Rachel. There was probably no need to speak quietly, but I did anyway.

She gave a nervous laugh, keeping her voice low as well. 'Yeah, I'm really going to stand out here by myself.'

245

I shone the torch around the overgrown garden as we made our way to the front door. The beam picked out a series of objects in the grass. Shells, rocks and pieces of driftwood stuck up from the ground at irregular intervals. I thought they'd been left randomly until I saw an oyster shell protruding from a new-looking mound of soil, and realized what it was.

'Edgar's patients,' Rachel said.

The ones that didn't get better, at least. As I moved the torch a pair of gleaming eyes shone back at me from the darkness. An owl blinked at us from inside what looked like an old rabbit hutch. The bird and animal cemetery disappeared into the darkness as I shone the torch back towards the house.

The front door had long since lost any paint that might have once covered it. Warped and decrepit, it hung skewed in its frame. The handle rattled loosely in my hand when I turned it. The door wasn't locked. It juddered open on rusted hinges, and an ammoniac stink of animal faeces spilled out.

'God,' Rachel muttered, wrinkling her nose.

A dark hallway confronted us. I played the torch over the peeling and mildewed wallpaper and bare floorboards. There was no furniture, only a single, broken chair. The floor was covered with old newspapers and mounds of what looked like faecal matter I hoped was animal.

'Stacey?' I called.

There was no answer, but now I could hear faint bumps and fluttering coming from further inside.

'Here, let me try the lights,' Rachel said, moving past me to reach for a switch on the wall. She flicked it a few times, but nothing happened. 'OK, so much for that idea.'

Careful of where I walked, I stepped across the threshold. Rachel followed close behind as I went down the hallway. The smell was even worse inside, and I felt ashamed and angry that Edgar had been left to live alone in those conditions. Glad of the torch's heft, I went to the nearest door and pushed it open.

The quiet was shattered by an ear-splitting shriek.

Rachel grabbed my arm, making the torch beam jerk crazily. Caught in the light, a seagull glared haughtily from inside a make-shift wooden cage.

'Jesus . . .' Rachel let go of me but stayed close.

I shone the torch around the bizarre scene in the room. Now the source of the noises I'd heard was explained. It was a kitchen, or at least had been. The encrusted sink was almost buried under filthy dishes and empty food cans, and the walls were stacked high with cages. Glowing eyes stared back at us from ancient bird and hamster cages, rabbit hutches and even an old fish tank. Most were occupied by seabirds, but there were small animals as well: rodents, rabbits, a hedgehog and even a young badger, all of them injured, some with splinted wings or legs. Inside the grimy oven, which was missing its door, a young fox watched us from behind a screen of chicken wire.

'How can he have lived like this?' Rachel asked in a hushed voice. 'Wouldn't somebody have known?'

Apparently not. Leaving Edgar's menagerie to the shadows, we went back into the hallway. I shone the torch along its length, wondering if I should check the bedrooms upstairs next. I didn't relish the prospect.

'Wait, shine the torch back,' Rachel said, pointing. 'There, on the floor.'

Picked out like a theatrical prop in the beam of light, an object was lying by a half-open door.

A woman's shoe.

It lay on its side, the ankle strap broken and the white leather mud-stained. I could hear Rachel breathing beside me, fast and tense. I shone the torch back on the doorway, trying to see through the gap into the room.

'Stacey?'

There was no answer. Rachel stayed close behind me as I went down the hall. I thought about telling her to stay where she was, but I knew she wouldn't take any notice. I put my hand on the door.

'Stacey?' I said again, gently pushing it open.

There were more cages in here, though not so many, and most of these were empty. A grubby tapestry hung on one wall, embroidered with the first verse of 'All Things Bright and Beautiful'. A large chesterfield stood with its back to the doorway, stuffing sprouting like fungus from the cracked leather.

A bare foot hung over the end. In the torchlight its toenails looked black, but I knew from seeing them in daylight they were varnished bright red.

'Stay here,' I told Rachel.

She didn't argue, but I wasn't trying to spare her. I knew from the unnatural stillness of the foot what I was going to find, and the fewer people who disturbed this place now the better.

I didn't want to go inside myself, but I had to make sure. I took a few more careful paces into the room, until I could see what was on the sofa.

In the light of the torch, Coker's daughter lay splayed and unmoving on the cushions. Her blond hair framed a face that was unnaturally swollen and dark. The open eyes bulged as though in surprise, the sclera shot through with broken blood vessels.

I shone the torch away, sickened. As the darkness hid her again, I took a few steadying breaths, shaken by what I'd seen. I'd known when I'd gone into the house that there was a good chance she'd be dead. I'd been prepared for that.

What I hadn't been prepared for was that Stacey Coker was naked from the waist down.

22

BLUE LIGHTS STROBED the darkness, casting a sapphire hue on the underside of the trees that crowded around the old house. Police cars and trucks lined the lane leading to it, squeezed into the undergrowth at each side to leave clear access. Floodlights had been set up in the garden, if it could be called that, casting moving shadows of the white-clad CSIs against the dilapidated walls.

I sat sideways in the open door of a police car, my feet resting on the wet ground outside. The rain had stopped, but the damp freshness of the air was polluted by exhaust fumes from the cars and generator. The white Land Rover had gone and so had Rachel, led away to give her statement as more police arrived. I didn't know if Edgar was still here or not. The last I'd seen of him was when he'd been taken from the Land Rover and put into a patrol car. His eyes were scared and uncomprehending as he stared at the bright lights and chaos transforming his home. As he shuffled past me there was a soft pattering sound, and I saw a growing wet patch spreading on his crotch. Even knowing what he'd done, I felt a stirring of pity.

Until I remembered the teenager's body sprawled on his sofa.

I hadn't given Rachel any details when I'd left the living room, but she'd seen enough from my face. It was a relief to go out into the fresh air and leave the squalor of the house behind, although

249

the image of what I'd seen still burned in my mind. I would have happily left Edgar locked inside the Land Rover until the police arrived, except that there was still the small matter of calling them first. The mobile reception was as fitful as ever, and I'd no idea how far we'd have to go to find a signal. In the end we were forced to get back in the car and drive until I could make the call.

It was a tense journey. Rachel drove while I kept a watch on the gangling figure in the back as I waited for a signal for my phone. He sat placidly enough, but after what I'd seen it felt as if we were sharing the car with an unpredictable animal. One that was all the more dangerous because it seemed so harmless.

We didn't have to go far before the signal bars flickered into life. Rachel and I both got out of the car while I phoned Lundy, not wanting to talk in front of Edgar. Late as it was, the DI answered. He sounded tired, and heaved a sigh as I told him what had happened, though without going into details.

'Ah, Christ. How bad is it?'

I glanced at where Rachel was leaning against the Land Rover. She looked small and lost, staring at the ground as the wind ruffled her hair. 'Very.'

Lundy told me to go back and stay outside the house until they got there. It seemed the most natural thing in the world to slip my arm around Rachel while we waited. She leaned against me word-lessly, and we stood like that until the first police car arrived. Lundy came half an hour later, by which time the house had been secured behind a flimsy barrier of flapping police tape. He stopped for a few words, asking if Rachel and I were all right. Then he went to talk to the CSIs and the rest of the crime scene team before disappearing into the house.

Rachel and I were separated shortly afterwards. No one suggested I leave as well, though there was no real reason for me to be there. Whatever had happened here, it wasn't anything a forensic anthropologist could help with. Frears got to the house soon after Lundy. The pathologist's smooth face looked puffy and pale above the blue coveralls, as though he'd not long been awake.

He favoured me with a tight smile as he walked past, snapping on a pair of gloves.

'Been keeping busy again, Hunter?'

I watched him disappear into the house as well. It was another twenty minutes before Lundy appeared in the doorway, his bulky shape recognizable even before he pulled down his hood and removed his mask. He stopped to speak with the crime scene manager, and I got to my feet by the police car as he came over.

'You were right. Looks like she was strangled,' he said without preamble. His face was red and flushed, with deep lines where the mask had dug in.

I'd expected as much from the dead girl's congested features and bloodshot eyes. 'How long has she been dead?'

'Frears thinks between nine and twelve hours.'

That meant she'd been killed some time that afternoon. While I'd been getting jittery about dinner with Rachel, Edgar had been choking the life out of Coker's daughter.

Lundy unzipped his coveralls and fished inside a pocket for a tissue. He blew his nose noisily before continuing.

'There are other injuries as well. She got bruising on her head by her right temple, and there's more on her torso. Probably from the crash rather than here.'

I nodded: she'd have been thrown about as the car had rolled, and the injury to her head was in keeping with her striking it against the door of the car.

'Does Frears think she was assaulted?'

The big shoulders lifted in a shrug. 'There's no visible trauma to indicate it, but he won't know for sure until the post-mortem. For her and her family's sake I hope not, but you've got to assume the intent was there or she'd still be fully clothed.' Lundy sighed again and shook his head. 'Tell me again what happened.'

I went through the encounter with Edgar, including his agitated state and what he'd said when Rachel tried to question him. He listened without comment until I'd finished.

'If Stacey Coker came out of the bend and found Holloway in

front of her it'd explain why she went off the road. And if he saw the car headlights in the water he must have been nearby. They wouldn't have stayed on long.'

'Holloway?'

'That's his name. Edgar Holloway.' Lundy looked at the floodlit house. 'This is going to open up a whole new can of worms.'

'Because of his daughter, you mean?'

His eyebrows climbed. 'How'd you hear about that?'

I explained how Rachel had told me about the disappearance of Edgar's young daughter. The DI rubbed his jawline with the back of a hand.

'Must be what? Twenty-odd years ago now. The Rowan Holloway case was one of the first cases I worked on when I moved here. Caused quite a stir locally. Nine years old, went out one morning in the school holidays and didn't come back. We never did find out what happened to her, although . . .'

'Although . . . ?'

He smiled, wearily. 'I was about to say although her father was suspected at one point. He was home by himself the day Rowan disappeared, so inevitably he came under scrutiny. I'll need to dig out the file, but from what I can recall the investigating officers marked him down as an oddball. Reclusive even then, didn't like mixing with people. His wife worked in a shop in Cruckhaven, and I think he was a naturalist of some kind. Wrote text books for schools, or something like that. Thought nothing of letting their daughter wander off by herself in the Backwaters, so they got a lot of flak when she went missing.'

'Was Edgar ever charged?'

'No, there was never any proof, and her teachers thought the girl seemed happy enough at home. He had some sort of break-down afterwards, as far as I can remember, and the investigation sort of fizzled out after that.'

'Did his daughter have blond hair?'

'Now you mention it, she did. But it seems a stretch to think he mistook Stacey Coker for his daughter just because they'd both got

252

hair "like sunshine", or whatever. Rowan was only nine when she disappeared. She'd be in her thirties now.'

'I'm not sure Edgar would be capable of rationalizing it like that. And it was dark, so perhaps at first all he saw was the blond hair. That might have been enough for him to pull her out of the creek and bring her back here.'

Lundy dug in his pocket again and produced a packet of antacids. 'Maybe, but that's one for the psychiatrists. And if Stacey Coker reminded him of his daughter, it makes what happened in there even worse, wouldn't you say?'

That unpalatable thought hung between us for a few moments. 'You said earlier about opening a can of worms,' I said. 'You didn't just mean because of Rowan Holloway, did you?'

'No.' He crunched down on a couple of antacids. 'People are going to be asking now why Holloway was allowed to fall off the radar like he has. Social services are going to have some explaining to do, because he obviously shouldn't have been left on his own out here. And after this we can't ignore the possibility that he might be responsible for more than his daughter's disappearance. This is going to stand the Emma Derby investigation on its head.'

Jesus. I rubbed my eyes, too tired to think straight. 'You seriously think he could have something to do with that?'

'God knows. But we'll need to search every inch of this place. Inside and out.' He shook his head, considering the shells and pieces of driftwood dotted like markers throughout the overgrown garden. 'I don't look forward to that. We're not going to know if there's any human remains under there without digging up the whole lot. It was bad enough with the dog's grave at Villiers' house, and this place is like a bloody pet cemetery.'

I hadn't thought about that, but he was right. Aside from the tangle of shrubs and briars that would have to be cleared, the rotting animal carcasses buried here would confuse a cadaver dog.

But the mention of Emma Derby had reminded me of something else. 'Has Rachel said anything about the motorbike?'

'Not to me, but I haven't seen her since she went to give her statement. What motorbike?'

I'd rather Lundy had heard about it from her, but he needed to know. I told him about the photograph of the gleaming Harley-Davidson on the sand dune, and how Emma Derby's old boyfriend might have made a reappearance.

'Let me get this straight, she's only just noticed the sea fort *now*?' he said, frowning.

'She recognized the bike but thought it must be an old picture. And the fort's hard to make out. It's only because you can see it in some of the other beach shots that you can tell what it is.'

I heard myself sounding defensive. Lundy sighed. 'And she's no idea when it might have been taken?'

I shook my head, but he wasn't expecting me to answer. He passed his hand across his face.

'Wonderful. So what else did she say about this . . .'

'Mark Chapel. Only that her sister knew him in London and he used to produce music videos. And he owned a Harley like the one in the photograph.'

'Like it or the same one?'

'I don't know, but I didn't want to ask too much. She knows we've found another body, and I didn't want her making the connection.'

Lundy looked baffled. 'Connection? You've lost me.'

'Between the motorbike in the photograph and the biker jacket and boots the body from the creek was wearing.'

Comprehension spread across his face. 'Christ, I'm getting slow. OK, I'll need to take a look at the photo myself. And we'll see what else we can find out about this Mark Chapel character. Might come to nothing, but we need to rule him out, if nothing else.'

He looked past me and straightened, making a visible effort to throw off his fatigue.

'Here's the chief.'

I turned and saw Clarke making her way between the parked police vehicles. Her pale trench coat was unbuttoned and flapped around her as she marched towards us. She looked tired and dishevelled, but mainly annoyed as she stopped in front of me.

'Frears is still in the house, ma'am,' Lundy said, resorting to formality.

She gave him the barest nod, but it was clear I was the main focus of her attention. The frizzy ginger hair threatened to escape from the plain black band that held it back as she glared at me, tight-mouthed.

'Just so I'm clear, Dr Hunter, can you explain to me why you went in the house without calling us first?'

'I knew there might be an injured girl who needed help.'

'And you thought you were the best person to give it? Rather than, oh, say, the emergency services?'

'The emergency services weren't here. I was.'

'So because of that you decided to contaminate a crime scene.'

My own patience was wearing thin. I was tired as well, and I'd spent the past hour replaying what I'd done, wondering if I could have prevented any of this from happening.

'I didn't know it was a crime scene when I went in. I was careful where I walked, I didn't touch anything, and I came out as soon as I realized. So yes, I'm very sorry. But not as sorry as I'd be if I'd let someone die while I stood out here twiddling my thumbs.'

I realized I'd raised my voice. Lundy fidgeted uncomfortably as Clarke stared, the pale-lashed eyes cold under the ginger hair. Here it comes, I thought.

There was a noise from the house. A stretcher was being carried out, the black body bag on it dully reflecting the flashing blue lights as it was taken to the black mortuary van. Clarke watched it for a moment, then sighed.

'I need to speak to Frears.'

Lundy gave me a look that could have been either warning or reproach before he went with her. As they disappeared towards the floodlit house there was the sound of the black van's door being slammed. I looked around to see a medic closing the other door as well, shutting the interior and its cargo from view.

I was driven back to the boathouse, but it was still after three before I got to bed. Even then I couldn't sleep. It might have been my imagination, but I thought I could still smell the unwashed animal odour of Edgar Holloway. And whenever I closed my eyes I could see Stacey Coker's swollen face, the terrible stillness of the blood-red eyes. I lay awake through first the boisterous barking of the seals, then the gulls' dawn clamour. The sky was already lightening by the time I finally drifted into an uneasy sleep.

When my alarm woke me it seemed as though I hadn't slept at all. After a long shower and a rushed breakfast I felt a little more human. Rachel didn't pick up when I tried calling her, but she'd had a late night as well. I'd no idea what time she would have got back, and she'd have an unenviable morning breaking the news to Jamie.

Leaving a message to say I hoped she was OK, I drove to the mortuary. No one had told me not to, so until I heard otherwise I was going to carry on with my job. There was no sign of Frears, but he'd either worked through the night on Stacey Coker's post-mortem, or would be preparing to carry it out that morning.

I didn't envy him.

It meant I could work without interruption on my own, which suited me. Lan offered to help, but I assured her I could manage. Changing into scrubs and a rubber apron, I went into the cool and ordered quiet of the examination room and shut the door behind me with something like relief.

The overnight simmering had finished the process months of submersion in the creek had started. What soft tissue there had been left had now fallen from the joints and bones of the body from the barbed wire. I systematically removed them from the foul stew the detergent solution had become, then rinsed them off and set them aside to dry. It gave me the chance to examine the sternal rib ends, auricular surface and pubic symphysis, all bones that would help reveal how old this individual had been when he died. While I worked, I tried not to speculate too much about Emma

Derby's motorbike-owning former boyfriend. This could still be someone else, and the biker jacket and boots might be a coincidence after all.

If it wasn't we'd know soon enough.

As I removed the cleaned bones, I was tempted to spend longer examining the multiple fractures the skeleton had sustained, especially to the right leg. But they could wait. If what I'd seen in the X-rays was borne out, there was no question of what I needed to pay attention to first.

The real story lay in the cranium.

Useful as X-rays are, they're only two-dimensional. Where there's extensive trauma, damage caused by one injury can overlie another on the film, making it difficult to get a clear picture of what has happened. That was the case here. The day before, I'd removed the already loose and badly damaged mandible before putting the skull in to soak. Even before the jawbone had been properly cleaned, I could see the deep bifurcation in its centre that in life would have given the owner a well-dimpled chin. Setting it aside, I'd cut between the second and third vertebrae with a fine-bladed scalpel to sever the vertebral column. Then I'd put the cranium to macerate in a pan by itself. I didn't want any small bone fragments that detached from it to become mixed up with those from anywhere else.

Now, rinsing it off, I noted that the CSI hadn't been far off the mark when he'd said the injuries were caused by a boat propeller. Some kind of fast-moving rotary blade had gone through the delicate facial bones like balsa. Fast moving because the kerf – the cut to the bone left by the blade – was clean-edged, with very little splintering. And rotary because of the shape of the cuts: shallower at either end but deepening in the middle, suggestive of a circular motion.

The wounds ran parallel to each other, more or less horizontally across the face. One several inches long had sliced across the upper arch of the eye orbits and what's known as the nasion, the recessed section of the nasal bridge that sits between them. Another cut ran

257

just below it, bisecting the zygomatic bones of both cheeks. Below this the cuts ran much closer together, in places merging so it was hard to distinguish individual wounds. Most of the lower nasal area had broken into several pieces, while the maxilla – the upper jawbone that would have housed the front teeth – had fragmented completely below the nose. Looking at pieces of this now, I could see the bone had an unusual porosity about it, giving it almost the appearance of pumice.

It would take painstaking reconstruction to determine what had happened. A lot of bone was missing, loose shards falling away or picked off by aquatic scavengers. Very few teeth remained in their sockets, and none that did were intact, sheared through by the spinning blade's passage.

But it was the cuts themselves I wanted to examine. I mixed up a batch of silicon putty and carefully spread it into the two most distinct cuts. Once it had dried, each cast would show the kerf in detail, revealing what sort of pattern the blade had left on the bone. Leaving the putty to set, I turned my attention to an object that had sunk to the bottom of the vat. This was what I'd first noticed on the X-rays, almost hidden among the black-and-white jumble of overlying injuries. It was a thin, leaf-like bone, one edge rough where it had been snapped off from the skull.

I was still studying it when the door opened and Frears breezed in.

'Afternoon, Hunter. Wasn't sure if you'd be here today.'

I set the wafer of bone down, wondering if Clarke had said something about taking me off the case. 'Why not?'

'Don't look so serious! I meant after all the drama last night. You're a glutton for punishment, I'll give you that.'

I relaxed, telling myself not to be so jumpy. 'Have you done the post-mortem?'

'On the girl? Finished it before lunch.' The pathologist seemed in a better humour today. 'You can probably guess most of it. Bruising on the throat, crushed windpipe and broken hyoid, all consistent with strangulation. The other injuries were in keeping with a car accident. Cracked ribs, abrasions, bruising. There was a hairline fracture to the skull but no internal bleeding. She'd have had a nasty concussion but it wouldn't have proved fatal.'

'Would she have been conscious?'

'Hard to say. I doubt she'd have been in any condition to get herself out of the car. But if you mean was she conscious when she was strangled, that's anyone's guess. No signs of a struggle, though, which suggests not.' He took a pair of surgical gloves from a box and began pulling them on. 'In fact that was the only odd thing about it. Rather surprising given her state of undress, but there was no evidence of sexual assault. Nothing suggestive of rape or even recent sexual activity. It seems our boy looked but didn't touch.'

That was something, although it would be cold comfort to Stacey Coker's family. I thought about the pathetic wretch huddled in the back of the Land Rover the night before, the terrified way he'd skittered away from us in the road. How Rachel had soothed him, like a child or frightened animal. *Don't worry, he's harmless.*

Frears snapped the tight nitrile gloves into place and went over to where the cranium sat in a metal tray. 'So, how are you getting on with our friend from the barbed wire? Been taking casts of the propeller wounds, I see?'

'They weren't made by a propeller.'

That got his attention. 'Really?'

'They were made by something spinning very fast, but they're more like grooves than cuts,' I told him. Wounds from a boat propeller are made by each of the individual blades repeatedly striking the bone. That wasn't what I'd seen here. 'It looks like they were caused by some sort of solid disc.'

'Curiouser and curiouser. How long till the casts are set?'

'They should be ready now.'

I went to the skull and gently tapped the silicon putty. It was solid, so I carefully eased out the rubbery impressions. In cross-section the kerf was square, the sides meeting the flat bottom at right angles. The inside surfaces of the wounds were rough, show-ing clear signs of abrasion.

I took a pair of calipers to measure the width of one cast while Frears examined another. He gave a grunt of surprise. 'I see what you mean. I'd expect the kerf from a propeller to be smooth, but this is rough as a bear's arse. Almost like it's been sandpapered. Some sort of power tool, do you think? Circular saw, perhaps.'

'I was thinking more of an angle grinder,' I said, putting down the calipers. 'The cutting discs are abrasive and flat-edged, and seven millimetres is a standard width. That's the same as these wounds.'

'Being doing your homework, I see.' Frears nodded thought-fully. 'Yes, that'd do the trick. The wounds would superficially resemble those caused by a boat prop, so if the body was found it wouldn't automatically be flagged as suspicious. Although that begs the question of how our man came by his broken bones. And if we're ruling out a boat accident, we have to consider the possi-bility that he might have been alive when someone took an angle grinder to his face. Now there's a cheery thought.'

It had occurred to me as well. Post-mortem bone is dry and brittle, and reacts differently to trauma compared to bone that's still living. The fractures and cuts here looked to have been inflicted when the bone still had some elasticity, which meant the trauma was peri-mortem, or from around the time of death.

Unfortunately, it could be difficult to determine if that meant just before the victim died, or just after. I'd no illusions about the cruelty some people are capable of, and grim as the possibility raised by Frears might be, I'd seen worse. But I didn't think that was the case here.

'I doubt it,' I said. 'I've not had a chance to examine them properly yet, but the breaks to the tibia and fibula don't look like they were caused by him being struck with anything. I'd say they were the result of a shearing force. Something kept the lower leg immobile while the rest of it was wrenched sideways, hard enough to dislocate the hip as well as snap the bones. Then there's the broken neck. Two of the vertebrae are fractured, but the skull isn't. How could he have been hit hard enough to break his neck without trauma to the cranium?'

The pathologist picked up the skull. 'You're thinking it was a fall?'

'I can't see what else it could be. Coming off a motorbike at speed or being hit by a car might cause similar injuries, but there was no sign of any abrasions to the body or clothing,' I said. 'A fall's more likely, and if the lower leg hit something or got caught on the way down the momentum would have snapped it. The rest of the fractures are all consistent with an impact. My guess is his skull was cushioned by an arm or shoulder when he landed, but the sudden whiplash snapped his neck.'

Frears was nodding. 'And then someone took an angle grinder to his face to try to conceal his identity and make it look like he was hit by a boat.'

'I think there might be more to it than that.' I picked up the fragile, leaf-shaped piece of bone. 'What do you make of this?'

Frowning, Frears took it from me. 'It's part of the vomer. What of it?'

'It was pushed up into the cranium.'

'I don't . . . Oh.' Still holding the bone, he hurried to where the X-rays were clipped to the light board. He stared at it for a moment, then shook his head. 'Well, bugger me. That's something you don't see every day.'

The vomer is a thin, vertical blade of bone that sits at the rear of the nose and divides the nasal opening in half. On the X-rays it had been obscured by the more obvious facial trauma, hidden behind the jumbled mosaic of damaged bones. But it could just be made out, a ghostly white shape with its tip still embedded in the frontal lobe of the decomposed brain.

'When I first saw it I assumed it must have been forced up by a spinning blade or disc,' I told him. 'But that would have sliced straight through the vomer as well, not pushed it inwards. And certainly not at an upward angle like that.'

'Quite.' Frears sounded annoyed with himself. 'Can't see it happening in a fall, either.'

Neither could I. The body would have to have landed face-first, which would have caused extensive trauma in itself. I'd seen no sign of that. And it would have taken a powerful blow at exactly the right angle to drive the vomer up into the frontal lobe like this. Which made this either a freakish accident . . .

Or an execution.

23

'PALM STRIKE.'

Lundy paused to blow his nose. It was late afternoon, the sun breaking out fitfully from behind dark clouds. The DI sat in the passenger seat of my car, still looking a little drowsy from his endoscopy. I'd called him to brief him on the day's findings, forgetting he'd told me he was due to have it today. I'd begun outlining what I'd found when he'd apologetically told me he was still at the hospital and couldn't talk freely. He'd been given a sedative for the procedure and told not to drive for the rest of the day, he said. His wife, who was supposed to be picking him up, had been delayed collecting their granddaughter from an after-school class.

The hospital was close to the mortuary, and I'd done as much as I was going to for the day. The cleaned bones of the barbed wire victim had been rinsed and left to dry. I'd taken a preliminary look at the most significant of them, especially those with fractures or damage, but I'd decided against carrying on with the reassembly until the morning. Lack of sleep and the events of the previous night were beginning to catch up with me. It was better to leave it until I was rested than miss anything through a lapse of concentration.

So I told Lundy I'd drive him home. I was glad of the company, and the distraction. I hadn't heard anything from Rachel. I'd tried calling her again but she still wasn't picking up. I didn't want to crowd her, knowing she'd have enough to deal with in the aftermath of Stacey Coker's murder. Even so, her silence was preying on my mind.

Lundy looked tired when I picked him up outside the hospital entrance. When I asked how it had gone he'd just said, 'Oh, fine,' with the air of someone not wanting to talk about it. Instead he'd asked if I'd found out anything else from the remains.

He'd perked up noticeably when I told him about the vomer, and explained how only either a very precise or a very lucky blow could have caused an injury like that.

'Palm strike?' I queried.

'It's the sort of thing you pick up if you're taught hand-to-hand combat or some types of martial arts. Instead of breaking your fingers punching someone, you ram the heel of your hand into their face.' He raised his own hand to demonstrate: palm thrust out, fingers curled back in a vague claw shape. 'Nasty, but if you want to stop someone getting frisky it'll do the job. An ex-para showed me when I was in the TA, along with a few other dirty tricks.'

'You were in the Territorial Army?'

He chuckled. 'There was less of me back then. You want the third exit at the roundabout.'

Lundy had assured me I wouldn't need the satnav. He didn't live far out of my way, but traffic was heavy.

'So a palm strike could cause an injury like that?' I asked once I'd negotiated the roundabout.

'Theoretically, but I've never come across it myself. You're sure someone didn't just stave it in with a club or something?'

I couldn't say for sure what the dead man had been hit with, but I doubted it was a weapon of any sort. Although the damage to the lower face made it hard to be certain, anything hard-edged like a brick or hammer would have been more likely to leave depression fractures bearing its shape.

'I don't think so.'

'Then if we're talking bare hands, a palm strike sounds most likely,' Lundy said. 'But you'd have to hit someone bloody hard, and at exactly the right angle to manage that. Ordinarily, you're more likely to wind up with a bloody nose or broken front teeth.'

'This did more than break his teeth. It looks like the jawbone immediately below his nose actually caved in,' I told him, slowing as a lorry pulled into my lane without indicating. 'A lot of the bone from there is missing, and what's left looks spongier than it should.'

'Spongier?'

'It was full of tiny holes, like cinder toffee. Could be a genetic bone defect, or perhaps he'd had some sort of infection in it. Either way, something weakened the structure enough for a palm strike – assuming that's what it was – to make it collapse and push the vomer up into his brain.'

Lundy nodded thoughtfully. 'So we're looking at that as probable cause of death?'

I'd discussed that with Frears, without reaching any conclusion. 'Hard to say. It's not a survivable injury, but it doesn't mean that's what actually killed him. If I'm right about the fractures, the fall would have been fatal by itself. My guess is the blow to the face came first, followed by the fall, because there'd be no point hitting anyone if they had those sorts of injuries. But I can't tell you how much time there was between one and the other.'

'At least it means he was dead or unconscious before someone ground half his face off,' Lundy said with a grimace. 'Still, you can see the thinking behind it. You kill someone in a fight, accidentally or otherwise, so you camouflage the evidence behind other injuries. Try to make the death look like a run-in with a boat and destroy any identifying features in one go. Then tangle the body in barbed wire and sink it in a deep section of the Backwaters, hoping if it is found that it'll look like an accident.'

'It was never going to work,' I said. 'Not once the body was given a proper examination.'

'No, but you've got to hand it to them for trying. Next left here.'

I took the turning he'd indicated. We were into a residential area now, pleasant semi-detached houses with cherry trees lining the grass verges. The pink blossom gave the street a celebratory look, like the setting for a wedding.

Lundy was stroking his moustache, a sign I'd come to recognize meant he was thinking. 'What else have you been able to find out?'

'Not much. He was tall, an inch or two over six foot, and between thirty and forty years old. But that's as much as I can say for now.'

'Any thoughts on how long the body had been in the water?'

'Probably several months, but without knowing if it was drifting or submerged on the barbed wire the whole time that's not much more than a guess.'

'For the sake of argument let's assume it was on the barbed wire. How long would you say then?'

I thought for a while before answering. 'Bearing in mind it's been winter and then a cold spring, somewhere between six and eight months.'

Lundy nodded. 'Emma Derby went missing just under seven months ago.'

That fact hadn't escaped me.

'Any luck tracing her ex-boyfriend?' I asked, knowing where this was leading.

'Not yet. I put someone on to it but then I had to go and have that bloody tube shoved down my throat. I haven't even had chance to look at this photograph of the motorbike you told me about.'

'But you're thinking Villiers might have killed Mark Chapel as well as Emma Derby.'

'I'm thinking the stars certainly seem to be aligning that way. Obviously, if Chapel turns out to be alive we're back at square one. But adding Emma Derby's old boyfriend into the mix could explain a few things. I can't see Villiers reacting well to having a rival, so you've got a potential motive for murder right there. And a palm strike's the sort of thing he could have picked up from his military background. You don't have to like playing at soldiers to remember what you've been taught.'

He pointed at a house on the other side of the road.

'This is us. You can pull in by the driveway.'

I drew up to the kerb. Keeping the indicator on, I left the engine running, ready to set off again. The scent of cherry blossom and wet grass drifted into the car when Lundy opened the door, but he didn't get out.

'Thanks for the lift. You want to come in for a cuppa? My wife isn't back yet so I can break out my stash of biscuits without getting shouted at.'

'No thanks. I'd better get off.'

I didn't want to intrude into the policeman's home life, and I thought his wife would want to hear about his hospital visit when she came home. But Lundy stayed where he was.

'Actually, I'd appreciate it if you did.' Behind the glasses, the blue eyes were candid. 'There's something else I want to have a word about.'

The house wasn't what I'd expected. It was a post-war semi that had been renovated and extended. The front garden had been turned into a Mediterranean-style patio, while inside was bright and modern, with comfortable but contemporary furniture. I sat in a small conservatory while Lundy busied himself making tea in the adjacent kitchen. He'd waved away my offer of help.

'They only told me not to drive. I can still operate a kettle.'

He seemed in no hurry to get whatever he had to say off his chest, so I let him get round to it in his own time.

'How did Coker take the news?' I asked as he poured boiling water into two mugs.

'As you'd imagine. I went round to his house to break it to him last night.' He shook his head. 'Doesn't bear thinking about what he's going to be feeling today.'

No wonder Lundy was looking tired. It must have been nearly dawn by the time he got home. 'Does he have any other family?'

'A son in the army. He was overseas but he's back in the UK now. I dare say he'll get leave after this.'

I was glad Coker had someone. It wouldn't make it any easier, but it was better than being alone.

'What about Edgar?'

Lundy grimaced, bringing over the tea and a packet of chocolate biscuits. 'It's hard to get much sense out of him. There's going to have to be a full psychiatric assessment, but from what we can gather you were right about him being in the road. Stacey Coker must have swerved to avoid him – the tyre marks show it was a sudden manoeuvre – and cracked her head when the car went in the creek. We're fairly certain Holloway pulled her out and took her back to his house, but things get a bit confused after that.'

'Confused how?'

He spooned sugar into his tea. 'There's a question over why he'd rescue and take her back to his house if he was going to kill her. That could have been his intention all along, but it doesn't seem likely that he was capable of that sort of planning. So then you're left with the idea that he started off trying to help, maybe getting her mixed up in his mind with his own missing daughter, maybe not. Then once he got her back home and saw how helpless she was, he got carried away.'

'Is that what you think?'

He pursed his mouth to take a sip of hot tea. 'It's possible.'

'But?'

'There are a few things that don't add up. Did Frears tell you there's no sign that she was sexually assaulted?' He dabbed his moustache and set his mug down. 'Well, that was surprise number one. When you find a young woman who's been strangled and stripped from the waist down, it generally means one thing. And even if Holloway didn't assault her, we should have found some evidence from when he undressed her. But we didn't.'

That surprised me as much as the lack of assault. 'Nothing at all?'

'Not below the waist. There were Edgar's hairs on her sweater, and his fingerprints were on her watch, probably from either pulling her from the car or carrying her afterwards. But that's all. Even though her jeans had been unfastened rather than torn off there weren't any prints on the fastener or zip. And the gold chain she wore round her throat had been bunched up and twisted when she was strangled, but there wasn't even a partial fingerprint on it.'

'He could have worn gloves,' I said, although I doubted that it would even have occurred to Edgar to cover his tracks.

'The only gloves we've found were in his pockets, and they were a manky pair of mittens covered in bird muck. If he'd worn those there'd be traces all over her.'

An unpleasant feeling was uncoiling in my gut. 'So how do you explain it?'

'I don't. Not yet. And then there's the bruising on her throat. Have you seen the size of Holloway's hands? They're bony, but *big*. Like shovels.' Lundy held up his own hand, which was thick and stubby. 'His fingers are half as long again as mine, but the bruises we've found don't have anything like that sort of span. OK, that sort of thing is open to interpretation, maybe he bunched up his hands or something. But the measurements suggest she was strangled by someone with much smaller hands than his.'

Someone wearing gloves. The feeling in my gut was growing stronger. 'What would anyone else be doing at Edgar's house? And why kill an injured girl?'

'Beats me.' Lundy absently took a biscuit from the packet and dunked it in his tea. 'But if someone *was* there, chances were they wouldn't have been expecting to find Stacey Coker. Must've given them a nasty shock, seeing her. And, more to the point, if she was conscious she'd have seen them.'

I thought it through, examining the theory from different angles. They all pointed the same way.

'You think Leo Villiers killed her? So she wouldn't tell anyone?'

Lundy finished the biscuit and brushed the crumbs from his

moustache. 'Honestly? I don't know. It seems like we're starting to lay a lot of crimes at the door of a man we thought was dead a few days ago. But if we're right and he is still alive, then he's far and away the likeliest suspect. The notion of a third party killing Stacey Coker to keep her quiet makes more sense than Holloway pulling an injured girl from a car, carrying her all the way home and then strangling her. Or taking off her clothes without molesting her or leaving any traces of himself. That just doesn't sit right with me.'

Me neither. 'So the fact she'd been partially stripped . . .'

'Window dressing.' His tone was hard. 'Someone killed her and then staged it to send us haring off in the wrong direction. Same as they did with the body on the barbed wire, making it look like it had been hit by a boat.'

Lundy's scenario had an awful plausibility about it. Stripping Stacey Coker made it look as though her murder was sexually motivated. And Edgar was the perfect scapegoat. Not only had he already been under suspicion for his own daughter's disappearance decades earlier, he lacked the capacity to explain and perhaps even comprehend what had really happened. We'd assumed that when Rachel and I found him he was running from what he'd done. But if he'd returned home to find the girl he'd rescued dead and half naked, he could just as easily have been running from what he'd *found*.

Even so, there were still elements that didn't fit. I could believe that Leo Villiers might have faked his own death after murdering Emma Derby, perhaps even killed her ex-boyfriend as well. From there it wasn't a big leap to suppose that he'd also murdered Stacey Coker so she couldn't tell anyone he was still alive. That still left one unanswered question.

'What would Leo Villiers be doing at Edgar Holloway's house?' I asked.

Lundy offered me the packet of chocolate biscuits, helping himself to another when I declined. Evidently his throat wasn't bothering him too much after his procedure. 'Good question. When we were searching the place we found a shotgun cartridge at the back of one of the cupboards. Bismuth-tin number five bird-shot, same size and brand we found in Villiers' house. Looked as though it might have rolled out of a box and got stuck in a crack.'

'Just one cartridge?'

'Just one. No fingerprints on it, and no sign of any shotgun either. But the dust in the cupboard was disturbed, as though something fairly big had been moved from there recently. We're still searching the rest of the place. There're still some floorboards to take up and we've barely even started in the garden. If there was a shotgun, though, I doubt it was Holloway's.'

I thought about the ramshackle house, with its unlocked front door and nothing inside but cages of sick and injured animals. 'So Villiers was using it as . . . what? Some sort of safe house?'

'More likely somewhere he could hide things he didn't want anyone else knowing about. There's no sign that anyone except Holloway was living there, and no one in their right mind could stand the stink anyway. Christ knows how even Holloway managed to get by as long as he did. He wasn't getting any help from social services and the house didn't even have any power. There was an oil-fired generator but it hadn't been run for Christ knows how long. And what did he do for food?'

'He could have foraged.' There was no shortage of eels and shellfish, and I knew from Rachel that sea vegetables grew in the saltmarsh. Edgar would know the Backwaters better than anyone, and if he'd once been a naturalist he'd know what was edible and what wasn't.

'He could, but he'd find lean pickings during winter,' Lundy said. 'How'd he survive all this time? The doctor who checked him out said he was suffering from malnutrition, but didn't think it was long term. Plus we found empty food tins scattered about his house, so where did they come from?'

I was still berating myself for not realizing Edgar was mal-nourished. I'd seen how thin he was; I should have noticed the signs. 'Why would Villiers take him food?'

'Seems out of character, I know, but Holloway's not likely to have gone shopping for himself. Maybe Villiers took Edgar a few cans to keep him happy while he used his house to stash things like the shotgun. Ideal place when you think about it. Middle of nowhere, nobody to see you come and go, and nobody living there who's likely to make a fuss.'

That much made sense. And it would explain why Villiers had gone into the house while Stacey Coker was there. Lundy finished his biscuit and washed it down with a drink of tea.

'Of course, there's one thing wrong with that theory,' he said, setting down his cup. 'Why would someone like Leo Villiers even know Holloway existed, let alone know where he lived? Wealthy man like that, access to serious money and resources, what's he doing grubbing about in some recluse's hovel? Come to that, why is he still *here*? Why hasn't he left the country or buggered off somewhere miles away, where he wouldn't be recognized?'

'I don't know. Why?'

'I haven't a bloody clue.' Lundy took another chocolate biscuit and snapped it in half. 'It wasn't a rhetorical question, I've really no idea. And that niggles me. Makes me think we're coming at this from the wrong direction. You know those optical tricks, where things are arranged to look a certain way from a specific angle? It's all about perspective, and I can't shake the feeling that ours is wrong. We're looking at this the wrong way.'

He'd continued breaking the biscuit as he spoke, absently snapping it into smaller pieces he let drop on to the plate. His manner had changed, and I found myself growing suddenly wary.

'Is this what you wanted to talk to me about?' I asked.

He smiled and put the remaining pieces of biscuit down. 'Sort of,' he said, wiping his fingers. 'I'm poking more holes in my own theory, but it occurred to me the one body we still haven't found is Emma Derby's. She's at the centre of all this, so if it *is* her ex-boyfriend's body we found on the barbed wire, how come we didn't find hers there as well?'

That had been bothering me too. I had a bad idea I knew where this was leading. 'If there'd been two bodies there we'd have known right away it wasn't a boating accident. And we don't know for sure the one we found was Mark Chapel's.'

'True,' he conceded. 'But if it *does* turn out to be him it's going to raise awkward questions for some people. Leo Villiers might be the main suspect at the moment, but that doesn't mean there can't be others. The fact is, if Emma Derby's former boyfriend turns up dead we're going to have to take another look at her husband.'

'I thought you said Trask had an alibi? Didn't you clear him yourselves?'

'We did, and he does. But just because he's in the clear for his wife doesn't mean he is for her boyfriend as well. Not this one, anyway. At the very least we're going to have to interview him all over again. His son too, probably.'

Christ. As if the tensions in Creek House weren't bad enough. 'Why are you telling me?'

Lundy looked at me reprovingly over his glasses. 'I'm not daft. I know you're friendly with Rachel Derby.'

'I'm not going to compromise the inquiry, if that's what you're worried about.'

'Calm down, I'm not saying that. Good luck to you. I've got a lot of time for her. She could have stayed in Australia instead of coming over here to help a family she barely knew. Not many people would step up like she has.'

'Then what are you saying?' I asked, less heatedly.

'Just that it's one thing getting involved with a victim's family. A suspect's is something else. I'm not saying Trask is one yet, but that could change pretty quickly if it turns out to be Mark Chapel's body in the mortuary.' Lundy regarded me over the top of his glasses. 'If that happens you're going to find yourself with a potential conflict of interest. For the family's sake as well as your own, you might want to think about maintaining a bit of distance until this blows over. At the very least you need to find alternative lodgings. Staying at a property owned by a potential suspect . . . I don't have to tell you how that could look.'

He didn't. Much as I hated to admit it, Lundy was right. I felt angry, but more at myself for not seeing this coming.

'It's too late for me to find anywhere else tonight, but I'll go back to London tomorrow,' I said, a bitter taste in my mouth.

The drive to the mortuary would take longer, but there wasn't much left for me to do there anyway. I couldn't pretend there was a good reason for me to stay in the Backwaters any more. Not because of the case, anyway.

Lundy nodded, embarrassed now he'd spelled out the situation. It was a relief for both of us when we heard someone opening the front door.

'Sounds like them.' He straightened, hurriedly popping a last piece of biscuit into his mouth. He gave me a wink. 'Don't tell my wife.'

He was twisting the packet shut when the kitchen door opened and a small whirlwind burst in.

'Granddad, Gran says I can—'

The little girl broke off when she saw me. Lundy's face had split into a huge smile. 'There she is! How's my big girl?'

His granddaughter smiled but cast glances at me, suddenly shy. She had a pretty elfin face under a wild tangle of hair. Still beaming, Lundy picked her up and planted a kiss on her cheek before plonking her down on his knee.

'Kelly, this is Dr Hunter. He works with Granddad. Aren't you going to say hello?'

The girl lolled her head against him, looking at me from under long eyelashes. 'Hello.'

'She's not normally this quiet,' Lundy said, giving her a squeeze. The police officer had been replaced by a doting grandfather. 'We normally have to hand out earplugs.'

'Make the most,' his wife said, bustling in with a rain-spattered coat and shopping bags. She was an attractive woman, with short blond hair and a no-nonsense attitude. 'God, this weather! Sun one minute and rain the next. And they're forecasting storms tomorrow. You must be Dr Hunter?'

She gave me a smile as she took off her damp coat. 'David,' I said, getting to my feet to help with the shopping bags. Lundy had done the same, one burly arm still holding his granddaughter. His wife waved us both away.

'Thanks, I can manage. I'm Sandra. Pleased to meet you.'

'Dr Hunter came in for a cuppa after bringing me from the hospital,' Lundy told her, sitting down again.

'I expect he ate all the chocolate biscuits, as well,' she said, raising an eyebrow at the packet on the table.

Lundy looked affronted. 'Well, it seemed rude to stop him.'

'See what I have to put up with?' His wife's smile didn't hide her concern as she spoke again to her husband. 'How did it go?'

'Oh, fine.'

She gave a nod, and I knew the subject was closed until they were alone. 'Are you going to stay and eat with us, David? You'd be very welcome,' she asked, unpacking the bags.

'Thanks, but I was just about to leave.' I should get out of their way, and I needed time to think anyway. I turned to Lundy. 'Thanks for the tea. And the biscuits.'

'You're welcome. Just try not to eat them all next time.' He stood up, mock-groaning as he set his granddaughter down. 'The rate you're growing I'm not going to be able to lift you for much longer. You help your gran while I see Dr Hunter out.'

'He said his name was David!'

'He's a grown-up, he's allowed more than one.' Lundy came out with me into the hallway. He still seemed uncomfortable after our earlier conversation. He jangled the change in his pocket. 'You OK?'

'Fine.' I shrugged. 'Don't worry, there won't be a conflict of interest.'

'Glad to hear it. Anyway, I'll talk to you tomorrow.'

I felt tired and depressed as I drove back to the boathouse. I was already beginning to wonder if I'd done the right thing by committing myself to going back to London, but staying at the boathouse any longer would put me in an untenable position. I couldn't tell Rachel about any of the new developments, and yet keeping them from her felt as bad as lying.

But I couldn't just leave without giving her a reason. Or was I flattering myself that she'd really care? She'd got more to worry about than a man she'd only known for a few days.

There was something else bothering me as well. Lundy had said that Rachel could have stayed in Australia, that she didn't have to come over to help out the Trasks. Yet she'd told me she'd already been in the country for a friend's wedding when her sister went missing. I turned that over in my mind, not liking where it led.

Lundy didn't know Rachel was here when her sister disappeared.

I knew it didn't necessarily mean anything, that the DI might simply have forgotten. Or got his wires crossed, because the police would have checked her out along with the rest of the family as a matter of course.

Wouldn't they?

I flinched as the sudden trill of my phone jarred me from my thoughts. My stomach knotted when I saw Rachel's number on the display. I pulled over to the side of the road, earning an irate blare of the horn from the car behind as it shot past. Rain blustered against the windscreen as I looked down at the phone, letting it ring again before I answered.

'Can you talk?' Rachel sounded anxious, and I immediately forgot everything else.

'What's wrong?'

'Nothing . . . I don't know. Look, can you come over?' She lowered her voice, as though not wanting to be overheard. 'I've found something.'

24

IT HAD STOPPED raining when I pulled up outside Creek House. The light had almost gone from a gunmetal sky, and the gale of the previous night had died to a fretful breeze that set the marsh grass whispering like static. Although it wasn't yet high tide, the creek in front of the house looked ready to overflow, the seabirds on its choppy surface paddling furiously against the tidal drag. There was a restless quality to the landscape, a sense of pensiveness.

Or perhaps it was just me.

Rachel hadn't wanted to say much more on the phone, leaving me no wiser as to what she might have found. My imagination had rushed to fill the void on the drive over, competing with a guilty conscience because I was flouting Lundy's warning. In the end, it came down to a simple choice. Which was I going to put first, my continued role in the investigation, or Rachel's plea for help?

So here I was.

As I walked through the dripping branches of the silver birches, I told myself that technically I wasn't doing anything wrong. The body from the barbed wire still hadn't been identified, and Mark Chapel could still be alive and well somewhere. Until it was proved otherwise, Trask wasn't actually a suspect.

But the rationalization rang hollow, adding to the sense of

nagging disquiet that had formed after what Lundy had said about Rachel.

I went up the steps and knocked on the front door. I could hear music playing inside, and then Jamie opened it. He regarded me dully, then dropped his gaze.

'Dad's not here. He's with a client.'

His eyes looked reddened. With everything that had happened, I'd not really thought how Stacey Coker's death would have affected him.

'That's OK, I came to see Rachel,' I said, relieved that Trask was out.

Wordlessly, Jamie stood back to let me into the hallway. The music was coming from one of the ground-floor bedrooms: some sort of girl band by the sound of it. Jamie shut the front door and turned towards the room where the music was playing.

'Fay, turn it down!' When there was no response he went over and banged on the door. 'Are you deaf? I said turn it *down*!'

There was an indignant but inaudible reply from inside, then the volume was lowered.

'Yeah, you too,' Jamie said to the closed door, then turned to me. 'Rachel's upstairs. Go on up.'

'Thanks.' I hesitated. 'I'm sorry about Stacey.'

He looked startled, then almost resentful. Giving a grudging nod, he began to turn away and then stopped. 'What's going to happen to Edgar?'

'I don't know.'

'Will he go to prison?'

I hesitated, but honesty was better than evasion. 'I doubt it. He'll probably be sent to a psychiatric hospital.'

That was true regardless of whether he was guilty or not. It would be a long time before he saw the Backwaters again, whatever happened.

Jamie's hands were clenched into knots. He struggled for a moment, looking on the verge of tears.

'Did he . . . was she, you know . . .'

I started to say that I couldn't tell him anything; that I wasn't even part of that investigation. But I'd already crossed more lines than I cared to think about.

'I don't think so,' I said quietly.

His next words seemed to spill out.

'It's my fault. Everything, it's all my fault.'

'You can't blame yourself,' I said, knowing that was easier to say than do. No matter what anyone told him now, his abiding memory of Stacey would be watching her drive off after they'd argued.

'No? How do you know?' He dashed a hand across his eyes. 'Fuck! I just wish I could go *back* . . .'

There was nothing I could say to that, and empty platitudes wouldn't help. I watched Jamie go into his room, and then went upstairs to find Rachel.

I paused at the top. The open-plan kitchen and living area was empty. The huge floor-to-ceiling window cast a dark reflection, but the only person in it was me.

'Rachel?'

'Over here.'

Her voice came from behind the freestanding bookshelves at the far end of the large room. Behind them, partitioned off from the rest of the living area, was a small work studio. Rachel was sitting at a glass-topped desk, studying a laptop. The glow from its screen reflected back warmly from the huge window it shared with the dining and living area. Her smile seemed hesitant as I went over.

'I didn't hear you arrive,' she said.

'Jamie let me in.'

A shadow crossed her face. 'He's taking what happened to Stacey hard.'

'What about you?'

'Oh, I'm all right. You know.' She gave a small shrug. She was wearing faded jeans and a baggy cable knit sweater with the sleeves rolled. The black hair was pulled back from her face with

279

an Alice band. She looked natural and unselfconscious, and I felt a dull ache under my breastbone. 'It still hasn't sunk in, to be honest. Going to Edgar's house and . . . and everything, it all seems a bit unreal. I still can't believe he'd do something like that.'

He didn't. But I couldn't tell her that. 'I called you earlier,' I said.

'I know, I was going to phone back before, but . . .' She trailed off. 'Look, can I get you something to drink? I just made coffee, but there's beer or wine?'

'Just coffee, thanks.'

Her unease added to my own. I followed her into the kitchen, standing silently while she poured steaming black coffee into a mug from a cafetière. 'Milk, no sugar, right?'

'That's right.'

She added milk and handed me the mug. I sipped the hot liquid, my curiosity growing as she crossed to the top of the stairs and looked down. Music still played from the lower floor, but no one was in sight. Satisfied, she led me back behind the bookshelves. They made an effective partition, hiding us from anyone coming up the stairs, but with enough gaps between the rows of architectural text books and journals for us to see anyone who came up.

'Grab a chair,' Rachel said, sitting down at the desk. I pulled over a lacquered wood dining chair. 'Sorry for all the mystery, but I wanted to talk to you in private. I'd have come to the boathouse, but Andrew's visiting a client in Exeter. And after what's happened I didn't think it was fair to leave Jamie to babysit Fay.'

'OK,' I said, waiting.

She took a deep breath, her eyes going to the open laptop. From where I sat I could only glimpse its screen. The blue glow gave the enclosed space the private, meditative feel of a library.

'I told the police about the motorbike photograph,' she said. 'You know, that it might belong to Emma's ex, and that it was taken around here.'

I said nothing, but my guilt went up a notch.

'They're looking into it, but I got to wondering if Emma had any other photos of Mark kicking around. Ones she hadn't framed. You remember I told you we'd had our computers stolen in the burglary? Most of Emma's pictures were stored on them, and we can't access any cloud back-ups because Andrew doesn't have her password. But she had a few boxes of hard-copy prints, so this morning I started going through them. I found these.'

She slid a plain cardboard folder across the desk. I opened it and took out the thin sheaf of glossy photographs. The top one was of a tall man in tight black jeans and T-shirt. He was in his mid-thirties, good-looking and well built, with tousled brown hair and a heavy stubble. There was a cockiness about him even in the photograph, and more than a hint of narcissism in the not-so-casual pose, arms folded to accentuate his biceps as he grinned at the camera.

'That's Mark Chapel,' Rachel said. 'It's an old photo but she obviously hung on to it.'

I would have known who it was. Although it was hard to gauge from a photograph, he looked tall, probably a couple of inches over six feet. But it was the stubbled chin that clinched it for me. Mark Chapel had a strong, heavily pronounced jawline, slightly flared at the angle of the base and with a deep, photogenic dimple in its centre.

I'd seen one just like it earlier, on the mandible belonging to the body pulled from the creek.

I went to the next photograph. At first I thought it was a smaller version of the motorbike print from the boathouse. It showed the same gleaming machine standing on the sand dune, the same criss-crossing of contrails in the deep sky. Then I looked closer and realized it wasn't quite the same: the vapour trails were more diffuse than I remembered, and the angle of the shot was subtly different.

I leafed through the next few photographs. Each of them was a slight variant of the same shot.

'Emma used to call them her outtakes,' Rachel said. 'That's why she preferred digital to film. She could shoot as many as she liked, and then print the ones that came out best. If you look at the last two you can see the sea forts much more clearly.'

She was right: in the final two bike photographs the three surviving towers of the sea fort were plainly visible in the background, rising from the waves like a scene from *War of the Worlds*.

'And you're sure it's the fort here?'

'I'm certain. Here, take a look.'

She spun the laptop round so I could see. On the screen was a website about the Maunsell sea forts. It showed a photograph of the same arrangement of three towers I remembered from going out to the Barrows with Lundy, but in much better detail. The fort was a remarkable structure. Each of its derelict towers was an angular, box-like structure supported on four spindly legs that sloped inwards like a pyramid. Only one of them was still intact, the other two having partially collapsed over the years. A caption under the image read, *Remaining towers of the Maunsell army fort off the mouth of the Saltmere estuary.*

'It's the same fort you can see behind the motorbike,' Rachel said. 'And I found this as well.'

She shuffled through the photographs from the folder and selected one.

'See? You can make out the bike's number plate on this. I thought the police could use it to confirm if it's Mark's. Even if he doesn't know anything the police will probably want to talk to him.'

I was sure they would, if his remains hadn't been found decomposing on the barbed wire. But Rachel didn't know anything about that. As far as she was concerned, the body from the creek bore no connection to her missing sister, and Mark Chapel was still alive.

'Is something wrong?' she asked.

'No, I was . . . just thinking that Lundy will want to see these.'

Not looking at her, I put the motorbike prints to one side and turned to the remaining photographs. There were around a dozen, all of them taken out at sea and looking back towards the shore at a large Victorian house surrounded on three sides by trees. The viewpoint threw me for a moment, but then I recognized the distinctive bay windows of Leo Villiers' estuary home. The photographs varied from long shots of the entire house to zoomed-in close-ups. Some of these showed the terrace, but most were of individual windows through which the rooms could be seen.

Rachel was leaning against my arm to see the photographs as well. 'Do you recognize it? It's Leo Villiers' house.'

She looked at me expectantly. Making an effort to concentrate, I leafed through the photographs again. There were no people in any of the shots, and they had the rushed look of snaps rather than the poster-art feel of Emma Trask's other photographs.

'Sorry, I don't get it. Am I missing something?'

'Doesn't anything strike you as odd about them?'

I went through the photographs once more, seeing no more than last time. They just looked like reference shots, probably from when Emma Derby had been hired to redecorate Villiers' house.

'No, should it?'

Rachel looked disappointed. 'Where do you think they were taken from?'

I looked again. The photographs were all looking back towards shore, obviously taken from out at sea. 'From a boat, I expect.'

'That's what I thought at first. But look at the *angle*. It's too high up.' Rachel sounded excited. 'You couldn't get that sort of vantage point from a boat. And the sea around the estuary mouth is too clogged up with sandbanks for anything bigger to get close enough to take these.'

She was right. I thought back to when I'd been to the house when the dog's grave had been found, trying to visualize the view out to sea. It didn't take long.

'You think she took them from the sea fort?' I said.

'She must have. There's nothing else out there but water.'

Rachel's face was flushed. She looked pleased with herself. I turned back to the laptop, looking at the photograph on the fort website. Even the sole tower that hadn't collapsed looked in poor condition, a rusted hulk stained with salt marks.

'They look derelict. Aren't they sealed up?' I asked, doubtfully.

'I've no idea,' Rachel said. 'They're supposed to be, but I've never been out there. I don't think anyone has, not since it was a pirate radio station back in the sixties.'

'So why would Emma have gone out to an old fort?'

'I don't know. Maybe she went with Mark Chapel. He was in the music business, he'd have loved that whole pirate radio thing. The point is she obviously *did* go. You've seen the photographs: where else *could* they be taken from?'

I couldn't fault her logic, I just couldn't see that it mattered. 'OK, so she took photographs of Leo Villiers' house from one of the towers. What does that prove?'

Rachel shook her head, forehead creased in frustration. 'Maybe nothing, but ever since I found these photos I can't stop thinking about it. Emma was always impulsive, and taking herself and her camera off somewhere like that without telling anyone would be just like her. What if she had an accident, or managed to get inside and then got locked in? I know it sounds stupid, but the police never found any trace of her. What if this is why?'

It didn't sound stupid, but Rachel didn't have the whole picture. As far as she was concerned, Leo Villiers' body had been found in the estuary. She didn't know he'd apparently faked his own death, and might even have murdered Stacey Coker. Or that it looked as though her sister's ex-boyfriend Mark Chapel was also dead, his face ground off and his body dumped in the creek less than a mile from this house.

So much for assuring Lundy there wouldn't be a conflict of interest.

I looked up, and felt a shock when I saw a face staring back at me through the window. It was my own, I realized a second later, my reflection caught alongside Rachel's in the blackened glass.

'Have you mentioned any of this to anyone else?' I asked.

'Not yet. Andrew's been out all day, and there's no point

worrying him if it turns out to be nothing. I almost phoned Bob Lundy, but I wanted to make sure I wasn't grasping at straws. Do you think I am?'

No, I didn't. I didn't know how a derelict sea fort figured in any of this, but it was another potential lead. And I hated that Rachel had taken me into her confidence when I couldn't be as honest with her.

'I think you should tell Lundy,' I said.

'You think he'll take it seriously?' she asked doubtfully, picking up the photographs again.

'I think he needs to know.'

I looked down at the photographs without seeing them. The pressure that had been building up in me ever since the conversation with Lundy made it hard to think about anything else.

Rachel was watching me. 'What is it? Is something wrong?'

Just ask her. 'When your sister went missing . . . You told me you were over here. In the UK.'

She looked puzzled. 'That's right, for a friend's wedding. It was in Poole.'

'Lundy seemed to think you were still in Australia.'

I watched her expression change, puzzlement deepening to something else as a flush rose up her neck. 'Well, I wasn't. I went through all this with the police at the time.'

'OK.' It was hard to meet her stare now. 'I just wondered why he didn't know.'

'Maybe because it wasn't him I told, it was some PC. I don't expect Lundy can remember every little detail. Or maybe he didn't think it was important. I mean, he's only a DI, what does he know?'

I should never have said anything, I realized, not without thinking it through. 'I didn't mean to—'

'If you like I can dig out hotel receipts. Would you like to check my plane ticket as well?' She didn't give me a chance to answer. 'Jesus *Christ*, are you *serious*? You think I did something to Emma? Or Leo Villiers? Or both of them, perhaps!'

'No, of course not.'

'Then why did you ask?'

Her face had darkened. She seemed close to tears, but more from anger than anything else. I shrugged helplessly. 'Because . . .' *Because I had to. Because I've been fooled before.* 'It was a mistake.'

'A *mistake*?'

There was a sound from the stairs. Jamie had come up, probably drawn by the noise. He gave me a flat look before speaking to Rachel.

'Everything OK?'

'Everything's fine.'

He gave me another look before turning and going back downstairs. My face was burning as I rose to my feet. 'I'd better go.'

'Yes, I think you had.'

Neither of us spoke as we went downstairs. The flush had subsided to twin patches of colour in her cheeks as Rachel opened the front door. I hesitated.

'I'm going back to London tomorrow.'

'Oh.' There was a flicker of something, then her face closed down. 'Andrew'll sort out the bill for the boathouse. You can post the key through the letterbox when you've locked up.'

Feeling shell-shocked, I stepped out into the damp night air. Anything I said right then would only make things worse, but I hated to leave like this. The wind was still fitful, carrying the threat of more rain and a saline tang from the sea as I turned to her.

'Bye,' Rachel said.

The door shut with finality.

I kept replaying what had just happened as I trudged back through the copse, as though that would somehow change the outcome. *Idiot, idiot, idiot.* Christ, what had I been thinking, blurting it out like that? Well, at least Lundy didn't need to worry about a conflict of interest any more. I doubted Rachel would even want to speak to me again.

Lost in my thoughts, I almost walked into the man coming the other way through the trees. Trask stopped on the path, seeming as surprised to see me as I was him. He had a battered leather satchel slung over a shoulder and a tubular drawing holder tucked under his arm. The external light from the house made his face look more deeply etched than ever.

'Here again?' he said, sounding guarded.

'I came to see Rachel.'

'Ah.' He eased the satchel strap on his shoulder. 'Awful about Stacey Coker. Absolutely awful. I'd never have believed Edgar Holloway was capable of something like that. How's her father?'

'I haven't seen him.' I didn't want to be brusque but the less I said to anyone now the better. 'I just called round to say goodbye. I'm leaving tomorrow.'

Trask's look became suddenly keen. 'Finished already?'

'I need to get back to London,' I said noncommittally. 'Anyway, thanks again for the tow. And for letting me use the boathouse. I still need to settle my bill.'

Trask irritably waved the offer away. 'Christ, don't worry about that. Not after what you did for Fay.'

'Really, I—'

'I insist. Are you likely to be back this way again?'

I thought about how things had been left with Rachel. 'I doubt it.'

'Well . . .' There wasn't much else to say. He gave a brisk nod. 'Safe travels.'

We shook hands awkwardly, then Trask carried on through the trees to the house. I went back to my car. Some people, like Lundy, you meet and feel you've known all your life. Others you brush by without either making or leaving an impression.

But I was too busy worrying over my row with Rachel to dwell on Trask. I tried to tell myself that it was for the best. She'd been through a lot, and these past few days had been so emotionally charged that my own judgement was probably skewed. It wasn't as though anything had actually *happened* between us anyway. We hardly even knew each other.

Telling myself that made no difference. I might not trust what I felt for her, but whatever it was, it was strong enough to make me miserable as I drove away.

Brooding about that, I didn't notice the glow at first. A turn of the road brought it into view, an unsteady light in the darkness off to one side. It wasn't far away, and even with my sketchy knowledge of the Backwaters I could tell it was the rough location of Edgar's house. The police must still be searching the place, I thought.

This wasn't the pure white of floodlights, though. It was a sickly yellow light that flickered against the black skyline. I glanced at it again, feeling a growing unease. The police wouldn't leave a crime scene untended. Not until it had been fully searched, and I couldn't see how they could have explored those thickets of undergrowth in the gardens already. And then the glow suddenly leapt higher, and any doubt as to what it was vanished.

Something was on fire.

I wasn't sure I could find my way to Edgar's house in the dark. Rachel had driven us there the night before, and I'd been too preoccupied with the disturbed man in the back seat to pay attention to where we were going. But there weren't many roads to take, and the blaze was an effective beacon anyway. The flames were clearly visible against the night sky, lighting up nearby trees with erratic shadows. Then I turned on to the bumpy dirt track leading to Edgar's and the fire lay dead ahead.

The house was engulfed. Sparks spewed up from it, and plumes of dirty smoke rose into the night sky. One of the nearby trees had caught fire as well, and the crackle of flames spreading through its branches sounded like snapping bone. A length of police crime scene tape, still secured at one end, flapped madly in the updraught. A police caravan was parked at the end of the track, and just behind it was a pick-up truck. In the feverish light from the fire I could make out the words *Coker's Marine and Auto* on its side.

Beyond that, silhouetted against the flames, were struggling figures.

The heat beat against me as I jumped out of the car and ran towards them. I squeezed past the truck, able to make out the bulky figure of Coker wrestling with a police offer. It was a female PC, struggling to hold the thrashing salvage yard owner in an arm lock. A male officer was on his hands and knees nearby, hat lying on the floor as he shook his head groggily. As I ran up Coker threw off the policewoman, his face shiny from snot and tears in the firelight. As he raised an arm to hit her I grabbed hold of him.

'OK, enough!'

He wrenched free and swung a fist at my head. He was off balance but it still caught me a glancing blow on the cheekbone. I clutched at his arm, trying to pull him away from the police-woman, and something barged into me from behind.

I landed in the dirt, convinced Coker had hit me again, but it was the male PC. He drove his shoulder into Coker's middle, wrapping his arms around him in a rugby tackle. By now the woman had recovered. As Coker clubbed at her partner she caught hold of an arm again, twisting it behind him.

'Fucking get *off*!' he roared as the two of them wrestled him to the ground. He landed with a heavy thump, but still struggled. I clambered to my feet but before I could go to help the female officer shot me a warning look.

'Stay where you are!' she yelled, struggling for something at her belt. She gave Coker's arm another wrench as the policeman wrapped his arms around the flailing legs. 'Stay down! Lie still or I'll spray you!'

Coker swore and fought them, almost kicking free. Grim-faced, the woman sprayed a short burst from a gas cylinder into his face. There was an agonized bellow and the big man thrashed around even more.

And then, abruptly, all the fight went out of him. He sagged back, putting up no more resistance as the two officers dragged his arms behind his back and handcuffed him. He was keening now, and with a shock I realized he was crying.

'He killed her. He killed my Stacey!'

The broad shoulders were shaking with the force of his sobs. The police officers stepped away, panting. Off to one side I noticed a large plastic petrol container, lying on its side with its lid trailing in the mud.

'You OK, Trevor?' the woman asked her partner.

'Yeah. Caught me a good one, though.'

He looked barely out of his teens. I could see now they were police community support officers, not PCs. All the way out here, with the house already searched, it must have seemed there wasn't much risk of anyone trying to disturb it.

The firelight gleamed on the blood covering the young PCSO's lower face. I took a tissue from my pocket and held it out to him.

'It's OK, it's clean,' I said. It earned a suspicious glare.

'Who are you?'

They visibly relaxed as I explained. By the time I'd finished Coker's sobs had subsided but he was still crying. He seemed spent, barely aware of us any more.

'Poor bastard,' the male PCSO said, when I told them about his daughter.

'Yeah, poor him,' the woman said, massaging her shoulder as she gave the prone man an unfriendly look.

A loud rushing noise made all three of us jump round as the roof of Edgar's house collapsed. Gouts of flame shot into the air, streaming sparks as a blast of hot air swept over us. I hoped all the animals had been taken away before Coker set the blaze.

'Shit,' the policewoman said. 'They're going to have a fit.'

While she went back to the caravan to call in, I walked back down the track to my car. I'd left the lights on and the door open when I'd jumped out. As I passed Coker's pick-up truck I glanced in the back. In the light from the flames I could see a small portable generator surrounded by coils of greasy rope and lengths of chain. Various power tools were half covered by an oily tarpaulin.

One of them was a heavy-duty angle grinder.

25

LUNDY PRODDED WITH his foot at a piece of charred timber that lay in the sodden grass. The remains of Edgar's house were blackened and roofless against a grey sky. Except for the walls not much of the structure remained. Most of the top floor had gone, leaving only a windowless brick shell.

The air was thick with the stink of wet soot and burnt wood. A tall sycamore close to the house was charred and scorched, half its branches reduced to charcoal. Heat still radiated from the house, and the ground in front of it was littered with scorched debris. Lundy looked at it and sighed.

'I hate fires. Between the fire brigade and the blaze there's bugger all left afterwards.'

At least no one had been inside this one. 'Was there much left to search?'

'Not in the house. We'd pretty much done with that, so we were waiting for more equipment to start clearing the garden. But it'd be nice to have it left in one piece.'

Coker had made a thorough job of destroying Edgar's home. The petrol had ensured there was little left for the fire teams to save once they arrived. They'd tried anyway, two engines blocking the lane at the end of the track while their hoses poured water on to the flames. Then they'd set about raking the smouldering remnants of furniture and cages outside so the fire couldn't start up again.

Lundy hadn't been out to Edgar's the night before. I'd decided against calling him. Even if there'd been a phone signal anywhere near the burning house, there was no point disturbing him at home when he'd learn about the fire soon enough anyway. He'd want to hear about the photograph of Mark Chapel, but that wasn't so urgent it couldn't wait till morning. And that would give Rachel an opportunity to tell him about the sea fort. It would be better coming from her than me.

After giving the police my statement, I'd left the firefighters still bringing the blaze under control and driven back to the boathouse. I'd slept badly, but by the time I got up one thing at least was clear in my mind.

I knew I couldn't go back to London without talking to Rachel again.

I'd rehearsed what I was going to say, and felt my frustration mount when her phone went straight to voicemail. I'd started to leave the usual bland message and then stopped.

'Look, I'm sorry about last night. I can't explain now, but . . . I was wrong, OK? Call me.'

Ending the call, I'd screwed up my face. *Bloody fool, is that the best you could do?* But it was done now. I'd been about to call Lundy next, but he beat me to it. He was on his way to Edgar's house to view the damage, he told me. Could I meet him there?

'You can tell me all about it then,' he'd said.

I'd got to the house first, and been kept behind a new cordon of police tape by a PC until Lundy arrived. He'd seemed subdued, and still did now as he regarded the burnt-out house.

'Were there any animals still inside?' I asked.

'No, the RSPCA and RSPB came out yesterday morning and took them away. And the ones he'd kept in the garden. They said it was like he'd triaged them, keeping the sickest inside and the ones that weren't so bad out here.'

That didn't sound like the behaviour of someone who'd rescue a girl and then turn into a crazed killer once he got her home. 'What about Coker? Will he be charged?'

Lundy sighed, regarding the house again. 'No way round it after what he did.'

'There were mitigating circumstances. I saw him; he wasn't in his right mind.'

'Doesn't change what he did.' He shrugged, as though realizing he sounded uncharacteristically harsh. 'I'm sure it'll be taken into account. But we can't ignore something like this, regardless of what state of mind he was in.'

'And the angle grinder I saw in his truck?'

'The lab hasn't found any blood or bone tissue on it, and it'd be a bugger to clean off if he used it on someone's face. There'd still be traces. And Coker having power tools is neither here nor there. So do I, come to that. We'll search his yard, but I doubt we'll find much.'

'Has he said anything?'

'Only that he's sorry Holloway wasn't in the house. As a father I can't say I blame him. The problem is he's taken it out on the wrong man.'

I looked at him. 'Is that official?'

'We're not telling anyone yet. But there's not much doubt that whoever strangled Stacey Coker had smaller hands than Holloway, and they were savvy enough not to leave so much as a hair or fingerprint behind. The psychologists doubt he'd be capable of anything like that, and probably not of murdering her either. At least not as he is now,' he added. 'There's still a question mark over what happened to his daughter, but I don't think we'll ever know the story there.'

'So what's going to happen to him?'

Lundy took off his glasses and rubbed his eyes. 'I expect he'll be sectioned. We can't just release him, he's not fit to fend for himself. He might not have murdered Stacey Coker, but she wouldn't have crashed if he hadn't been wandering in the road. So there's that, as well. However you look at it, he won't be coming back here.'

I looked at the burnt-out shell that had been Edgar's home for decades. 'Then what'll happen to this place?'

'That's where it gets interesting. You remember I wondered what the connection could be between Holloway and Leo Villiers? I couldn't understand why Villiers would even know this place existed, let alone feel confident enough to keep a shotgun here. Well, we looked into it and guess what? Turns out the house is owned by the Villiers estate.'

'Edgar's their *tenant*?'

Lundy smiled, more like his usual self. 'The estate owns land and properties all over this area, but I didn't twig that this was one of them. And it gets better. Sir Stephen handed the local tenancy side of the business to Leo a few years back. Nice independent income, and he probably hoped it'd get his son more involved with the running of things. Didn't work out, but it means Leo Villiers is Holloway's landlord.'

I looked at the blackened house, remembering its squalor and dilapidation. 'He was charging him rent for this?'

'That's the thing. He wasn't. Holloway wasn't claiming benefits and didn't have any income we're aware of. He can't have been paying rent for Christ knows how long. We found a gull nesting on a pile of old bank statements, and according to them he used to get publishing royalties from the text books he wrote. But that wouldn't have been enough to live on, and it must have dried up long since. I dare say the family lawyers will try to tell us it was a charity case, but I can't see Villiers letting anyone live rent free from the kindness of his heart.'

Neither could I. Whether he'd intended all along to take advantage of his vulnerable tenant or not, it wasn't a kindness to let Edgar live alone out here anyway. Villiers might not have harmed him directly, but he'd allowed him to exist in barely animal conditions, slowly starving as his mental health disintegrated along with his home. That was a form of cruelty in itself.

'When are you going to let people know it wasn't Villiers in the estuary?' I asked.

'That's down to the chief. There's an argument in favour of keeping quiet so we don't tip Villiers off, but that's running out of steam fast. After everything that's happened word's bound to be getting out, and after Stacey Coker I don't know how much longer we should keep a lid on it anyway. The priority now is finding the bugger before anyone else gets hurt. Anyway,' Lundy said, glancing at his watch, 'you said you'd got something on Mark Chapel?'

I'd forgotten about that for the few moments we'd been discussing Edgar, but now the heaviness settled on me again as I remembered the previous night. 'Rachel found a photograph her sister took of him. He has a cleft chin, the same as the mandible we found with the remains from the barbed wire.'

'I noticed that myself,' he said. 'You could have parked a bike in it.'

'You've managed to trace him?' I asked, surprised.

'Not exactly. He went missing seven months ago, around the same time as Emma Derby.'

Even though I'd been expecting it, the confirmation was unwelcome. I didn't like the way any of this was beginning to look. 'That can't be a coincidence.'

'No,' Lundy agreed. 'Unfortunately, because he lived in London no one made the connection. And the dates don't quite tally. Last time anyone saw Chapel was the Friday before Emma Derby vanished on the following Monday. He got fired from the music video producers the year before so he was working at a place that makes videos for corporate websites. Pretty low-end stuff. Said he was going away for the weekend but didn't say where, and then never showed up for work the next week. No one thought much of it because he'd been having a lot of time off anyway. Dental problems, he claimed. We can probably take that with a pinch of salt, but it meant it was another week before he was reported missing. His boss only bothered then because Chapel had taken video equipment with him. He'd been threatened with the sack already, so when he didn't appear everyone assumed he'd nicked it.'

'What sort of dental problems?' I asked, thinking back to the skull I'd examined.

'No idea. Is it important?'

'An abscess or infection could have weakened the bone around the front teeth, and made it give way when he was hit. If Mark Chapel was being treated for that it'd be something else pointing to it being his body we found in the creek.'

'If he was it'll be on his dental records,' Lundy said, not sounding particularly impressed. 'Either way, the timing's much too convenient to ignore. With Trask away on his work trip, Emma could have arranged to hook up with her boyfriend without worrying about being caught. Chapel drives over here on his bike, and then whatever happened to them happened.'

'How do you know he drove up on his bike?'

The DI gave a grim smile. 'I did some digging after you told me about the photograph of the motorbike. A burnt-out Harley was found six months ago in a ditch a few miles from here. No registration plates and someone had ground off all the serial numbers, but it fits the description of the one registered to Chapel.'

Like the indentation in the mandible, it wasn't proof in itself. But a picture of what had happened to Emma Derby's former boyfriend was starting to emerge. And now something else occurred to me.

'They could have met at the boathouse. It was Emma Derby's pet project, and I got the impression Trask didn't have much to do with it.'

Lundy considered. 'It'd take a brass nerve for them to be right under Trask's nose, but Chapel would have to stay somewhere and there's not many places round here. Have you seen anything to make you think he was there?'

'No, but I haven't really looked in the dock underneath the flat. It's full of old junk.' I'd only been inside the lower level briefly, when I'd wanted something to help retrieve the training shoe. I hadn't paid much attention to what else might be in the clutter.

'Well, I'm heading there next. I can take a look then.'

'You're going to the boathouse?'

'Rachel Derby's bringing the photographs she found. She doesn't want Trask to know, so she said she'd see me there.' He looked uncomfortable. 'She, ah, also wanted me to know that she'd been in the country when her sister went missing. Said she'd told us at the time, which it turns out she had. I didn't take her statement so I assumed . . . Anyway, everything checked out. She was at a friend's wedding somewhere.'

'Poole,' I said.

'Right.' Not looking at me, Lundy took out a handkerchief and wiped his nose. 'Sorry if that's made things awkward.'

I didn't know whether I should feel relieved or more of a fool than ever. 'It's OK.'

He put the handkerchief away. 'So, are you off to the mortuary now?'

'Yes,' I said, and abruptly made a decision. 'If it's OK by you I need to stop off back at the boathouse first, though.'

'Forgotten something, have you?'

'Something like that.'

I saw Lundy smile to himself as he turned away. But he fell quiet as we walked back down the track to where we'd left our cars. He unlocked his and then stood without opening it.

'Can I ask you something?'

My first thought was that it was about Rachel, but then I noticed the worry in his eyes and realized this was something different. 'Of course.'

'The hospital rang this morning. I was supposed to be seeing the consultant for the results in a couple of weeks, but they've brought it forward. To tomorrow.' He cleared his throat. 'You used to be a GP. I just wondered if they ever do that sort of thing for . . . you know. Good news.'

No wonder he'd seemed subdued. 'It depends on the consultant, I suppose. Or perhaps the equipment was faulty and they need to do it again. Could be any number of things.'

I wished I could offer something more reassuring. I really didn't know, but if I were Lundy I'd be worried too.

'That's what I thought. Probably a lot about nothing.' He gave a brisk nod, the police officer again. 'Right, I'll see you there.'

Lundy said he had a call to make before setting off, so I left him outside Edgar's and drove to the boathouse. Neither of the Trasks' Land Rovers were there, which I took to mean Rachel hadn't arrived yet. But as I parked I saw her waiting by the front door. She had the same folder under her arm that she'd had the photographs in the evening before. I climbed out of my car, simultaneously nervous and glad to see her.

I walked over, with no real idea of what I should say. Neither of us spoke for a moment. 'Are you OK?' I asked.

Her face gave nothing away. 'I thought you were going back to London.'

'I am. Later.' *Come on, talk to her.* 'Lundy told me you'd spoken to him.'

She looked at me without saying anything.

'About last night,' I ploughed on. 'I shouldn't have . . . I didn't mean to upset you.'

'How did you think I was going to feel?'

'I'm sorry, it's just . . . the situation's complicated.'

'You think I don't know that?' Rachel was looking at me with a perplexed, almost exasperated expression, but at least she seemed calmer now. I heard the sound of a car engine approaching, and knew I only had a few more seconds.

'Look, I can't leave it like this. I want to see you again.'

I hadn't planned to blurt it out, and from Rachel's expression she hadn't expected it either. She appeared at a loss, and then just when it seemed she might answer Lundy's car crunched on to the cinders.

Rachel gave me a last troubled look as the DI heaved himself out of his car. He flexed his shoulders stiffly, rubbing the small of his back as he looked up at the dark smear of cloud out to sea. 'Going to be raining in a bit.'

'Do you feel it in your bones?' Rachel asked, and I was glad to see her smile.

'Radio 2, actually. Same sort of thing.' He nodded at the folder. 'Those the photos?'

'Yeah.' She looked down at the folder. 'I feel a bit weird about this. Andrew still doesn't know anything about it. I'm not comfortable going behind his back.'

'No point upsetting him if there's no need,' Lundy said reasonably. 'Maybe we could go inside to take a look?'

Both Rachel and Lundy looked at me. I felt my face colour. 'I, uh, I posted my key through the letterbox when I left.'

When I'd gone to meet Lundy at Edgar's house I hadn't thought I'd be coming back here again. Lundy gave me a wry look but made no comment.

'It's OK, I've got a spare.' Rachel pulled out her sister's heavy key ring, jangling through them before finding what she wanted.

I let her and Lundy go in first. The DI bent to pick up the key I'd posted. He raised his eyebrows as he turned to me. 'Shall I give this to Rachel or might you change your mind again?'

Deciding the less I said the better, I followed him inside. I'd tidied the place before I left, leaving the quilt and bedding folded on the sofa. The Tupperware box Rachel had brought dessert in stood on the side, a few pieces of the dog food cake still in it. It had been too rich for me to finish, but I thought that would come well down my list of transgressions. While she set her folder down on the table, Lundy headed over to the stack of framed photographs leaning against the wall. The motorbike one was still at the front.

'I'm certain it's Mark Chapel's,' Rachel said as he studied it. 'And you can see the sea fort in the background. Here, it's clearer on these other prints.'

As she turned to open the folder, Lundy caught my eye and gave a short nod, confirming that the motorbike matched the burnt-out one they'd found. He came over to the table where Rachel was spreading out the smaller photographs.

'These were taken from the beach by the sea wall,' she said, shuffling through them. 'It's the same bike and location, and the sea fort's definitely the one by the mouth of the estuary. And here, these photographs of Villiers' house. Emma must have shot them from one of the towers. There's nowhere else they could have been taken from.'

Lundy's face remained impassive as he went through them. 'Have you any idea why she might do that?'

'Not really. She was doing remodelling work on the house, but that was all interiors. And if she needed to photograph the outside she could have done it from the front lawn. She didn't need to go all the way out there.'

Lundy went through the photographs again, then tapped them into a neat stack and put them back in the folder. 'Can I take these? We'll return them when we've made copies.'

'I suppose so, but they aren't mine . . .'

'Don't worry, we'll look after them.'

Rachel nodded, but still looked unhappy. 'What should I say to Andrew?'

'Nothing just yet. Best let us look into it first. No point him jumping to conclusions if there's no need.'

Especially not when he might be a suspect, I thought. I hated keeping the truth from Rachel, and her next words made me feel even worse.

'So are you going to talk to Mark Chapel?'

I was glad she'd asked Lundy and not me. He tucked the folder under his arm. 'That sort of thing's up to DCI Clarke. Before I go, can I have a quick look downstairs?'

'In the dock, you mean?' Rachel shrugged, surprised. 'If you like. Why, what are you looking for?'

'Oh, nothing in particular. I'd just like a shufti while I'm here.'

'It was checked when Emma went missing. There's nothing down there but junk.'

'I'd still like a look, even so.'

I could see Rachel wasn't convinced. We waited while Lundy put the photographs in his car, then went outside to the creaking timber steps that led down the side of the boathouse to the creek. A boat was moored at the end of the jetty, and when I saw it I realized why neither of the Land Rovers had been parked outside. Rachel hadn't come by road. It was the same fibreglass dinghy that Trask and I had taken to search for his daughter, its line pulled tight as it pitched about in the current.

Rachel stopped on the wooden landing next to the hatchway in the boathouse wall and unhooked the rope holding the hatch cover in place.

'Is that the only way in?' Lundy said doubtfully. The hatchway opening was no more than four feet high and two wide, and promised to be a tight fit for the DI.

'The gates at the front are padlocked,' Rachel told him. 'I don't have a key.'

There was an edge to her voice. As Lundy pushed open the hatch cover, hinges squeaking as it swung inwards, she turned and looked at me. Her expression said she knew she wasn't being told something, but then there was a clatter and a curse as Lundy climbed through into the dock. The DI's voice echoed hollowly from inside the boathouse.

'Ow. Bloody thing drops down inside.'

'Sorry, I should have warned you,' Rachel said, not sounding it. Turning away from me, she ducked her head and stepped nimbly through the hatchway after him. I followed her through, pausing in the dank atmosphere to let my eyes adjust to the darkness. The gloomy interior had the same musty odour of damp earth and salt water I remembered from before. The dock was partially flooded, and light from the slopping waves danced on the walls. The wooden walkway ran along the back wall and both sides, cluttered with old nets, cork buoys and other boating paraphernalia. I stayed by the hatch with Rachel as Lundy picked his way towards the shuttered gates, having to step over the holed fibreglass canoe.

'I wouldn't go too far,' she told him. 'The decking's pretty rotten.'

He stopped, taking her at her word. Framed by the strips of light coming through the gate's slats, Lundy looked down at the water below us.

'Does it all drain out at low tide?'

I could see from the stiff angle of Rachel's neck and shoulders that she was growing angry. Her voice confirmed it.

'Why wouldn't it?'

I knew Lundy was thinking about Mark Chapel's submerged body, wondering if something might be hidden under the water inside the boathouse as well. But it had been low tide when I'd been in here for the oar, and there had been nothing more sinister on the muddy creek bottom than rocks and dirty strands of weeds.

'No reason,' Lundy said. He looked up at the timbered ceiling. There was nothing to see up there, the rough beams barely visible in the shadows. 'Shall we go back outside?'

I stepped through the hatch on to the small landing, relieved to be back in fresh air. I started up the steps as Rachel emerged, but paused when I realized she wasn't following. She stayed on the landing, her face set and angry as she waited for Lundy to come out. The DI stepped through the hatchway with a grunt.

'I'm not built for this,' he grumbled, looping the rope over the hook to hold the hatch cover shut. Straightening, he turned to leave then stopped when Rachel didn't move.

'What's going on?' she demanded.

'What do you mean?'

'I mean there's something you're not telling me.'

'I can't go into details about an investigation, you know that. Now, why don't we—'

'I'm not asking for details, I'm just sick of not being told anything. You wanted to look in there for a reason. And you ducked the question when I asked if you're going to talk to Mark Chapel. I'm not stupid. It's obvious *something's* going on.'

Lundy sighed. 'You're just going to have to trust me.'

'*Trust* you? I'm the one who's stuck my neck out and gone behind Andrew's back, and now you won't even say *why*?' She shot me a brief glare, including me in the accusation before confronting Lundy again. 'Why are you being so cagey about Mark Chapel? Do you think he had something to do with what happened to Emma?'

'No, it's nothing like that.'

'Then *what*, for God's sake? And if you haven't even questioned him yet how do you know . . .' She trailed off, her eyes widening. 'Something's happened to him, hasn't it?'

Lundy looked cornered. 'Like I said, I can't go into details.'

The colour had drained from Rachel's face. She raised a hand to her mouth. 'Oh, God, the body on the barbed wire with Fay. Was that him? That was *Mark*?'

'Nothing's been confirmed,' Lundy ploughed on, but Rachel was staring at me.

'You knew, didn't you?'

Oh, Christ. 'I couldn't say anything, I'm sorry.'

'I told him not to,' Lundy cut in. 'This is an ongoing inquiry, we can't—'

'I can't believe this!' Rachel looked stunned. 'What happened to him? Did Villiers kill them *both*?'

Lundy seemed to struggle for a moment, then sighed. 'We don't know.'

'Well, if he didn't, who . . .' I saw the realization hit her. 'Oh, no, you can't think *Andrew* . . . ?'

'We don't think anything at the moment,' Lundy said doggedly. 'But until we know more this has to stay strictly confidential. You can't tell anybody. Do you understand?'

But Rachel wasn't listening. She looked pale. 'I feel sick.'

'Do you want to sit down?' I asked.

'No, I don't want to bloody sit down!' she snapped, then turned to Lundy. 'What about the sea fort? What are you going to do about that? Or is that confidential as well?'

'The marine unit will probably go out and take a look,' Lundy said, with the air of a man under siege.

'When? Today?'

'No, I don't know when it'll be. But even if your sister did go out there—'

'*If?* You've seen the photographs!'

'—then I can't see that it's relevant. They took away the main access ladders from the towers years ago, so she can't have got inside. And if she made those prints afterwards then she obviously came back, so it's not as if there's any need to rush out there.'

I thought Rachel was going to argue. She stood facing Lundy with her arms crossed, an angry flush on her cheeks.

'Fine.'

She turned and went down the last few steps to the jetty, heading for the boat. Giving Lundy a glance I went after her.

'Where are you going?'

'Where do you think?'

She didn't so much as break step, forcing me to hurry to keep up. 'You're going out to the fort?'

Rachel didn't answer. She didn't have to: she'd intended to go out all along, that was why she'd brought the boat. My exasperation rose as she bent to untie the mooring line.

'Look, will you just *stop* for a second?'

'Why? I'm tired of waiting around. If no one else is going to do anything then I will.'

'You've no idea what condition the fort's in. You don't even know if you'll be able to get inside.'

'Emma managed.'

'And you said yourself she might have had an accident. Two of the towers have collapsed already.'

She continued untying the line. 'If I don't come back you can raise the alarm.'

'Come on, this is . . .' I wanted to say *stupid*, but thought better of it. 'I know you're angry, but going out on your own isn't going to help anyone. Just think about it.'

'I have. And I'm going.'

'Then I'm coming with you.'

That made her stop. Finally she looked at me. 'I'm not asking you to.'

'No, but I'm coming anyway.'

The jetty shook from Lundy's heavy footsteps. From the sour expression on his face I guessed he'd heard.

'I don't have to tell either of you my views on this, do I?'

'No.' Rachel gave the mooring line an angry tug. 'I know no one else thinks this is important, but Emma must have had a reason for going out there. I'm going to find out what it is.'

Lundy blew out his cheeks. 'I can't stop you, but I wish you'd at least wait. The weather forecast's atrocious.'

'That isn't till later,' Rachel told him, coiling up the line. 'I'll be back long before then.'

The DI looked out across the creek, shaking his head at some internal conversation. 'Oh, bloody hell,' he muttered.

26

LUNDY LEFT ME with Rachel while he called the inquiry team to let them know what he was doing. He climbed back up the steps to the top of the bank on the pretext of finding a signal, although it was more likely that he wanted to explain without us overhearing. Ordinarily I'd have appreciated the chance to talk to Rachel. Now I didn't know how to begin.

But I didn't have to. 'So is that what last night was about?' she said, banging aside the items inside a small locker in the stern of the boat. 'You were checking up on me as well as Andrew?'

'It wasn't like that.'

'Really? Because that's how it feels.'

'Look, I didn't know for sure about Mark Chapel until I saw the photograph. And I couldn't have told you anyway.'

'Seems like there's quite a few things you can't tell me.'

'That's right, I can't,' I shot back, my own temper fraying. 'What would you have done if I had? Tell Trask your sister was seeing her old boyfriend again as well as Leo Villiers?'

That made her pause. 'I don't know,' she admitted. 'But I don't think for a minute Andrew's done anything wrong.'

I didn't point out that's what everyone says. No one wants to believe someone close to them could be a murderer. I'd made that mistake myself in the past.

The jetty bounced as Lundy came back along it. The DI looked vaguely troubled.

'Everything OK?' I asked.

'Can't get hold of anyone. I've left a message, though, so they know where I am if they need to get hold of me. Assuming they can reach me out there,' he added sourly.

Lundy waited for Rachel to respond, but she seemed chastened now. He cast a worried eye on the boat as she pulled another life-jacket from the locker.

'You sure this thing's big enough to take out of the estuary?'

Rachel put the lifejacket behind her and closed the locker. 'It'll be fine. I've taken it out in a lot worse weather than this.'

Lundy scratched his neck doubtfully. 'Well, if you're still set on it, we need a few ground rules. If the weather turns nasty, or if it looks too rough once we're out in the estuary, we turn back. Same when we get out to the fort. If there's anything I don't like the look of, we're turning the boat straight round. I'm sticking my neck out over this as it is, so I don't want any arguments. That clear?'

Rachel nodded meekly. Lundy sniffed, obviously expecting more resistance.

'Right, then. Just so we know.'

I steadied the boat for him as he clambered awkwardly on board. The two of us sat on the bench seat in the middle while Rachel sat in the stern next to the tiller. Lundy wrestled his way into the lifejacket she gave him, struggling to make the straps meet across his barrel chest before abandoning the attempt.

'Don't suppose you've anything any bigger?'

'Sorry, they're all one size apart from Fay's.'

He regarded the lifejacket draped on either side of his stomach and shook his head. 'I must be mad.'

But once we were under way it didn't seem to worry him. As the small boat picked up speed, he sat with his face turned to the wind, showing every sign of enjoying himself despite the circumstances. I saw him pop a couple of antacid tablets in his mouth, and remembered what he'd said about the hospital calling him. It occurred to me that could be the reason he'd not put up more of a fight when Rachel insisted on doing this. He was bound to be worried about what the hospital wanted: perhaps the trip to the fort was a welcome distraction.

Rachel sat at the tiller, dark hair streaming back in the wind. She wore the red waterproof jacket I'd first seen her in under her own lifejacket, and seemed more relaxed herself as she guided the boat between the banks of the creek. Seeing me looking, she gave a smile. But it was an uncertain one, and I wondered if she was having second thoughts. The stiff wind turned the water's surface fretful and dull. There was no rain as yet, but the sky was a leaden grey, with a darker band on the horizon.

'You said the forecast was bad?' I asked Lundy over the drone of the engine.

He nodded. 'Supposed to be getting a bit feisty later on. It's a spring tide tonight as well, so that should be fun. We'll need to be back well before then.'

After a few minutes the creek merged into the estuary. Out here it was more exposed, and the chop gave way to marching waves. The boat juddered with rhythmic thuds as they smacked against the prow. Each impact flicked beads of cold spray against us, leaving a taste of salt on my lips.

The sea fort's towers lay dead ahead, but the visibility beyond the estuary mouth wasn't good enough to see them clearly. A slight haze, more like smog than a sea mist, obscured the tall structures, reducing them to vague skeletal shapes in the distance.

The boat slowed, its engine noise dropping as we entered the Barrows. All around us low, smooth humps rose from the waves. Rachel manoeuvred through them, scrutinizing the water for disturbed or smoother patches that might indicate a sandbank hidden below the surface. Once we were through the bottleneck she gunned the engine again, and we had to brace ourselves as the boat pitched against the bigger swells. As we approached the mouth of the estuary, Leo Villiers' house came into view off to one side. It stood on the wooded promontory, the curved glass of its bay windows reflecting black as they faced out to the open sea.

Then we were past, and heading out of the estuary. Up ahead, the old army fort's remaining towers rose from the waves. They looked even stranger seen from this close, alien and forbidding relics that had lived past their time. The towers were set a short distance apart, each consisting of a square, two-storey metal box supported on four inward-sloping legs. Flimsy-looking gantries and catwalks sprouted from their sides, now warped and rusted.

The nearest tower looked the most intact. Rachel headed for it, but Lundy leaned towards her.

'Go by the others first,' he told her, raising his voice to be heard. 'Let's rule them out before we take a look at this.'

Rachel obliged, looping the boat around the outside of the towers. But it was already clear that if her sister had taken the photographs of Villiers' house from the fort, she hadn't done it from either of the two towers that stood further out to sea. The first was little more than an empty shell. Fire had blackened the metal walls of the platform, though judging by the ochre coating of rust it wasn't recent. The roof was gone, and so was the external framework of walkways and ladders I'd seen on the website photographs. The structure had been completely hollowed out, and as though to emphasize the point a seagull flew up through a gaping hole in the platform's base, flitted past glassless windows, and emerged above the roofless structure a moment later.

The second tower had fared even worse. The upper structure was completely gone, leaving the four spindly legs to rise from the sea like the corners of an incomplete pyramid. Lundy took off his glasses and wiped the salt spray from the lenses.

'OK, let's take a look at the other.'

Rachel took the boat in towards the last tower. Even out here the sea was silted up and shallow. I could see the paleness of seabed where a sandbank had formed around the third tower, even breaking the surface in places. Swells smacked against the structure's legs, creating a criss-crossing chop that buffeted us as we approached. The sound of them became more resonant as Rachel brought us in underneath.

Up close the tower was bigger than I'd expected. The legs were tubular and made from reinforced concrete, now badly spalled and draped with seaweed below the waterline. It swirled from them like green hair, and every now and then there was an echoing boom as a larger wave crashed into the hollow tubes.

I looked up as we passed beneath the shadowy underside of the tower, sixty feet above my head. The girders that formed its base were badly rusted, stained white with bird droppings that added an ammoniac sharpness to the smell of seaweed. Rachel bumped the boat alongside a mooring platform set between the fort's splayed legs and quickly tied a line around a mooring post. As the swells jostled the boat, she went to get hold of the rusty ladder that extended down into the water.

'I'll go first,' Lundy told her. 'If anybody's going to get dumped in the sea, it's better off being me.'

Timing the swells, the DI hauled himself up the ladder and onto the steel platform. Brushing the rust off his hands, he stamped on the platform, making the whole thing clang and quiver.

'Seems solid enough. All right, up we come.'

Rachel went next, clambering easily up the rungs. I followed slightly less elegantly, but managed not to fall in. The ladder was blistered with corrosion, and the platform itself was little better. But Lundy was right: there seemed no imminent danger of its collapsing.

Following Rachel and Lundy's example, I took off my lifejacket and looked around. Another ladder, this one newer-looking, ran up to a small gantry suspended above us. From there, a flight of metal steps led to a heavy-looking door into the fort itself. There was no other way in that I could see.

'Look,' Rachel said, pointing back towards the coastline.

Across the open sea, Leo Villiers' empty house stood facing us on its rocky promontory.

Rachel took a pair of compact binoculars from a jacket pocket, and studied the house through them before handing them to Lundy. 'It's the same view as the photographs.'

'Came prepared, did we?' he commented as he raised the binoculars. 'Not quite the same view. It's too low down.'

'So she must have taken them from inside. Let's go and look,' Rachel said, her impatience returning.

Lundy considered the ladder rising to the underside of the tower. 'This shouldn't be here. I'm not happy about . . .' he said, and then broke off as his phone rang.

The musical trill sounded out of place, but at least it meant we were close enough to the shore for mobile coverage. That settled the question of Emma Derby's not being able to call for help if she'd had an accident. Lundy fished in his pocket for his phone as it continued to ring.

'I need to take this,' he said, checking the display.

He moved to the other side of the platform to answer. Rachel watched him go, then turned back to the ladder and began to climb.

'Rachel . . .' I said, exasperated.

'There's no point standing around.'

She was already halfway up to the small gantry. I looked across at Lundy, expecting him to remonstrate. But the DI didn't seem to have noticed. He'd turned away from us, and stood with his head cocked, listening to whatever was being said on the other end of the phone.

Great. With a sigh, I began to climb as well. This ladder was an extendable one, made from lightweight aluminium rather than rusted steel. Lundy had said the original access ladders had been removed years ago, presumably to keep people out of the towers. Someone hadn't let that stop them.

I wondered who.

I pulled myself through an opening on to the gantry. It was smaller than the platform below and caked with white droppings. The wind was stronger up here, cold and biting. Clambering to my feet, I saw that Rachel had already gone up the metal steps to the tower door. She tugged on the handle.

'It's padlocked.'

On one level I was relieved. Finding Stacey Coker's body was still fresh in my mind, and if the tower held any surprises it was better for the police to find them rather than Rachel.

But after coming all this way I knew I'd be disappointed if we had to turn back now. Rachel gave the door a frustrated thump. 'Do you think there's another way in?'

'I doubt it.' The fort had been built for coastal defence: it was supposed to be hard to get into.

'Have we got anything to smash the padlock?' she asked as I went up the steps.

I could imagine what Lundy would say to that. 'No, and I don't think that's going to break in a hurry anyway.'

Both the padlock and the hasp it was fitted to were new, made from heavy-duty stainless steel. They looked as though they'd resist anything short of a sledgehammer.

Rachel rattled it in frustration. 'This is ridiculous! How did Emma get inside if it was locked?'

I didn't know, but I was beginning to feel uneasy. 'Come on, let's go.'

I turned away, but Rachel stayed where she was. Crouching by the door, she reached in her pocket and pulled out her sister's heavy bunch of keys. She went through them, then selected one and tried it in the padlock.

'What are you doing?'

'Trying Emma's spare keys. I've no idea what some of them are for, and she must have got inside somehow.'

'We should get back to Lundy,' I said impatiently, as she tried another.

'Just a couple more.'

'You're wasting your—'

There was a *snick* as the lock came open. Rachel grinned down at me.

'Ta-da.'

I felt the hairs prickle on the back of my neck. It was one thing if her sister had made a single trip to the fort to take photographs. But if Emma Derby had padlocked the tower – and presumably was responsible for the replacement ladder as well – that suggested she'd been out here more than once. No one would go to all that trouble over an abandoned sea fort without good reason.

Not unless there was something inside they didn't want anyone to find.

Rachel was already taking the padlock from the hasp. Before I could say anything a piercing whistle came from below. Going to the edge of the gantry, I looked down and saw Lundy, craning his neck with two fingers poised in his mouth. He took them out when he saw me.

'We need to go,' he called.

'There's something here you should see,' I shouted back. There was a groan of dry hinges behind me. Glancing round, I saw Rachel struggling to swing open the heavy door.

Lundy's voice echoed up to me again. 'It'll have to wait. Something's come up. I need to get back.'

Whatever it was, it must be serious. The DI looked shocked, I realized, looking down at where he stood on the lower platform. No, not shocked. Stunned.

'OK,' I called, and turned back to Rachel. 'Come on, we'd better—'

The doorway was empty.

Shit. I ran up the steps. The heavy steel door stood open, revealing a dark corridor with flaking metal walls. It disappeared into shadow, but there was no sign of Rachel.

'What's going on?' Lundy's voice sounded annoyed as it bounced off the metal roof.

I turned my head to shout. 'Rachel's gone inside.'

The DI's muttered 'Jesus wept' carried up to me, then I heard his footsteps ringing on the ladder. I stepped through the doorway, unable to see far in the dark interior.

'Rachel?' I yelled. 'Rachel, we need to go!'

There was a muffled response from somewhere deep inside the

tower, but it was too distorted to make out. I swore, torn between going after her and waiting for Lundy. But from the laboured pace of his footsteps on the ladder, it would take the DI longer than us to reach the top. Swearing, I went further inside.

It was cold in the tower. The air was clammy, with a peppery smell of mould and rust. Once in the corridor I found it wasn't as dark as it seemed from outside. Dirty light fell through small, rectangular windows, the glass brown with filth. Bright squares of daylight spilled through broken panes, revealing an antiquated generator standing like a sentinel at the foot of a flight of steps. More rooms were visible beyond it, but they were only hinted at in the gloom. Every surface was crusted with muck and salt, while corrosion lent a ruddy tint to the flaking metal walls and floor. It was like a sepia photograph brought to life.

Fragments of rust and old paint crunched underfoot as I went past the generator to the stairs.

'Rachel?'

'Up here.'

Her voice echoed down the steps from the floor above. I started to go up, but a clattering from outside announced that Lundy had reached the gantry. A moment later the DI appeared in the open doorway, red-faced and out of breath.

'Where the hell is she?'

'The next floor. The door was padlocked but her sister had a key.'

'Bloody hell!' He shook his head, his breathing laboured. 'We've had this all wrong. All of it.'

'What do you mean?' I asked, but he waved it away.

'Later. Let's go and find her.'

I paused to jam the heavy steel door back against the wall, testing it to make sure it wasn't going to swing shut, and then hurried after him. Our footsteps rang on the metal steps as we climbed to the next level. At the top was another corridor, branching off to one side as well as straight ahead. Open doors gave glimpses of ruin. The rooms had been stripped except for empty metal shelves, upended bedsteads and broken chairs. A faded pin-up of a smiling young woman in a swimming costume was still fixed to one wall, winking at the camera. Looking up I saw the steps continued to the roof, but the door leading out to it was closed.

'Rachel? Where are you?'

'In here.' Her voice came from a room at the far end of the corridor, where a steel door stood ajar. 'You need to see this.'

Lundy's usually placid expression had been replaced by a tight-lipped anger as he marched in front of me down the corridor. Whatever he'd been told over the phone, it had seriously rattled him.

'That was bloody stupid!' he declared, pushing open the door and going in. 'I told you not to . . .'

He stopped.

After the dark squalor of the rest of the tower, the room was a surprise. Daylight flooded through its windows, and apart from empty metal brackets still fixed to the floor there was nothing left of its military origins. A glass booth had been built against one wall, where a peeling poster advertised a long-forgotten concert by The Kinks. Inside the booth two antiquated turntables sat on a desk, along with an empty microphone stand.

I'd known the fort had been a pirate radio station during the 1960s, but someone had been using it much more recently than that. The room had been decked out like a studio flat. The cold metal floor had been covered by a Turkish rug, and a folding table and chairs stood in front of a portable gas heater. There was a stainless-steel camping stove as well, while an improvised futon had been made by laying an inflatable double mattress on wooden pallets. There were other domestic touches: battery-powered lanterns had been covered with colourful pieces of cloth, and dog-eared paperbacks and empty wine bottles stood on a bookshelf made from house bricks and planks of wood. Fixed above the bed, a computer-printed sign in crimson text declared, *If you're not living your life, you're already dead.*

But the room still had a sense of abandonment. The damp salt air had curled the book covers, and a black rash of mildew spotted the rumpled duvet on the bed. The mattress had partly deflated, most of the air seeping out so it sagged limply over the pallets.

'Home sweet home,' Rachel said, in a small voice.

Lundy was looking around, taking everything in. 'Have you touched anything?'

She shook her head, hands pushed deep in her pockets. 'No. Take a look through the window.'

The rain made a tinny sound on the metal walls, and I thought I could feel the tower sway in the wind as Lundy and I went to the window. The glass was much cleaner than the others I'd seen, but it was already hazed by a new accumulation of salt. Though not enough to obscure the view of Leo Villiers' house, facing us across the open sea.

'This is where Emma took the photographs,' Rachel said.

Without answering, Lundy went to where the deflated mattress drooped forlornly on the pallets. He scanned the mildewed duvet before sniffing at the crushed roll-ups discarded in a saucer on the makeshift bookshelf.

'Did your sister smoke dope?'

'No, she didn't smoke anything. She hated cigarettes.'

Lundy straightened. 'Well, someone here liked a joint.'

'That'd be Mark Chapel. Emma told me he used dope.' Rachel shook her head angrily. 'This whole place is just . . . *him*. Camping out somewhere like this, in an old pirate radio station. And that stupid sign! God, I can almost hear him saying it!'

She gestured angrily at the printed slogan taped above the bed. But Lundy's attention was on something else. His knees cracked as he bent to examine something on the floor.

'What is it?' I asked.

'Looks like a lens cap,' he said without touching it. 'Says "Olympus".'

'That's the same make as Emma's camera,' Rachel said. 'Christ, I could bloody shake her! What was she *thinking*?'

The DI had started to get up, but then seemed to notice

316

something else. I followed his gaze and saw dried splashes on the floor. Against the rusty metal they weren't immediately obvious, and at first glance could have been wine or coffee.

But I could see from Lundy's face that they weren't.

'Oh God, is that blood?' Rachel asked.

Lundy climbed stiffly to his feet as another gust of wind thrashed against the tower. 'We're done here. Let's go before—'

A sudden *clang* rang through the tower. It came from below us, somewhere on the lower level. We froze as it resonated through the steel structure and slowly died away.

Lundy turned to me. 'Did you wedge the door open?'

He didn't whisper but he kept his voice down. I nodded. I remembered the solid weight of the steel door, how stiff and reluctant the hinges had been as I'd forced it back against the wall.

'Maybe it came loose . . . ?' Rachel spoke in hushed tones as well.

Neither Lundy nor I answered. It was too heavy to swing shut by itself, and it would have taken a stronger wind than this to move it. The silence inside the fort seemed to gain weight. The DI drew in a breath, as though asserting something to himself.

'Wait here.'

He went to the door. I started after him. 'I'll come with you.'

'No you won't. Close the door and keep it bolted till I get back.'

He stepped out before I could argue. Moving softly for such a big man, he pulled the door to behind him, easing it shut with a dull clunk.

His footsteps died away outside. In the silence that followed, Rachel hugged herself. 'It could still just be the wind. If the door's open it might have blown something over inside.'

She could be right. The wind was definitely growing stronger, its low moaning accompanying the boom of waves breaking against the tower's hollow legs. Perhaps the door hadn't been wedged as firmly as I'd thought. Suddenly it seemed ridiculous to be hiding in there while Lundy checked the empty corridors by himself.

'What are you doing?' Rachel asked as I went towards the door.

'I'm going to see where Lundy is.'

'He said to wait.'

'I know, but—'

An explosive *BOOM* shattered the quiet. It reverberated through the metal walls, far louder than the noise that had preceded it. There was no question of it being the wind this time, and no mistaking what it was.

A shotgun blast.

Rachel was staring at me, eyes wide with shock. Despite Lundy's instructions we hadn't bolted the door, and as the gunshot died away I reached for the handle.

'No!'

She pushed in front of me, ramming the top bolt shut before I could stop her.

'You're not going out there,' she said, facing me with her back to the door.

'I need to find Lundy—'

'*And do what?*' Her face was scared, but determined. 'That was a *gun*, what do you think you're going to do?'

I didn't have an answer. God knows, I was scared enough myself, but I couldn't leave Lundy out there. I reached past her for the bolt. 'Lock it behind me.'

'No, don't be—'

The soft protest of unoiled metal came from the door. We stared as the handle turned down. The door shifted slightly, creaking as it pressed against the heavy bolt that Rachel had just slid into place. Out of reflex, I started to say Lundy's name, but it died on my lips. If it had been the DI in the corridor he would have said something.

Whoever this was, it wasn't him.

Rachel backed away, moving close to me. I felt her flinch as

318

something thumped against the door. The top bolt rattled but held, and as the handle shook again Rachel darted forward and shot the lower bolt home as well.

The door shuddered once more, then fell quiet. The silence was unbearable. Rachel turned her head towards me to speak, and as she did the shotgun roared again.

The entire tower rang like a struck bell as the door bucked from the blast. Twisting away, I hunched over Rachel as the noise hammered at us like a physical blow. Certain the door must have given way, that the old bolts couldn't have withstood the impact, I risked a look over my shoulder.

The steel door was intact, its bolts securely in place.

My ears rang painfully as the sulphur stink of gunpowder filtered into the room. Rachel's face was white as we stared at the door. Nothing happened. My ears were still ringing but now the thudding of my heart drowned it out.

'Have they gone?' Rachel whispered.

I didn't answer. Whoever it was could still be waiting out there. But the silence seemed to have a different quality now, as though the corridor outside were empty. There was only one way to find out.

Rachel tried to pull me back as I unfastened the top bolt. 'What are you doing?'

'I can't leave Lundy.'

I reached down for the lower bolt. The steel edge of the door was deformed halfway down: the blast had been aimed at where a single lock or bolt would be. I slid the last bolt partway back but left a half-inch of the metal rod still in place. I paused, listening for any sign that someone was still outside, hoping if they were they'd be fooled into giving themselves away.

Nothing happened.

I turned to Rachel. 'Get ready to open it, then bolt it again as soon as I'm out.'

She shook her head, vehemently. 'No, we should—'

'Count of three,' I told her.

She closed her eyes, then suddenly hugged me. 'Be careful.'

I silently mouthed the numbers, then gave a nod. As Rachel tugged the bolt back, I yanked the door open and rushed into the corridor.

It was empty.

A blue haze filled the air, and the reek of gunpowder was much stronger. I realized Rachel hadn't closed the door. She had followed me out, her eyes wide as she stared down the corridor.

She shook her head. 'I'm coming with you.'

There was no time to argue. I started towards the steps, trying to walk as quietly as I could. Halfway along the dark corridor I paused, making sure the door to the roof was still closed and bolted. As I did I heard the distant sound of a receding engine outside.

A boat was leaving.

But any relief I felt was replaced by a growing dread. 'Lundy?' I yelled. 'Lundy!'

The shout echoed into silence. And then I heard something: a low, hoarse sound coming from the steps. I ran to the top and saw him.

Lundy was lying halfway down. He was on his back, one leg crooked under him and both arms straight by his side. His entire front was covered in blood. In the dim light it looked as though he had something on his stomach and chest. Then what I was seeing resolved itself into exposed intestines and ribs.

The steps were slippery with blood. It had already started to congeal, clotting into viscous piles where it had dripped down from one step to the next. I was vaguely aware of Rachel behind me as I knelt by the DI in the cramped staircase.

'Lundy? Bob, *Bob*, can you hear me?'

He was still alive. His chest still rose and fell slowly, as though with great effort. The noise I'd heard was his breathing; asthmatic and laboured. His expression was surprised, and every now and then the cornflower-blue eyes behind the blood-flecked glasses would blink as he gazed up into the shadows.

'Oh, God,' Rachel breathed. 'Oh, God, look at him!'

I tore off my coat, wadding it up to hold against the terrible wound. 'Go outside,' I told her, pressing down on the coat with both hands. 'Find a signal and phone for help.'

'Shouldn't I—'

'Just do it. *Now.*'

Still keeping up the compression, I moved to one side so she could squeeze past. She tried to avoid the blood on the steps, but there was too much of it. As she eased by I noticed a footprint already in the congealed mess lower down.

But I didn't spare any thought for that. Shifting my position to ease my arms, I continued to press down on the wound. My balled-up coat was already soaked, and my hands were sticky with blood. It was pumping out more slowly, but I knew that wasn't my doing.

'OK, Bob,' I told him, trying to keep my voice calm and reassuring. 'Rachel's gone for help, so all you need to do now is sit tight till it gets here. I just want you to stay awake and focus on my voice, OK? Can you do that, Bob?'

Lundy didn't respond. His eyes remained fixed above him as his chest slowly rose and fell. I carried on talking. I talked about his wife, his daughter and granddaughter, about the little girl's birthday party and anything else I could think of. I didn't know if he could hear me but I talked anyway, because it felt like I should and there was nothing else I could do for him. I kept talking when Rachel came back and stood silently at the foot of the stairs, and I still carried on when the big chest stopped moving and the laboured breathing fell quiet, even though by then I knew I was talking to myself.

27

THE RAIN DRIPPED off the edge of the sea fort's tower in sway-
ing silver curtains. Every now and then a squall of wind would
blow a sheet of it into its shadowy underside, a cold spray that ran
down necks and sleeves, chilling to the bone.

The sandbank that had built up around the tower had been
exposed by the low tide, revealing a smooth brown island by one
of the legs. Dappled with seaweed and the rusted carcasses of tin
cans, it had been colonized by dozens of small, pale crabs. They'd
emerged cautiously into daylight, pincers raised as they made
scuttling runs that left stippled patterns in the wet sand.

I watched them from the edge of the docking platform under the
tower. The tide had begun to return, and now the crabs were disappearing as the sea reclaimed the sandbank. I'd be sorry to see
them go. Watching them had been a welcome distraction from the
activity going on above my head. A blanket was draped around my
shoulders, replacing the ruined coat I'd left inside the tower. The
marine unit's RHIB was moored to the platform next to the smaller
boat I'd come out in with Rachel and Lundy, bobbing on the waves.
A larger launch was anchored in deeper water further out,
wallowing on the heavier swell.

As we'd waited outside the tower for the emergency services to
arrive, Rachel had wiped tears from her face.

'It's my fault. He didn't even want to come out here.'

I told her it was no good blaming herself, that there was no way to have foreseen any of this. I doubted it made any difference. The shock of what had happened was numbing. I felt useless myself, unable to even hold her. Lundy's blood was still caked on my arms, cold and sticky, but I couldn't wash it off before the police got there. They would need to test our hands for gunpowder residue to rule us out as suspects. And so I stood while it dried on me, a clotted coat smelling of iron and offal that cracked when I moved.

A fast coastguard launch arrived first, bringing paramedics who'd clambered up the ladders to Lundy. The urgency was in contrast to the way they'd re-emerged a short while later, empty-handed and defeated. They'd offered blankets and hot coffee while we waited for the police. The marine unit had arrived next, vaguely familiar faces I recognized from the estuary recovery. They'd been followed by a bigger police vessel, discharging the first of what seemed like an endless stream of CSIs and crime scene personnel. Or perhaps it was the same ones coming and going.

I didn't keep check.

Rachel had been taken back to shore to be interviewed and make a formal statement. Although I'd not asked to stay, no one suggested I leave. I could guess why, and so I'd waited on the platform out of everyone's way, watching the busy crabs. It was a relief when my hands had been swabbed by a member of the forensic team and I could finally clean Lundy's blood from my hands. I'd crouched down on the platform and plunged my arms in the sea, rubbing the caked mess from my skin and letting the cold saltwater carry it away.

It was mid-afternoon when the coastguard launch returned with more passengers. It bumped alongside the platform, and I turned and waited as DCI Clarke and Frears climbed out. Both wore coveralls, and the DCI's face was bleak. She looked over at me as she accepted help out of the boat from a police officer, but went straight to the ladder without a word. Behind her, the pathologist appeared uncharacteristically solemn as he clambered on to the platform. He saw me and paused, as though in two minds.

'Dr Hunter. Glad you're all right.' He looked up at the tower, shaking his head. 'Bloody bad business.'

I nodded. It was.

A bloody bad business.

I went back to watching the crabs on the diminishing sandbank. Only a small patch remained above the surface when the first seagull found them. Within a few minutes several more had joined it, their cries echoing under the tower. I was still watching nature run its course when I heard someone coming back down the ladder. I waited until footsteps approached behind me, and then turned to face Clarke.

The DCI's pale eyes were red-rimmed, and the wispy ginger hair was even more dishevelled than usual. Her voice held a quaver, but I thought that was barely contained fury.

'What the hell happened?'

I went through it one more time, even though I knew she would have already been briefed. She didn't interrupt, but her mouth compressed into an ever tighter line.

'Jesus Christ,' she said when I'd finished. 'Jesus *fucking* Christ! Whose idea was it?'

'Mine.'

I could tell she didn't believe me. Or perhaps she already knew: Rachel wouldn't have spared herself in her statement. But I wasn't about to point any fingers. No one had forced Lundy to come out here. Or me either, come to that.

Clarke gave me a hard look, then stared off at the waves through the curtain of rain. A wisp of escaped ginger hair flapped unnoticed in the wind.

'And you didn't see who it was? Nothing at all?'

'The engine sounded like a small boat's, but that's as much as I can tell you.'

She sighed, impatiently pushing the loose strand of untidy hair out of her face. 'Christ, what a mess.'

'What about forensics?' I asked. 'Can you tell anything from the footprint?'

'Not much. It's only a partial, and there's no sole pattern or any identifying marks. Doesn't look like it's been worn down, so probably a smooth-soled shoe. Most of the surfaces are too rusty for fingerprints, but we've found two distinct sets in the room and five on the aluminium ladder. We're assuming that three of those will be from you, Rachel Derby and . . . and DI Lundy. We don't know about the other two yet, but they aren't recent. If we're right about the set-up here I think we'll find they belong to Emma Derby and Mark Chapel.'

I thought so too. The natural oils in older fingerprints would have been dried out by weathering and the salty air. I'd have to have my fingerprints taken at some point to exclude those I'd left, and so would Rachel and even Lundy. But if the five sets the police had found could all be accounted for, that meant whoever had climbed up to the tower to shoot Lundy had been wearing gloves.

The same as Stacey Coker's killer.

'He knew we were here,' I said.

'He? I thought you didn't see who it was?'

I bit back an angry retort. But she was right, and I should know better than to make assumptions. 'OK then, whoever it was knew we were here.'

'We don't know that.'

'Why else would they have come out? By the look of it no one had been inside the tower for months, and it can't be an accident they turned up at the same time as us. Not with a shotgun.'

'So what are you saying? Someone tipped them off?'

The only person who'd told anyone we were going out to the sea fort was Lundy. He'd called in to let his team know, but I couldn't believe one of his colleagues would set him up to be murdered.

'Or they were keeping a watch on the fort somehow, I don't know. I just don't believe the timing was a coincidence.'

'I don't like it either,' Clarke said flatly. 'But the alternative is that someone came out here to deliberately execute a detective inspector. And two civilians, given half a chance. What would they gain by that?'

'To keep anyone from knowing what was inside.'

'And shooting a police officer's really going to keep a lid on that.'

Her voice was heavy with scorn, but she had a point. Even if Lundy's murderer had succeeded in killing all three of us, the tower would have been searched as a matter of course when Lundy didn't report in. Shooting him had only escalated the situation.

'I didn't say it made sense,' I said wearily. 'But our boat was moored outside, so it was obvious *someone* was here. If the intention wasn't to kill us why come into the tower?'

'I don't *know*, Dr Hunter, all right? If I did I'd be a hell of a lot closer to catching the bastard!' Clarke massaged her temples, taking a second to compose herself. 'Look, we know someone was keeping ammunition and probably a shotgun at Edgar Holloway's house. Maybe they wanted another hiding place now that's gone and panicked when they realized someone was out here.'

I remembered the persistent attempts to get through the bolted door. That didn't seem panicked to me, but there was no point labouring the point. Clarke didn't have any more answers than I did.

'What about the stain on the floor?' I asked. 'Is it blood?'

A gust of wind blew a sheet of rain under the tower on to us. She didn't seem to notice. 'We think so, but I doubt it'll tell us much. It's probably from either Emma Derby or Mark Chapel, but between the rust and the salt air we'll be lucky if we can say which.'

'I think it's Mark Chapel's.'

Clarke regarded me. 'I'm listening.'

I'd had plenty of time to go over it while I'd been watching the crabs. It was better than thinking about Lundy lying in the tower. 'You know it's probably his body we found on the barbed wire?'

'I've been briefed,' she said irritably. 'Go on.'

'Someone hit him hard enough in the face for a piece of bone to be driven into his brain. An injury like that would have shattered his nose. It'd have bled. Perhaps not a lot if he died straight away, but enough to explain the patch of blood.'

'You're saying he was killed here? That's reading a hell of a lot into one bloodstain.'

'Not if you take into account the multiple fractures on Chapel's body. They were the sort you'd expect from a fall, and one hip was literally wrenched from its socket. That would take a huge amount of force. I couldn't work out how it could have happened until I came here.'

I indicated the scaffold-like arrangement of landings and ladders descending from the tower's entrance.

'That's high enough to do it,' I went on. 'The easiest way of getting his body down from the tower and into a boat would be to drop it from the top. It'd have tumbled against the ladder on the way down, and if a foot got caught between the rungs the momentum would snap bones *and* dislocate the hip.'

A fall like that would also explain why Chapel's cervical vertebrae were broken while, except for its facial injuries, his skull remained undamaged. Like his limbs, his head would have been twisted and jerked around like a rag doll's during the descent, with enough force to break his neck. From that height his skull could easily have been fractured as well, but my guess was that either the fall had been checked by his leg catching on a rung, or else his head had been cushioned by an arm when it hit the steel platform.

I stayed quiet while Clarke frowned up at the dripping underside of the tower, thinking it through for herself. I'd worried at first over why anyone would take a body all that way into the Backwaters instead of dumping it at sea. But the reasoning wasn't hard to follow. This close to shore there'd be a good chance it'd be washed up somewhere along the coast. Weighting it down was another option, but as silted up as the sea was around here there'd be no guarantee low tide wouldn't expose it.

In the Backwaters, though, there was a good chance the body would never be found. And even if it was there'd be no reason to associate it with the sea fort. While it wouldn't have been practicable to remove all traces of habitation from the tower, once anything identifying had been disposed of – with the exception of an overlooked lens cap and a small stain in the rust – it became an abandoned camp rather than a crime scene. There'd be no reason to think Emma Derby and Mark Chapel had ever been there.

And nothing to link Leo Villiers to any of it.

I looked across the sea towards the house on the promontory. It seemed shrunken from down here compared to the view from the tower window, blurred by spray and rain.

'They were blackmailing Villiers, weren't they?' I said.

If I hadn't felt so exhausted I might have realized something was off from Clarke's sudden stillness.

'Why do you say that?'

I was too tired for games. 'What else could this be about? If they just wanted somewhere to meet they could have used the boathouse. They didn't have to come all the way out to a sea fort. OK, Chapel might have liked the whole pirate radio thing, but enough to camp out here? And right opposite Leo Villiers' house? They didn't do all this for fun. They were spying on him.'

It was the only explanation that made any sense. The long-lens photographs Emma Derby had taken, even the video camera Chapel had stolen from work, it all pointed one way. The pair had used the sea fort as a hide, staking out Villiers' home so they could observe him from a distance. And he'd killed them for it.

Clarke's face was a mask. 'What could they have seen worth blackmailing him over?'

That was where my reasoning broke down. Political ambitions or not, Villiers didn't seem a natural fit for blackmail. He'd seemed almost to cultivate a bad reputation, flaunting his indiscretions rather than being ashamed of them.

'I don't know,' I admitted. 'He'd have destroyed any photographs or footage that was on their cameras. And any backups would have been lost in the burglary.'

'Burglary?'

It was obviously news to her. But then a DCI probably wouldn't have been told about a petty crime spree. 'The Trasks had all their computers stolen. Not just them, there was a spate of burglaries around the same time.'

'When was this?' she asked sharply.

'Not long after Emma Derby went missing,' I said, feeling the fatigue that had been clogging my mind begin to fall away. 'You think that was why they were stolen? The other burglaries were just a smokescreen?'

Clarke ignored the question. 'Would she have any other backups?'

'Not that I know of. Rachel – her sister – told me they don't have the password to any cloud storage.'

And if Emma had printed out any hard copies, she wouldn't have kept them at home where her husband might find them. In all probability they'd have been with Chapel at the sea fort, from where Villiers would have taken them, along with the cameras.

Evidently Clarke was thinking along the same lines. 'Shit.'

Until now I'd been numb. Since Lundy's shooting I'd felt trapped in a bubble, watching events around me without feeling a part of them. Now it burst.

'You can't keep this quiet any longer,' I said, my voice harsh. 'People need to know that Villiers is still alive.'

Clarke looked out over the windblown sea. 'It's not that simple.'

'Why? Jesus, what more does he have to do?' I didn't care how powerful Sir Stephen Villiers was, even he couldn't muzzle this any longer. 'This isn't just about Emma Derby any more. He's murdered three, no, *four* other people that we know of! He shot a *police* officer, for Christ's sake!'

'You think I need reminding?' Clarke flashed back. Our raised voices drew looks from two CSIs on the upper gantry. 'I've known

329

Bob Lundy for fifteen years! I went to his granddaughter's *christening*, so don't think for a *minute* I'm not going to shift heaven and hell to catch the bastard who shot him! But it wasn't Leo Villiers.'

I stared at her. Belatedly, I remembered the phone call Lundy had received earlier, how he'd explained that we had to go back. *We've had this all wrong. All of it.*

'How do you know?' I asked, my anger draining away.

Clarke glared for a moment, then turned away with a frustrated shake of her head.

'Because he's been in custody all morning.'

28

LATE THAT MORNING, a woman had pushed open the heavy glass doors and walked into the police headquarters building. The young constable behind the desk was on the phone. He glanced at the woman, noting in a not entirely professional assessment that she was attractive and well dressed as he gestured that he wouldn't be long. The woman waited patiently, but as the call went on the PC detected signs of nervousness. And impatience. One hand was knotted whitely on the shoulder strap of the Hermès bag; the long fingers of the other tapped a staccato rhythm on her arm.

Finally, the young constable ended the call and turned to her. The woman was very striking. Mid-thirties, model tall, with thick, almost black hair and great bone structure. Her clothes were well cut and obviously expensive, and although he didn't know what perfume she was wearing, the PC decided he liked it. He leaned on the counter, giving his best smile as he asked how he could help.

The woman's voice was a surprise, low and honeyed. And hesitant. She told him she wanted to speak to either DCI Clarke or DI Lundy. Only those two would do, she said, with a hint of attitude. When he asked for more information, she declined, repeating again that she would only speak to Lundy or Clarke. This time it wasn't a request, and the PC's smile dimmed. He stopped leaning on the counter.

There was something vaguely familiar about her, he realized. Retreating behind his usual desk formality, he picked up a pen and asked for her name. When she told him he thought he must have misheard. He asked her to repeat it, and this time there was no mistake. The young PC stared at her, open-mouthed.

Then he snatched up the phone.

Lundy was unavailable. He was on his way to the Backwaters to meet me, and it would be some time before the message reached him. But by luck Clarke was already at headquarters, preparing for what promised to be a terse budget meeting. Distracted and already in a bad mood, when a detective sergeant said there was someone asking for her at the desk downstairs, her response was typically curt. Then he told her the visitor's name.

Clarke cancelled her meeting.

In the observation booth, Clarke stared at the monitor showing the woman sitting in the other room. The visitor tried to seem calm, but her demeanour gave her away. She drummed her fingers, shifting uncomfortably in her chair as she glanced uneasily at the video camera. By now word had spread, and other officers had crammed into the observation booth to see for themselves. It wasn't every day someone supposedly dead strolled into a police station, and certainly not like this. Recovering from her own shock, Clarke ordered everyone out except for those directly involved with the investigation. Then, taking a few moments to compose herself, she squared her shoulders and went into the interview room.

The dark-haired woman looked up warily as the DCI entered. They'd met before, although Clarke wouldn't have recognized the person sitting in front of her. Not in a million years. Now she knew who it was, though, knew what to look for, there was no doubting it. Still, the formalities had to be dealt with.

The woman lifted her chin when Clarke asked who she was. There was a mixture of nervousness and defiance as she met the detective's gaze.

'My name's Lena Merchant,' she said. 'But I used to be called Leo Villiers.'

The cold and rain were forgotten as I stared at Clarke. 'You're serious?'

It was a stupid thing to say, but I was still stunned. The DCI looked as if she was having a hard time accepting it herself.

'Very. Villiers is transsexual. Or transgender, I should say. That's the big secret he's been hiding. He's still pre-op but he's undergoing "transition", I think it's called. He – or she, I suppose, now – spent the last few weeks at a private clinic in Sussex. Sort of a retreat for people with gender identity issues who want privacy and space. Those who can afford it,' she added, with something like her normal acidity.

I was struggling to take this in. 'That's where he's been all this time? Since he disappeared?'

'That's how it looks. He'd cut himself off from any outside contact, so he'd no idea what was going on. He was there when Emma Derby went missing as well, that's why he wouldn't provide an alibi. He couldn't admit where he'd been without revealing he was transgender, and he wasn't ready for that then. I don't think he intended to come out like this now, except he saw a news report yesterday and read about his own body supposedly being found in the estuary.'

Christ. Lundy had been right about Villiers hiding something. It just wasn't what everyone thought.

'Do you believe him?' I asked, not entirely convinced even now.

Wisps of ginger hair whipped unheeded across her cheeks as Clarke considered. 'We still need to verify it. But yes, I do. The clinic backs up his story, and he's agreed to release his medical records. It's not surprising his father didn't want anyone seeing them. It's all in there, going back years. Villiers was referred to a psychiatrist after a failed suicide attempt, and it came out he'd always felt he was female but didn't want to admit it. Even to himself, which given his background I can't say I blame him for. Doesn't alter the fact he was a shit, but it starts to explain why.'

It did. I'd come across transgender patients when I was a GP. The fact that someone could be born with a gender identity that didn't match their biological sex was recognized medically, but society was slower to accept anyone it perceived as different. Although there was more awareness now, some people still chose to keep their condition a secret.

But this showed Leo Villiers' behaviour in a whole new light. Not just the blatant womanizing, which now seemed like a desperate attempt at denial. Suddenly the drinking and depression, even his supposed suicide note, took on a whole new relevance. He hadn't been planning to end his life, just change it.

As Lundy said, it was all about perspective.

I looked through the blurring rain towards the house on the shore. 'That's why he was being blackmailed.'

Clarke nodded. 'He was sent pictures last year. Someone had photographed him through the windows, putting on make-up and a wig, trying on dresses. There was an anonymous letter claiming there was video footage as well, and that everything would be put online unless he paid half a million within the week.'

'He didn't know who sent it?'

'No, but he guessed Emma Derby was involved. She was a photographer and had access to his house while she was doing the interior design. Villiers had a dressing-up room where he kept his women's clothes but he left it unlocked one day while she was there. He thinks she must have found it and put two and two together. And I think now he was telling the truth when he denied they'd been having an affair. Not for lack of trying on her part, apparently, so she'd a motive to want to hurt him.'

I thought about what Rachel had told me about her sister, remembered the carefully posed self-portrait in the boathouse. Emma Derby would have been angry and humiliated to be turned down by Leo Villiers, which showed the public scenes and frosty atmosphere reported by witnesses in a very different light. It hadn't been the end of a relationship, but the rejection of one.

'What about the half-naked woman the cleaner saw in his

bedroom?' I asked, already having a good idea what she'd say.

'That was him. Or rather her.' Clarke shook her head. 'He'd started to get careless. He was finding the whole charade hard to sustain by then, and when he got the blackmail demand he panicked. He didn't have that sort of money to hand, so he basically ran away. Took himself off to the clinic to try and decide if he wanted to transition or not. In the end he didn't feel ready to commit, and came back home expecting the shit to have hit the fan. Which it had, just not how he expected.'

God, I thought, trying to imagine it. Villiers had exchanged one nightmare for another. Instead of having his secret made public he'd found himself the main suspect in Emma Derby's disappearance. And he couldn't prove his innocence without revealing his secret. For the first time I felt something I wouldn't have believed myself capable of feeling for Leo Villiers.

Sympathy.

'So why did he wait so long before going back to the clinic?' It was still too much of a leap to think of Villiers as 'she'.

'He was a mess,' Clarke said simply. 'He'd no idea what was going on, and now there were all these questions and pointed fingers to cope with as well. He was drinking and on tranquillizers, and says he really did consider suicide. We were almost right about that much, at least. The final straw was when his dog died.'

'His *dog*?'

'I know.' Clarke gave a wintry smile. 'He got it as a pup when he was kicked out of university, and according to him it was the only thing that didn't care who or what he was. When it had to be destroyed he says something snapped. He stayed long enough to bury it and then just walked away. Literally. Got on a train and left everything behind. House, car, money, the lot. He says he doesn't want anything to do with any of it any more.'

Clarke sounded sceptical about that much, at least. But put in this new context Villiers' reaction didn't seem hard to understand. Sometimes all it takes is one final stress to bring everything crashing down. And while our circumstances were very different, I didn't find it hard to imagine a life becoming so unbearable that the only way to survive was to walk away from it.

I'd once done the same thing myself.

Still, while this explained why none of Villiers' bank accounts or credit cards had been used since he'd disappeared, it posed a different question. 'If he wasn't using any of his own money how did he pay for the clinic?'

'Oh, he's not exactly penniless.' Clarke irritably brushed the flapping strand of hair from her face. 'His mother left him a trust fund that'll see he doesn't starve. Merchant was her maiden name, so cutting himself off from his old life obviously doesn't extend to that. It's only anything connected to his father he doesn't want anything to do with.'

Remembering Sir Stephen's behaviour I guessed that might be mutual. I thought about the cold-eyed insistence that the body found in the estuary was his son's. Lundy had said all along that Villiers' father was hiding something, and now we knew what. *My son is dead.*

As far as Sir Stephen was concerned, perhaps he was.

'Does Villiers know who it was we found in his clothes?' I asked.

Clarke nodded tiredly. 'That's why he came back. Anthony Russell, twenty-six-year-old former model and dancer. Indonesian on his mother's side, worked at a dressing service in London where trans men and women can try on clothes in private. He was another of Villiers' secrets. They usually hooked up in London but he'd occasionally come out to Willets Point. He was the same sort of size as Villiers and used to borrow clothes when he stayed. Except for his shoes. Russell's feet were bigger.'

And had hammertoes, I thought. It was a common complaint for dancers. I'd told Lundy I thought the dead man could have been athletically built, but I'd not made the connection. I felt dully annoyed at my mistake. Still, the part-Indonesian ancestry could well explain the skull's mix of characteristics. As well, perhaps, as the gardener's sighting of a prowler on Willets Point. Not a burglar or a refugee, just another part of Villiers' private life he wanted to keep secret.

Something else occurred to me. 'Was Russell colour-blind?' I asked, thinking about the garish purple sock in the cheap training shoe.

'I've no idea. Why?'

'It doesn't matter.' I felt too tired to explain.

Clarke gave me an odd look as she continued. 'Russell was the only person who knew Villiers was transgender. But they fell out when Villiers told him he was going to transition. Apparently Russell had expensive tastes and a recreational drug habit, so the idea of a poor, transitioned Villiers was a lot less attractive than a rich, closeted one. Villiers ended up throwing his house keys down and storming out, telling Russell he could help himself if that was all he cared about. He didn't expect to be taken literally, but when he read about the body he guessed who it was.'

'Does Villiers have any idea who might have killed him?'

'No, but Russell used to like playing around with his shotguns. Shooting bottles, taking pot-shots at seagulls. Although Villiers doesn't think he would have shot himself intentionally, he thought he could have done it by accident when he was drunk or high.'

'Is that what you think?' I asked.

'I think if it was that simple we'd have found the gun by now. And I'm a long way past believing anything about this case is accidental.'

The sound of someone climbing down the ladder made us both turn. But it was only Frears. Awkward in the bulky coveralls, the pathologist made an ungainly descent before coming over. He gave an awkward shrug.

'What you'd expect.' There was none of his usual flippancy. 'Single shotgun blast to the abdomen and lower chest, massive trauma and blood loss. Looks like the gunman surprised him half-way down the steps. Minimal spread, couldn't have been fired from more than six or seven yards away. The pellets we've found look like bismuth birdshot, probably number four or five. Not huge, but at that distance it wouldn't make much difference.'

The shotgun cartridge found at Edgar's home had been number five birdshot, and bismuth rather than lead. The same as the cartridges at Leo Villiers' house.

'If it's any consolation I doubt he knew much about it.' Frears sounded almost apologetic. 'With an injury like that his system would have started to shut down from shock almost immediately. Frankly I'm surprised he survived as long as he did.'

As though on cue there was activity above us. We fell silent as Lundy's body was carried out from the tower. Strapped to a stretcher, the body bag was brought down on to the upper gantry. Then, while one officer went down the ladder first to steady it in the wind, it was slowly lowered on a rope to the platform. I started forward to help as it neared the bottom, but the area around the ladder was already crowded. Hands reached up to take the weight as the stretcher and its burden were set down on the platform.

Clarke watched, tight-lipped, as Lundy's body was carried over to the waiting launch.

'What'll happen now?' I asked her as Frears headed after it.

'Now?' she echoed bleakly. 'Now I go to see Sandra Lundy. Then I'm going to continue questioning Leo Villiers, or Lena bloody Merchant, to find out what else he knows. There've been too many assumptions made in this investigation from the start, especially about Emma Derby's role in all this. When it comes down to it we still haven't found her body, which is starting to make me wonder. And after what's happened today I'm not taking anything for granted.'

As her meaning sank in, I felt a shiver down my spine that had nothing to do with the cold. It had been assumed from the start that Trask's missing wife was a victim of Leo Villiers. But if we'd been so wrong about that it threw doubt on everything else as well. Emma Derby's disappearance had started all this, yet out of all the victims her body remained conspicuously absent.

What if Rachel's sister was guilty of more than blackmail?

'What do you want me to do?' I asked.

Clarke tore her eyes away from the scene on the launch. 'Once you've given your statement you might as well go back to London.'

'London?' I said, surprised. 'I've still got some things to finish off at the mortuary . . .'

'They can wait. You're too involved now. I can't afford any more complications because one of my consultants got tangled up with a victim's family. Not after this.'

'But I can still—'

'I'm not asking, Dr Hunter,' Clarke said, her voice suddenly hard. She sighed. 'Look, I appreciate what you've done, and I know you want to help catch whoever did this. But you can't. You need to let us handle it from here.'

I was on the point of arguing. Then I saw the strain in her face and remembered Lundy, and any argument drained out of me.

I nodded.

She started to walk away, then turned back. 'One more thing. Until we know what's going on, I'd appreciate it if you don't see anyone else connected with this investigation. That means anyone, OK?'

Ginger hair blew about her face as she stared at me, making sure there was no misunderstanding. Then she turned on her heel and marched to the launch.

Below me on the diminishing sandbank, the gulls fought raucously over the last of the pale crabs.

The weather was filthy as I was taken back to shore in the marine unit RHIB. Gusts of wind blew the rain in near-horizontal sheets, merging it with the spray thrown up by the blunt bow. The open cockpit lacked any sort of shelter, and I was shivering despite the waterproof jacket I'd been lent. It was heavy, but the bright-yellow plastic was unlined. The marine unit officers were politely distant towards me, but I didn't mind. I wasn't in the mood to talk either.

The larger coastguard vessel had taken Clarke and Frears

339

further down the coast, where there was a deep-water harbour from which Lundy's body could be taken to the mortuary. The RHIB was heading back to the oyster quay, where a mobile incident command unit had been set up. Bouncing and pitching on a towline behind us was the small boat that Rachel, Lundy and I had taken out to the sea fort.

It seemed an impossibly long time ago.

The overcast sky was already hastening the day towards a premature dusk as the RHIB bumped against the quayside. I climbed up the same steps as I had the morning we'd recovered the body from the Barrows. There was something dreamlike about walking again across the puddled concrete when I went to give a formal statement in the police trailer. More than once the police officer taking it had to repeat herself when my attention wandered.

'Sorry, what?' I asked, realizing I'd drifted away again.

'I said, do you want to see a doctor?' The young woman's round face was professionally concerned. 'You might be suffering from shock.'

She could be right, but I didn't need a doctor. The only person I wanted to see was Rachel, and I still had no idea what to do about that. She should have been allowed home by now, but I didn't think turning up at Creek House would be a good idea even if Clarke hadn't expressly warned me against it.

But no matter what the DCI had said, there was no way I could leave without speaking to Rachel, at least. I was already taking out my phone as I left the trailer, walking into the lee of the boarded-up oyster factory for shelter while I called her. When it went to voicemail I left a message to ring me and then tried to think what to do next.

The numbness I'd felt earlier had descended again. I knew Clarke would be angry that I'd tried to contact Rachel, but it didn't seem to matter any more. Objectively, I was aware that the state of suspension I was in was only temporary, that it was only a matter of time before everything that had happened caught up. For now, though, I was running on automatic, focusing only on whatever was directly in front of me.

Which right now was how to get to the boathouse where I'd left my car. None of the police had offered to drive me back, and even if I'd wanted them to I wasn't going to ask at a time like that. I spent several minutes standing with the rain dripping off the plastic hood of my borrowed coat, staring blankly across the broken surface of the estuary, before I realized the answer was right in front of me.

One of the marine unit officers was in the process of untying Trask's little boat from the RHIB when I offered to take it back to the boathouse, where it could more easily be collected. There was a brief discussion over the radio, but the police had more important things to deal with than delivering a boat back to its owner.

'You sure you'll be OK handling it in this?' the marine unit sergeant asked, looking at the white-flecked waves in the estuary.

'I'm only going to the creek.'

'OK, but don't hang about.' He glanced at the moody sky, water streaming from his yellow waterproof. 'It's a spring tide, and the weather's going to get worse before it gets better. We've been told to get everyone off the sea fort in the next hour whether they've finished or not. You don't want to be taking a boat far.'

I told him I wouldn't, but I didn't really care about the weather. I'd sailed in bad conditions when I was younger, and I'd be running with the returning tide rather than against it. The engine started on the second go, and as soon as I pulled away from the quayside I felt the current take hold. Even though I'd been expecting it I was almost caught out. I fought the boat as it tried to get away from me, then brought the bow round and headed up the estuary towards the creek.

Once I was out in the middle it was easier. The estuary was rougher than I'd seen it, but not so much so that it threatened to overwhelm the small craft. I was glad to have something to occupy my mind, and the waves' grey rhythm was hypnotic. Rocking with the boat's motion I found myself thinking of absolutely nothing beyond the simple task of keeping the bow on course. Then a larger swell thumped against the fibreglass hull, and I flinched as the shotgun's *boom* seemed to echo in my head again.

As quickly as that, the numbness was gone. I took deep breaths of the cold salt spray as the full impact of what had happened finally hit home. There was too much to process. The revelation about Leo Villiers, my dismissal from the investigation and uncertainty over Rachel. All of it faded beside Lundy's murder. The memory of that made me feel physically winded. No matter what Clarke had said, someone had come out to the sea fort with the intention of killing everyone on it. Someone who had already murdered four people, at least two of them only guilty of being in the wrong place at the wrong time. And now that Leo Villiers had been ruled out, we had absolutely no idea of who had done it.

Or why.

Distracted, I almost missed the opening to the creek. When I realized how fast it was coming up I quickly steered towards it, but I'd misjudged the strength of the tide. The engine pitch rose as I opened the throttle, turning at a sharper angle to compensate. Now the waves were hitting the boat side-on. I clutched at the seat as a larger one smacked into the hull, sending freezing water over the side and almost overturning it. As the little boat settled I looked around, only now noticing how conditions had deteriorated. The estuary was a mass of frayed waves, already lapping close to the top of the banks, and the level was still rising. I'd been too preoccupied to worry about the marine unit officer's warning. I couldn't afford to ignore it any more.

The mouth of the creek was sliding past at an alarming rate. There was no way I could make it, not without exposing the side of the boat to the full force of the waves, and I'd come close enough to tipping over once as it was. Wiping the spray from my eyes, I turned the bow away until I was running with the tide once more. By now I'd passed the creek, but there was no helping that. Looking back, I tried to gauge the rhythm of the swells before gunning the engine and swinging the boat into a tight turn. It began to roll, lurching as waves slapped against its side, but then the bow came round and I had it aimed directly into the waves, heading back up the estuary towards the creek.

It meant I was fighting against the full force of the tide and wind. The engine laboured, and the boat barely seemed to make any headway as it slammed into one wave after another. For agonizing minutes the creek didn't seem to come any closer, and I thought I'd have no choice but to either run higher up the estuary or try to make for the nearest shore. Gradually, though, the whipping grasses that fringed the mouth of the creek drew nearer, until at last I was in its relative shelter.

The chop here was still heavy but nowhere near as rough as it was in the more exposed estuary. I tasted salt as I wiped the mingled rain and seawater from my face, relaxing my grip on the tiller as the tide carried the boat towards the Backwaters. Now it was less of a struggle to keep on course, I could appreciate how abnormally high the waters were. The swollen creek was already topping the lowest sections of its banks, spreading out on to the surrounding fields. And the tide hadn't peaked yet.

Even though I'd known this part of the country was prone to flooding, had seen the evidence in the high-water marks left on trees and buildings, it hadn't really struck me before how quickly it could be inundated. The weather wasn't even especially bad: compared to an Atlantic storm I'd once been caught in on the Outer Hebrides this was no more than a squall. But the Hebridean islands were fortresses of cliff and rock. Here the low-lying ground was subject to the whims of the sea, vulnerable and easily overwhelmed.

Like now. I barely recognized the landscape around me as I steered the small boat up the creek. Sandy hummocks had become miniature islands, and reeds and long-stemmed grasses sprouted from the water's choppy surface. It was growing dark, too, as what little daylight remained was choked off by heavy rain clouds.

But I didn't have much further to go. I still had no idea what I'd do when I got back to the boathouse, and as though the thought had prompted it my phone rang. Easing off the engine, I let the tide carry me along as I took it from my pocket.

It was Rachel.

'I got your message,' she said, her voice breaking up from the poor reception.

'I wanted to see how you were. Are you back at the house?'

'Yeah. I caught a taxi after I'd given my statement. Where are you? I can hardly hear you.'

I turned my back to the wind, trying to shield the phone from the rain. 'On the creek. I'm taking the boat back to the boat-house.'

'You're out in this?'

'Not for much longer.' I broke off while I avoided an entire bush that must have uprooted from the bank and was now being carried upstream. 'What shall I do with the boat?'

'It doesn't matter, just leave it there.' She sounded upset. 'Have you heard?'

For a moment I was confused, thinking she was talking about Lundy. Then I realized she didn't mean the shooting. This was something else.

'Heard what?'

Her voice faded, then came back loud enough to hear: '. . . police . . . taken Andrew for questioning.'

Oh, Christ, I thought. Clarke hadn't wasted any time. 'I thought he was meeting a client? Can't they confirm where he was?'

'The client cancelled at the last minute. Andrew drove into Exeter anyway, but he didn't see anyone so he can't prove it. The police picked him up in front of Jamie and *Fay*, for God's sake! Did you know about it?'

'No, of course not,' I said, correcting the boat.

'Like you didn't know about Mark Chapel, you mean?'

I stared at the dirty water pooling around my feet, too weary to respond. But Rachel quickly went on.

'I'm sorry, I shouldn't have said that. I just . . . I don't know what's going on any more! I keep thinking about . . . about what happened earlier. And now this. It doesn't seem to stop.'

Rain dripped from my hood, running in cold rivulets down my sleeve as I tried and failed to come up with an answer. 'Shall I come over?'

'It's better if you don't. Fay's in a state and Jamie's beside himself. He almost lost it when the police took Andrew.'

'Tomorrow, then. I'll call you.'

Clarke wouldn't like it, but if I was off the investigation it was none of her business. There was a pause. I thought the signal had died until Rachel spoke.

'What will you do tonight?'

I hadn't thought that far ahead. I couldn't bring myself to go back to London, but I didn't have the boathouse key any more. Even if I did, I wasn't confident the flat would stay dry if the creek continued to rise like this. Where it had broken its banks it was starting to merge into a single body of water with the smaller channels and ditches. I looked out across the spreading floodplain, its full extent masked by the rain and deepening twilight.

'I'll find somewhere to stay.'

'OK, but the roads around the Backwaters are going to be impassable if this keeps up. Be careful.'

I said I would, wiping the rain from my phone before tucking it inside the waterproof coat. At least Rachel, Fay and Jamie would be safe. These were the sort of conditions Trask had designed Creek House for, and its concrete pillars would raise it well above any flood.

I needed to get to higher ground myself. I opened up the engine again, wanting to get off the creek and away from the Backwaters as soon as I could. But I daren't go any faster. I didn't want to run aground, and with the creek overflowing it was becoming hard to see where its banks were. Trees and hedges seem to grow from a spreading lake, and off to one side I saw water streaming across a low stretch of road almost as fast as the boat was travelling. It would be touch and go to get my car clear in time, and I was relieved when I finally saw the boathouse up ahead.

The jetty was already submerged. Only the top half of the timber gate that closed off the boathouse dock was still visible, and waves now covered the lower steps almost to the small landing by the hatchway. But the creek's bank was higher here, and the flooding hadn't reached as far as the boathouse itself. That was just as well, since my car was parked behind it. As I drew closer I was relieved to see it was still on dry ground. Then, as the boat approached the jetty, I saw there was another car parked next to mine.

Even in the fading light I recognized the sleek black lines of Sir Stephen Villiers' Daimler.

29

ICUT THE ENGINE, letting the powerful current carry me the last few yards. Even so, I still hit the jetty too fast, the fibreglass hull thumping into it hard enough to jar my teeth. I threw the line around a post before the boat could be swept upstream, making sure to leave enough slack to allow for the still-rising tide before I clambered out.

The water covering the jetty almost reached my knees. Careful of my footing, I sloshed along it to the boathouse, which seemed to have shrunk to almost half its height as waves slapped against its stone walls. As I made my way to the steps, I saw that the wooden cover for the hatchway had come loose. It was banging against the wall, the rope that had secured it swinging in the wind. I didn't bother stopping to shut it. It would only blow free again, and I was in a hurry to get on to dry land.

I wanted to find out what Sir Stephen was doing there.

Water streamed from my legs as I hurried up the steps, wondering what could be urgent enough to bring Leo Villiers' father out in this. As I reached the top of the steps I saw his driver, Porter, walking away from the boathouse towards the big black car. He wore a thick overcoat but no hat, apparently indifferent to the weather. The wind and rain must have drowned out my approach, because he didn't notice me until I spoke.

'Looking for me?'

Porter spun round. He stared, then gave a perfunctory smile.

'Where'd you come from? Scared me to death.' He flicked away a cigarette he'd had cupped in his hand. It hissed in the wet cinders as he gestured towards the Daimler. 'Sir Stephen would like a word.'

I'd no idea what Leo Villiers' father might want, and I'd no wish to speak to the man anyway. But I could hardly refuse. Hoping it wouldn't take long, I started to walk over to the Daimler as Porter opened its rear door.

'He's here, Sir Stephen.'

He stood politely by the black car, gloved hands folded in front of him. My boots squelched as I walked, and I was conscious of how wet and bedraggled I was. But the unease I felt had nothing to do with that. I slowed, wondering how Sir Stephen knew I'd been staying at the boathouse. Or why he hadn't phoned if he wanted to talk. I found my eyes going to the cigarette stub Porter had discarded.

I stopped.

The driver stood patiently by the car's open door, water trickling over his bare head. The pockmarked face had dark flecks on it, like shaving cuts. I took in the black leather gloves, the smart black brogues that were now muddy and smeared. They were city shoes, the sort that would have smooth leather soles.

Like the footprint in Lundy's blood I'd seen at the sea fort.

'Dr Hunter?' Porter said, still standing by the open car door.

I found my voice. 'I thought Sir Stephen didn't like you smoking.'

His polite smile remained in place. 'And I'm sure I'll be reprimanded for it. Now, if you don't mind . . .'

I couldn't see into the back of the car. The door had opened towards me, and the darkly tinted windows hid whatever was inside. I looked over at the boathouse.

The door stood ajar, the frame splintered by the lock.

The rain beat down as Porter and I faced each other across the cinders. He pushed the car door shut with a heavy *thunk*.

'Worth a try.'

My heart was pounding. I didn't know why he was here, but I knew what it meant. And as my fatigue dropped away, I also knew that he wouldn't let me go now I'd seen him. Any more than he had Stacey Coker.

Or Lundy.

Porter gave a snort when he saw me look towards my car. 'Yeah, go ahead. I'll just wait here while you unlock it.'

I abandoned that idea: there was no way I was getting past him. Trying to seem as unconcerned as he did, I nodded at the small flecks of blood on his pockmarked cheeks. 'Not a good move, shooting a steel door. You're lucky you didn't lose an eye.'

'Yeah, lucky. That's me.'

He glanced past me to the steps leading down to the jetty, as though checking there was no one else he'd missed. Almost absently, he flexed his folded hands, snugging the fingers of the leather gloves down tighter. 'So where is it?'

'Where's what?'

'Look, I've had a shit day and I'm really not in the mood. Just tell me where it is.'

I felt I was in some surreal nightmare. 'I've no idea what you're talking about.'

There was no smile on his face now. 'Don't fuck around. Where's the *money*?'

'What money? I don't—'

'Look, you stupid bastard, I'm giving you a chance here,' he spat. 'Villiers' five hundred grand, it was hidden in the cupboard at Holloway's house. Where is it?'

None of this made any sense. Five hundred thousand was the amount Emma Derby and Mark Chapel had demanded for the photographs. But according to Clarke, Leo Villiers hadn't paid his blackmailers.

Worry about that later. 'The house burnt down . . .'

'I *know* it burnt down, but the money was already gone by then.

Somebody took it, and Holloway wouldn't have any use for it even if he knew what it was. The only other people who went there before the police were you and Derby's sister. So I'll ask you again. *Where's the fucking money?'*

'The police searched the house, they must have—'

'The police went there after I did,' he said with exaggerated patience. 'If they'd found it the old man would have heard, and so would I. Try again.'

I was getting past the shock now, beginning to piece this together. 'The old man' must be Sir Stephen. I didn't know where the money had come from, but Porter had obviously been hiding it at Edgar's house. And while I'd no idea who had taken it, I knew what he'd found at the house instead.

'Was it worth killing Stacey Coker for?' I asked.

If I'd had any doubts, his reaction ended them. An expression that could have been shame crossed his face, but only for a moment. 'I asked you a question.'

'Did she actually see you, or did you just strangle her anyway?'

'Last chance. Are you going to tell me?'

There was no sign of any remorse. I started to say again that I'd no idea, that I didn't know anything about any money. But even if he believed me Porter wouldn't let me live to tell anyone. I'd seen first-hand what he'd done to Mark Chapel, a martial arts enthusiast who was younger and bigger. I'd no illusions about my chances in a fight. That left one option.

Porter shrugged and started forward. 'OK, if that's how you want it.'

'It's in the car boot.'

He stopped, watchful as I searched through my pockets for my car keys. I pulled them out, holding them up for him to see.

'Here.'

I threw them too hard, hoping he'd miss the catch. But his hand shot out and snatched the keys from the air. He stared at me.

'It's all there,' I told him.

'It better be.'

I could feel myself shivering from adrenalin as Porter went to my car. Keeping his eyes on me, he thumbed the fob. I forced myself to hold his stare as the door locks clicked open. Still watching me, he reached for the boot. I stood there as it popped open. He lifted it and looked inside.

I turned and ran.

I heard him swear and come after me as I clattered down the steps to the jetty. The boat had seemed my best chance, but looking out to where I'd left it I saw my mistake. I'd been gambling on having enough of a head start to jump in and cast off before Porter could catch up. Even though I wouldn't have time to start the engine, the rushing current would carry the boat away as soon as it was untied.

But I'd forgotten about the slack I'd left in the line so it wouldn't be swamped by the rising waters. The tide had carried the boat out to its full extent, and now it was tossing around on the end of the rope like a leashed animal, a good two yards from the end of the flooded jetty.

I'd never haul it back in time.

Porter's footsteps thudded on the bank as I jumped on to the small landing on the steps. The wave tops had almost reached it, and the jetty itself was all but invisible under them. I'd cornered myself, I realized. There was nothing for it but to jump into the flooded creek and take my chances. But as I was about to fling myself down the last few steps and into the water, there was a movement off to one side. The hatchway's loose cover was banging in the wind, offering a glimpse of the dock's dark interior. As Porter's feet sounded on the timber steps behind me I made up my mind and ducked inside.

I splashed down into blackness and cold, choppy water. Gasping for breath, I grabbed the hatch cover and tried to slam it. The cover bucked as Porter threw himself against it, forcing a hand through the gap. Water sloshed in my face as I struggled to keep him out, the submerged decking creaking and cracking under me in protest. Something bobbed nearby, and in the thin light coming through the hatchway I recognized the broken oar I'd taken into the Backwaters. Keeping my weight against the wooden cover, I snatched up the oar and brought the jagged end down on to Porter's gloved hand. I stabbed it down again and again, until with a grunt he yanked his arm back.

The cover banged shut. A moment later it jerked against me as he kicked it, but I'd got the advantage now. I kept my shoulder to the rough timber planks, riding out the kicks until he stopped.

Water slopped in the sudden quiet. I could hear Porter breathing heavily outside.

'Very fucking clever. What're you going to do now?'

I hadn't a clue. The hatch opened inward, so providing I stayed where I was he couldn't get in. But I couldn't get out either. Shivering, I looked around. The water was waist deep and still rising. Vertical bars of grey twilight seeped through the slats of the gate. I could make out an assortment of boating junk floating around but none of it looked of any use. Pushing away the holed canoe that was bumping against me like a persistent horse, I took my phone from my pocket. It was dripping wet but I tried it anyway. The screen stayed dead.

There'd be no help coming. I tried to stay calm and think. The water level inside the boathouse already seemed higher, but that would hold for the outside as well. The creek was cold but not life-threateningly so, and Porter would be in a hurry to get away. He'd murdered a police officer. He couldn't afford to waste time here, or wait until the rising waters forced me out.

Then I remembered he had a shotgun, and any relief was snuffed out.

'You still there or have you drowned?' he called.

I pressed my hands against the hatch cover, gauging the rough wood. Solid as it was, it wouldn't be any protection against a shotgun blast. I spoke through it.

'Don't make this any worse for yourself.'

My voice sounded ragged from cold and exertion. There was a sour laugh from outside.

'I don't intend to. Soon as you tell me where the money is I'll go.'

Back to that again. 'I told you, I don't know about any money.'

'You just said it was in your car, so why should I believe you?'

'Because this isn't helping either of us. You killed a police officer. You seriously think you're going to get far?'

'Worry about yourself. Water must be getting pretty high in there. Bet it's cold round your bollocks.'

I was trying to ignore the cold, thinking instead about the shot-gun. The Mowbry must be in the Daimler, but if Porter went to get it I could make a break for the boat. Evidently that had occurred to him as well, or he'd have gone for it already. 'Did you know Leo Villiers is still alive?'

'No shit.'

Of course he knew, I berated myself. That was why he was running. With Villiers not just alive but demonstrably innocent, it would be only a matter of time before the police began looking at other suspects. Including him.

'Did his father tell you?' I asked, aware that the longer he stayed down here, away from the shotgun, the more the odds swung in my favour.

'You think the old man would admit his son's turned up as a woman? Like he's going to broadcast that.'

The soft slosh of water told me Porter was moving around out-side. I listened for any sign that he was going back up the steps, ready to make a dash for the boat if he did.

'So how did you find out?' I pressed.

'I was driving him when the police called to break the news. Got to keep Sir Stephen happy, haven't they?'

'He talked to them in front of you?'

'Like I said, you'd be surprised what you get to hear when you're taken for granted.'

There was a note of bitterness there. I filed it away, more con-cerned with what he was doing outside. I could hear him moving through the water, trying to be quiet about it. 'Is that how you found out we were at the sea fort?'

'Yeah, I wasn't expecting that. Made my arse pucker when I heard, I can tell you. Couldn't wait to drop the old man off so I could find out what you were doing out there.'

His voice was coming from further away, from the direction of the jetty rather than the steps. I strained to make out what he was doing, hoping he wasn't untying the boat. 'You shouldn't have killed Lundy.'

'Tell me something I don't fucking know.'

'Then why did you do it?' I almost shouted, unable to keep the rawness from my voice.

'I didn't have any choice. I didn't even know he was with you until I saw him. From what I'd heard it sounded like it was just you and the sister who'd gone out there.'

'So you were only planning to kill us? And then what? Try and pass it off as another boating accident?'

'I didn't plan to kill anyone, all right? I only wanted the fucking money back! Christ, you think I *wanted* this?' The sloshing was getting louder: he was coming back from wherever he'd been. 'Look, things have got out of hand. If I turn myself in will you put a word in for me?'

That was the last thing I'd expected. His voice sounded closer: he was right outside again. I hesitated, shivering in the cold water. I didn't trust him but I couldn't see where this was leading.

'OK,' I said carefully. 'But you have to—'

I was almost knocked off my feet as the hatch cover bucked under a new assault. Water surged as I heaved against it. I could hear Porter panting on the other side. He'd almost caught me out, but now the attempt had failed he didn't have the leverage to force his way in. The cover jumped from a last desultory blow before he gave up.

'Come on, this is fucking stupid,' he panted. 'Just tell me where the money is and I'll let you go.'

'For Christ's sake, I don't *know* about any money!' Frustrated,

I kept my shoulder against the hatch while I looked round for the broken oar. Grabbing it, I jammed it at an angle between the decking planks and the hatch cover. It wouldn't keep Porter out for long but it might give me a few seconds if he tried anything again. 'Who'd you steal it from anyway? Or were you blackmailing Leo Villiers as well?'

'I'm not a fucking thief! And if I'd wanted to blackmail the Villiers I'd have done it years ago.' He sounded genuinely affronted. 'I was trying to bail them out, same as always. That Derby bitch and her boyfriend had got photos of Leo dressing up, and wanted half a million not to go public. Half a *million*. Jesus. Little Leo shit himself and did a runner when he found out, so then they went to his old man. I told him not to pay, but oh no. Couldn't have everyone knowing his son liked to play at Barbie, could he?'

The bitterness was back. I could hear Porter moving away from the hatch again. *Now what?* I looked over at the gate that barred the opening to the creek. The wooden slats were more than half covered by the slopping waves.

Remembering its rusted padlock, I hoped it would hold.

'So then what? You killed them and took the money?' *Come on, what are you doing out there?*

'I wasn't going to let some chancers muscle in, not after all I've done for the Villiers.' I could hear him prowling around outside, trying not to make a noise as he waded through the water. 'Any idiot could see the photos were taken from the sea fort. They wanted the money leaving at the oyster sheds, so after I dropped the bag off I went to Willets Point and kept watch. Waited until I saw a boat go to the fort and then took Leo's dinghy out there. Thought I'd get the money back and maybe put a bit of a scare into them, but that was all.'

His voice was still moving, but sounded more muffled now. It was hard to pinpoint where he was.

'So what went wrong?' Christ it was cold. I hugged myself, straining to hear Porter's movements.

'The fucking boyfriend.' Porter sounded disgusted. 'He had to show off, act the big hard man. Giving it all that "don't fuck with me, I'm a blackbelt" shit. Like it was a fucking dojo. So I hit him.'

'A palm strike,' I said. My teeth had started to chatter.

There was a pause. 'That's right. I thought a busted nose might straighten him out. Didn't mean to kill him, but the wanker had it coming.'

'Did Emma Derby have it coming as well?'

There was no answer. I listened, desperate for some clue as to what he was doing. The water was lapping up to my chest now, leaching the remaining heat from my body. I didn't know how much longer I could stay in there.

'What did you do with her body?' I asked, trying to keep my voice from shaking. 'Did you take her into the Backwaters as well after you'd dropped her from the tower?'

'You're half right.'

He sounded distracted. I'd no idea what he meant, but I was too cold to worry about it now. 'What about Sir Stephen? Does he know?'

There was silence. Of course he didn't, I thought dully. Porter wouldn't have been able to keep the money if his employer knew what he'd done. The cold was slowing me down, making it hard to think. But I needed to get him talking again, to get some idea of where he was.

I'd started to frame another question when the dim light coming through the timber slats was suddenly blocked. I turned to see a shadow passing behind them, and then the chain securing the padlock clattered as Porter heaved on it. I abandoned the hatch as the gate shook, frantically wading towards him, but in my panic I forgot I was on the raised decking. I'd only gone a few paces when my foot slipped off the edge, and suddenly I was plunged into deeper water.

That saved me. As I floundered back onto the decking, the gate abruptly fell quiet. The shadow vanished from behind it as Porter began splashing back along the jetty. He was making no attempt to be quiet any more as he rushed for the hatch he'd drawn me away from. If I'd reached the gate I'd never have made it back in time, and it was still touch and go now. The heavy plastic coat acted as a drag as I laboured through the chest-deep water. It was like running in a slow-motion nightmare. I could hear Porter wallowing along the side of the boathouse, racing to beat me to the untended hatch.

He reached it first. I saw the wooden cover jerk as he tried to get in, only for it to be checked by the oar I'd wedged in place. There was a *crack* as the shaft snapped, and then I threw myself against the wooden panel and forced it shut. I braced myself, spitting out a mouthful of salty water as I rode out Porter's furious blows.

'*Fucker!*'

The hatch cover stopped jumping. I could hear Porter panting outside, swearing in frustration. I leaned my head against the cover's rough wet planks, breathless and shuddering from the cold. I was soaked through, and the water was still rising. But this was the third time Porter had almost tricked me. I wasn't moving away from the hatch again until I was sure he'd gone.

'Look, this is fucking stupid,' he said, his voice rasping with frustration. 'I only want the money. Soon as you tell me where it is I'll go.'

I didn't even have the strength to yell any more. 'I keep telling you, I don't know about any money. It doesn't matter how many times you ask, the answer's the same. I don't *know*!'

There was silence from the other side, but the sound of his breathing told me he was still there. Finally, he spoke.

'Your choice. Don't say I didn't warn you.'

I heard him wading through the water, then his feet were clomping up the steps. I tensed, thinking about the shotgun, and uncertain if this was another trick. 'What's that supposed to mean?'

His voice came from higher up: he'd reached the top of the bank. 'Only two people could've taken the money from Holloway's house before the police got there. If you don't know where it is, that leaves Derby's sister.'

'No, wait!' I shouted. 'She doesn't know anything. *Wait!*'

But his footsteps had already receded. Panic rose in me at the thought of Porter going after Rachel. It crossed my mind that this was another ruse to lure me outside, but it didn't matter. Grabbing the broken oar, I threw the hatch cover open. Nothing happened. I looked outside. The creek was swollen and fast, but in the dusky twilight I couldn't see anyone waiting. Then I heard a car engine start up.

Porter was leaving.

I felt no relief, only a terrible sense of urgency. My mind was racing as I began clambering out through the hatch. There was no way to warn Rachel or call the police with my useless phone, and Porter had my car keys. My only hope was the boat. If it was still there then I had a chance.

I was half out of the hatchway before I realized the sound of the engine was growing louder. It wasn't deep or powerful enough to be the Daimler, and suddenly I understood why. As tyres crunched over the cinders at the top of the bank I turned and threw myself back into the boathouse.

Then my car burst through the wooden railings above me.

30

I FELL INTO THE freezing water as the wall behind me shuddered with a huge, rending crash. I couldn't see, couldn't hear. Couldn't breathe. I thrashed around but I'd lost any sense of direction. Something struck my head. I flailed away from it, convinced the entire wall was coming down, and then my head broke the surface. I sucked in a lungful of air and breathed in saltwater as well. Coughing, I fought for breath as I struggled to stay afloat. My feet no longer touched bottom and the heavy jacket had filled with water, threatening to drag me under. The air was full of dust, still ringing with echoes of the impact, and I flinched and twisted round as something bumped against my shoulders. The humped shape of the upturned canoe floated behind me, swinging in a slow circle on the churned water.

I threw an arm over it, clinging gratefully to the smooth hull. Panting, I looked over at where I'd been standing moments before. In the fading light coming through the gate, I saw that the stone wall was bellied inwards around the hatchway.

Wedged into the opening was the crumpled wing of my car.

I felt a wave of despair. The water was lapping well over half-way up the walls, and still rising. If it continued at this rate it wouldn't be long before the whole lower level was underwater, and me along with it.

But Porter would have reached Creek House before then. It wasn't only Rachel who'd be there. Trask was in police custody, but Fay and probably Jamie would be home. Porter had already killed an injured teenage girl and an unarmed police officer.

He wouldn't leave any witnesses alive.

I kicked towards the submerged decking, but when I tried to climb on to it the rotten boards pulled free of the damaged stonework, dumping me back into the water. I'd seen enough, though: the hatch was hopelessly blocked. Grabbing on to the canoe again, I tried to force my sluggish brain to think. The shadows inside the boathouse were growing deeper. The twilight outside was fading into night, and soon it would be too dark to see. Still holding on to the canoe, I swam over to the gate. There wasn't much chance I could open it when Porter had failed, but I had to try. The padlock and chain were on the outside. Letting go of the canoe, I kicked to keep myself afloat and squeezed my hands through the narrow gaps between the gate's slats. The coarse wood took the skin from my knuckles as I groped with dead fingers for the padlock. It was crusted with rust, unopened in years. I wrenched on it as hard as I could, then tugged on the gate itself to see if I could break the waterlogged timbers.

But they were solid, and I couldn't waste any more time. Letting go, I groped for the canoe again. I wasn't going to get out through the gate or the hatchway, which left one last possibility.

One Porter wouldn't have known about.

There wasn't enough light to see the ceiling, but it was out of reach. Shuddering from the cold, I cast around the junk floating around me until I saw the broken oar drifting nearby. Its shaft was splintered from when Porter had tried to get through the hatch, but it was still long enough for my purposes. Swimming to the middle of the boathouse, I supported myself with one arm over the canoe and stretched above me with the oar into the shadows. Relying purely on touch, I began dragging its blade back and forth across the rough timbers. There was a bump as I felt it snag on something.

The bolt for the trapdoor into the flat above.

I'd cursed it when I'd stubbed my toe on the ring concealed under the rug, but now it was my only hope of getting out. Praying it wasn't locked or nailed shut, I tried knocking the bolt back with the oar. But it was too clumsy and I quickly abandoned the attempt. If I was going to unfasten it I'd have to do it by hand. I tried lunging up for the bolt, but the ceiling was still too high. That left the canoe. There was a jagged hole in it larger than my fist which would make it sink if I righted it, so instead I climbed on top of its upturned hull. That didn't work either: as soon as I put my weight on it water gushed through the hole and the canoe sank under me.

I slid off, letting it bob to the surface again. I looked around, but even if there was anything else among the floating junk I could use, it was too dark inside the boathouse now to see. *Come on, there must be something.* I'd kept my cumbersome jacket on for the minimal insulation it offered. More importantly, the thick plastic was waterproof.

Kicking to keep my head above water, I struggled out of it. Fumbling with my icy hands, I wadded it up and packed it into the hole in the canoe's hull. It made a crude plug, but it was the best I could do. Hoping it would hold for long enough, I dragged myself on to the overturned hull. The canoe slipped out from under me. Spitting out saltwater, I tried again. The canoe bucked around, but this time I managed to haul myself on top until I was sitting astride it.

Now the ceiling was only inches above my head. But the canoe was already beginning to sink. Twisting round awkwardly, I groped blindly at the rough underside of the trapdoor until I felt the bolt. Gripping it with bloodless fingers, I tried to prise it back. It was seized shut. The canoe was sinking quickly now, so ignoring the bracket's sharp metal edges I began yanking on the bolt as hard as I could.

Without warning it shot back, showering my face with flakes of rust. There wasn't time to feel relieved. Putting both hands on the trapdoor, I pushed. The canoe bobbed lower, but the trapdoor didn't move. Setting myself, I tried again. This time there was a slight shift. I heaved at it again. The door rose a little higher, allowing me to get an arm through.

As the canoe foundered under me, I hauled myself up and forced my other arm into the narrow gap. Then, legs kicking in space, I heaved my head and shoulders through as well. A heavy weight pressed down across my back. I'd emerged underneath the big rug, which was pinning the trapdoor on top of me. It took all my strength to drag myself the rest of the way in, but at last I pulled my legs up into the flat. Gasping, I lay face down on the floorboards. Pinpricks of light swirled in the darkness as I breathed in the sticky scent of varnish. I wanted nothing more than to lie there, but I forced myself to move. Crawling out from under the heavy rug, I rose unsteadily to my feet. The flat was in darkness. Tottering like an infant, I felt for the light switch, shuddering with cold and trailing water with every step. All my instincts clamoured for me to rush after Porter, but I was no use to anyone like this. If I wasn't already hypothermic I soon would be. I needed warmth and calories. Fast.

I blinked, dazzled, as the overhead light came on. Porter's search for the money had left the flat in disarray. Drawers and cupboards had been emptied, their contents strewn about, but he'd inadvertently done me a favour. He'd tipped over the sofa and in doing so had shifted it from the rug. If not for that I doubt I'd have been able to open the trapdoor at all.

My fingers were numb and dead as I tore off my shirt, and I shook uncontrollably as I rubbed myself with a towel from the kitchen. The overnight bag with my spare clothes was in the car boot, but the jacket I'd borrowed from Trask was still in the cupboard. I pulled it on over my bare skin, grateful for the warm lining. I couldn't do anything about my trousers and boots, but they were going to get wet again anyway. The Tupperware container of dog food cake from Rachel was still on the worktop. Ripping off the lid, I crammed the remaining pieces into my mouth, forcing myself to swallow the rich mix of chocolate and carbohydrates. Then I was out of time. Pausing only long enough to snatch up a kitchen knife from the scattered cutlery, I ran for the door.

Night had fallen outside. The rain had stopped, and patches of clear sky and stars were visible behind streamers of torn cloud. But the wind hadn't eased, and even before I rounded the boathouse corner I could hear the rushing of the creek. My car was canted down the bank among the wreckage of the steps, more than half-covered by water. The creek had spread far beyond its banks, transforming the marsh and fields into a lake. Only the higher ground around the boathouse remained above the flood, and if the creek carried on rising that would soon be covered too.

I'd worried that the boat would be gone, that Porter might have untied it to strand me here. But it was still there, its pale shape dancing at the end of the mooring rope. Supporting myself against my car, I slithered down the bank and into the water. Cold waves slapped against me as I waded out on the submerged jetty. Taking hold of the dripping rope, I dragged it towards me and clambered in. The knot fastening the line was under water, so I sawed at it with the kitchen knife until it parted with a twang. The boat immediately began to move. I let it carry me along while I crouched by the motor and tried to start it with numb fingers. It fired on the second attempt. Opening the throttle as far as it would go, I huddled down in the boat and sent it roaring up the flooded creek.

But even as I did I knew I'd be too late.

Porter would have reached Creek House by now. I'd spent too long getting out of the boathouse, and he'd have driven the big Daimler as fast as he could on the narrow roads. And I'd no idea what I'd do once I reached the house. Porter was ex-services, and a kitchen knife was no use against a shotgun. As the cold wind chapped my face, I wondered why he hadn't gone for the stolen Mowbry when he'd had me trapped. Even if I'd managed to make it to the boat before he came back, I'd still have been within range of the shotgun. I felt a flicker of hope that he might no longer have

363

it, that he'd got rid of it after shooting Lundy. But I couldn't afford to let myself believe that. More likely he'd decided he didn't need it.

Not when he could drop my own car on me instead.

The moon emerged from behind ragged clouds, silhouetting flooded trees and casting a silver glow as the boat cut across the black waters. If not for the tufts of grasses and reeds sprouting from the waves it would have been impossible to tell where the creek's banks were. Trying not to think what might be happening at Creek House, I focused on keeping the boat in the deepest part of the channel, away from any floating debris. Then, in the opalescent moonlight, I saw something that put everything else out of my mind.

The flooding had rendered any landmarks and features unrecognizable, but off to one side I could see the long, winding hedgerow that ran beside the road.

Stranded in a flooded dip was the black Daimler.

The boat rocked, almost capsizing as I jumped up to look. The door on the driver's side stood open, allowing small waves to lap over the sill. Porter had made the same mistake as I had on the causeway, either underestimating the water's depth or hoping the car would make it through. It hadn't.

There was no sign of Porter himself. I scanned the darkened road, hoping to see him stranded nearby, but except for the car it was empty. Then the creek curved away, and the Daimler was lost to view.

For the first time since I'd climbed from the boathouse, I allowed myself to hope. Although I didn't fool myself that he was going to give up, without his car Porter would have to make his way through the flood on foot to Creek House.

There was still a chance.

I gripped the throttle tightly, as though that might wring more speed from the motor. The boat was already going as fast as it could, but even with the help from the current it seemed maddeningly slow. For what felt like an age there was nothing other than the floodplain and darkness. Then, through a screen of waving branches, I saw the lights of Trask's house.

I willed the boat to go faster, but it continued at the same imperturbable pace. The lights slowly grew bigger, resolving into the broad strip of floor-to-ceiling windows. A smaller yellow square from one of the bedrooms hung in the darkness below them. Gradually, I began to make out shapes and colours inside. Movement. For an agonizing minute the house was obscured as a bend in the creek concealed it behind a copse of trees, then it emerged from behind them.

Waves were lapping all around the concrete pilings, but Creek House sat serenely above the floodwaters. The upstairs windows gave a clear view of the lighted room on the other side. I could see Rachel with Fay on the sofa, the young girl curled peacefully against her as she read from a book. In the smaller window below I could see Jamie sitting at a desk, staring moodily at a computer screen.

Safe.

Thank Christ. I slumped on the bench seat, suddenly weak from the strength of my relief. Framed by darkness, the windows displayed the brightly lit interior of the house like a silent film. As I drew nearer I could see Rachel's mouth moving as she read to Fay. Downstairs in the flickering light from his computer, Jamie sat with his head in his hands.

None of them so much as glanced outside. The double glazing would blanket the sound of the boat's approach, and I'd seen myself how impenetrable the glass became at night. Once the lights were turned on the sliding doors became a huge mirror; even if anyone in the house looked out, all they'd see was their own reflection.

But that hardly mattered: the important thing was I'd made it in time. I aimed the boat at the floating jetty, already thinking how best to handle this. I didn't want to waste time on lengthy explanations, not with Porter still at large. The priority was to get everyone out of the house as quickly as possible. Everything else could wait until they were safely in the boat and we were well away from here.

I was almost at the jetty when Rachel broke off from her reading. She glanced over her shoulder at the stairs, and downstairs at the same time I saw Jamie raise his head as well. I felt suddenly cold as I realized why.

Someone was at the door.

Rachel said something to Fay and put the book down. She started to get to her feet, but in the room below Jamie straightened and called something. Then he stood up and went out.

To answer the door.

'No!' The boat rocked as I jumped to my feet. 'Rachel! *Rachel!*'

Frantic, I waved my arms, but she couldn't see or hear me. I was invisible behind the window's dark mirror. As the boat droned the last few yards I could only watch as she turned to listen to something downstairs. Suddenly both she and Fay gave a start. Rachel shouted something and jumped to her feet. She ran towards the stairs but she'd only taken a few steps when Jamie came sprawling from the top of them.

Behind him was Porter.

Wet and caked in mud, the driver yelled and gestured at Rachel. Looking confused, she shook her head. He took a step towards her, finger stabbing. Scrambling up from his hands and knees, Jamie launched himself at him, then reeled back as Porter drove a hand into his face. The windows muted Fay's screams as her brother tumbled downstairs.

Porter was already turning back to Rachel. She stood in front of Fay, her expression scared but determined.

'PORTER!' I screamed. 'LEAVE THEM ALONE, I'M OUT HERE!'

The wind carried my shouts away. I saw Rachel snatch up a lamp and fling it at Porter's head. It sent crazy shadows as he ducked, before shattering noiselessly on the wall. Rachel made a grab for a vase, but he caught hold of her arm. Wrenching her away, he hit her across her face. She dropped to one knee, and I saw Porter take hold of her hair.

'NO!' I yelled. And then they were lost from sight as the boat passed below the window.

By now I'd reached the jetty, but I didn't slow. The propeller bit into mud and gravel as I opened the throttle and sent the boat over the flooded bank and along the side of the house. It carried me a few more precious yards before it ran aground. As it slewed to a stop, I leapt out and splashed through the knee-deep water. I was clutching the knife I'd taken from the boathouse, but I'd no plan, no idea what I was going to do as I rushed up the steps. The door stood open, the hallway beyond in darkness. I barged it aside and headed for the stairs.

As I started up them the crash of a shotgun rang out.

I staggered as though I'd been hit myself. No, I thought, numbly. No, no, no. Then I was running up the stairs. I burst into the room at the top.

And stopped.

A lazy drift of smoke hung in the air. The upper floor stank of gunpowder and blood. Rachel was kneeling by Fay, hugging the girl to her. They were both crying, but apart from a livid graze on Rachel's face neither appeared hurt.

The shotgun blast had taken Porter between his shoulder blades. He'd been flung into the bookshelves, and now lay sprawled among the scattered books. I started to go over, until I saw the extent of the wound in his back and realized there was no point.

I turned to where Jamie stood nearby. Blood streamed from the teenager's nose, and the haunted look in his eyes was as eloquent as any confession. He still had the shotgun raised to his shoulder, but offered no resistance when I gently took it from him.

The photograph Lundy had sent hadn't done the Mowbry justice. It was a beautiful piece of craftsmanship. Two over-and-under barrels were set in a honeyed walnut stock, inset with ornate silver side panels. Engraved on them in flowing script were two initials.

LV.

31

THREE WEEKS AFTER the flood, Rachel called to say we needed to talk. She didn't say why, but I could tell by her voice that something was wrong. She sounded different. Distant.

We met in a café in Covent Garden. The ease I'd felt with her before was absent today. I watched her walk across the room, the worn sweater and jeans replaced by a slim-fitting dress, and her thick dark hair taken back. She looked lovely.

'I'm going back to Australia,' she said, looking into her coffee. 'I wanted to tell you in person rather than over the phone. I thought I owed you that much.'

I couldn't say her announcement came as a surprise. A blow, yes. But not a surprise.

We'd continued to see a lot of each other in the days after I returned to London. To start with there had been long conversations over the phone, followed by dinner in Chelmsford one evening. Then she came to London for the weekend. I thought it might feel strange for us to spend time together in such a different environment, but any nervousness was forgotten the moment she arrived. Being with her seemed natural, as though we'd known each other far longer than the few weeks it had actually been.

After the grim horror of those last days in the Backwaters, the weekend had seemed one of those charmed periods that occasionally touch our lives, apparently endless yet over too soon. Spring was hurrying into summer, and the bright sunshine seemed to promise a fresh start after the dour winter months. When Rachel left it was understood that she'd come out again soon. For longer next time.

And then something changed between us. It was hard to say how, exactly, and I told myself it was only to be expected after what she'd been through. That she had a lot on her mind.

Now I knew what. I felt numb, the sort of deadness that precedes the pain of a bad injury. *It's your own fault. You were expecting too much.* I stirred my own coffee, giving myself chance to absorb the news. 'That's sudden, isn't it?'

'Not really. I've been treading water for too long as it is, I need to get my life back. Too much has happened here. And I keep thinking about Bob Lundy. I can't . . .' She broke off as her eyes filled up. 'Shit. This is exactly what I wasn't going to let happen.'

She shook her head when I reached for a tissue, taking a paper napkin to angrily dab her eyes.

'You can't keep blaming yourself,' I told her, knowing it wouldn't do any good. We'd had this discussion before, though not like this.

'Yes, but if not for me he'd never have gone out to that bloody place. If I hadn't been so pig-headed he'd still be alive.'

'What happened to Lundy wasn't your fault. He was a police officer, he was doing his job.'

And I knew the DI would do it again if he had to. In the week following his murder I'd gone to see his wife at their home. The cherry tree blossoms that had lined the road had largely fallen now, the delicate pink petals turned to brown mulch in the gutters. Sandra Lundy had been quietly dignified as she'd asked how her husband had died. I'd told her it had been saving the lives of Rachel and myself, that if not for him we'd have been killed as well. She covered her eyes for a moment, then smiled.

'That's good. He'd be happy about that.'

I didn't mention the call-back from hospital that Lundy had

been worried about on the morning he'd been shot. It was possible she might not even know about it, and I couldn't see how it would serve any purpose to tell her now.

Rachel had taken the DI's death hard, but I'd thought she'd been coming to terms with it. She'd certainly given no indication that she wanted to return to Australia.

'There's something else, isn't there?' I said, looking at the smooth lines of her face as she balled up the napkin.

She took a moment to answer, making minute adjustments to her cup and saucer.

'Pete's been in touch.'

'Pete?' I asked, though I could guess.

'The marine biologist I told you about. Who I split up with.'

'The one with the twenty-two-year-old post-grad in a bikini.'

I regretted the jibe straight away. A smile quirked a corner of her mouth, but it was sad rather than wry.

'Yeah. He heard about . . . what happened. Even made the news in Australia. He was worried, wanted to see if I was OK.' She looked across at me. 'He wants to give it another go.'

I looked out of the café window. Tourists thronged outside, more than I could count. A street musician was playing a jazzed-up version of 'What a Wonderful World' on a guitar. 'And what do you want?'

'I don't know. But we were together seven years. It wasn't all bad.'

Until he ran off with someone else, I thought, but managed to keep it to myself this time. 'So . . . ?'

She gave a lost shrug. 'So I've said we can talk about it when I get back.'

I sat very still, feeling as though the ground had shifted under me. 'You're definitely going?'

'I – I have to. Too much has happened, I need some time to work things out. And it's not like I'm needed any more.'

Isn't it? Her hands were resting on the table. I reached out and laid mine on one of them. 'Rachel—'

'Don't. Please, I can't . . .' She broke off. 'This is hard enough already.'

The numbness had been replaced by a disappointment that pressed down on me with a physical weight. 'So there's nothing I can say?'

She looked at me for a long moment, her thumb lightly stroking my hand. Then, with a gentle squeeze, she let go. 'I'm sorry.'

So was I. I forced a smile as I moved my hand back to my cup. 'When are you going?'

Some of the tension seemed to leave her. 'As soon as everything's tied up here. Andrew's found a place to rent in Chelmsford until things are sorted out. It's a nice area, and there's a good school nearby for Fay. He's going to put Creek House on the market as soon as he can. They can't stay there, not after everything that's happened. It's not going to be easy for them, but maybe a fresh start will help.'

'Sounds like a good idea.'

In hindsight, there had been something unhealthy about the beautiful house on the edge of the saltmarsh. For all its modern aesthetic, all the planning Trask had put into its design, it had been an unhappy place. It seemed forced upon the landscape rather than a part of it, and that applied to the people who lived in it as well. Trask had been a careful man, but he'd been so busy safe-guarding his family against the Backwaters he'd forgotten that tragedy can come from the inside too.

I hoped the house's next occupants would have better luck.

The street musician was winding up the song, to scattered applause. People drifted away as he bent to count coins in his guitar case.

'What will you do when you get back?' I asked.

'I don't know yet. Maybe see if my old job's still open.' She hesitated. 'Will you be OK?'

I turned away from the window. My smile felt more natural this time, but then I'd had plenty of practice. 'Sure, I'll be fine.'

She looked at her watch. 'I'd better go. I just wanted to see you again, to explain. And I never really thanked you.'

'For what?' I asked, confused. I couldn't see what there was to thank me about.

Rachel gave me a quizzical look.

'For finding Emma.'

By dawn the morning after Porter's shooting, the floodwaters had disappeared. In their wake was a miles-long swathe of mud and shingle. The tidal surge hadn't been bad compared with others that had inundated the east coast in the past, and certainly nowhere near as severe as the storm tide of 1953. A few hundred houses had been evacuated, roads rendered impassable and sea walls breached or washed away. But everyone agreed it could have been worse. No one had died.

At least not because of the flood.

Wearing yet more borrowed clothes of Trask's and wrapped in a blanket for the second time that day, I was checked out by paramedics who arrived at Creek House with the police. They'd seen to the others first, all of whom needed attention more than I did, one way or another. I'd barely spoken to Rachel after the shooting. Once I'd called the police I'd hurried them all downstairs, away from the body of Lundy's killer. Rachel had taken Fay into her room to console the hysterical girl, while I'd stayed with Jamie. That was more to make sure he was all right than to prevent him from going anywhere. I didn't think he'd try to leave.

He'd had enough of hiding.

The paramedics suggested I go to hospital, but I'd refused. I knew the warning signs of hypothermia or a resurgent infection well enough, and didn't have either. Two mugs of warm, sweet tea and dry clothes borrowed from Trask's wardrobe had stopped the worst of the shivering. I felt exhausted, but I could rest later.

I wanted to see this through.

Clarke came to see me after I'd given yet another statement at police HQ in the early hours of the morning. She arrived in the beige interview room with two polystyrene cups of tea, one of which she handed to me. I wasn't sure if it was a peace offering but accepted it anyway.

'How are you feeling?' she asked, sitting down across from me.

I shrugged. 'OK. How are the others?'

The DCI looked tired, the skin of her face pale and drawn after the long night. I knew I didn't look any better. 'Rachel Derby's just got some bruising. The little girl's suffering from shock but we released Andrew Trask earlier, so at least he's with her again. We might have more questions for him later, but under the circumstances . . .'

Under the circumstances, letting a young girl be with her father was the humane thing to do. Especially when her brother had just killed a man in front of her.

'And Jamie?'

'He's got a broken nose and a couple of loose teeth, but they're the least of his problems. How much did he tell you?'

'Most of it,' I admitted.

Some I'd been able to piece together myself. From the moment I'd seen Trask's son holding the hand-crafted shotgun I knew what it meant. I'd wondered why Porter hadn't used the Mowbry at the boathouse, but the reason was simple: he didn't have it. He never had. It had been hidden at the bottom of Jamie Trask's wardrobe ever since the teenager had accidentally shot Anthony Russell.

It hadn't been long after his father's abortive attempt to confront Leo Villiers that Jamie had seen a light on at Willets Point. He'd been returning home from a night out with friends, and while he wasn't exactly drunk, he wasn't exactly sober either. No doubt he was worried what his father might do now Leo Villiers was back. But it wasn't just the alcohol, or concern for his family, that made the teenager head out to the house on the promontory.

'Did he tell you about him and Emma Derby?' Clarke asked.

'Not in so many words, but I guessed,' I said. It wasn't difficult: once Jamie had begun to open up his feelings for his stepmother had become obvious. 'How far had it gone?'

She took a drink of tea, grimacing as she set it back down. 'It doesn't look like anything actually happened between them, but she'd been egging him on for a while. Flirting, leaving the door open when she was showering, that sort of thing. Probably just a bit of fun as far as she was concerned, but it was enough to mess with his head. It got so he didn't want to be alone in the house with her when his dad was away. That's why he was staying with friends when she went missing, because he didn't trust himself.'

It wasn't surprising. Teenage hormones on one hand, guilt on the other: it was a volatile mix.

Clarke shook her head, radiating disapproval. 'Christ knows what she was thinking. She should have known better.'

Yes, she should. Rachel had told me how Jamie had abruptly split up with Stacey Coker even before learning she was pregnant, and now it was clear why. It was no secret there were cracks in Trask's ill-matched marriage, and for someone like Emma Derby – vain and bored, missing city life – the teenager's infatuation must have been a flattering diversion. She'd won over her stepdaughter by playing the big sister. For her stepson she'd taken a different approach.

'Did Trask know?' I asked.

'He hasn't admitted it, but he must have had suspicions. Teenagers aren't the best at hiding their feelings, and I can't imagine Emma Derby tried too hard to be subtle. It's academic now, but I wouldn't be surprised if Trask didn't *want* to know. Probably scared of what he might find out, especially after his wife went missing.'

Christ, I thought, the emotional undercurrents in the Trask household didn't bear thinking about. No wonder the relationship between father and son was so strained, or that Rachel had said being around them was like walking on eggshells. She'd not become involved with the family until after her sister had disappeared, so had missed the interplay between Jamie and his stepmother.

But there was no ignoring the tensions in the house afterwards. And for Jamie, months of jealousy, grief and guilt had reached a tipping point when he saw the light on at Leo Villiers' house and thought his stepmother's lover and killer had returned to Willets Point.

The teenager's voice had been dull and nasal, muffled by the frozen peas he held to his broken nose, as he'd told me what had happened that night. Pumped up by alcohol and adrenalin, he'd parked outside Villiers' house and been about to bang on the door when he'd heard glass breaking on the terrace. He'd gone round to the front and seen a man wearing a long coat standing on the water's edge, collar turned up against the chill. On the terrace around him were empty glasses and bottles, some of them shattered as though they'd been used for target practice. A shotgun had been propped against a tree nearby. More to keep it out of Villiers' reach than with any intent to use it himself, Jamie had picked it up.

The man heard him and turned. Even in the dark it had been apparent it was a stranger. Panicking, Jamie had thrust the over-and-under barrels at the man's face, stammering a demand to know where Leo Villiers was.

And the shotgun had gone off.

'It blew Anthony Russell back into the water,' Clarke said with a sigh. 'It was a spring tide that night, so the body must have been carried over the Barrows into the estuary rather than out to sea. Probably ended up in the fringes of the Backwaters, which is why it wasn't found for weeks.'

Four of them, in fact. Once in the maze of creeks and channels, the body would have sunk to the bottom. Exposed to air and sea-birds twice a day at low tide, and picked over by aquatic scavengers, eventually it had refloated and drifted back out into the estuary.

And then Lundy had called me.

'What'll happen to Jamie?' I asked.

Clarke stared moodily into her polystyrene cup. The sight reminded me of Lundy doing the same thing only a few days before. 'Porter was self-defence, no one's going to blame him for that. But intentionally or not, he still shot Anthony Russell. He'd have been better off coming to us straight away. As it is . . .'

She hitched a shoulder, indicating it was out of her hands. Which it was: Jamie had killed an innocent man and then concealed it. Although he hadn't intended to, he'd helped set in motion a series of events that had claimed yet more lives. Even allowing for mitigating circumstances, he'd be facing a custodial sentence. With luck and a sympathetic court, he'd be young enough to reclaim his life afterwards. But any plans for university and a normal life were now a long way in his future.

And yet, if not for the shotgun he'd had hidden, Porter would in all likelihood have killed Fay and Rachel, as well as Jamie himself. I was too tired to decide if that was fortuitous or ironic.

'Have you found the shotgun Porter used at the sea fort?' I asked.

'Not yet, but we're still searching his flat. He lived in quarters in Sir Stephen Villiers' main house, so you can imagine how well that's gone down,' Clarke said drily. 'There was an empty cartridge box in his bin, though. Number five bismuth birdshot, the same brand as Villiers used.'

And the same type of shot that had killed Lundy. But Clarke wouldn't need reminding of that.

'The thinking at the moment is that Porter took a shotgun and shells from Leo Villiers' house when Sir Stephen sent him to clean up at Willets Point,' she continued. 'We knew there could be a second gun missing from the gun cabinet, but since Villiers had it moved into the cellar when the house was renovated no one could say for sure. We're still trying to locate the shotgun, but my guess is Porter would have dumped it in the sea on the way back from the fort.' The DCI looked across the table at me, the harsh overhead lights emphasizing the shadows under her eyes. 'Lucky for you.'

It was, although I didn't feel that way. On an intellectual level I realized I'd had two narrow escapes inside twenty-four hours. Emotionally, though, too much had happened for it to have sunk in.

But I thought Clarke was probably right about Porter getting rid of the shotgun. The weapon tied him to the shooting of a police officer, and he'd just had his face peppered with shards after firing it point blank at a rusted steel door. Even if the blowback hadn't damaged the barrel, he must have decided it was too risky to keep.

Looking back, I could see how events had slipped out of his control ever since he'd gone out to the sea fort to confront Emma Derby and Mark Chapel. And when Leo Villiers, who must have seemed the perfect scapegoat, returned from the dead Porter's own situation had become untenable. I could well believe he was telling the truth when he'd said things had got out of hand. But that was small consolation to the people whose lives had been destroyed because of it.

'The empty cartridge box wasn't the only thing we found at his flat,' Clarke went on. 'He was a magpie. The place was full of stolen items. Nothing big or obvious, mainly stuff like watches and jewellery. We're still checking records, but we think at least some of them came from burglaries reported in the area last year.'

'Around the same time Creek House was broken into?' I asked.

Clarke tipped her head in acknowledgement. 'It looks as though you were right about them being a smokescreen. Porter would have known there'd be copies of the photographs on Emma Derby's computer, but he didn't want anyone thinking the Trasks had been specifically targeted. There weren't any stolen computers in his flat, so he must have got rid of those. But we did find a USB flash drive hidden behind a loose skirting board. We're still going through the files, but the blackmail photographs are on there. Shots of Leo Villiers dressing in women's clothes, all taken at long range through the windows of his house. There's some film footage we think is from the video camera Mark Chapel took from work, but it's poor quality and doesn't show much.'

'You haven't found the camera itself?'

'Not yet. Porter was too savvy to keep anything that could easily be traced back to Emma Derby, but he obviously decided to hang on to the photographs. Makes you wonder if he planned to use them himself someday.'

Porter had been indignant when I'd suggested he was a blackmailer, but then he'd also denied being a thief. Although he might not have seen himself as either, he'd evidently left his options open in case he changed his mind.

'He told me he wasn't going to let them "muscle in" after all he'd done for the Villiers,' I said. 'What do you think he meant?'

Clarke raised the polystyrene cup again before thinking better of it. She set it back down with a sour expression. 'I'm not sure, but the whole set-up seems odd. There doesn't seem to have been any love lost between Porter and Leo Villiers, yet Sir Stephen sent him to clean Willets Point when he realized we were going to search the house. And why send his driver to deliver half a million pounds in blackmail money rather than one of his security team?'

'He'd been employing Porter for twenty-odd years. He must have trusted him.'

Clarke gave me a sceptical look. 'Exactly. But Sir Stephen doesn't strike me as naïve, and Porter wasn't what you could call the trust-worthy type. We know he kept his boss's money, and there were various bits and pieces at his flat we think he lifted from Leo Villiers' house. Silver cutlery, gold cufflinks, a pair of high-end Zeiss binoculars, stuff like that. So how come a hard-nosed business leader like Sir Stephen put so much trust in his light-fingered driver?'

I rubbed my face, trying to organize my thoughts. Clarke was right, there was something wrong. I just couldn't see what it was. 'What does Sir Stephen say?'

'Do you mean about his employee being a mass murderer or his son coming back from the dead as a woman?' She pushed her cup of tea away as though it were to blame. 'He's making no comment about Leo, but he must have known he was transgender or he wouldn't have stopped us seeing his medical records. Maybe he thought Leo really had murdered Emma Derby, as well. It'd explain why he was so keen for us to believe his son was dead. He knew there was a big fat can of worms waiting to be opened, and he was hoping to keep a lid on it.'

'And what about Porter?'

'Sir Stephen doesn't have much to say about him at all. His lawyers have assured us how shocked he was, and said their client isn't responsible for the independent actions of his employees. Oh, they also pointed out that Sir Stephen had his car stolen, so he's a victim himself.'

'You're joking.'

'I kid you not. I offered them the number of Victim Support, but funnily enough they declined.' She gave a snort of disgust. 'As far as the blackmail goes, they're refusing to confirm or deny anything. My feeling is they don't want people knowing Sir Stephen gave in to blackmail, so they're hoping to bury it.'

'Can they do that?' I asked.

'They can try. There's no concrete evidence that Derby and Chapel actually blackmailed Sir Stephen, except for Porter's version of events. And even that's second-hand.'

Jesus, I thought, sickened. Blackmail or not, I couldn't feel any sympathy for Leo Villiers' father. There was a coldness to him that was unnatural, and a sense of entitlement and arrogance in the way he thought he was above the law. But then, with his money and connections, perhaps he was.

'There is one more thing,' Clarke said slowly. 'The RSPCA took away the birds and animals from Holloway's house before the fire. But when we made a start clearing the garden yesterday afternoon we found a sports holdall in the undergrowth. Looked like it'd been used for a sick seagull or something. As well as bird shit it was full of fifty-pound notes.'

I stared at her. 'He used the money for a *bird's nest*?'

A faint smile tugged at the corner of Clarke's mouth. 'I know. It was close to one of the trees that caught fire, so if it hadn't been so wet it'd probably all have gone up in smoke. The notes were pretty scorched but it looks like most of it's there. Five hundred thousand pounds propping up a seagull's backside.'

Christ. I sat back, stunned. Porter had been wrong when he'd said Edgar wouldn't have any use for the money. At another time it would have been funny. 'What's going to happen to it?'

'Well, that's an interesting question. Obviously if the money belongs to Sir Stephen it should be returned to him, bird shit and all. But for that to happen he'd have to admit to being blackmailed. So unless he does we'll have no choice but to regard it as Holloway's property.'

We shared a smile at that, both of us appreciating the poetic justice. And for me there was also an element of relief. Although I hadn't wanted to acknowledge it, Porter's accusation had lodged like a thorn at the back of my mind: *If you don't know where it is, that leaves Derby's sister.* I wondered what it said about me that I'd still harboured a doubt about her, even now.

Clarke was getting to her feet, signalling the interview was at an end. 'I think we're done here. Are you OK to get yourself back to London?'

I said I was. My car was a write-off, but I still had my wallet. I could catch a taxi to the train station and be back at my flat within a couple of hours. There was no longer any point in staying here, even if I'd had anywhere to stay. Rachel would have enough to deal with at the moment, and I needed sleep. Just the thought of it made my body feel twice as heavy as it should.

But there were still things I didn't understand, frayed threads of questions that tiredness and caffeine only seemed to tangle more. 'How would Porter have known about Edgar's house in the first place?' I asked, pushing back the chair as I stiffly stood up. 'Has Leo . . . I mean Lena Merchant said anything about that? There must have been some reason why the Villiers estate let him live rent free.'

'Sorry, I can't discuss that.'

The sudden curtness surprised me. Clarke hadn't seemed to mind talking about other aspects of the case. But I wasn't the only one who hadn't slept, and the DCI still had this unholy mess to sort out. Perhaps she felt she'd already shown me enough courtesy for one night.

Or day, as it turned out. I'd lost track of time in the windowless

380

room, but when I left the police headquarters a thin grey dawn was breaking. It was far too early to call Rachel, and my water-logged phone wasn't working anyway. Clarke told me they'd need to hold on to my bags and belongings from my car for the time being, so I took a taxi straight to the station.

I dozed fitfully on the train, and caught another cab to my flat rather than contend with the morning rush hour on the Tube. It seemed strange to be back in the bustle and grime of London after the reedy isolation of the Backwaters. There was an unnerving sense of disorientation as I walked up the familiar garden path to unlock the front door. The sticky smell of fresh paint threw me until I remembered the attempted break-in before I'd left. It seemed a long time ago.

There was a bill from the decorator on the floor among the junk mail, courtesy of my upstairs neighbour. I dropped it on the kitchen table, feeling restless and out of sorts. My head hummed from fatigue, but I'd reached that fretful stage of tiredness I knew wouldn't let me sleep. Putting on the TV more for distraction than any desire to see the morning news, I filled the kettle to make coffee.

When I turned round again the sea fort was on the screen.

Seeing it here, in my flat, felt utterly surreal. For a moment or two I thought I was hallucinating as an overhead shot from a helicopter showed tiny white-clad figures moving about under-neath the tower. But of course the murder of a DI would be big news, more so than ever after the shooting of his killer.

I switched off the TV. There seemed no air in the room. An image of Lundy bleeding out on the metal steps came to me, so vivid I could almost smell the blood and gunpowder. I tried to busy myself making coffee, but a nagging disquiet persisted. I was familiar enough with the way my subconscious worked to know that the TV news had shaken something loose. It wasn't just the shock of seeing the sea fort, or the reminder of Lundy's death. I was overlooking something. I just didn't know what it was. *Come on, what is it? What have you missed?*

I poured myself a coffee, picturing the fort again. I visualized the ladder climbing to the gantry and how the sea had boomed and echoed underneath the tower. Waves breaking against its hollow legs, the wet drape of seaweed as gulls fed on the exposed sandbank . . .

That's when I realized. I put my coffee down, cursing my stupidity. Like so many things, it had been staring me in the face.

Crabs.

32

THE MARINE UNIT had to wait until the next low tide before they went out to the sea fort. Clarke hadn't wanted me to go along. Her initial scepticism had faded as I'd made my case, but her reluctance had been harder to break down.

'You need to get some rest. You're no use to anyone half asleep, and you've been up all night,' she argued.

So had she, but I knew better than to mention that. So I countered that I felt fine, that I could snatch a couple of hours' sleep while we waited for the tide. She knew as well as I did that, if we found what I was expecting, they'd need a forensic anthropologist. And even if they could find someone at such short notice, a newcomer wouldn't know the case half as well as I did.

Finally, Clarke agreed. After we'd finalized arrangements, I set my alarm and then collapsed on to the bed for two whole hours. I woke feeling grainy and far from rested, but a hot shower and breakfast helped. By the time I caught the train back to police headquarters for Clarke's briefing I felt almost human again.

But going back out to the sea fort was more unsettling than I'd thought. The marine unit launch slogged through the post-storm waves, forced to anchor a little way off from the mooring platform. The police tape tied around the ladder and upper gantry made a low thrumming in the wind as we were ferried across by dinghy. I looked up at the rusted tower high above me, but my business wasn't up there today.

It was lower down.

The sandbank around the tower was still underwater when we arrived, but by the time the forensic teams and equipment had been disembarked, a smooth brown curve had broken through the surface. It quickly grew, and as the CSIs stepped out on to the soft sand the first of the small crabs appeared.

I should have pieced it together sooner, although when I'd watched the tiny creatures the day before I'd still been in shock from Lundy's shooting. But the information had still registered in my subconscious, gradually working its way out like a splinter until it could be plucked free. Crabs were scavengers. They fed on dead flesh, even when it was badly decomposed. And for so many of them to have colonized the sandbank meant there must be a plentiful food source buried inside it.

Like a body.

'Are you sure about this, Hunter?'

Frears stood next to me on the platform, watching the pale crabs scuttle away from the CSIs' spades as their refuge was destroyed.

'Sure enough,' I told him.

Ordinarily I might have had some anxiety that I was wrong, that I'd brought all these people out here on a fool's errand. Instead I felt a quiet certainty. The crabs had been a catalyst, bringing together all the separate pieces that were already there. *You're half right*, Porter had mocked when I'd asked if he'd hidden Emma Derby's body in the Backwaters after dropping her from the tower. I hadn't known then what he meant, but when he'd gone out to the sea fort to confront the blackmailers it had been in Leo Villiers' boat. I'd seen it at Willets Point, a small dinghy moored to the wooden dock at the rear of the house.

Too small to carry Porter and two bodies.

He wouldn't have realized his mistake until after he'd let them fall onto the mooring platform, sixty feet below. Once he'd done that he was committed. It wouldn't have been practical to carry their dead weight back up a near-vertical ladder, so when he found there wasn't room in the boat for both, his options had been limited. If he let the tide carry one of his victims away, he knew they'd eventually be washed ashore and discovered. But the low tide would have revealed another alternative.

He could bury one of the bodies in the sandbank.

Porter would have chosen Emma Derby for practical reasons. He would have been exposed out in the open under the fort, in a hurry to get away, and she was the smallest. She wouldn't need as big a grave. I doubt he'd have had a shovel with him, but the wet sand would have been soft enough to dig with an oar blade. He wouldn't have had to go down very far. Only deep enough for the tide not to uncover what was buried there.

Seawater seeped into the hole as the CSIs scraped the sand from what was left of Emma Derby. The crabs had been busy during the months she'd lain under the sea fort's tower. Most of the exposed skin and soft tissue had been picked away, leaving behind bones and cartilage crusted with dirty-white adipocere. The sand-caked hair had sloughed off but it was still long and dark, plastered about the empty eye sockets and bones of the face. Although there was no resemblance to the beautiful and confident woman whose photograph I'd seen in the boathouse, I wasn't in any doubt.

We'd found Rachel's sister.

I didn't attend the post-mortem. That had been one of Clarke's conditions of my being present at the recovery: I could observe and advise on handling the delicate remains but that was all. Although I was loath to admit as much, it was probably for the best. I'd been getting by on reserves and adrenalin, and by then both had run out.

And so, for the second time that day, I'd returned to London. I slept for six hours, then got up and showered before throwing together a late supper from what I had left in my fridge. I'd tried calling Rachel, and felt a coward's relief when it went straight to voicemail. The news about her sister needed to come from the police rather than me, and I didn't want to speak to her before she – and Trask – had been told. I was wondering if I should try her again when my landline rang.

It was Clarke, calling to let me know the results of the post-mortem.

'No fingerprints, obviously, so we're cross-checking with dental records and DNA,' she said. I was still getting over my surprise that the DCI had bothered to phone: I hadn't been expecting her to. 'But the clothes and jewellery match Emma Derby's. After what happened with Leo Villiers I'm wary of jumping to conclusions, but this time I think we're safe to assume it's her.'

'How did she die?' I asked, massaging my back. My muscles had seized up from the punishment they'd had in the flooded boathouse.

'Frears thinks she was strangled. Her hyoid bone was broken, and so was her neck, although that could have happened in the fall. She'd suffered the same sort of multiple fractures as Mark Chapel, so Porter obviously dropped them both from the tower.'

The probable cause of death came as no shock. Porter had strangled Stacey Coker as well, another unexpected witness he'd wanted to silence. But I felt no satisfaction at hearing it confirmed.

'We found Leo Villiers' dinghy in the estuary,' Clarke continued. 'Probably washed there by the flood, but it looks like that's what Porter took out to the sea fort. There are fresh tyre marks on Villiers' lawn that match the Daimler's, so he must have gone back to Willets Point for the car afterwards and then left in a hurry.'

She didn't have to say why, or explain the bitterness in her tone. 'Was the other shotgun in the boat?'

'No, but we found gunpowder residue on the outboard motor. We think it came off his gloves, which again makes me think he got rid of the gun overboard on his way back. And there were traces of blood as well.'

'Chapel's?'

As soon as I said it I knew it couldn't be. Seven months' exposure to rain and saltwater would have rendered anything belonging to him virtually unidentifiable.

'Not Chapel's, no. But we can assume Porter cleaned the boat after he'd taken the body to the Backwaters anyway. The blood we found was recent, and there were two different types. One was the same as Porter's, so it probably came from his face after he caught a ricochet from the steel door. The other was off his shoe.' There was a fractional hesitation. 'It matches Bob Lundy's.'

We were both silent. Clarke cleared her throat.

'We've notified Emma Derby's family. Hard news coming on top of everything else, but hopefully they'll get some closure now. Oh, and one other thing,' she continued briskly. 'You were sent an email by accident. I'd be grateful if you'd delete it.'

It seemed an uncharacteristic mistake for Clarke to have made, but after the last twenty-four hours she was entitled to a small slip-up. 'OK,' I said, rubbing my eyes. I wouldn't have given it any more thought, but she hadn't finished.

'I imagine it was probably somebody who didn't get any sleep last night,' she went on, and now her tone of voice had subtly changed. 'I don't expect it'll be of any interest to you, but I'd prefer it if you didn't mention it to anyone.'

Now curiosity was beginning to kick in. 'No, of course.'

'So we're clear, then.'

'I'll make sure it's deleted,' I said carefully.

'Thank you, Dr Hunter.'

She hung up. *What the hell was that?* Puzzled, I went to my computer. The email was waiting in my inbox, sent only a few minutes before. There was no subject or message, only an attachment. I hesitated, then opened it.

The attachment was a copy of a witness statement. When I saw whose it was my tiredness was suddenly forgotten.

Leaning forward, I began to read about the events of twenty-five years ago.

*

The summer when Leo Villiers turned nine was marked by a rare heatwave. August temperatures climbed to Mediterranean levels, prompting drought warnings and water shortages. The days were hot and still, the nights humid and close.

But Leo didn't mind. He enjoyed the sun, and at the family's summer home on Willets Point there was a sea breeze to take the edge off the baking heat. And away from the boarding school, with its teachers' censorious gaze and the other boys' pack-like mentality, he felt able to relax. When he was alone he could be himself.

It was when he was with other people that he felt different.

At Willets Point Leo was usually left to his own devices. Except for Sunday lunch and his parents' occasional shooting party where he was expected to put in a showing, his mother and father let their son amuse himself. That was fine by Leo. He was used to being on his own, and found it easier than having to face his parents. Especially after what had happened at Easter.

Even though he'd known he shouldn't, one afternoon Leo had sneaked into his parents' bedroom to try on his mother's clothes. The confusion and unhappiness he'd come to accept as normal seemed to fall away as he looked in the mirror and saw himself transformed. For all that the clothes were too big, the person staring back at him seemed a truer reflection of who he was. It was the everyday Leo that was a sham.

He'd only meant to spend a few minutes in there, but he'd lost track of time and been caught. Again. He'd never seen his father so angry. It had been terrifying, even more so than his usual cold disdain. Leo had turned to his mother, hoping she'd intervene, but she'd turned her face away.

The memory still made him ashamed and miserable. He'd hoped things would get better once they came to the house on Willets Point, but they hadn't. To make things worse, his father's usual driver had had to go into hospital and a replacement had been hired for the summer. A younger man, with smirking eyes and a pockmarked face. His name was Porter.

Leo didn't like him. Porter had been a soldier and had driven in the army, and on days when Leo's father didn't need the car, he'd been instructed to look after his son. So instead of being able to come and go as he pleased, Leo found himself accompanied everywhere. There were drives to the beach, walks along the sea wall and into the Backwaters. Porter never played or talked with his young charge, but would smoke silently, clearly bored and resenting his babysitting duties. It seemed as though the entire summer was going to be ruined.

Then, one day when they arrived at the beach by the sea wall, a young woman was waiting. Porter smilingly told Leo to come back in an hour, and Leo was happy to oblige. From then on, that became the norm. The beach became their usual destination, and each time Porter would meet someone there. Sometimes it was the same young woman, sometimes another. The thought of telling his father never crossed Leo's mind. The arrangement suited him as well. He was left alone, free to wander where he liked.

That was how he met Rowan.

She appeared while he was sitting by himself on the sand dunes one afternoon, a plain girl with freckles and straw-blond hair. Leo hadn't had much contact with girls, but he found Rowan much better company than the boys at boarding school. She lived in the Backwaters, and said her mum worked in a shop in Cruckhaven while her father stayed at home most of the time. He wrote books on nature for schools, and in the past used to take his daughter out with him into the saltmarshes during the holidays.

But that didn't happen so much any more, she told Leo, not since her dad became ill. She didn't know what was wrong with him, but he would shut himself away in his study for days. Even when he came out he hardly ever spoke, and Rowan's mum had told her he needed to be left alone. So now she was left to entertain herself as she liked.

And, for an hour each day, so was Leo.

From then on the two of them met every afternoon. They didn't always stay on the dunes. They would walk in the hot sun, often all the way into the Backwaters, which Rowan loved. She was familiar with every ditch and channel, knew which parts were safe even at high tide and which parts to avoid. They would talk, each of them telling the other things they'd never spoken of to anyone else. Rowan told him how she heard her mum crying and sometimes shouting at her dad, who was becoming ever more distant. In turn, Leo told her how he hated boarding school and the boys who went there. He even admitted he was frightened of his father.

One afternoon, he told her about dressing in his mother's clothes.

His face burned after he'd said it, but Rowan didn't seem to think there was anything wrong. She told him she did the same herself, and Leo felt a wave of unaccustomed happiness. For the first time in his young life he'd found someone he could talk to freely. Share his secret with.

Later, he couldn't remember who came up with the idea, only how excited they both were about it. Plans were breathlessly made for the following afternoon, and then it was time to go. As he hurried away, Leo was so distracted he didn't see Porter until he spoke.

The driver was standing between two dunes, a streamer of blue smoke curling from his cigarette. Leo quickly looked back to see the small figure of Rowan disappearing down the beach. Watching her go, Porter smirked and wagged a finger at Leo. What would your father say, he asked?

Leo's heart was pounding. His first thought was that Porter had heard what he and Rowan had been planning. But the driver had been too far away, and once Leo realized that a new emotion took over. He found himself hating that smirking face, almost shaking at the thought of his cherished new friendship threatened by his father's employee. He'd say he doesn't pay you to smoke or meet girls, Leo said.

Porter's pockmarked cheeks had darkened, but it wasn't mentioned again.

The following afternoon, as they set off in the car, Leo waited until the house was out of sight and then asked to be let out. Porter was reluctant, but Leo had learned that secrets worked both ways. And when he revealed he'd seen the driver taking boxes away from the summerhouse in the grounds, Porter pulled over. He wasn't smiling any more, and swore under his breath when Leo got out and said he could go.

But he still did as he was told.

In the quiet as the car engine died away, Leo hurried to the summerhouse. Hidden behind a thicket of trees and bushes, the small, single-storey structure was built from overlapping planks nailed to a rough timber frame. It was meant to resemble a Swiss chalet, and years ago it had been used for entertaining. But that was before Leo was born: now, weathered and warped, it was only used for storage.

A door stood in the middle of a small covered porch, on either side of which were cobwebbed windows. Leo looked around to make sure no one was watching. He'd sneaked in here many times before, but he had to be careful.

His parents would be furious if they found out.

He felt in the window box, where dead and desiccated weeds clung to the dust-like earth. The key was still there, so Leo fitted it into the lock and opened the door. It squealed on dry hinges as he pushed it open. The chalet was hot and airless. A dry, scratchy smell of sun-baked pine tickled his nose as he stepped inside. It was full of cardboard boxes and wooden packing cases. There were old suitcases and trunks as well, though not so many since Porter had taken some of them away. Leo had watched from the trees, unseen, while the driver had let himself in, emerging a few minutes later with the first of several boxes and small pieces of old furniture. He'd loaded them into the car boot before driving off, but even though Leo didn't think his father knew, it never occurred to him to say anything.

He only cared that one particular suitcase hadn't been touched.

When Rowan arrived she looked uncertain at finding herself in this new place, so close to the grand house. But Leo felt full of confidence. The anticipation he'd felt all day infected them both as they began exploring the suitcase's contents. Leo thought the clothes might have belonged to his mother, but it must have been a long time ago. The short dresses and skirts were brightly coloured and much too small for her now.

Neither he nor Rowan minded the smell of mothballs as they began trying on the clothes. Costume jewellery and shoes first, strapped sandals with platform heels and gaudy necklaces. Then blouses and skirts. Small as the clothes were, they were still too big but that hardly mattered. Inside the chalet, with sunlight streaming through the old muslin curtains, it felt like they were in another, private world. Leo felt dizzy with a sense of homecoming, a feeling he would try, and fail, to recapture with alcohol when he was older. He had on a bright-blue dress, Rowan a matching orange top and skirt, giggling as she slid bangles over his hand. One of them was tortoiseshell, almost luminous as the sun shone through it, and afterwards Leo would remember the bone-like rattle they made as they slid down his wrist.

He still had his arm raised when the door was torn open. He saw Rowan's face change as she looked behind him, and then he was wrenched around. He found himself staring into a face so contorted at first he didn't recognize his father. Leo's head snapped back and forward as he was shaken, then a blow to his cheek knocked him to the floor. Stunned, he saw a flash of orange as Rowan ran for the door, only to fall as his father reflexively lashed out. Leo was yanked up and shaken again, so hard he couldn't see. His father was shouting at him, but he couldn't tell what. And then, quite distinctly, he heard another voice say, 'Oh, fuck!'

The next thing he knew, Porter was pulling his father away, pushing in between them. Leo fell back into the boxes, hearing only disconnected sounds. Then he was being half-carried, half-dragged towards the door. Rowan was on the floor, unmoving in her too-big orange clothes. She was very still. He couldn't see her face, but there was a large, dark mark on the corner of a wooden packing crate next to where she lay. It looked sticky and wet.

That was his last sight of her. The door closed, hiding her from view, and after that things became muddled. Leo could remember being put into the car, and someone – either Porter or his father, he wasn't sure – dragged off the dress and roughly bundled him into his own clothes. Sometime later he heard his mother's voice, asking how he'd managed to have such a silly accident. And then he was in cool sheets, drifting away in a darkened room.

Next morning, without explanation, Leo was driven back to the Villiers' main house. He slept for most of the journey, waking every now and then to see the back of Porter's sunburned neck in front of him. Years later he would suspect he'd had a concussion, but at the time he welcomed the numb, fogged state that stopped him from thinking clearly. At one point he roused himself enough to ask about Rowan.

She went home, Porter answered without turning round.

No one ever mentioned the incident again. Leo's recollection of it soon faded and became dreamlike, until he could barely remember the young girl he'd made friends with that summer. If he did happen to think about her, or that afternoon in the chalet, it brought such a stifling sense of panic that it was easier not to think about it at all.

Eventually, he convinced himself it never happened.

It was years before he set foot in Willets Point again. By then his mother had died, and Porter had somehow become his father's permanent driver. Leo himself had already embarked on the path of unhappiness and rebellion that would characterize his adult life. When he was expelled from the military academy, instead of returning home for the inevitable scene with his father, he followed an impulse he didn't fully understand and hitchhiked to the house where he used to spend his summers.

It was like being back in a barely remembered dream. The house had been shuttered for years. The chalet had gone, mysteriously burnt down years before. There was nothing to say it had ever been there, and a large magnolia tree had been planted on the spot where it once stood. Rain had dashed the petals from the candle-like buds, and the grass around the tree was dappled with their dirty-white splashes. The sight was obscurely disturbing. It stirred a vague memory, like an old photograph glimpsed on the bottom of a murky lake.

But it wasn't until years later, when another half-understood impulse led him to set up home in his one-time sanctuary, that he came to hear how a young local girl had left her parents' house in the Backwaters one hot summer afternoon and never been seen again.

I read through Leo Villiers' statement twice. Then, as Clarke had requested, I deleted both email and attachment. Turning off my computer, I kneaded the bridge of my nose. All along, I'd assumed the series of tragedies in the Backwaters were recent ones. But the events that had brought me out here had been merely the latest shoots of a crime whose roots stretched back more than two decades.

I felt bone tired and sickened. Porter had seen his employer kill a young girl, and treated her death as an opportunity. Small wonder he'd been taken on permanently after that. He and Sir Stephen were bound together by what they'd done, and while Porter might not have regarded himself as a blackmailer, his silence wouldn't have come without a reward. Perhaps that was why he'd reacted to Emma Derby and Mark Chapel as he had. They were interlopers, trespassing on what he'd have regarded as his personal territory, and he'd responded accordingly. *I wasn't going to let some chancers muscle in*, he'd said at the boathouse. *Not after all I've done for the Villiers.*

And what exactly *had* he done, I wondered? Did his involvement only extend to keeping quiet, or had he proved his value in a more practical way? Porter's duties certainly went beyond driving. Sir Stephen had him clean the house on Willets Point to remove any incriminating evidence, and then deliver a sports bag full of money to the blackmailers. What other favours had there been?

Rowan Holloway had never been found, but I couldn't imagine the grey-suited businessman would have dirtied his own hands disposing of her body. Not when there was someone else who'd do it for him.

I got up from my desk to make myself another coffee. Even though Leo Villiers – it was still hard to think of the person at the centre of this as Lena Merchant – wasn't the killer we'd all believed, he didn't emerge from this blameless. He might have been a child when his father killed Rowan Holloway, but he'd elected to remain silent as an adult. In his statement he admitted letting Edgar live rent free and sending him monthly food parcels in an attempt to appease his conscience. In doing so, he not only condemned the father of his childhood friend to a solitary existence, but set the stage for the final act of the tragedy.

He'd made Porter deliver the supplies.

If his intention was to punish the driver by reminding him of his part in the crime, it failed. All it did was gift him with another opportunity, in the form of a secluded house and an uncomplaining tenant. And when it appeared that Leo Villiers had committed suicide, Porter stopped bothering with the food parcels anyway. He'd been prepared to help cover up the killing of Edgar's young daughter. I couldn't see him losing any sleep over letting her father starve.

Now Porter himself was dead, along with five other people. And the only person who'd emerged unscathed was the man who had started it all.

Sir Stephen Villiers.

I sat down with my coffee, then got up and added a splash of whisky to it. There was precious little chance that Rowan Holloway's killer would face charges for what he'd done. Although I didn't doubt what I'd read – it fitted too well with what we already knew – an unsubstantiated childhood memory would never be enough to warrant prosecution. Especially not one that had supposedly been suppressed for years, and that by his own admission Leo had chosen to conceal until now.

The unpalatable truth was that, with neither evidence nor a body, there was little the police could do. They had ample cause now to conduct yet another, more exhaustive search at Willets Point, and it had crossed my mind that the magnolia tree planted on the site of the old chalet might have more than soil concealed under its roots. But Sir Stephen wouldn't have wanted such tangible evidence of what he'd done to remain on his property, not since there was a much better alternative nearby.

Perhaps Mark Chapel's body wasn't the first Porter had hidden in the Backwaters.

The maze of waterways would no doubt be searched again as well, but the chances of finding Rowan Holloway were remote. After all these years, there would be little of the young girl left to find. Just lonely bones sunk into the mud.

Yet the police couldn't ignore the allegations, not when they'd come from Sir Stephen's own son. I would have liked to ask Clarke what was going on, but I knew the DCI wouldn't appreciate that, and doubted she'd tell me anyway. She'd stuck her neck out enough as it was.

So there was nothing I could do but wait, and hope something happened. Days passed without any mention of Sir Stephen Villiers so much as being questioned, let alone arrested. I shouldn't have been surprised. He'd been ruthless enough in protecting the family name when it was his son who'd been a suspect. Now it was his own reputation, not to mention liberty, at stake, he'd be exerting all his power and influence. It was galling to think he could emerge unscathed even after this, yet as the furore over the killings in the Backwaters started to die down, I began to think that Rowan Holloway's killer was going to go unpunished.

I wasn't the only one.

When Leo Villiers posted his story on social media, not even Sir Stephen's legal team could suppress the storm that followed. The heir of a wealthy and powerful man hadn't only come back from the dead, but done so as a woman. As if that weren't enough, now he was accusing his father of killing a young girl over two decades before.

The revelations caused outrage. An old school photograph of a smiling Rowan Holloway, blond and engagingly gap-toothed, was shown everywhere as the story of her disappearance was revisited. Predictably, Sir Stephen hid behind his lawyers, who deflected questions with assertions of innocence or bland 'no comment's. The businessman himself said nothing, but news footage of him hurrying into his car – a dark-grey rather than black Daimler now – told its own story. His face looked drawn, even more colourless than before, the bones of his skull picked out by the flash of cameras. Before I turned off the TV in disgust I had the unprofessional, and unsympathetic, thought that he looked like a dead man in waiting.

It turned out to be prophetic. When news broke that Sir Stephen was critically ill after a massive stroke, his lawyer issued a statement blaming the stress caused by all the media attention. It could well have been true. There's nothing unusual about being able to commit a crime. What sets some people apart is their ability to live with it. Sir Stephen had lived with his for twenty-five years, untouched and apparently unmoved.

What he couldn't live with was other people knowing about it.

His former son gave no interviews, either before or after his father died two days later. Disliking the air of voyeurism that now surrounded the case, I tried to avoid the gossip and speculation that rushed to fill the vacuum. But it was impossible to ignore altogether. One particular video clip was shown again and again. It was outside the glass doors of a building I recognized as the police headquarters I'd been to myself. There was movement inside, then the doors opened and someone emerged.

Leo Villiers had been a good-looking man, and Lena Merchant was a striking woman. She was elegant and smartly dressed, with well-cut, medium-length dark hair. I'd never met Villiers, and it was strange now to see this person I'd heard and read so much about. She was immediately engulfed by microphones and cameras, and I expected her to hurry away from the attention. Instead, she calmly walked through the jostling scrum, head held high as she ignored the questions fired at her. There was no shame, no embarrassment. Not any more.

Just a dignified silence as she walked away from her old life and into a new one.

Epilogue

I PUT THE SKULL back in the box and rubbed the back of my neck. The vertebrae there clicked as the stiff muscles reluctantly acclimatized to the idea of moving again. Not for the first time, I told myself I needed to set an alarm to remind me to take breaks while I was working.

Not for the first time, I knew I wouldn't.

I set the box in a cupboard under the workbench. The skull was an historic one, an archaeological relic found on Salisbury plain. It was over seven hundred years old, and there was damage to it that the archaeologists thought could have been made by an axe. It was possible. People were no less inclined to kill each other in the fourteenth century than they were today. Still, I was unconvinced. The wound had been made by something with an edge, but not a bladed one, and there was a curvature about it that didn't shout axe to me. While I couldn't categorically rule out some other type of weapon, I'd seen similar injuries before, and had a pretty good idea what might have caused this. A glancing blow from a horse's hoof might be less dramatic from an historical perspective, but it was no less fatal to the person receiving it.

I would have to examine it further to be sure, but there was no rush to do it now. The skull had kept its secret for several centuries: another day or two wouldn't make any difference. It was a Saturday

399

morning, so there was no real reason for me to be at the university anyway. I'd only gone in because I hadn't wanted to sit around my flat. The skull made a convenient excuse.

But the thoughts that had driven me here in the first place were still waiting, and without the distraction of work to keep them at bay now they crowded in again. I automatically looked at my watch, catching myself too late to keep from seeing the time.

Two more hours.

The café was closed at weekends, but I made myself a coffee in the department's tiny kitchen. There was no one else around. The corridors were empty and silent, which as a rule didn't bother me. Today, though, the emptiness weighed more heavily than usual.

If I hadn't been exactly welcomed back at the university with a fanfare of trumpets, there was a definite sense that things had changed. I'd escaped any mention in the news coverage of what had happened in the Backwaters, which was hardly surprising. With so many more sensational aspects to report, no one cared very much about the peripheral involvement of a forensic anthropologist. That suited me. I hadn't enjoyed the attention the previous year, when my name and photograph had appeared in media reports after the Dartmoor case. My job was supposed to be behind the scenes, and I preferred to keep it that way.

But professionally it was another matter. My connection with such a high-profile police inquiry didn't hurt the department's reputation, and the new head's attitude towards me had noticeably thawed. 'Good to see you back in the game,' Harris had beamed on my first day back. Nothing about what had happened in the Backwaters could remotely have been described as a 'game', but I took his point.

I should have been relieved not to find myself back in the job market, but that didn't seem so important any more. I sipped the hot coffee and took another look at my watch. Half past twelve.

Another hour before Rachel's flight would take off for Australia.

We'd only seen each other once after she came to Covent Garden

400

to tell me she was leaving. It had been at Lundy's funeral, a formal affair with police dignitaries as well as rank and file officers paying tribute to a colleague killed in the line of duty. The sombre mood seemed out of keeping with the cheerful DI I'd known, and it was a relief when it was unexpectedly lightened. The reading was from Ecclesiastes, and as the bishop intoned about 'a time to plant and a time to uproot' a young girl's voice suddenly piped out.

'But Granddad *hated* gardening!'

A ripple of laughter went around the church, and the solemnity was broken. I thought Lundy would have liked that.

There hadn't been an opportunity to really talk to Rachel at the funeral, and even if there had it was neither the time nor the place. We'd spoken several times on the phone afterwards, though, and I'd begun to sense she was having second thoughts about leaving. I'd told her how I felt, but I'd resisted the urge to pressure her to stay, knowing the decision had to be hers.

In the end she'd made it.

She hadn't wanted me to go to the airport. I could understand why, but I'd still been bitterly disappointed not to see her one more time. Our last conversation was a strain for both of us. She'd promised that she'd be coming back to the UK at some point, for Jamie's trial if not before. He'd finally been charged with Anthony Russell's murder, although there was a good chance that would be dropped to a lesser charge of manslaughter before it came to court.

But we both knew his case wouldn't be heard for months, and a lot could have changed by then. Rachel had a life and career in Australia, one that involved swimming on the barrier reef rather than grubbing for eels in the Essex mud. And she was going back to make a go of a broken relationship, with a man she'd lived and worked with for seven years. He even surfed, for God's sake.

I didn't say any of that. Rachel was right, this was hard enough already. So I went along with the fantasy that it wasn't goodbye. I told her to take care, kissed her one last time. And then she was gone.

My coffee had gone cold. I poured it down the sink and began washing out my mug. When my phone rang I felt a brief hope it might be Rachel until I saw that the number was withheld. Work, then. Trying to ignore the disappointment, I answered.

'Dr Hunter? It's Sharon Ward.' The voice was familiar and so was the name, but just then I couldn't place either. 'DI Ward?' she added, tentatively.

'Yes, of course.' The name came back to me from a year or two ago. I'd met her when a dismembered body part had, in a very literal way, turned up on my doorstep.

'Have I caught you at a bad time?' she asked.

'No, I was just . . .' I tried to gather myself. 'What can I do for you?'

'I need to have a word with you about the attempted break-in.'

'Break-in?'

'The one at your flat . . . ?'

I'd assumed the call must be about a case. The break-in seemed like an age ago, and I'd practically forgotten all about it. I made an effort to focus. 'Right. Sorry.'

'Can we meet?'

'Sure. I'm around all next week, so pretty much any day then.'

'Actually I was thinking of sooner. Whereabouts are you?'

'At work. The university.' She had my attention now. A DI didn't get in touch about a failed burglary, far less want to meet to discuss it. Not unless there was something else going on. 'Why, what's happened?'

'I'd prefer to tell you in person. How long will it take you to get home?'

'I can be there in an hour.' I'd left my hire car at home but the Tube shouldn't be too busy on a Saturday. 'Look, are you going to tell me what this is about?'

There was a pause. I felt an awful presentiment, a conviction that an already bad day was about to slip into uncharted territory.

'We've had a hit from one of the fingerprints we found on the front doorway,' Ward said. 'It was Grace Strachan's.'

The name seemed to resonate down the line. I felt a sense of dislocation, as though this wasn't really happening. From a long way off I heard the DI's voice continue.

'. . . apologize for not contacting you sooner, but with budget cuts being as they are routine break-ins are bottom of the queue. No one realized until now, and I called you as soon as it was flagged up. Dr Hunter, are you still there?'

'Yes.' I felt distantly surprised at how calm I sounded. 'Are you sure?'

'It's only a partial, but it's definitely hers. The thing is it was lifted from the strip of putty on the window frame, and the oil in that's made it impossible to date. So we don't know how long it's been there. It *might* have been left when she attacked you, but we just can't say. Obviously, given what happened last time, we don't want to take any chances. That's why I want to see you at your flat. I think . . . well, I think we should take a look at what sort of precautions you need to take.'

There was a rushing in my ears. I realized my hand had gone to the healed scar on my stomach. *Given what happened last time . . .* She meant when I'd almost bled to death after Grace Strachan stabbed me in my own doorway. But that was years ago. There'd been no sign of my attacker since then, so how was it possible she'd come back now? Grace had been a murderous psychotic who'd only escaped detection because she'd had help. As time passed I'd allowed myself to believe that she must be dead. If she wasn't . . .

I mumbled some sort of agreement and lowered the phone. I was barely aware of the journey back to my flat. Buffeted by feelings I thought I'd left in the past, I descended the escalators to the Tube in a bubble of shock. As the carriage rumbled through the tunnel I checked the time. Rachel's plane would be in the air by now. I actually felt relieved. If Grace Strachan was back then everyone close to me was in danger.

At least I knew Rachel was safe.

Walking from the station I found myself scanning the street in a way I hadn't done for years. I went up the path to my flat and stopped by the front door. The woodwork had been repainted after the joiner had replaced the lock and repaired the damage. Any fingerprints that had been there would have been covered over. There was no way of determining now if Grace Strachan's was an old one or not. I told myself it might have survived all this time, that this could all be a false alarm. But I didn't really believe it.

I couldn't afford to.

There was no one home upstairs, but at some point I'd have to let my new neighbour know. That was a conversation I didn't look forward to. When I let myself into my own flat, the rooms and furniture seemed familiar and yet utterly strange, as though I were only now seeing them. I went into the kitchen and filled the kettle. I didn't want anything to drink, but it gave me something to do.

My coffee cooled untouched as I waited for Ward to arrive. Even though I was expecting it, the doorbell's cheerful chime made me flinch. I hurried to answer it, pausing in the porch with my hand on the front door. There was no peephole. I'd always resisted having one fitted, not wanting to give in to paranoia after the attack. But it meant I couldn't see who was outside now. A sense of déjà vu settled over me as I stood in the black-and-white tiled hallway, then I opened the door.

'Can I come in?' Rachel said.

Acknowledgements

It's been a longer than anticipated gap between the previous David Hunter novel and *The Restless Dead*. A number of people and organizations helped along the way. Thanks are due to Tim Thompson, Professor of Applied Biological Anthropology at Teesside University; Tony Cook, the National Crime Agency's Head of Operations at CEOP; Patricia Wiltshire, Professor of Forensic Ecology at Southampton University; Dr Martin Hall, Research Entomologist at the National History Museum; Essex Police Press Office; Kay West, former president of transgender support group the Beaumont Society; GIRES (Gender Identity Research and Education Society); and Robin Adcroft, chairman of sea fort renovation group Project Redsand Trust. Without their assistance with factual aspects of the story, *The Restless Dead* would be a poorer novel. It goes without saying that any errors or inaccuracies are my fault, not theirs.

Thanks also to my agents Gordon Wise and Melissa Pimentel at Curtis Brown, my editor Simon Taylor and the team at Transworld, my German editor Ulrike Beck and all at Rowohlt, my parents Frank and Sheila Beckett, my sister Julie for the dog food cake, Ben Steiner and SCF.

Finally, as ever a heartfelt thank you to my wife Hilary, for being there with me throughout.

Simon Beckett worked as a freelance journalist for national newspapers and magazines before turning to write fiction full time. A visit to the Body Farm in Tennessee was the inspiration for what has become a number one bestselling series of thrillers featuring the forensic anthropologist David Hunter – *The Chemistry of Death*, *Written in Bone*, *Whispers of the Dead*, *The Calling of the Grave* and now *The Restless Dead*. He is also the author of five standalone psychological thrillers, including *Stone Bruises* and *Where There's Smoke*, which have also been international bestsellers.

To find out more, visit www.simonbeckett.com